Also By Roxanne Tully

The Blue River Springs Series

1. *Wild Rose*
2. *Fallen Willow*
3. *Saddle Storm*

The Hideaway Springs Series

1. *The Runaway*
2. *The Ruined*
3. *The Rogue*

The Blades of Heart Series

1. *Becoming Mine*
2. *Hatefully Yours*
3. *Timelessly Ours*

Wild Rose

ROXANNE TULLY

embla books

First published in the UK in 2025 by

embla books

An imprint of Bonnier Books UK
5th Floor, HYLO, 105 Bunhill Row,
London, EC1Y 8LZ

A CIP catalogue record for this book is available from the British Library.

ISBN: 9781471420146

Also available as an ebook and an audiobook

2

Typeset by IDSUK (Data Connection) Ltd
Printed and bound by CPI (UK) LTD, Croydon CR0 4YY

MIX
Paper | Supporting responsible forestry
FSC® C013604

The authorised representative in the EEA is Bonnier Books UK (Ireland) Limited.
Registered office address: Block B, The Crescent Building, Northwood, Santry,
Dublin 9, D09 C6X8
Ireland
compliance@bonnierbooks.ie
www.bonnierbooks.co.uk

For the brave way you keep going—even when it's messy. This one's for you. And for the hope that you'll find exactly where you're meant to be.

Playlist

Wildflowers and Wild Horses – Lainey Wilson
Every Rose Has Its Thorn – Poison
According To You – Orianthi
Beautiful Crazy – Luke Combs
Broken and Beautiful – Kelly Clarkson
Love Somebody – Morgan Wallen
Some Days – Brent Morgan
Save a Horse (Ride a Cowboy) – Big & Rich
Bless the Broken Road – Rascal Flatts
I'll Come for You – Nickelback
Better Place – Rachel Platten

1

Wilder

The summer heat has arrived early, baking the fields surrounding Blue River Ranch. I inhale the earthy aromas of soil and mowed grass, which hit my senses in the same way each time—dusty and familiar. The main house—my house—is up on a ridge. A high enough rise from the river that flows along the ranch and its borders, giving a full view of our land, and just about every main structure.

I swipe the sweat off my forehead and make a call I *know* will get loud—I wouldn't want to wake sleeping beauty.

My older brother, Dallas, and I run the ranch as equal partners—or so we're meant to. But I'm the unofficial wrangler of every problem that crosses our gates, while he's—hell, fuck knows what he's doing these days. Claims to be busy researching weather and planning for the off-season. But everyone on this ranch knows he's still hiding.

Still mourning.

We all miss Millie, but not the way he'll miss the woman he planned to spend the rest of his life with.

Before her, we lived together in this main house. Then when he started planning a future, he started building his own over by the riverbend. The house is finished for the most part. But not one of the Thorne men—Dallas included—thought he should be alone after Millie's death. So he's been back here with me since the funeral two months ago.

Truthfully, I'd rather my brother hide out under my roof than anywhere else. He's the oldest, the firmest, hell, the scariest out of the three of us Thorne brothers. But I've never seen him so lost. So broken.

I don't bother him. I let him sleep in, let him get into trouble at the local bars, let him *pretend* he's going to get his act together soon and come help me run this damn place.

But I'm no stranger to a broken heart. And I know it doesn't heal overnight, which means I'm going to need help this summer. Lots of it.

Minutes into my phone call, I'm gripping the railing around my porch, my jaw tight as I listen to the supplier rattling excuses about why his shipment of hay is delayed—again.

"Maybe you should've thought about that before overbooking your trucks," I snap into my phone, running a hand through my dark hair. "I've got thirty-seven horses counting on that feed."

Kruper, or Kramer, whatever his name is, mutters something about placing an order earlier, and I nearly lose my shit before I remember I don't have time to find—nor deal with—another supplier.

Patience and a deep breath. I'm not going to yell.

Not today.

The guys are still steering clear of me after last week's mishap with the tractor that ended up in the creek. Still think it was the new kid I hired for the season.

After a few more tense minutes of Kramer reassuring me we'll have the hay by Friday, and me reminding myself that my options are limited, I hang up and toss the phone onto the wooden bench behind me.

"Not enough fucking hours in the day."

"You talkin' to yourself now, cowboy?" Wesley's voice cuts through my grumbling.

I turn to my best friend—and the ranch chef—as he climbs the steps with a crooked grin and a rag slung over one shoulder. There's the usual glint of mischief in Wes's green eyes, but I can tell something's off. Something's . . . weighing on him. Wes always looks too carefree for his own good, except when he isn't.

"When the alternatives are you and Dallas, I'll take talking to myself," I say, crossing my arms like I've got everything under control and taking a seat on the bench.

Wes steps up and leans against the railing. "Rough morning?"

I snort. "What gave it away? The fact that I've been on the phone with vendors since I woke up or the fact that half the shit Dallas is supposed to do is slipping through the cracks, and there's not a damn thing I can say about it?"

"Neither—it's the scowl," Wes says with a grin. "You could curdle milk with that face."

I shake my head with a smirk. Wes has always had a way of cutting through my frustration. That's why we work so well together. Why we stayed friends since rooming together in college, even though we were from different worlds. Two fresh-out-of-high-school boys looking for a room off campus, him studying culinary arts while I majored in business.

It was always understood that Dallas and I would take over the ranch. Dad had a way of getting it into our blood, teaching us how to fix fences before we were tall enough to see over them. I always imagined Dallas taking the lead more—he was the oldest, the one who'd follow Dad out into the rain at late hours to check on the cattle. The natural leader of the Thorne brothers.

Our younger brother, Silas, didn't follow any footsteps—unless they led him to the frozen lake with his skates. He's nine years younger than Dallas and six younger than me. That kid was in no way born with hay in his hair. He's now in his fourth year with the Denver Kings hockey team after being drafted from Denver University.

College wasn't something Dad talked much about, probably because he never went himself. Hell, I almost didn't either, but Dallas insisted one of us had to. If only for the business skills to keep up with today's world.

But I didn't go far—and certainly not on a full scholarship like Silas. I went to a small college outside of Denver for business. Which, coincidently, was also on the list of the best culinary schools in the country.

Best move I ever made. Best *friend* I ever made.

A year after we graduated, when Wesley's dreams of becoming a top chef in a big city became too stressful, I offered him a job here at the ranch. Dad didn't like the idea of a full-time chef for staff. Back then, it was biscuits and anything hot and ready. Usually cooked by "whoever lost the bet." But with a growing business and opening our working ranch for tours, guests, and events, having a head chef run our kitchen and restaurant made the most sense.

Wes was reluctant at first, but he's come to love it here. And hell, if he was starting to have regrets now, I don't know if I could handle it.

"What's on your mind?" I ask, crossing my arms. "You've got that look."

Please don't tell me you're leaving.

Wes rubs the back of his neck, hesitating. "It's Rose. Lost her job at the gallery, so she's back at that bar in downtown Manhattan, workin' the late shift." He shakes his head, and I feel his pain.

Working late at a bar is bound to face some risk. I don't know much about city crowds, but it can't be all that different from our locals—especially when they've been drinking. If I had a kid sister, that wouldn't sit well with me either.

I've only met Rose once. It was seven summers ago, when Wes's family were visiting the ranch. After brief introductions, I wanted to give the family some space, so I hadn't hung around. But later, as I rounded the corner of the stables, I found Rose lighting up a cigarette.

Straight dark hair, bright green eyes as mischievous as her brother's. Pretty—and young. Too young for me to notice just *how* pretty she was.

Knowing how Wes felt about smoking, and looking out for his sixteen-or-somewhat-year-old sister, I reached over, gently knocking it out of her hand.

"Does Wes know you smoke?" I asked.

She didn't seem the least phased by the implied threat. Instead, she gave me a once over, starting at my boots, where the dusty cigarette bud lay, to the brim of my hat, blowing the last of the white smoke out of her mouth as she did.

Then met my eyes. "Not unless you plan on telling him, and I don't think you want to do that."

"And why's that?"

She reached for a new one and lit it without a care in the world, then stuck the pack in my shirt pocket. "Might just have to tell him you gave it to me."

I smirked. "I do hope you have a plan B."

Her emerald eyes dropped to my chest. "You're wearing the proof, dude."

I let her take a drag before lifting it from her fingers and bringing it to my mouth. I don't know why I did it. I didn't smoke, but I imagined it was because the less she did right then, the better I'd feel.

"You always this pleasant?" I asked.

She took back the cigarette, putting her lips on the spot where mine were seconds ago. "Only with people who threaten me."

"Look, I'll let you finish this one, but if I see you sneak another, at the very least, I'll need to tell your brother." I met her eyes with a smirk. "Then he can tell your parents."

I wasn't sure what I was doing. I didn't plan on meddling in anyone's private business. And I sure as hell didn't plan on making a bad first impression on my best friend's parents by ratting out their daughter.

Her eyes flashed with alarm, but she stood her ground. "I'm not afraid of you."

I frowned. Crap. Maybe I'd taken it too far? I never intended on scaring her. Teasing, maybe. But not intimidating. "Am I giving you a reason to be?"

She glanced back at our three-story walk-up. "I don't know, are you?" she asked cautiously, handing me the half-smoked cigarette and then popping a stick of gum.

I put it out and looked into her eyes. Seeing that behind her tough-girl exterior, she might be a little vulnerable, maybe even scared? At the very least, she didn't want to disappoint her family. And that was something I could relate to.

"Never," I assured her.

"Anyway," Wes goes on now, "I told her I could help her find something else, similar to what she was doing at the gallery, but she doesn't want it. Said the cash tips she makes bartending are keeping her from getting evicted. I fucking can't with this girl."

What I know about Rose now—and that's plenty, going by the eyes of her older brother—is that she moved to New York for a bachelor's in psychology at NYU, but dropped out mid-way through her senior year to become an artist.

A questionable choice that has too many holes, but not my business.

"What was she doing at the gallery?" I ask.

"I don't know. It was a gallery. Tour guide?"

"If you don't know what she did—and she clearly wasn't happy—why send her back?"

"Because it's safer."

I nod slowly and sit back. Who am I to argue with that?

"Rose has a talent for finding trouble—and New York is the kind of place that sharpens that unfortunate skill. I've got to get her out of there."

"Well, don't come lookin' to me for advice. I've got my own shit to deal with. Dallas came home drunk again last night, and I need to deal with inventory, timesheets, and"—I blow out a breath—"fuck knows what else. I need to go to the Saddle Room and run through some schedules. After that, I'll check on the south pasture and work my way up."

My head is all over the place. I worry about my brother. I worry about the ranch. Mostly, I worry about the town talk. If Ricky and Dusty Callahan from Callahan Ranch get wind of the disorganized mess we're becoming, they'll use it in the worst way.

Not to mention, they've got that big annual rodeo coming up that'll make us take a hit with sales and bookings.

Wesley keeps his gaze on the fields. Just when I think he's in his own head and barely listening, his eyes find mine with a hint of a smirk playing on his lips. "Sounds like you need help."

I'm about to tell him I've needed help for weeks when the meaning behind his words hit me. I glare up at him. "Don't even think about it."

Wes holds up his hands innocently. "I'm just saying, maybe Blue River is exactly what Rose needs. She's great with people, well-mannered—"

"Well-mannered?" I burst out with a laugh. "I've been your best friend for ten years, and for the last *six*, been hearing 'bout how you always have to step in and clean up her mess."

He shrugs like I didn't just flat-out contradict him. "Lord knows you could use the extra help around here. And she's a helluva lot more well-mannered than you or Dallas at the moment, I might point out."

"I ain't ever been well-mannered."

"Great. Then you two will get along just fine."

"The answer is no." Immediate and firm no. "This place is hard work, and Rose is . . ." I struggle for the right choice of words. "She's not exactly built for ranch life."

"She's tougher than she looks," Wes argues. "And she's not a kid anymore, Wilder. Besides, you wouldn't have to babysit her. I'll make sure she pulls her weight."

I shake my head. "I don't have time to train some city girl who's never been near a horse; I need someone to help me run this place. This is the busiest time of year, Wes. We're already spread too thin for me to be watching her between tasks."

"She wasn't always a city girl, and we had plenty of horses down in South Carolina—not totally country, but close enough."

I roll my eyes. "You're missing the point."

"One summer. And hell, if she's not workin' out here, I could use her help in the kitchen. That's all I'm asking."

"I yell," I remind him carefully.

"She's got thick skin."

Yeah, but I remember cutting through it just fine when she thought I'd rat her out.

"I ain't about to bite my tongue. No matter whose sister she is."

"You really should consider anger management."

"Forget it."

"It's fine, it's fine. Rose worked for some ill-tempered people in New York; she's used to it."

That makes my chest tight with a different kind of rage. Protectiveness. Hell, I may not know her, but she's Wes's kid sister. Of course I'd feel protective of her.

I sigh. "I gotta look at the budget."

Wesley gives me a look. He damn well knows more help is in the budget. And we've got plenty of room.

I sideways glance at him and push off the bench, knowing I'm going to regret this. But Wes has been there for me through some tough times. This is the least I can do.

"Six weeks."

"Eight."

"Six. I'm not committing to the full summer."

"Deal. She can stay with me."

I shake my head. "I've got an extra cabin." Wes doesn't live on the ranch. He's got a one-bedroom apartment not too far out of the gates.

My friend hesitates.

I sigh. "Oh, is a cabin not good enough? Too country for her?"

Wes drags his hand through his hair. "No, it's just—she'll be all right here? Alone?"

I nod, understanding. My cowboys might be pricks to each other but they're respectful of women. Any sign of disrespect, they're off my field.

The only thing that could hurt her is if there's another attack from our rival. Last summer, the Callahans set a trap to spook our guests. A gun went off during a big event and riled up the livestock. It was a disaster. Slowed us down for weeks. "I'll keep an eye on her. Come to think of it . . . I might give her Millie's old cottage while she's here."

Wes glances back at the house, where we assume my brother is still asleep. "You sure?"

"It's meant for long-term, really. Ginger used to live there before Millie. It's fine." I point a finger at him. "But she'd better be ready to work because I'm not going easy on her."

Wesley's grin returns in full force. "She'll be ready. I know she will. I think she needs a break from the city, you know? She's always so jumpy when I call or ask to come visit. Maybe when she's done here, she'll calm down. Hell, maybe a bull ride will give her enough thrill to keep her satisfied for a while."

I grin. "Or send her packin'."

Wes drops the subject of his sister and starts talking about the week's menu. But I'm barely listening.

I can't shake the nagging feeling that I've just agreed to a whole new level of chaos for the summer.

2

Rose

My brother's voice carries a mix of exasperation and worry as it booms over the phone.

"Rose, unless you've got a better idea, this isn't up for discussion. I got you a summer gig here in Colorado—what've you got to lose?"

I squeeze my eyes shut and lean against the kitchen counter of my miniature New York City apartment.

I hate to admit how tempting it sounds. Getting out of the city, breathing fresh air for a change . . . or hell, just *change*.

Change is healthy, right? Even if it's temporary.

Not to mention my feet could use a break from having to walk home twelve blocks from my bartending job downtown at two in the morning because I don't dare ride the subway that late.

Or get in a car with a stranger . . .

But what would it *mean* if I go?

That I'm failing miserably here in New York and need my brother to rescue me? I can't do that.

It's exactly the kind of thing he expected when I told him I was moving to Manhattan for school. That the city would somehow swallow me whole, be too fast-paced for me to handle, or worse . . . I would get hurt.

Mom and Dad didn't mind so much since they were both hoping I'd follow in Wesley's footsteps and "go away for school."

And sure, I did drop out more than three quarters of the way into my degree. But I had my reasons.

I'm not meant to be a therapist.

That little fact became clear to me when I went to therapy and saw it for what it really is.

A sham. A dumb, stupid tactic to get people to talk for as long as they need to without ever giving them a real answer.

Without ever healing them. I want no part in it.

A world of art instead . . . just sounded *right*. Still does . . . I think.

I only hesitate because it's not easy making steady income as an artist.

But hey, at least I'm in the right city for it. With its world-class museums, vibrant street scene, and endless diversity, the sky's my limit here—even if my brother does hate the idea of me making it my permanent residence. All so I can pursue a career that is impulsive, risky, and my personal favorite—not *practical*.

Even in middle school, when all the other girls joined drama club or tried out for cheerleading, I was sneaking into metal and woodworking class to see if I could weld something without setting my hair on fire.

My parents never complained about my choices. They want me to be happy. It's always been my brother whose protective nature warns me that my free-spirited lifestyle will catch up with me.

In the form of bills, responsibilities, and reality checks.

He didn't laugh when I replied with, *I'd probably bounce that reality check*.

Truthfully? I'm not laughing either. In many ways, I know he's right. But I'm not ready to tell him that yet.

"Wes, I told you, I'm doing *fiiine*." I stretch the word I desperately need him to believe. Even if I don't believe it myself. "And did I mention? I don't need you covering my rent this month. I've totally got it. Actually, I think I've got next month too. The tips at the bar have been—"

"Really? You're fine? And how long until I hear you quit or got fired because your boss was 'toxic'?"

"It's Manhattan," I shout back. "Toxic bosses are a package deal, bro." I try to sound like I love the city vibe. And I think I'm pulling it off. Because I did love it here for a while. What's not to love? It's got everything you could want.

We're from a small town in South Carolina. And as much as I loved it, I wanted to explore a broader life—it's why I applied for every scholarship under the sun for NYU. I was meant for New York vibes, not small-town charm.

Not that it did me any good.

After "the accident"—which is how I refer to it as I refuse to call it what my therapist did, "the incident"—I've been living in fear of living in fear.

So I do things impulsively, bravely, and spontaneously. Art is spontaneous. Art heals.

With art, you can't lie to someone and tell them it's going to be OK.

But no . . . art didn't solve my problem either. Because I'm still restless some nights.

I try not to be a cliché.

I try not to let my fears control me.

So those nights when I'm restless . . . I'm *reckless*. Desperate to prove that I can handle myself. I'm not scared. I'm not *scarred*.

How reckless, you ask?

Well, a few weeks ago, I started talking to a fellow artist at the Painter's Room, a place downtown where new artists showcase their work. Mine are usually watercolor or charcoal. His are photography. *Nude* photography.

He showcases them in silhouettes, and for a moment, I was drawn to them. They were so . . . tasteful and sexy, I just had to ask about it. How he makes everything around them so colorful and brilliant, and you can almost see the woman's mood.

It's magnificent.

At least . . . in the moment.

I was so interested . . . and reckless . . . that I asked if he would photograph me. I didn't expect him to, but he handed me his card and said he'd only do it if I agreed to be paid. Since the work would be featured in his book, I'd need to sign rights for him to use it.

If I told my brother, he'd have a fit and call it borderline prostitution.

Me? I call it expressing myself through art.

But a tiny part of me wonders . . . *how far is too far?*

Yes, that was exhilarating, and I can't wait to see the images when Patrick's done with them, but . . . is that really me? Or was I just trying to prove something?

And if so? To whom?

"Rose," Wesley sighs. "I know how stubborn you are. I came prepared."

"Gonna pull the mom and dad card on me again?" I try to sound bored with the threat I know is coming.

"No," he starts because he secretly hates being predictable. "Fine, yes. It's me or them, Rose."

I grumble, but it's more for his benefit. Because I'm not going to lie, I've considered moving back home.

My brother sighs. "OK, what about going back to school?"

"What? Who has time for that?" I don't ask if he means art school or back to NYU to finish my degree. Because either way, I won't be able to afford this place on a part-time salary, or the tuition.

"*You* would if you let me help you. Rose, I'm your brother. I know your independence is important to you and being young and carefree has its appeal, but so is looking at the future. After the summer, let's talk. If you're still itching to get back to New York, I'll help you look for some scholarships and get you back into school. Even schools like . . ." He sighs. "Chelsea Art Academy."

My eyes widen at his offer. Is this a trick or is Wes really coming around? "Thought you said it's not *practical*."

"Fuck practical. This is what you want. We can get you a work-study program and maybe you can keep"—he sighs again, like coming on board with me is truly painful—"bartending on the weekends."

A grin spreads across my face. "Thanks, Wes." I consider the summer offer again for a beat, not quite ready to commit. "I really can take care of myself. I just . . . need to get my groove back."

He scoffs. "Where'd ya lose it? What's it look like? I don't think I've ever seen it."

"Wow. Harsh. You know, it's not my interest in art that makes me impulsive."

"Art? No. Quitting four jobs in the past year because of 'artistic differences' is impulsive."

"I'm going to embarrass you," I warn. Or maybe I'm fishing for some affection and reassurance that I could never do such a thing. That I'm *not* an embarrassment.

"It's *Wilder*. I'm pretty sure he could pass a certification test on my kid sister."

"Wonderful," I grumble. "Tell me you talk smack about me without telling me you talk smack about me."

"All right, I gotta get back to the kitchen before they burn something. We all set, then?"

I groan with a soft laugh. "Wes. I'll shrivel up and die out there."

"It's not that hot."

"I meant from boredom." Now I'm just having fun with him. Because I'm pretty sure I've already made my decision.

"You've got *me*," he cheers like he's the poster boy for good times.

"And the shriveling has started," I mutter.

"Well, it's not like you're going to be hanging out with me much. You'll be in the main office—or the Saddle Room, that's Wilder's office—I'm not entirely sure what you'll be doing. But he needs—"

"Wait, I thought you were hiring me to be your sous chef."

He laughs. Just *laughs*. Like I've said something hilarious. "Rose, if I let you in my kitchen, we'll *both* be out of a job."

The likelihood of Wilder cutting him loose is about as likely as me getting a call from Juilliard with a full scholarship based only on my Instagram posts.

Zero.

"So this is office work? Like papers and filing and stuff? I thought it was a farm."

"It's a ranch. Wilder needs help with the day-to-day. Vendor deliveries, inventory, billing, payroll, scheduling, things like that."

"Sounds like busy work."

"It is."

"And how much does it pay?"

"I didn't ask. But it comes with free housing and food. Hear great things about the chef."

I grumble, but it's not genuine. I've missed my brother's cooking.

"This isn't forever. It's just . . . a reset." Even as he says it, I can hear that he's still worried.

Wes's voice softens. "And who knows, maybe the scenery here will give you some inspiration."

There he goes, winning me over with art references. "The whole summer though? That seems like a long time to commit to something."

"Yeah, well, it's not exactly the whole summer. It's six weeks."

"Not until the end of August?"

"Well, you know. In case you . . . well, it's just . . . we want to make sure you'll really fit in here."

Heat floods my face when I realize what's happening here. "Wesley, did you have to twist his arm to hire me?"

"Couldn't if I tried."

"I don't mean physically," I grit.

"That's it. I'm not arguing with my little sister. Now start packing."

"You jackass. What did you say? Does he feel like he has to babysit me? Well, I'm telling you right now, I'm not about to be anyone's problem."

"No. Of course not. Wilder's not a softie like that. He truly needs the help, Rose." Something about his tone makes me believe him.

But I don't indicate as much.

He sighs again. "Look, remember a few weeks ago, I told you about his brother Dallas?"

"The one who lost his fiancée in a barn fire?"

"Yeah. He's been . . . well, unavailable, and Wild's been having to fill in—everywhere. We're not sure when Dal will be ready to get back to work. If he's not spending all day in bed, he's at Bones, one of the local bars here. He doesn't ride, barely talks to the staff anymore, he's just . . . not himself. Now Wilder's runnin' the place on his own."

I purse my lips. "Wasn't there a third brother?"

"Silas. Yeah. He doesn't have much to do with the ranch. Plays hockey for the Denver Kings."

"Oh, right. Can I be *his* assistant?"

Wesley chuckles. "Your enthusiasm is misplaced."

I grumble, partly to myself, "Yours would be too if it'd been a while since—"

"Rose, come on, boundaries."

I laugh. "All right, all right. I'll start packing. But be warned, if I hate it or if it's 'toxic,' I'm booking myself a one-way ticket back home."

I glance around the space. *Or as close to 'home' as I can afford right now.*

I hear him typing away. "It's a deal. I'm sending you flight information for Monday."

"It better not be before noon."

"Oh, that's another thing. This is an early-morning job. Not one that starts at four in the afternoon. You need to readjust your sleep schedule."

My chest tightens.

I can try.

But even I know that unless I intend on being a zombie at my new job, I won't be making it on time. Maybe Wilder will let me come up with a new *custom* arrangement.

Yeah, that'll work. I've had one conversation with the man ages ago, and I can only imagine how much his ability to rationalize with a woman has grown.

"Six weeks," I agree with a newfound worry.

"A reset," he reminds me.

Hours after hanging up and throwing some clothes on my bed to consider before packing, I catch Willow up on my new summer plans. She's my best friend—if not *only* friend. We met in college when I mistakenly walked into the music room where she—seemingly alone—was sitting in front of a piano, rocking out to a solo concert in her head.

We've been inseparable since.

Rose: I can't believe I said yes to this.

Willow: I can. You need to get out of the city. Sheesh, I wouldn't mind the fresh air myself if I could afford a plane ticket.

Rose: I'll miss working with you.

Willow plays piano at the downtown bar where I bartend; it's how I got the job. The owner there worships the ground she walks on, so when she recommended me, I pretty much started the next day.

Willow: Have you worked out your hours for this gig yet?

Rose: Early. *Real* early.

Willow: You're kidding.

Rose: I'll be fine.

3

Wilder

First of July and I already feel like I've dropped ten pounds of sweat this season. The heat doesn't usually bother me. The workload I'm stuck with now does. The *stress* does. The weight I'm bearing to keep this place running smoothly.

And make it look like we can afford to be one man down.

I ride across the pasture slowly, back toward the house, scanning the fields for routine inspection. It's not dusk yet, but I'm shot as hell since I was up at four this morning, rearranging the week's schedules to accommodate last-minute tours. OK, so maybe they weren't *last*-minute, per se. Maybe I'm working them *into* the schedule last-minute.

And somewhere deep, *deep* in the back of my worries is Wesley's sister. My last and only interaction with her was less than . . . well, mature. So excuse me if I'm less than confident that she could be of any use to me here.

I shake my head. Focus.

Did I check everything?

The fences seem to be holding up well. That's good.

It's not like me to be forgetful. My head's been somewhere else these last few rounds. And with the heavier workload, I can't afford things slipping through the cracks.

One brother's head wrapped in a fog is enough for this ranch.

My muscles ache, and my brain hurts from the amount of unreliable suppliers I never realized we work with. The pressure is mounting.

But nothing hurts like the knot of worry in my chest for Dallas.

He's no closer to healing than the day he had to say goodbye.

Reaching the house, I take a deep breath, bracing myself for another afternoon of trying to get Dallas out of bed and outside.

To my surprise, I hear him in the kitchen. The scent of citrus and something herbal hits my nose as I make my way inside.

His back is to me, facing the kettle. "Morning," he calls out.

"It's after four, Dal."

Dallas turns with a shrug. "Oh well." Older by three years and taller by an inch, my brother is a constant reminder of how different we are. He navigates the world with a natural serenity. His composed demeanor is frustrating for someone like me whose mind runs a mile a minute, constantly buzzing with worry, judging everything I lay my eyes on, and overbearing myself with burden.

I'm not proud that Rose comes to mind when I think of these burdens I'm taking on for the sake of others, but it's just how I see things right now.

I judge everything poorly until I'm proven otherwise.

It's not lost on me that I've found flaws in every supplier I've come to know since taking over inventory for the last two months.

Setting down my hat, I eye the dark stains on my marble counter, slices of lemon on a wooden cutting board, and stalks of washed basil in a bowl. "What you up to?"

He barely glances up. "Lemonade."

"That's a lot of lemons. Expectin' company?"

"I didn't make it right . . ." he mutters, his focus deep.

I point to the dark drops of liquid on the counter. "Tea?"

"Millie liked black tea lemonade." He tries a sip of the mixture. "Too sweet."

I nod slowly. "So . . . an Arnold Palmer."

"No. Millie couldn't pronounce it." He grins a little before it's gone. "Said it was a tongue-twister."

I exhale a small laugh. "Hardly."

He looks up. "How are things?"

I blink in surprise, since he hasn't asked about the ranch in a while. "Great. I mean . . . we're managing. How are you?"

He nods. "I dreamt of her last night. Woke up thinking it was her birthday or somethin'." He shakes it off and turns, dumping the mixture and muttering something about trying again.

"Well, go easy on those lemons. We don't grow those here." I chuckle, finding no humor in any of this nonsense.

His back is to me again, but he nods. I'm about to leave him to his mixing when he says, "Heard you hired yourself an assistant."

I pause and turn back tentatively on my heel—like I've done something wrong. "Yeah, well, thought we could use some help around here."

He meets my eyes for the first time today. Maybe in days. "'Cause of me?"

"Nah. It's probably long overdue, you know? Someone who can deal with the suppliers better than you or I can. Keep things in order."

"Someone who doesn't yell as often as you do? Who knows, she might teach you a thing or two about catching more bees with honey." He flicks his gaze to me again. A slight smirk. "She cute?"

"It's Wesley's kid sister," I practically snap.

"Ah, yes. Was wondering when he'd cave and relocate Rose."

"You know about her?"

"Yeah, I hang out in the kitchen occasionally. Might'a heard a thing or two about the untamable little sister. Surprised you agreed to it."

This is probably the most normal I've seen my brother in weeks. Though a shower wouldn't hurt.

"Not like I've got a choice."

His gaze in response is empty. Like he knows he's the source of our troubles but can't help it.

And hell, I don't blame him for checking out.

I thought I knew heartbreak after Bonnie left me, but this doesn't compare. Having the love of your life die in a fire that shouldn't have happened—on your ranch—is a tragedy beyond words.

But there should never be any comparison. Bonnie is and never will be *half* the woman Millie was.

And my dumb ass nearly gave up everything for her.

The sound of a car kicking up a trail of dust from the long driveway breaks our silent standoff.

I rub the back of my neck. "That's Wes back from the airport . . . with Rose."

Dallas looks uncomfortable for a moment, scanning his concoction like it's evidence of his grief.

"I'll uh . . . I'll come out there in a minute. Introduce myself."

What's the point? She'll probably never see you beyond the porch steps.

"Don't worry about it. You just . . ." I glance down at the mess on my counter. "Work on that iced tea. I'm going to need some later." I offer a small grin, but my brother remains unaffected by my efforts.

"Where she stayin'?" he asks, and there's an edge to the question. It's not conversational, it's almost a demand.

My gut twists. I'd expected this part to be easy. But looking at him now, it's anything but. "Millie's cottage."

Jaw tight and eyes on the counter, he nods. "It's cool," he assures, like I'm not an equal owner of everything on the property. "She'll like it there," he rasps.

"It's temporary. I didn't think a regular cabin would—"

"I said it's fine," he barks.

I nod, taking a step backward to the door. "Check in with you later." What I mean is I'll check in *on* you later, but I'm not in the mood for another defense.

I step outside, cross my arms over my chest, and lean against the post under the overhang.

Wesley hops out of his truck first, already shaking his head, car still idling.

My eyes narrow to the passenger seat. The girl I haven't seen in six years is silhouetted by the dipping sun. Her face is turned down and to the side like she's looking for something—her profile as sharp as the glass she's behind. She flips the visor down, looking up at the tiny mirror as she applies something on her nose and cheekbones. Probably sunscreen.

Wes pulls three giant suitcases from the back.

I can only imagine what they each contain. Stylish jeans and dresses, a variety of boots she'll complain about getting dirty, maybe a set of organic cotton sheets.

"Need some help?" I call without movement.

Rose emerges from the truck, a backpack slung over her shoulder and a pair of sunglasses perched over her nose.

Her hair is dark brown, falling in long, silky waves over her shoulders. She's small, with a deceptively delicate frame. Because from what I remember about this wild Rose, she's anything but delicate. She doesn't face me when she steps out—she faces the river, or maybe it's the mountains behind it that catch her attention.

Or hell, maybe it's just her being a brat.

Judging by the annoyed look on my best friend's face—and the defiant tilt of her chin—I can tell there was a fight on the way over.

Fucking great.

Wes comes around and mutters something that gets no reaction out of her.

I imagine it was something like "Behave" or "Don't embarrass me."

I can't help but scan her once more. Even if it is her backside I'm getting. Other than her longer hair, she doesn't appear to have grown much since I last saw her. She barely reaches Wes's shoulder, let alone my towering six-foot-four frame. She looks about as suited for ranch work as a kitten in a dog pen.

Wes climbs the steps of my porch, putting on a smile for me. Albeit a tight smile, but credit to him for trying.

I smirk, patting his back as he reaches me. "Rough ride?"

He sighs. "Just got a call from the kitchen. Jack needs help packin' up the take-home meals tonight. I was hoping to give Rose a quick tour before showing her to the cottage."

I follow his gaze. Something tells me that's not the only reason he's ditching her right now. She's still watching the fields like we're not over here talking about her. "Remind me why I'm doing this?"

"Because you need help around here and she's available—and to help me out. Honestly, if she didn't come back here with me, I'd have seriously considered moving to New York."

I frown at this new information. *Wes considered leaving?*

"You didn't tell me that."

"Good thing I didn't have to." He winks and slaps my shoulder. "Ro," Wes calls, waving her over.

I catch her shoulders lift, a sharp inhale that promises a sigh, but then she stops—like time catches her mid-motion. Her head turns toward us, and for a heartbeat, everything stills. Slowly, deliberately, her shoulders fall with a soft exhale, and she pushes her sunglasses up onto her head.

Pouty, bee-stung lips part slightly, and my mouth goes dry.

With a hard swallow, I tear my gaze off them—meeting her eyes—and it's not any better.

"*Hell*," I growl low at the sight.

Maybe it's the way the sun hits her, or the way those dark silky locks frame that round face, but fuck, her eyes are striking. They're green, like I remember, but packed with raw, magnetic intensity.

Closing her mouth with a swallow, Rose scans me. And I'm not sure if she's deciding if she could take me in a wrestling match . . . or checking me out.

Something tells me that's a package deal with Rose.

You'll never truly know what goes on in her head.

"You say something?" Wes asks.

"Uh . . . was she always this . . . small?"

He laughs. "Yep, you just got broader since you saw her last."

I lick my lips. "Let's head down. Doesn't look like she takes too well to commands."

My buddy mutters a "thanks" and follows me down the steps.

"Rose." I keep my tone sharp yet friendly, but don't offer a hand. It's hard enough keeping my expression neutral as I come within a foot of her.

Touching her right now would be as foolish as my reaction when our eyes met.

"Rose, you remember Wilder."

She steps back, making a point of looking up at me, shielding her eyes. "I don't remember him being a giant."

I cock my head. "Still got your manners intact, I see."

"Still haven't found yours, I see." She extends her hand, making a show of my rudeness.

"Rose," Wes warns from behind me.

I stare back, my eyes drawn to every damn feature.

She's fucking stunning.

And Christ, what is that smell? Like grapefruit and . . . coffee? Shouldn't she smell like an airport or luggage or something that isn't so . . . damn good?

"Kitchen," I say, then twist my neck to look at my friend. "You said Jack needed you?"

Wesley jerks at my boss-like demeanor. "Right. Rose, I've got to get back to work, but I'll swing by later, OK? Wilder will get you settled."

"Don't bother, I can take care of myself."

He sighs. "I'll see you tomorrow then; stop in the kitchen for breakfast. I tucked a map into your backpack."

Rose doesn't respond with anything more than a glare.

When he hesitates, I give him a reassuring nod, and he hops back in his truck, pulling away without a second glance.

I watch him make his way off my lot. The blow of his words up on the porch still hitting hard.

He was going to leave Blue River?

Losing Wes in the kitchen is one thing. But he's been my best friend since college. I can't imagine running this place without his support. Sure as hell not getting it from Dallas these days.

I turn back to Rose, determined to make this work—for Wes.

Now that he's gone, the corner of her lip twitches. She swings her backpack from around her shoulder and shoves it at my chest. "I imagine you have someone who can bring my bags to my room? After a super quick tour—if one is even necessary—I'm going to need a nap. So I do hope they're equipped with blackout curtains. And then . . . what do you have for transportation? Because I took a look at that map, and there's no way I'm walking."

The glimmer in her eye gives away that she's playing with me. But on the off chance she's serious, I step closer, my imposing frame towering over her. "Let's get one thing clear—this isn't a vacation. You're here to work, not sightsee."

Her eyes widen as she scans her surroundings like I'm delusional. "What's there to see?"

"Plenty. So try to keep up." I check my watch and start walking. "I've got exactly one hour to give you that 'super quick tour' and I expect you to take notes. Because tomorrow, when I send you to the Cattle Quarters at six a.m. for feeding, you'll need to know what I'm talking about."

She bursts out a laugh, slightly breathless as she tries to keep up with me. "Six a.m.? You're kidding, right?"

I'm surprised she's not shocked at me giving her ranch-hand duties. But I keep walking.

"Welcome to Blue River Ranch. Our days start early. Also, I was kidding about the feeding; you're not going anywhere near my animals. I'll assign you tasks daily and expect them done right the first time. If you don't understand something, ask questions. No wandering about the ranch, keep your eyes alert at all times and your phone on in case I call, and I *will* be calling or forwarding you messages. A lot. That clear?" I stop and pivot back to let her catch up.

But she's closer than I anticipated and slams into my chest with an "*Oof*" from our collision, bouncing back from impact.

I catch her wrist, my voice rough as sandpaper as I pull her back. "Sorry, didn't realize—"

"That I could keep up?" she asks, winded and blinking up at me. "I'm from New York. We don't dawdle."

I scowl, annoyed that this girl seems to have an answer for everything, but at the same time, still holding her wrist like I need some reassurance she's all right.

Her voice is shaky as she tears her gaze off where we're connected and looks up. That smooth throat of hers working as she swallows. She pulls her hand free, composing herself. "Shall I call you 'boss' too? Or do you prefer 'sir'?" Her lip quirks mischievously.

I clear my throat, trying to stay composed as my mind races to whatever she's implying. But my body betrays me as heat rises to my skin. "I don't care what you call me," I snap. "As long as you answer when I do and you show up on time. I've got a ranch to run, and I'm pretty much on my own, so I need you to take this seriously and hold some level of respect."

She stares at me, any humor wiped from her face. "What exactly has my brother been telling you about me?"

I leave her question unanswered but note the hint of hurt in her eyes.

"I need some confirmation that I'm understood."

She perks a brow. "Yes, sir."

"Cute," I mutter, before stalking toward my red truck parked near the gate of my long driveway. I don't usually park it this far from my house but needed to unload a delivery earlier onto a tractor.

I open the passenger door and toss her backpack inside.

I feel her sprint behind me. "Whoa—we can't just leave my stuff." She points back to the house where the three suitcases sit on the gravel driveway. "Two of those suitcases are art supplies. They'll get fried out here."

That makes me pause. *She brought more art supplies than clothes?* I flick my gaze to her worried one. "I'll text my brother to bring them inside." I cock my head. "Get in."

Her eyes narrow at my tone. "Still single, I presume?" she mutters before sliding in, giving me another whiff of that tangy scent.

I don't bother confirming her assumption and shut the door, then quickly shoot Dallas a text to bring the suitcases inside the house and I'll pick them up later.

Our first stop is the main office, which is nestled at the entrance to the property.

"Blue River Ranch," Rose says as she looks up at the hand-painted wooden sign on the building. "In Blue River Springs . . ." She squints up at me. "How original."

Without comment, I yank the door open and hold it for her.

Following her inside, I'm hit with the scent of burnt coffee and leather.

Rose must notice it too as she inhales softly with a frown, then scans the dark paneled walls that showcase photographs of the ranch's history.

"Well, afternoon, Wild," Ginger greets me. But it's not her usual greeting. She's looking at Rose. "This must be the new assistant."

"Ginger, this is Rose, Wesley's kid sister. She's going to be helping us out this summer until we—" My office manager and I lock eyes in an unspoken exchange. "Well, until we're adequately staffed again. Rose, this is—"

"Oh, you're no *kid*." Ginger waves me off and pushes out of her chair, coming around the reception desk.

"Look at you, you're as grown up as I am." She takes Rose's delicate hands into hers with a firm grip.

To my surprise, Rose beams at her.

"Can't argue with that," I mutter. Despite her mature age of sixty-two, Ginger is as serious as a kid in grade school.

"This is Ginger," I continue with a sigh. "Our office manager and the glue that's been holding this place together since my father opened it thirty years ago."

Rose smiles. "Oh, you must be Gingerbread. Wes has told me so much about you." Rose hugs the woman that's been like a mother to me for decades—even when my own was still with us.

"Oh." Ginger presses a hand against her chest. "That boy's as sweet as those cookies he bakes me." She grips Rose's hands. "Now you listen, this grumpy cowboy here gives you any lip, you come talk to me." She winks.

I roll my eyes. "You two about done?"

Rose ignores me, her eyes shimmering with gratitude. "That a promise? Because I started twenty minutes ago and I've already got enough to fill your afternoon."

Ginger gasps. "Wilder Thorne. Your best friend's little sister? Where are your manners?"

I rub the back of my neck and avoid Ginger's eyes. "Heard her say she could take care of herself just fine. Come on, we need to make more rounds."

"Is this where I'll be working?" Rose almost sounds excited as she takes in the guest welcome area.

"No." I start walking toward the back. "Let's move." I stroll past a few tourists browsing a selection of ranch-branded merchandise. Rose eyes the shelves stacked with goods like scented candles, wooden spoons, and handwoven blankets. It's not quite a gift shop but fills the walls with more of that "touristy vibe" Dallas insisted we needed. Tourists were less impressed with old family photos and vintage memorabilia. I didn't disagree since it's just the kind of thing I learned in business school. Commercializing the ranch has made it more profitable but at the same time, created busy work for us.

It's been a joint effort over the years and business has sure been booming as a result. But it comes with a price. Bigger staff, double the vendors, upkeep of each structure. And the bane of my existence, bookkeeping.

After a quick intro to the rest of the office staff, I cock my head to the exit. "Let's move on."

"Oh, sweetie, wait up," Ginger calls, placing a bag on the counter. "I swiped this from the gift shop just for you." She eyes me. "Sure the boss won't mind."

Rose dips her hand into the bag, pulling out a pink cowboy hat. At this point, I've got a migraine in my future with all the eye rolling.

"Oh," Rose breathes, slight disappointment in her voice. "It's so pretty. Thanks. You got a blue one?"

"Blue?"

"It's my favorite color."

Ginger frowns. "Blue cowboy hat . . . no, I don't think so. We sell a lot of the pink ones, though. Thought with a name like Rose, you'd be a fan . . ."

Rose blinks, then smiles gratefully. "This is perfect. Thanks, Ginger."

My office manager gives me one final glare of warning to "be nice" before shooing us out.

I hold the door open for Rose, hearing Ginger behind me typing away into the computer and muttering "blue cowboy hats."

The next stop is one of the barns, one of the larger ones that overlooks the south pasture. I can tell from her expression the smell hits her hard but I give her credit for not saying as much.

My tour is quick, like with any newcomer. Partly because I'm not one hundred percent sure she's listening. And partly because I'm not sure how long she'll really be able to hack it here.

I gesture at the open space as we walk past the wide door. "This one's mainly used for storage," I say, "and shelter during rain. You'll be in here quite a bit, signing for deliveries, keeping things in order. I'll need you to make sure it stays in good shape and stocked. You're not responsible for keeping it clean, but let me know if it needs it, and I'll get the boys on it." I turn to her, something I've been avoiding since her body was pressed against mine and I had the breath knocked out of me. "You'll have a set schedule," I tell her firmly. "Nothing too overwhelming, but busy."

Rose nods slowly as she processes everything.

"Any questions so far?"

"Just one. How do I get around? Will I get a horse?"

I chuckle. "No. You'll be on foot, mostly. Anywhere you need to go is within walking distance of the Saddle Room—that's my office. You can always pull me or Jeff aside if you need a ride somewhere. That's one of our cowboys. He's been with us for nearly a decade. Trust him more than I trust myself. I'll introduce you tomorrow."

Rose blinks, her gaze blank. Something tells me she's not keen on the idea of depending on someone just to get around.

We hop back in my truck, but I don't move just yet. From where I sit, I point back to the main office, reminding her where it is. "You'll stop in there to pick up mail for Dallas and me. I'll need you to go through it. Any outstanding invoices need to be thoroughly reviewed. Way you do that is to confirm on time delivery and that inventory received is what's stated on the invoice. Ginger and Brett at the office can help you with that. Your signature on each one confirms you checked all the boxes. I'll approve it and you'll take it back to the office."

She frowns. "There's got to be an easier way to do all that. You got email here?"

"We do. But Ginger doesn't like email. She likes paper." I start the car and drive. "Also, all vendor calls will be forwarded to you. Any questions, you can talk to Brett or call Dallas—he's usually the one who deals with them."

She waves me off. "Oh, I don't need to bother him. I'll be fine. I'm great with people."

"They're not social calls. You're conducting *business* and ensuring we're getting what we paid for."

She gives me a pointed look. "It's *all* about how you talk to people, Wilder."

I'm certain this is the first time I have heard her say my name. Damn certain. Because I would have remembered the way it sounded from that soft, raspy voice.

It takes me a moment to realize she's merely modeling an example of just how she'd get more bees with honey. And hell, if it didn't work.

Because the second I heard my name from her lips, I wanted to hear it again.

I glance over to tell her that it won't work—if only to convince myself—but when I do, I hold back. Her eyelids are falling heavy.

She's tired.

It's barely another minute drive before I reach the cottage. I consider the distance. Sure, she can walk from point A to B of where she'll spend most of her time, but that might still get to be a little too much.

The thought makes me consider if I'm being a little rough on her before her first day. Like I'm expecting her to fail.

And that's not fair.

Not to mention if she hates it here and leaves, who's to say Wesley won't follow her back to the east coast?

My thoughts come to a complete halt when I see Dallas's car along the gravel road in front of Millie's cottage.

"The hell?" I mutter.

"Something wrong?" Concern laces her voice, which is unexpected. Or maybe what I'm hearing is more *anticipation* for something exciting. That's more in line with what I know about her.

And unfortunately, if it's a show Rose is itching for, she might just get one.

4

Rose

"Stay here a minute," Wilder tells me, and my heart is in my throat. Panic slams into me as he rushes out, leaving me alone in the car. I can't move—can hardly breathe as past events drag me under.

The sun has set and the lights are on in the house. I blink, making out the car parked in front of the charming cottage. It's familiar. In fact, I'm pretty sure I saw it back at Wilder's house just under an hour ago.

I breathe a sigh of relief. It's someone he knows. Someone who . . . lives with him?

Is it a woman? Will I be living *with* someone?

I watch him march across the gravel road to the porch steps before quickly deciding I want to know what's got him so worked up.

Jumping out, I follow behind him. My footsteps crunch on the gravel but he's too focused on who's inside to notice.

My eyes trail around the blue and white painted exterior. This *can't* be all for me for the short while I'm staying. I imagined I'd be at one of the cabins we just drove past. Wes said he stayed in one before he bought his apartment but that I wouldn't last a day in one of those.

It was almost insulting. But on the off chance he's right, I didn't challenge my brother. But this . . . this is more like a small house. Wilder's clearly taken me to the wrong place.

I'm still staring up at the siding when I feel myself—once again—crash against a hard body that's stopped short in front of me.

"Oomph," I exhale on impact.

Bouncing back, I blink, quickly realizing I've slammed against his backside this time.

And *damn,* he's hard everywhere. What is this man made of? They sure don't make them like this in Manhattan. Or South Carolina for that matter. I should be abundantly mortified that I just pressed myself against him, not once, but twice in the span of one hour.

But I'm not.

I'm buzzing with a new energy I can't quite place. But the heat filling my cheeks is about to spell it out for me.

Is it me? Would it have killed Wesley to warn me that this man is notorious for stopping short and I'd do well to stay within ten feet of him at all times?

Wilder spins back irritably. "What are you doing?"

I blink, needing a minute to think of something witty or bratty or anything to distract the man from thinking I either have two left feet or am trying to feel him up.

I scoff. "Trying to feel you up and making it look like an accident. What does it look like I'm doing? I'm *following* you, jackass."

"What did you say?"

"Oh, you don't like that? Boss–employee respect works both ways. So when *I* start seeing a shred of it, so will you," I snap.

I hear a chuckle from above the steps, and we both turn. A burly man who looks the exact definition of a cowboy beams down at me. "Well, you must be Rosie."

"It's just Rose."

He nods curtly . . . *respectfully*. "My apologies, Rose." He steps down.

"Dallas Thorne, good friend of your brother's, and the better-looking Thorne brother." He extends a hand. I take it, feeling the roughness of his palm against mine.

He's not wrong about being good-looking. But *better* looking? I'm not sure.

Dallas's hair, from what I can see under that black cowboy hat, is darker, while Wilder's is more sun-kissed. The older brother's got that tall, dark, and handsome look about him, a bearded rugged handsome. An *intimidating* handsome.

Wilder is more *GQ* magazine featuring cowboys, kind of handsome. Sharp jawline dusted with the hint of stubble, eyes a deep blue, steady, a little too knowing. A strong frame and lean muscles that I've felt *twice* today. From both directions.

The other difference? I didn't forget how to *breathe* when I saw Dallas.

"More like the oldest," Wilder mutters. "What are you doing here?" His voice is rough, and I'm not sure if he's angry at his brother for something or at me for snapping at him.

Feeling tension, I step between the brothers. "It's nice to finally meet you." I smile at Dallas. Then remember the last time I heard Wes speak of him. My face drops. "Oh, and I'm so sorry for your loss."

His eyes soften, gratitude filling them. *Thank God.* I never know what to say to people when they're grieving.

"Thank you, Rose." He gestures behind us. "This was hers. Well, for the last two years, at least."

My eyes go wide. "Oh, well then I couldn't possibly—"

"Nonsense. It's clean, furnished, and has the best view of the river—it's perfect. I just stopped by to bring those suitcases of yours. What you got in there, bricks?"

"Art supplies, mostly."

He rubs his chin. "Huh. Well, walls could use some fresh art, I suppose."

I hesitate and look at Wilder—not like he'd give me much to work with.

As expected, he ignores me and looks at his brother. "Since you're here, you, uh . . . want to help me give our new temp a tour of the place?"

Dallas gives a low headshake. "Nah, I didn't make it far past the front door," he says honestly, and my heart breaks a little for him.

Wilder takes a step toward his brother, his hands on his hips and his voice low. "When I asked you to pick them up off the driveway, I didn't mean—"

"I know. I wanted to." Dallas's kind but hurting eyes turn back to me. "You need anything, just give me a call." He tips his hat curtly, but there's no forced smile this time. "Be seein' ya."

"Thank you," I offer softly.

The two of us wait until Dallas drives off before facing each other.

Wilder gives me a scan as he releases a breath, then motions toward the entrance, like I'm the chore he's been avoiding all day. "After you."

It takes everything in me not to roll my eyes. Because let's be honest, I did just slam into this mountain of a man twice and he's now probably a little wary of me.

I reach the top step and my eyes are instantly drawn to the name painted on the white mailbox.

Millie Rivers.

I can't do this. It doesn't feel right.

I flip around, holding my hands up to pause, and—wouldn't you know, Mr. Mountain and his rock-hard chest walk right into them.

I squeeze my eyes shut. "Oh my God, I swear, I am not doing this on purpose."

There's a rumble that vibrates from his chest that makes me think he's amused. I look up to find the slightest hint of a grin.

I jerk my hands back like I've touched a boiling pot. His eyes drop to them. "Was there a problem?"

With your chest? Heavens, no. It's per—

The house. He means the house.

"No. It's just—I don't feel right staying here." I glance behind me "This place looks lovely, but it's . . . I mean, he's still . . ."

Another sigh. "Have it your way." He turns on his heel and starts down the steps. "Let's go."

I blink but don't question him yet. This man's made it very clear he doesn't slow down for anyone. I catch up first, mindful to keep a decent distance.

He walks past his truck and toward the elevated cabins lined up along the river. I move fast to keep up with his swift steps. I consider asking where we're going and about my things, but something tells me not to poke the bear right now.

We've walked what's equivalent to a long city block before he slows down and counts the cabins with his index finger before stopping at one. "That one should be open."

Wait—it's either the cottage or *this*? There's *nothing* in between?

My stomach twists with apprehension, but I don't say anything. If it's this or the cottage, then this will have to do. Hell, it'll just add to the adventure. Put me in touch with nature. Or spiders, whatever.

Its weather-beaten slats lean slightly to the right. Something that might not be noticeable to locals, but my artistic eye catches almost every imperfection.

Something tells me I'm about to have a field day of imperfections.

I pause at the stoop, warily eyeing the steps. But Wilder jogs up like it's nothing. Like they're not about to crack at the slightest gust of wind.

He pulls out a set of keys, not bothering to look back at me as he unlocks the door. "You comin'?"

I swallow, putting my hand on the wooden rail. "Right behind ya—a safe, crash-free distance behind."

Rolling his eyes, he holds the door open for me, and I know why. The jerk is waiting to see my reaction as I walk in.

Well, two can play this game.

I don't linger at the entrance. Nor pay any mind to the lone window on the front that has a crack running through it. I march right in.

I keep my eyes low, not wanting to give away too much. The wooden planks seem to be in good condition, not warped or anything. And the creaks they make with each step are faint, so there's that.

It's dim, the overhead light casting a yellowish glow on the small space. There's a twin bed, dresser, armchair and a kitchenette. It smells all right, I suppose. Or maybe I lost my sense of smell earlier, back at the barn?

"This is it," Wilder says gruffly, but I don't miss the faint smirk. "Will it do?"

"Well, it's not the Ritz, I'll admit," I say, showing good faith by tossing my backpack on the bed—with sheets looking older than me.

He laughs. He actually laughs. It's deep and gravelly, and it makes my stomach fizz. Even if it is at my expense.

The. Absolute. Nerve.

"I take it the bathroom is through there?" I ask, pointing at the door by the old dresser that will *not* be seeing any of my clothes. Art supplies, maybe. In fact, I may just use some to give it a little life.

He folds his arms, watching me as he offers a subtle nod.

Unzipping my backpack, I pull out a pack of disinfectant wipes I brought for the plane and hold it up. "Well then, I'll be right back."

"Rose." It's a mix of warning and calling my bluff, but I don't turn around.

Pushing the door to the bathroom open, I pause at the threshold. It's surprisingly clean. Small, yes, but not all that different from my apartment. Maybe a bit more rustic.

"Smells nice in here," I call out, still wiping down every surface.

"Sure it's not the coconut-scented toilet wipes you got in there?"

"They're hand wipes and they come in handy." I chuckle out loud at my own pun as I finish my business and flush.

"Bet you won't find it funny when the bears come around . . ."

I yank the door open. "Bears?"

"Only seen once or twice this year. Just keep your door locked."

I almost laugh at the irony.

Oh, don't worry, cowboy. I always do.

My eyes flicker to the wooden door nervously, resisting the urge to ask if I'm safe here. If there's a history of break-ins. Or . . . if he's got a few extra locks I can borrow.

I don't ask any of that. Not yet, at least. "So there's some huffing and puffing in my near future?"

He watches me for a moment, then shakes his head. "Nah, you're fine. Besides, I didn't say wolves. I said bears."

I march to the front door and carefully pull it open, to ensure I don't yank the knob right out of the wood. "Well then, let's test out this lock now, shall we?" I cock my head, gesturing for him to leave.

"Rose, come on, you are not staying here."

"And why not? Others do."

He goes into the logistics of the practicality of having cowboys live on the property. The types of emergencies that can happen at any hour and needing staff on site to tend to it.

"Well, I'm part of your staff now," I say with a shrug. I'm not sure what I'm trying to prove here. It could be the way he's been rolling his eyes at me like I'm some hopeless, spoiled city girl. Or that I like watching him squirm. Or maybe . . . this rustic living . . . is just the adventure I need.

"So are Ginger, Wesley, and several others who have homes outside these gates."

I sigh, still holding the door open.

"Rose, I don't got time for games. You're staying at Mil—you're staying at the cottage. End of story."

"Or what?"

Hands on his hips, he twists his neck. "Know what? Have it your way. Breakfast starts at five and ends at eight in The Shack—that's the kitchen. I suggest you get there at six since you're due in my office at seven."

Is he mental?

"Seven. Got it, boss. Am I to bring you coffee too? Extra foam, no sugar?"

"I don't drink coffee."

If I needed some sign that he's not perfect—besides his biting remarks, which I'm totally here for—that was it. *He doesn't drink coffee?*

"Explains why you're so grumpy."

With a final glare, he turns and marches down the steps. "I'll have someone drop off your bags here tonight."

I stand with my chin up and arms crossed like I've won. When the truth is—no one did. And I have a feeling there's going to be plenty of these rounds.

I shut the door and turn back to my little cabin, expecting to see a spider or roach skittering past me.

"Nope. No roaches here," I mutter under my breath. "Just bears and hot, grumpy cowboys."

12.42 a.m.

Willow: How's your first night?

I send her a pic of my cabin in reply.

Willow: Cute. But you're not really staying there are you?

Rose: It's OK, it was worth it.

Willow: What was?

Rose: The look on his face.

Willow: Your brother?

Rose: No. My boss.

5

Wilder

The first ray of sunlight hasn't even warmed the fields and my patience is already burning out. It's past eight and Rose was due in the Saddle Room an hour ago. I stare at the collection of vintage saddles mounted on the walls instead of getting my head into all the work I have ahead of me.

Since my new assistant is a no-show.

I run a hand through my hair and reach for the paperwork stacked on the desk, shuffling through it like I'm looking for something specific when I know damn well I'm not.

I toss the papers back down, berating myself for thinking I could make this work.

This was a mistake. Dad warned me never to do business with friends—which, let's be honest, is exactly what I did with Wesley. Except he's not the problem.

I grab my hat from the desk, shove it on my head, and pace to the window. Still no sign of her walking down from the cabins.

How hard can it be to show up on time?

Maybe her phone died. Maybe the sound is off on her alarm.

Maybe I had this coming.

Rose isn't exactly what I expected when she stepped out of Wes's car fifteen hours ago. Short shorts, burgundy boots, and green eyes that lock me in like a forest path, leading somewhere I can't resist.

This is a sign.

If she's distracting me this much without even being here—there's no way I could work side by side with her all summer.

Especially when she keeps slamming herself into me—accident or not.

Her throaty gasps from our collisions wrapped around me like velvet. I swear I kept hearing them all night in my head. If Dallas wasn't asleep in the next room, I'd have blasted music just to tune them out.

And the shower I took when I got home barely erased the lingering sensation of her touch.

When she bumped into me from behind, she steadied herself with a firm grip on my arm, and it felt . . . *good* to be that anchor for her.

I growl, dragging a hand down my face. It's bad enough having Wes's sister working for me. I don't need to complicate things by noticing how soft her skin is.

How her breasts felt pressed against me. Or the flush in her cheeks when they had.

Work. I need to work.

My boots thud against the hardwood as I pace my office. I could march up to her cabin and bang on the door. Give her a piece of my mind.

Except the thought of standing face to face with her, especially when she might still be in her pajamas . . . or worse, some city girl nightie, makes me rethink that fast.

Before I can make up my mind, the sound of an engine outside breaks the morning quiet. Peering out the window, I find Wesley's truck pulling up in front of the Saddle Room. I yank the door open and march out.

Of course she asked her brother for a ride. Heaven forbid she walks a little more than a city block.

Wait. There's no one in the passenger seat.

Wesley steps out with a large to-go cup and brown paper bag, his grin as easygoing as ever.

My jaw is tight as I weigh my options. Take out my frustration on my best friend. Or play it cool.

I swallow, taking my time as I walk over. "You bring me somethin'?"

"Rose didn't stop in for breakfast this morning. Figured you got her starting early, so I brought it over."

I clench my back teeth. Wesley's quick to notice, his grin dropping.

"Oh boy, what'd she do? It's her attitude, isn't it?"

I shake my head, forcing a laugh as I choose to play it cool. "Nah, she's fine. Just settling in, I think."

Wesley's brows furrow as he looks past me to my office. "Shouldn't you be prepping for the tour group comin' in later, instead of delivering coffee?" I ask, noticing how my tone is laced with annoyance.

I never said I was *good* at playing it cool.

Wes blinks at my unexpected brush-off. Thankfully, he doesn't confront me about it—not at work. Though it'll catch up with me later over beers, I suppose.

"Just wanted to check on her." He hands me the paper bag and hot coffee cup. "And maybe make sure she doesn't hate me for draggin' her out here. I may have made a cappuccino muffin batch this morning, extra chocolate chips." He winks for good measure and turns back to his car without another word. But his mood's changed, and I feel like shit.

"Hey," I call back. "What's a guy gotta do to get one of these? 'Cause *my* brother ain't bringing me anything but more work." I chuckle.

Wes is unamused, watching me for a long moment. Then glances at the door to my office. "She's not here yet, is she?"

I rub the back of my neck. "Probably still getting settled."

Wes shakes his head. "I'll swing by the cottage and check on her."

Panic flares in my chest. If he finds out Rose spent the night in the drafty old cabin—one I took her to in order to prove a point—he might just deck me for messing with her.

"Actually, I was just about to head that way," I say quickly. "And hell, she's probably already on her way."

Wes gives me a long look, then shrugs. "All right, just . . . keep an eye on her for me?"

I look away, acting bored. "You got it."

I watch him drive off, my stomach knotting tighter with each passing second. If this is any indication of how my summer is going to go—I'm putting a stop to it.

It's nearly nine when I storm back into the Saddle Room and pick up the phone. I don't bother with small-talk when the familiar elderly voice answers. "Ginger, I need you to do me a favor."

The door to my office bursts open and a brunette flies in like there's a blizzard outside.

My mouth goes dry at the sight. Wild-haired, flushed, and gasping for breath, is Rose. The girl I need to remind myself to look after the way my best friend asked.

"Never mind, I'm all set," I mutter to Ginger before hanging up.

Her pink lips close as she looks up at me apologetically and swallows hard. "I am so sorry."

Tearing my eyes off her face, I scan the rest of her. She's in a long-sleeved shirt again—blue this time, and a pair of denim shorts. And the burgundy boots from yesterday.

Before I can form words, Rose holds her hands up. "Before you yell, yes, I set an alarm—I swear I did. I thought I hit snooze, but apparently, I shut it off—I've been known to do that—plus I was out super late—"

"Rose," I bark, holding up a hand to stop her. She takes a deep breath.

"What do you mean you were out late? Where did you go?"

She shrugs. "I took a power nap, got up, had a can of soup . . . and then later, when I couldn't sleep, I took a walk."

I cock my head. "How much later?"

"Eleven."

I glare at her.

She frowns at me, placing her hands at her hips, still catching her breath. "Don't look at me like that, I can take a walk whenever I want. Just because I'm staying on your grounds, doesn't make it your business."

A mix of frustration and something else I don't want to name tightens my chest. "Rose, I'm not one to stop you from going out, but you don't know your way around. Especially at night. You can't be wandering around the ranch after dark. It's not safe."

She rolls her eyes. "It's not like I went out there looking for rattlesnakes and coyotes. I saw a bonfire over by the corral and figured it was a ranch thing. Bunch of nice boys were having beers and roasting marshmallows." She shrugs innocently as if she had no choice. "Didn't want to miss the party."

I crack my neck. It's not that I don't allow bonfires on the ranch—especially when we've got the fire pits for it. But I don't exactly love the idea of my best friend's sister walking into one.

My jaw tightens. "You did what?"

She blinks at my tone, her smile faltering. "I joined them for a little while. It looked fun, and they didn't mind. They all seemed really nice."

"Rose," I say firmly, stepping closer. "You can't do that. I've got decent enough men on my staff, but some are still fairly new. I don't know them all that well. Especially not what they're like when they're drinking." Her eyes are wide but she still seems confused. "You've got to understand what I'm saying. Some of these guys are only here for a few weeks before they move on. Bottom line is, I don't trust them all."

She tugs on her bottom lip. "Right."

Fisting a hand, I hold it against my mouth, fighting the urge to ask if she slept OK otherwise, because she looks like she could use another few hours. "Want some coffee?"

Green eyes light up, and it lifts something heavy off my chest. "Coffee?"

I point to my desk. "Your brother brought it by a few minutes ago. Said he didn't see you at breakfast and figured you were hard at work."

I take my seat and motion to the chair across the cluttered desk. "Let's go over a few things on the agenda this week, then I'll leave you to it."

She crosses to my desk but doesn't sit. "Wilder, I'm so sorry I held you back this morning."

My gut twists at the unexpected tenderness. The man in me wants to tell her it's all right and that maybe a good night's sleep is what she needed. But the boss in me—and fine, maybe the protectiveness in me—wants to scowl and yell at her for spending a late evening with strange men. If that's just her first night, what the hell kind of trouble do I have ahead of me?

She looks at me tentatively and continues, "If you could stop looking at me like that, I'd like to explain. It's just I'm used to late hours because I have trouble falling a—"

"Rose. Sit down, drink your coffee and let's get to work."

I need to take a step back. A bossy step back. Because fuck how much time I've already lost this morning. I want to go find Landry or Jeff and make them tell me who was at the gathering last night and if anyone showed any level of disrespect toward Rose.

She releases a breath and sits. "OK." She pops the lid of the cup and takes a sip, releasing a moan. "Wes makes the best coffee." She lifts her eyes to mine.

"Can we focus?" I shout, tossing down the stack of mail.

Her eyes drop to the papers as that throat works again to swallow. "They told me you do that. A lot."

"What?"

"Yell. I should tell you, I don't . . . do well with people yelling at me." She holds up her hands in defense. "And I in no way mean that as a threat, I swear. I just . . . well, I don't like it. And I might—"

I perk a brow. "Cry?"

"Slap you. It's . . . impulsive. I almost got arrested for assault against my old manager. Bitch had it comi—" She covers her mouth, her cheeks turning a deeper shade of pink. "You know what? I've wasted enough of your time, let's get on with it." She motions to the stack of papers.

She's agonizingly adorable.

What the hell did I get myself into?

6

Rose

"How was your first day?" Ginger stretches the last word as I walk through the door.

I roll my stiff neck and hand her the invoices Wilder approved for payment today and the schedule for the rest of the week. I helped him re-work it after he mapped out the week's events, tours, and the day-to-day staffing for every part of the ranch.

It took a considerable amount of time to figure it all out. But I think I impressed him with how effectively I spaced out his staff. I told him this was similar to what I did at the gallery. We had various exhibits, events, and tours where staffing needed to be properly distributed. With levels of talent and focus in mind, of course. That's where Wilder came in. But now that I have an idea of who does what—and a cheat sheet—I can help with scheduling each week.

Was it easy sitting shoulder to shoulder with him half the day? No . . . no, it wasn't. On several instances I had to remind myself to *focus*. But he smelled so . . . manly. The scent of leather and cedar clinging to him. Heat crept up my neck every time he shifted in his seat, making my breath catch.

God, I hope men are as oblivious to notice these things as Willow insists they are.

But what was a girl to do except grip her pen tighter and hold her breath because she could *feel* the vibration each time he hummed or spoke, that low rich voice entirely too close.

Thankfully, we won't always work side by side the way we did today. We covered enough of my responsibilities, including timekeeping, ordering supplies, and checklists for deliveries.

I'm sure I can do more. He seems so overwhelmed. But I'll take it one day at a time. Not to mention, I'm already on thin ice with the man.

"Not bad," I tell her. "I overslept, so I suppose it could have been better."

She perks a brow. "Heard there was a special guest at the bonfire last night. And that you were a real hoot."

"A hoot?"

"Had everyone pretty entertained with all your stories about Wesley pre-Blue River, and city life, and somethin' about how you're pretty sure it's illegal to force someone to live on a farm for six weeks with no way of getting to a Starbucks."

I put my hand on my hips. "They all laughed, but I was damn serious."

She chuckles. "I'll put it in the suggestion box."

Brett walks past Ginger, carrying a clipboard. "Could always try the shuttle that takes tourists to and from town. Don't think one runs at night though."

"Shuttle," I repeat, unimpressed.

"I'll pull up the schedule for you, dear," Ginger offers.

I sigh, about to ask Brett if there are other options.

Before I have a chance to, a young man in overalls and with dimples peeks his head through an open window. "Hey, Brett, you want me to take the golf cart and run the Bransons over to the north pasture? They wanted to see the wildflower trail."

Golf cart?

Brett sighs. "Yeah, all right. But stay with them and tell 'em we close in thirty minutes. I want those carts back in place before tomorrow's tours. We're short as it is without them being scattered all over the place."

"Got it." The young man disappears from the window, and I cock my head to see the direction he's heading in.

"That's cool, you give tours in golf carts?" I ask casually.

Brett sighs. "Yeah, we've got a couple smaller ones to get around the ranch quicker. The bigger ones, six- and eight-seaters, move tourists or staff when we need to run errands or carry equipment."

And no one thought to tell me about this? I want to ask, but I simply shrug. "Good to know there are ways to get around if I need to."

Brett holds up a hand, his expression a warning. "They're limited, Rose. We only use them for specific jobs, not for just getting around. Plus, the land's tough on the carts. They're not exactly free-for-all vehicles."

"Right." I nod. "Makes sense. But if necessary, you do use them for purposes other than driving around tourists?"

"Limited," Brett repeats, hitting every syllable. "Now where's that inventory list?" he asks.

With her gaze pinned on me, Ginger hands it to him over her shoulder. He clips it onto his board and disappears into the back.

Ginger lowers her head, giving me a scan over the rim of her glasses. "Don't even think about it."

"What?"

"Rose . . . he'll have your head."

I wave her off. "I'm not. Besides, Brett looks like he wouldn't hurt a fly."

She starts working on the invoices. "Wasn't talking about Brett."

I ate dinner with Wesley back at The Shack. It was the first time I'd seen the kitchen where he's worked for the last several years. And it was fun watching him run the place—even when he was supposed to be on break.

He offered to come to the cottage, but I still don't want to tell him I'm staying in one of the cabins instead. He'll only make a scene of it. Or call me out for being a brat.

We video-called our parents since they love when the two of us are together. Or at least that I'm not alone in the city without his "supervision." Needless to say, they were ecstatic at the idea of me moving here. I had to remind them it's just for the summer.

But the idea of staying a bit longer doesn't feel as ridiculous to me now. It's only my second night here but this whole open sky and easy silence thing is something I didn't realize I missed.

I asked Wes if he could take me out on the town tonight, but he said he had to be up early to prep for tomorrow's tours and events.

Last night, between the smokey air and crackle of the fire, the cowboys were telling me about a place called Bones located on the "it" strip here in Blue River Springs. Curious, I asked a few questions like, "What makes it so special?" and "Has anyone had a drink named after them for doing something stupid?"

The stories I got were all widely different—and very intriguing. The kinds of memories you can only make in a small town like this one.

Which only convinced me of one thing: I need to stop by and make my own.

But how?

The idea of the golf carts has gnawed at me all night. Limited or not, one of those babies could get me out of here, even if just for an hour.

Or, you know . . . until something exciting happens.

The faint chirping of crickets is the only sound breaking the silence when I step out an hour later. I scurry behind the row of cabins, heading in the direction of the main office. I don't know what I'm going to do when I get there.

I don't even know if the carts will be accessible.

Like an idiot, I slipped on one of the few sundresses I brought with me. It's light linen with blue flowers. Note to self: when sneaking around and borrowing without permission, always wear black—and a sweater.

It's a nice night, but there's the occasional chilly gust of wind. And I haven't got much but my adrenaline to keep me warm.

When my cell phone rings, I jump, shushing it like a fool. I glance at the caller ID and swipe to answer.

"Hey, girl," Willow says in that sweet, deep voice of hers I'll always envy. She's only two years older than me but has the maturity of a thirty-year-old.

"Shh."

"Uh-oh, what are we doing?"

"I'm sneaking out, and you're going to get me caught."

"Why are you sneaking? Is there a curfew?"

"Um . . . not exactly." I reach the main building and glance behind me, my paranoia getting the best of me.

"So, I'm just supposed to guess here?"

My heart thuds in my chest as I tiptoe around the building, ducking by a crooked security light.

I gasp when I reach the lot behind the building with all the carts. *Sure doesn't look like you don't have any to spare.* There must be twenty of them here.

"What's going on?" Willow hisses.

"I'm going into town in one of these." I snap a quick picture and send it to her.

She laughs at me. "That's hardly grand theft auto, Rose. How far you taking it?"

"I don't know. I'm not even sure how to drive one."

"Oh, my mom's boyfriend used to take us golfing. I can totally walk you through this. Do you see a key in the ignition?"

I reach the closest cart, which thankfully is the four-seater one. But I freeze when I see a shadow of a man move out from behind the building. With a gasp, I slide into the cart and dip down.

"What? Someone there?" Willow whispers.

I breathe into the phone.

"OK, stay hidden and don't move."

"Damn mosquitoes," I hear the guy mutter as his footsteps slowly fade away. Lifting my head to peek, I see him walking deeper into the night, waving a hand in front of his face.

"All good?" Willow whispers.

"I think so," I breathe, my pulse racing. Dipping my head, I gasp. "Wil, you're not going to believe this. The keys are in the ignition."

"Well, of course they are. Ranch security isn't exactly Fort Knox."

I shut my eyes and hold my breath. Then slowly turn the key. The engine hums to life. My eyes shoot open with a breath. "I am so getting busted."

"All part of the fun, isn't it?" Willow reminds me. "Now just like a car, put your foot on the brake and position the switch to *forward*."

"There's a lever," I say.

"Yeah, try that."

My heart rate kicks up as I pull it.

Willow's right. Getting caught *is* part of the fun. But so is *not*. And I'm not getting caught tonight.

The tires crunch softly against the gravel as I make my way down the road. The gate at the edge of the property looms ahead. I'd have to push the button to get them open. I don't know where—or who—that button calls. "I can't get through the gate," I tell Willow, panic starting to kick in.

"Oh well, you tried. Now head on back."

"No," I stammer. "I didn't get this far to turn around." I look one way across the ranch—nothing but a faint outline of fenceposts disappearing into the night. I turn in the other direction—same. Nothing but shadows stretching over dry grass. Beyond that, just darkness.

I turn the vehicle and drive along the fence.

"Where are you going now?"

"This cart isn't that big. There must be a big enough gap somewhere, I'm sure of it. This can't be the only way out."

"Rose, you are out of your mind."

"You just find directions for me to get to Bones in Blue River Springs. I'll worry about an exit."

She laughs. "Yes, ma'am."

It takes a few minutes, with Willow on the phone for moral support, but I find a small opening between bushes.

It isn't large enough for a golf cart. It almost looks like a discreet wildlife passage.

I wince as I push the pedal and move through the cluster of wild shrubs. Thick, twisted branches snap off as I power through, scraping against the vehicle. One somehow reaches my shoulder, grazing my skin painfully.

"Maybe I overestimated the size of that opening," I whimper as I cut through to the other side.

Willow chuckles. "That's what he said."

Remember when I said she had the maturity of a thirty-year-old? Scratch that part.

"I'm out," I breathe. Getting out was the end goal, but at what cost? It's not like no one is going to notice the vandalism of the vehicle, what's left of those bushes back there, and the scrapes along my upper arm.

The *one time* I didn't wear sleeves.

"Turn right," Willow directs in her best GPS automated accent.

I release a breath and push forward.

Worry about it later.

Exhilaration bubbles in my chest as the ranch lights fade behind me, replaced by the open night and distant town lights on the horizon.

One hour. Tops.

7

Rose

"What dress ya wearin'?" Willow asks as I walk down the block, silently reading off signs of storefronts as I pass each one.

"The linen with the blue flowers."

"The one that has the loose strap on one side that keeps slippin' off your shoulder?"

I lift said strap, hiking it up by the blue sewed-on rose. "That's the one."

"So no sleeves," my bestie confirms. "Look at you, daredevil."

Only Willow knows the reason I wear long sleeves, or at least three-quarter long sleeves. Especially around my family. Back in New York, I'm less neurotic about it—mostly.

"It's *night*. No one's going to come close enough to see the faint scars on my arm."

"You're going to get eaten alive out there. Wesley's got every right to worry about you," she mutters.

"I'm hanging up now. Thanks for your help."

"Love you. Call me when you get back to your spooky cabin."

"I'll text. Night."

I slip the phone in my purse and look up at the sign on the bar that seems to have the most action. "*This* is it?" They really need a New York lesson on what to consider the "it" bar.

It's a low-slung building with a small neon sign on the window with the bar name. There's a larger wood-carved one over the storefront, which I like better.

I pull the wooden door handle in the shape of a big bone and step inside like I belong.

I'm hit with the thick air of fried food, beer, and stale smoke.

Strings of dim colored bulbs hang from the ceiling. There's a soft glow over the bar, which stretches along one wall. A modern country song plays from a jukebox at the entrance.

I take an empty seat on the side of the bar, against the wall. From here, I can see everything, so this seems as good a spot as any to . . . people watch, I suppose.

I try to grab the bartender's attention. He's a middle-aged, brawny man with light hair. A smirk plays on his lips as he wipes glasses and chats with what I assume is a group of regulars.

The place is half full, which seems about right. Even in New York, this is average for a Tuesday night.

I hear a handful of conversations from where I sit. The one that piques my interest the most is an upcoming rodeo event a threesome of cowboys are discussing.

One catches me staring and lifts his chin. The other two follow his eyes.

"Hey, pretty lady," the blond one greets me. He's got an interesting silver and red bolo tie and judging by the way the others don't engage—including the one who caught me staring—he's the alpha in the small group.

And I decide . . . I don't like him.

"Hello," I offer non-committedly and turn back to the bartender.

"Where you come from?" the cowboy asks, shifting toward me.

"New York."

He chuckles and scans me. "What brings you by?"

I turn a hard glare on him. "If you're not here to take my order, please go away."

The other two cowboys look up at the man like I'd just insulted a prime minister.

"Hey, Benny," he calls. "Get Snow White here a drink on my tab."

The bartender rolls his eyes, which tells me this cowboy has no authority here, which is a relief.

"I'm good, thanks. I can get my own," I tell the cowboy, then turn back to the bartender. "I'll have anything off your specials. Make it colorful and virgin, please."

"Virgin, huh?" the cowboy beside me comments.

"The drink," I clarify, getting irritated.

He scratches his beard. "Good to know."

I tap my foot against the barstool, then shift to face him. "I heard you talking about rodeos. I've never been to one, so I was interested. It wasn't an invitation to buy me a drink."

He extends his hands as if to say he's an open book. "What do you want to know?"

I glance at him but don't answer.

He smirks, perking a brow. "It wasn't an invitation to one, just offering to feed a curious mind. Call me Rodeo Ricky."

I release a soft laugh as the bartender hands me a purplish drink with an umbrella. "Thanks."

"It's on him." I expect him to point to Rodeo Ricky, but he points to a man across the bar.

Not sure who I was expecting, but it certainly wasn't . . . my boss.

My *other* boss, Dallas, is sitting at the far opposite end of the bar. He'd be hard to make out if it wasn't for those distinct features I noticed yesterday when I met him briefly. He doesn't smile when I meet his gaze. He salutes me but doesn't come over. Almost to let me know he's here if I need him.

After I offer him a small, tentative smile—and wonder if I'm going to have to explain why one of his golf carts is parked outside—he turns a hard glare towards the intimidating cowboy.

"Ricky Callahan." The man stretches out his hand. Something unfriendly and suspicious lingers in the air between us, and I hesitate.

Ricky sets his hand down, then glances back at his friends. "New Yorkers," he sighs. "A rodeo, sunshine, is a celebration of cowboy traditions. Bull riding, roping, racing. We're pretty family friendly, with live music, even brisket." He smiles at that last one. "Unless you're more into sausages."

"I don't eat meat," I lie.

"You never tried mine," he probes.

"You have an answer for everything, don't you, Rodeo Ricky?"

He cocks his head, and there's nothing charming about it. "Sounds like you've met your match."

I catch sight of a woman watching us and wonder if she might be his girlfriend . . . or wife. But then I really look at her. To put it simply, she's *beautiful*. Wavy blonde hair, blue eyes, and rosy cheeks. The kind of woman to turn heads in a place like this. She's got a cool blue cowgirl hat on, white boots, and a denim romper.

I don't think I've ever seen a cowgirl in real life. I'm instantly jealous of how she carries herself.

I like her style, but I don't like the way she's looking at me.

As if deciding she'd seen enough, she walks over and slaps his shoulder—hard. "Read the room, Ricky, she's not interested."

Whew. Not the wife. Did not feel like getting a black eye tonight. "On the contrary, sis, Snow White wanted to know about the rodeo we got comin' up."

"Benny," she calls, and the bartender nods in her direction, not bothering to get her order before he starts mixing.

"You should come," she says dryly. "It's gonna be a wild ride." She looks across the room, and I don't follow her eyes. "We got *real* cowboys on Callahan Ranch."

Callahan . . . where have I heard that name before?

She reaches for the drink Benny hands her and moves down a few seats. One of Ricky's friends slides off his stool, offering it to her.

Rodeo Ricky turns back to me. "Got an invite from the queen herself. Can't say no now, sunshine." He smirks and shifts a little too close for comfort.

With nothing but the wall to my left, I don't have much to work with as I shift away.

An arm stretches between us. "All right, that's enough, Ricky," Dallas slurs.

I jerk back. He *reeks* of alcohol, his hair tousled, his large frame swaying just slightly.

Ricky grunts. "Thorne, I ain't on your property and neither is this lovely lady here, so why don't you take a step back. Try not to hurt yourself."

"She's our employee. Go talk to someone else."

Ricky pauses, eyeing me for a beat like I betrayed him or something. "Still ain't on your property, so why don't you just get back to your corner at the end of the bar where you've been getting toasted each night and leave us be."

Ignoring him, Dallas turns to me. But he doesn't get a word out before Ricky grabs his shoulder.

"I'm only going to ask once," Ricky warns. "Now leave before you embarrass yourself—and your ranch."

"I'll take my chances." Dallas's tone is cool and calm as he faces off with Ricky.

My heart rate kicks up, and I twist in my seat, slipping my phone out of my bag and shooting off a text.

Rose: Need help. I'm at Bones.

"Richard, not now," the blonde interjects.

Dallas's eyes don't leave his opponent as he greets her. "Hey there, Dusty."

Really? The woman Ricky referred to as the *queen* a minute ago is named Dusty?

"You want to tell your brother to go hit on someone else? Rose is our guest. Surely there's someone in Blue River he could haunt with those crooked teeth."

Ricky advances, but Dusty reaches for the large cowboy. "I said back down," she grits. "He's in no shape to fight."

Fight? I was afraid of that.

I realize I've yet to say a word, and I feel like I need to.

Real soon.

But how do I break through the intensity between the two men? And a woman who looks like she could take them both with just her sharp eyes and frightening tone.

She turns to me. "Do me a favor and get outside." My eyes widen. Is she threatening me? "It's about to get ugly in here," she mutters.

"I'm not leaving Dallas," I stammer.

She perks a brow. "Suit yourself."

"Growin' a little tired of you pickin' on girls who never asked . . ."

"Give it a rest, Dallas," Ricky warns. "You're alone, wasted. And I'm not feelin' very neighborly."

I notice the two other cowboys now step behind Ricky.

My stomach churns. I step between them. "That's enough. Why don't you boys get back to your rodeo talk, and I'm just going to mind my own business and have my purple drink. All right?"

Ricky smirks at me. But it's not friendly. He looks almost . . . dangerous. "Move, missy."

"What?"

"He said move."

Before I realize what's happening, Dusty lifts me off my feet and tosses me aside like a ragdoll, just as a fist is thrown at Dallas.

Fortunately, the woman's got skill, because I land on my feet. Unfortunately, someone bumps into me to see the fight, sending me stumbling backward into the wall. My dress snags on something—a nail, maybe—and I hear the unmistakable sound of fabric ripping.

Shit.

I pull myself up to find Dallas and several more men now standing by his side throwing fists at the cowboys.

I'm relieved he has help. And horrified at the same time. The urge to pull Dallas out of a situation I got him into is strong. But I can't. At the very least, I'll get trampled if I try.

My heart thuds against my chest. At what point does someone call the police?

I grab my purse off the floor and practically crawl to the door, ducking behind people being knocked all over the place.

I push to my feet, trying to stay close enough for him to hear me. "Dallas," I call.

He merely glances at me before his focus lands over my shoulder. Dallas dodges a punch and reaches for me.

I gasp when I'm lifted off my feet by his big hands on my waist.

For a second, I think he's hauling us both out of the bar, but instead, he practically slams me into another body before returning to the fight.

I stiffen for a moment before a familiar cedary scent wraps around me. My back is pressed against a broad chest. Hot, muscular arms secure me in place as I'm rushed outside. The beat of his heart is so fast, I'm dizzy with it.

Wilder sets me on my feet and spins me to face him.

I don't know how to help Dallas in a bar fight. I don't know how to get a mean-looking stranger to leave me alone.

But I thought I knew how to take on a grumpy cowboy about to do some yelling.

Unfortunately, when he looks like Wilder does right now, muscles flexed, jaw tight, sharp, stormy eyes . . . I've got nothing.

I'm not cold anymore but I feel naked right now, as he roams over the tears in my dress, the scrape on my shoulder.

"Dallas," I breathe, twisting my scarred arm out of the light.

"He'll be fine. It's his third one in the last two weeks." There's a fire simmering beneath his words, even as he's trying to comfort me that his brother will be all right.

My mouth drops open at the new information, but I manage to swallow. "I didn't call you here for me." I leave him to head back to the bar. He doesn't follow. Before I can pull the door open, Dallas steps out. His left cheekbone is red and he has dried blood on the corner of his mouth. But it's his arm that catches my attention.

"Oh my God, you're bleeding."

He holds a hand up. "I'm fine." Then he pins me with those eyes that are more a sad blue than penetrating—unlike his brother's. "You all right?"

I nod, but I'm not sure I am.

Dallas looks behind me. "I had it under control, you didn't have to come."

"Look better than you did last week," Wilder comments.

Ricky and Dusty step out. Dusty still looks like she walked out of a comic book for adults. And Ricky . . . looks like he should be seen by a doctor.

How the hell did Dallas manage that in his condition?

Ricky looks over at Wilder with one good eye, the other too swollen. "Well, if it isn't the other Thorne in my side. You boys do yourself a favor and bring your lovely new employee by Callahan Ranch for a real experience. She seemed very interested." He winks at me, and I have the strangest desire to spit on him.

Yeah, you better walk away, I think to myself when Dusty tugs her brother in the other direction. She flicks her gaze back to Dallas—more to his bleeding arm. "Might want to make sure there's no—"

"We got it, Dusty," Wilder assures her. After they walk away, he glares at his brother. "Give me your keys."

Dallas sighs and reaches in his pocket.

Wilder takes the keys and turns on his heel. "Let's go."

For a moment, I consider folding my arms and stubbornly insisting I'm staying. After all, I barely finished my drink.

But that would be immature, and Wilder is too . . . scary to provoke right now.

Plus, I really want to make sure Dallas is all right. I feel so guilty about the fight. Even if it was inevitable—tonight, I was the cause of it.

Dropping my head, I follow quietly, deciding I'll try that drink another night.

So what if the first man I meet is *the* man to stay away from. Now I remember why the last name Callahan sounded familiar. And not in a good way. Wesley's mentioned them once or twice as the Thorne family's rivals for more than a decade.

A gust of wind blows pieces of my dress around my legs, and I pull my strap up. Suddenly conscious of my exposed forearm, I rub it and keep my hand over it as if I'm cold.

Wilder opens the back seat of his truck and reaches in, snatching a dark grey blanket. It almost looks like one of those heavy blankets they wrap around people they pull out from a burning building. He cocks his head once, and Dallas slips into the back—where I was sure I'd be going.

Closing the door, Wilder turns and scans me once, as the wind continues to blow through the new slit in my dress.

The thick blanket is wrapped around me tightly—and he's anything but gentle about it. He grips both ends of the blanket in front of my chest, meeting my eyes, and for a moment I think he might say something. Maybe even ask if I'm all right?

But he lets it go and yanks open the passenger door. "Get in."

I swallow. "Only if you take me back to your place."

"Excuse me?"

"So I can take care of Dallas's arm."

"You're in no position to be making demands. Get in the car."

I'm about to argue, storm off or, hell, do something. But the only thing that slips out is a small, "Please?"

He blinks away with a resigned breath. "Fine. Get in."

I settle into the passenger seat, glancing back at Dallas. He's spread across the back seat, eyes open, staring up into space.

I gasp when Wilder's arm reaches across me from where he stands by my passenger door. He lifts my purse, reaches inside, and pulls out the keys for the golf cart.

Even through the thick blanket covering me, I'm sizzling from the proximity. Already wondering if my body's reaction to him will ever stop.

After shutting my door, he darts across the street to the "borrowed" vehicle and tosses the keys inside, and that's when I notice its condition.

"*Holy shit.*"

It's not like I picked up the golf cart shiny and new, but how did I not see what I did to it? The wheels are caked in dirt and mud. There are dark scratches along the roof and sides. Pieces of shrubs and branches are scattered inside.

God, I hope there's no other damage. Like to the engine or anything. Brett warned me about them not being built for certain roads.

Dallas glances back through the window, following my gaze. "Oof." He winces, then chuckles. "You're in trouble."

I narrow my eyes at him. "Not any more than you," I point out.

He smirks, then plays dead when his brother jumps in the driver seat. Wilder glances in the rear-view mirror with a furrowed brow, then takes off.

On the short drive back, he dials someone. "Hey, Jeff, sorry to bother you. You out?"

I don't hear the response.

"Figured as much. Would you do me a favor? I left one of the golf carts parked outside of Bones. Keys are by the pedals. Mind towing it back to the ranch for me?" There's a pause before he offers his thanks and hangs up.

An hour later, I step out of Wilder's house, releasing a deliberate breath.

As suspected, the sharp cut on Dallas's arm turned out to be the result of a broken beer bottle. I inspected it for any glass shards that might have pierced through the skin, pressing my thumb lightly near the wound.

Either there were no embedded pieces, or Dallas is extremely tolerant to pain.

Or just too numb.

I cleaned the area with a first-aid kit Wilder handed me, then dressed it, all the while conscious of his curious gaze on me. Before I left, I thanked Dallas for coming to my rescue tonight. Even if I was sure I could handle myself, I didn't want Dallas's efforts wasted.

I kept the blanket over my shoulders, covering the better part of my right arm while in their bright kitchen.

Now outside, in the dark, I hand it back to the owner. "Thank you for coming."

Maybe another night I'll ask about the rivalry with the Callahans. In New York, we don't have "rivals." We have enemies or annoying neighbors, or the occasional personal vendetta against the coffee vendor who charged three dollars for my coffee and then another ten for a tip.

Still disputing that charge.

Wilder doesn't respond to my gratitude. I consider turning back to him as we walk to his car, then remember my tendency to run into him.

When I'm a safe distance away from possible impact, I turn. "Is it OK if I stop by to check on him tomorrow?"

"House calls are a thing of the past, Doc." He meets my eyes and there's a question in his that makes me shift uncomfortably.

He takes a few steps until his intimidating frame towers over me, the intensity in his eyes making me feel both trapped and electrified at once.

"I don't think so," he replies gruffly. "You're going to be *very* busy tomorrow. And *very* tired."

A shiver runs through my veins. And my heart flutters. Why does my heart flutter? Whatever he's implying *can't* be good for me.

I roll my lips, having no response to his unspoken threat. Despite the tension, there's something magnetic about him—an edge that hints at control just barely restrained. He's angry, yes, but it's not hasty. It's measured, careful, and damn near intoxicating.

His eyes drop to the scrape on my shoulder. It nearly knocks me off my feet when he brushes his fingers lightly over the wound. I suck in a sharp breath, and he draws his hand back.

"I don't suppose this would be a good time to tell you the bush got it worse?" I smirk with a hint of laughter.

"Come on," he tears his eyes off me, "it's been a long night."

But I'm not ready. I'm picking up on something and . . . in Wilder's words from the other day, I'm going to need some confirmation.

"Will you just tell me what's got you so angry? If Dallas is going to be fine, then what is it? I snuck out with stolen property, big deal. When the shit hit the fan, I called, didn't I?"

He snaps his head back. "I don't know if Dallas is going to be fine. I didn't know if *you* were fine." He huffs out a laugh like I have no clue. "Do you know what it's like to have your staff call you in a damn panic because they thought someone broke in?"

My eyes widen, lips parting as the weight of my actions tonight starts to settle in.

"Found the path you managed to push through. We thought we were dealing with rustlers. I had my men combing the grounds, armed, on edge. All so *you* could take a little joyride through town." His voice is gravelly, cutting through the air like a whip.

His eyes are dark as he scans me again, the way he did earlier, as if checking for more scrapes and bruises. "And then you called for help," he exhales, finally pulling his gaze off me.

I suck in a breath, ready to unleash, about to make it painfully clear to this man that *I* wasn't the one who needed saving, it was for Dallas.

But my breath catches in my throat.

He's so rugged and feral right now, in a dangerous, intoxicating kind of way. In a way that makes me feel hot . . . and safe.

Because there's something *else* laced in his words, his eyes, that's unmistakable. His whole body trembled with it when he carried me out of that bar.

Fear.

Lifting my eyes, I watch him struggle with himself.

Then, I give my most heartfelt apology of the evening.

"I'm sorry I scared you."

8

Wilder

The organ in my chest constricts.

She thinks she scared me? "I'm a whole lot of things right now, Rose. Furious, disappointed, frustrated as fuck, but I don't scare easily." I keep my voice even, my glare powerful as I take a step closer.

It's not like I'm lying. I don't scare easily.

But when I read that text from Rose, I was paralyzed with fear.

In all the years I've known Wesley, and all the stories I've heard about his sister getting knee-deep in mischief, never, and I mean *never*, did I hear that she picked up the phone . . . and called him for help.

The things that went through my mind. The sheer panic that consumed me.

Instantly, I stopped the search for an intruder on the property and sent everyone home. Then I hopped in my truck and all but busted through the gates to get to her.

It was two minutes to get off the property. And a five-minute drive—at that hour and my speed—but I got there.

When Dallas tossed her into my arms—unharmed, breathing, whole—the relief that washed over me was profound. An overwhelming warm embrace.

She's watching me in that way I'm starting to hate—like she gets me, despite my walls. "Yes, you are all those things, and I'm not disregarding how upset you are with me." She shrugs like she's struggling for the right words. "Look, I'll be honest, you all left me here with no way to get around, so I'm not sorry I took matters into my own hands."

She winces at my scowl, and fuck, it's adorable. "But I am sorry for causing so much trouble tonight." She licks her lips, and I can't stop my eyes from dipping to them. Even poutier now with that frown. I'm about to shut her down to the best of my ability, but then, raspy, raw, and unguarded, she adds, "Especially to you."

And I'm royally fucked.

You're going to be very busy.

And very tired.

The second the words came out of my mouth, I regretted it. Because of the way her eyes flared with heat. And because my dick clearly misunderstood my meaning as well.

I couldn't just say, *You're going to clean up the mess you made.*

No, I had to get all creepy about it.

I crack my neck, loosening the tension from last night. The sun was already over the hills when I stepped out to do my morning rounds with Tuscan—my horse.

The air was already thick with heat, which reminds me of my first task of the day. Pulling his reins, I pause and scan the horizon of golden fields, smirking as I dial one of my off-site cowboys. One of the few I trust not to ask questions when I have an odd favor. "Hey, Jeff, mornin'."

"Mornin', boss. Got the cart settled back at the lot," he says cheerily. He doesn't ask what happened to it or why it was parked outside of Bones.

"Yeah, do me a favor. My new assistant offered to fix it up for us. Would you mind dropping it off at her cabin this morning?"

He hesitates. "It's going to need a little more than a dusting, Wilder."

"I'm aware. Just bring her everything she needs . . . a bucket, rags, whiteout, I don't care. Just drop it off, and I'll let her know."

"On my way."

"Thanks."

I roll my shoulders back and lift my hat to rub the exhaustion off my face. Sure hope she managed to get some sleep.

She's going to need the energy.

Wilder: Dropped off your first task of the day. Go to town.

Wilder: And I don't mean literally.

Twenty minutes later, after I've settled into my office, Jeff returns the keys, dropping them on my desk.

"Assuming you didn't want me to leave these with her?"

I look up at him as I shove the keys in my pocket. "Smart man."

He shakes his head with a chuckle as he walks out. "Gonna be an interesting summer."

My phone pings, and my heart rate ramps up as I reach for it.

Rose: Is punishment a kink of yours?

Jesus Christ.

Wilder: Good morning. Hope you slept well.

Rose: Is that a toothbrush?

I laugh out loud. "Oh, Jeff. Remind me to give you a raise."

I'm tempted to tell her that if that doesn't suit her, she could always use the ripped dress from last night as a rag, but that would be inappropriate.

Wilder: I hear you're creative.

A minute passes and I wonder if I've taken it too far. The cart isn't in terrible shape. And we do get them washed weekly because of all the dust and rain.

Rose: I'm going to be a little late to the office.

Wilder: You have one hour.

A little over an hour passes when my phone rings and I expect it to be Rose. I push off my chair and reach for it, shaking off the bubble in my gut from getting to hear her voice.

But it's not her. It's her brother.

"Hey." I've never had to try to sound nonchalant with my best friend before, so I'm not sure how that came out.

"Please tell me she's on time today."

I breathe a sigh of relief that he hasn't heard anything about last night.

For a reason I can't settle on, I don't want him knowing about it. Not yet at least.

"Already working on the first task of the day," I assure, pleased with myself as I glance out the window for the fifth time in the last few minutes, waiting for her.

He releases a breath. "Ah great, how's it going?"

"I'll let you know at the end of the week."

"That's a good sign. Well, tell her to stop in for breakfast soon. We're closing early to get ready for the Randerson Tour, and I don't exactly have time to run it over to her again."

I check the time and curse. There's no way I'm letting Rose skip breakfast because of a dumb golf cart.

I stand, march to my office door, and pull it open. Still no sign of her.

"You there?" Wes asks.

"Uh, yeah. You just worry about the crowd you got comin' in. I'll take care of Rose." The words are innocent, but I can't help but feel like a sleaze as I say them.

Because I haven't been able to get my mind off her all morning. All night for that matter.

And not just how she looked in that tattered dress.

Not even the anger that's still lingering.

But the way her body felt pressed against mine for a brief moment when I carried her out of the bar. The pang of disappointment I felt when I had to set her down.

Her tenderness with my six-foot-five burly brother in my kitchen last night when she felt for pieces of glass under his skin.

The remorse in her eyes for the trouble she'd caused me.

"You're the best. Make sure she gets her iron. I don't need her passing out on the job."

I frown. "Is she anemic?"

"No. Or at least not anymore. She had a terrible diet her last year of college. Lived off coffee, barely ate meat—or much of anything. Must have been midterms or the pressure of graduating, but eventually it resolved itself."

That's odd.

Or maybe I find it odd that her brother—who claims to know her better than anyone—doesn't know much about what it was that caused her poor diet for a short time.

I don't pay a ton of attention to my brothers. But when Dallas and Silas have a noticeable change that affects their health, I get answers.

As do they when it comes to any one of us.

"Good luck with the tour. Call me if you need anything."

Again, I dismiss him with business and don't wait before hanging up.

Within ten minutes, I'm in front of cabin four, jumping out of my truck.

Rose is lying on the dirt next to the cart I hardly recognize as one of mine, but I don't focus on it.

"Rose."

She yelps, a wooden stick flying out of her hands. It's not until it falls back down, brushing against her face, that I realize it's a paint brush.

"You scared me," she breathes, her dirty hands clutching her heart. A fresh blue smudge on her cheek.

My lips part as I take her in. Her hair is up in a messy bun, long, dark strands falling from every direction. She's in a white top covered in dirt and blue paint, but it's the long sleeves of her top that bother me. It's too hot for her to keep wearing those.

Rose wipes at her sweaty forehead. "Hey," she says breathlessly since I haven't bothered with a word yet. "I'm just finishing up." Then with a small smile, she steps aside, spreading her arms out. "What do you think?"

I've been so busy gawking at her that I barely noticed the golf cart. It shines like new. Inside and out. But then my eyes dip to the colorful roof contour. In bold, blue strokes, she's painted the words *Blue River Ranch*.

"I couldn't get the scratches out, so I . . . got creative."

I step forward, my brows shooting up. "Wow."

She holds up her hands. "Bet ya I can still make you mad." She waves me to the side of the cart, and I follow with caution.

I fight back a grin when I see it. The words *The Rose* are painted in bright pink with beautiful blue roses surrounding them.

"I named it." She beams. "Which means, it's mine. For the summer, of course. I need to be able to get around, and unless you're giving me a horse—and lessons—this will have to do."

She watches me, waiting for my reaction, consent, more scowling maybe . . . hell, I don't know. But I don't care about some stupid cart she just branded.

My eyes are on her. She looks exhausted and pale.

I rake my fingers through my hair. The fuck was I thinking having her do this first thing in the morning?

She must notice my irritation because her eyes go wide—like she's taken things too far. "I can change it ba—"

"You haven't eaten."

She frowns, then looks at the cart like it's obvious she's done nothing else this morning. "No."

I swallow hard and start back toward my truck. "Get in the truck."

After a brief pause, she sprints behind me. "So you *don't* want me to do the same to all the other carts? I can name one after you. How's 'Broody Ranger'?"

I reach into my pocket, spin, and give her the keys. "It's yours."

She pauses. "Wait, really?"

I look over her shoulder. "Doesn't look like I've got a choice."

She smiles giddily, her eyes lighting up her face. "And don't worry, before I leave, I'll paint her back to white."

I turn and march to my truck. "Get in the truck, Rose."

Confused, she follows and slides into the seat. "I can drive myself to work now," she says tentatively.

I start the engine. "We're not going to work."

My response seems to be enough. Glancing down at her appearance, she lowers the visor and sighs. "Visors with no mirrors are just a cruel trick," she mutters, then releases her hair from the tie. Dark silky strands fall around her shoulders, and I can't look away.

I don't even try.

Christ. Three days and I don't even know who I am anymore. "You look fine, Blue."

She turns her head to me. "What?"

I swipe my thumb across her cheek, smearing some of that paint off, and show it to her.

"Oh." She pulls on the edge of her sleeve and wipes it off. "Did I get it?"

I blink, feeling like I'm under some spell.

"Good enough. Here," I say gruffly. "This'll keep you quiet for a while." I hand her a coffee tumbler.

She stares at it, inhaling the aroma.

"Stopped by the house before coming to check on you. Dallas was up, mumbling something about his arm. Unlike me, he's a heavy coffee drinker, so there was a fresh pot."

She takes a sip with a relieved sigh. "Thank you."

I relax at the sound. Finally able to think straight. Next order of business is getting some color on those cheeks. And I don't mean from the sun.

"It looks good," I say after a long silence. "The Rose."

She beams at my compliment. "You really like it?"

That organ in my chest swells. And like a jerk, I backtrack. "I don't like that you did it all at once."

"Where are you taking me?" she asks as we pass the open gates.

"To the sheriff's office for vandalism."

She considers it for a moment. "Sheriff, huh? Is he cute?"

I laugh. "You got a thing for badges?"

"I got a thing for men telling me I've been a bad girl."

I had to ask.

"Breakfast, Rose. I'm taking you to breakfast."

She smiles. "OK, but then can we go meet this sheriff?"

She's toying with me. She has to be.

Rose takes another sip, leaning back against the passenger door, watching me. "Maybe I'll hold off on naming your cart just yet."

I smirk.

"How's Dallas?"

"Think he was hurtin' this morning. But I can't say I'm sad about it."

"Even if he came to my rescue?"

I perk a brow. "*Because* he came to your rescue. I should've let you both get eaten by the Callahan wolf pack."

"Dusty doesn't seem so bad. She seems kinda sweet."

I laugh.

"What's so funny?"

"You should tell your brother you think Dusty's sweet. You'll never hear the end of it. And he might just have you committed."

My eyes go wide. "Wesley? He's a teddy bear; he'd never hate on anyone." She winces. "Then again, I nearly cracked a rib when she threw me against the wall, but if she hadn't, I would have had my face creamed."

Bile rises in my throat. "Dallas didn't move you aside?"

"He pushed me behind him, but I thought I could help and jumped between the guys when things started to heat up."

"Jesus, Rose."

I pull up to the outdoor café in town, setting the truck in park and jumping out, my boots scuffing against the gravel.

Jerry, the owner, waves as he clears a table, then nods that he'll be right with us.

Rose is still by the passenger door and I nod her along, but she doesn't move.

Her eyes gaze past the storefronts and lampposts of the small street. I know exactly what she's fixed on.

The beauty of Blue River Springs. The mountains, the river that flows below, the evergreen trees lining the hills. That sweet smell of pine in the faint wind.

"Wow," she breathes. "I could just stare at these all day."

I expect to roll my eyes. I've got work to do and already spent the past hour fussing over her.

But I don't. I lean against the building with my arms crossed like I'm annoyed. But through my sunglasses, I watch her face, her eyes taking it all in. Her chest rises as she inhales.

Tearing her eyes off the scene, she turns to me, her cheeks rosy with that same flush. "Sorry, coming."

I sigh and hold the fence open for her.

I lean back in my chair, arms crossed loosely, watching Rose take another bite of her omelet. Perhaps it's the lighting, but the shadows under her eyes seem to have softened.

There's something quietly fierce about this girl. And maybe not so quiet too. Something that Wesley never mentioned.

Or misunderstood, perhaps?

I played back her "sorry, not sorry" spiel last night several times in my mind. And no matter how many times I heard it, not once did it sound . . . bratty. Impulsive, sure, but the girl wanted something.

And she went for it by any means necessary.

Also, if I'm not mistaken, she texted me at seven this morning, which means . . . she was going to be on time.

"What time did you get to bed last night?"

She looks anywhere but at me. "Hit the sack soon as I got in."

It's a lie.

Don't know why or how I know, but it's a lie.

Letting it go, I take a sip of my water. "How's your arm?"

Slowly, she slides her right arm off the table, setting it on her lap. "It's fine, why?"

"I meant your other arm." I shift my gaze to the covered skin just beneath her shoulder.

"Oh. It's nothing—" She smiles playfully. "Serves me right for getting into it with a thorny bush."

"Agree." I smile and wink.

And it does something to her, if the way her eyes flash and her gaze lingers appreciatively is any indication.

What is happening?

How did I get here? One minute ready to throw this untamable troublemaker out the door, and the next . . . feeling a flutter stir in my stomach because my smile made her happy.

This isn't right.

She's been here three days and every coy smirk, every lingering glance, every accidental touch drags me in deeper.

I need to pull back. Create some distance if I have any chance of making it through this summer unscathed.

She can't hurt me. No one can. Not after Bonnie.

A flicker of my ex's face threatens to surface but I push it down, burying those feelings where they belong. She sure as hell had none when she said goodbye.

I was ready to give it all up for her. Lost myself in something that was never real.

Rose isn't Bonnie. That much is clear from a mile off. But the risk is one hundred percent the same.

I need to shut this down before it gets any further.

But one wrong move, and others would suffer. Wesley, the ranch, and who knows . . . maybe even Rose.

No. I won't play this game.

These inappropriate comments, the brush of skin, it all stops.

Today.

9

Rose

It's my fourth day of work and I'm off to a late start, again. I've been at least an hour late every day this week.

This was stupid.

I should have said no to this job.

I should have known I can never have another normal night of sleep again. Or be the type to wake up at six a.m., work out, mix myself a green juice, and march out the door.

The way I used to be until senior year.

I started painting as a way of calming myself. Some people find comfort in warm milk; I make art. Only dozing off after pure exhaustion.

My body and brain must physically give out for me to fall asleep. Which happens around the two or three a.m. hour.

It's why bartending makes sense. If I'm not sleeping, I might as well be making money.

I throw on a pair of jeans and a dark blue blouse, curse the damn snooze button, then yank on my boots.

I almost forget to lock the door before breathlessly rushing out.

It's still surreal being here. Especially when I'm hustling and bustling, getting dressed like I'm late for opening night of The Rockettes. But every time I open this creaky door, it's like I'm walking out of my city apartment and onto a movie set.

The summer glow across the fields, the low rumble of tractors in the distance, the occasional faint neigh of a horse.

It's so full of life—but not.

It's steady. And I think I like steady.

For once, the world isn't spinning too fast for me to keep up with.

No constant reminder of something I failed even before I started. For once, I don't feel pressured to make sensible decisions in life.

A reminder of why I said yes to this gig. It's like a big timeout. To think about things I did wrong.

Or things I can't change.

I take a breath, bracing myself for an angry boss before walking into the Saddle Room.

He wasn't angry yesterday when I raced in late. In fact, he barely looked my way the last two days except when he was training me on something. On Wednesday, after we had breakfast, I spent the afternoon going through old mail piling up on both Wilder's and Dallas's desks, then finished payroll for the previous week.

Thursday, Wilder was out all day on the ranch but left a list for me.

I'm starting to think he's avoiding me. Maybe he's still mad?

Idiot. Of course he's still mad.

The man was probably born mad and will die a grumpy old man.

And it would be a shame. Because I'm sure the universe meant that body for love . . . not bitterness.

I swallow as I reach the door.

Maybe if I just walk in like this is my regular time now, he won't notice?

Maybe he's not even in yet? I could easily pretend I'd been here all morning, right?

Wrong.

Sharp blue eyes flick to meet mine. But it's barely a passing second before he looks back down to his papers. He's standing behind his desk, leaning with his palms pressed against the wood.

I imagine it crumbling to the floor under the pressure.

"You're early," he says, voice low and gruff. "I didn't expect you in until at least ten, given it's a Friday an' all."

OK. I deserve that.

"Figured I'd get a head start," I reply chirpily as I set my bag down on the smaller desk he'd designated as mine. "Don't worry, I'll catch up."

He doesn't look at me. "Skip breakfast again?"

I shuffle paper and don't bother looking at him. "How else will I be eligible to become next season's Miss City Girl unless I skip breakfast and live on coffee?"

I may need a little help waking up in the morning, but I'm going to earn this man's respect if it kills me.

Wilder doesn't respond, just nods toward the stack of papers on my desk. "You can start with supplies and vendors today."

I peer over to his desk. "Are those this week's time-cards already? I can work on those after I'm done here."

He grunts. "No, these are from last week. Payroll's a mess. The guys are already grumbling."

I frown. "That's impossible, I totaled each one up twice to be sure."

Granted, I failed Accounting 101, but who can understand the difference between debits and credits with the way Professor Levitz described it? The guy could say "Assets must equal liabilities plus equity" and "Let's have a party" and it would sound like the same thing.

Wilder still doesn't look up, punching into an ancient calculator. "Yeah, well, maybe you should have done it a third time," he mutters.

I cock my head to the side, giving him a pointed look, which he's determined to ignore.

Not on my watch.

Pushing back from my desk, I walk over to him and pull the card he's looking at out of his hands. "What was wrong with this one?"

With a sigh, he plucks it back. "Brock worked the week-end too. He should get overtime. He was underpaid."

Overtime. Right.

I look at the other stack, afraid to ask. "How many were wrong?"

He takes a moment, jaw tightening before he twists his head up at me. "I don't know, Rose. I don't know if the rates were right either."

My chest heats with anger, even if I am the screw-up here. But I swallow it down, putting on my grown-up shoes and leveling my tone. "I'm sure there are better things you can do with your time. This is why you hired me." I reach for the stack and manage to break them out of his grasp. "I'll just go through them again."

He catches the other end of the stack and holds tight.

"Rose, there's plenty for you to do. Leave this to me. There's no room for mistakes when it comes to payroll."

I'm infuriated. Sure, I made a mistake. But who wouldn't in their first week on the job. Although I do feel bad that I short-changed his hardworking staff. I want to make it right.

"Wilder, let go. I want to fix it."

"I admire that. But I'm already on it." There's an edge to his voice. Like he just wants me to get out of his space.

And maybe it's his coldness that's catching up to me now, but I am not backing down. "Let. Go."

"Rose," he warns with an effortless tug.

I tug a little harder. OK, a lot harder since there's no budging from his side.

With a groan, I give it my all until they're yanked out of my hand and I stumble forward—gasping as I crash onto him, his chair rocking under the impact.

My hands press against his chest as I find myself draped over his torso—and between his legs.

I feel him tighten . . . *everywhere*. Like I'm a bumble bee that might sting him with one wrong move.

"Jesus," he growls low, a muscle flexing in his strong jaw.

I'm weightless against him. Lightheaded. And instead of scrambling off him, my stupid hands itch to touch him more while they've got the chance.

I release a shaky breath and say something quick so he can't see right through me.

"Sorry, that was stupid." I push to stand, but his strong grip wraps around my wrist, keeping me close. But it's not intimate. It's more laced with concern.

Deep blue eyes pin mine. "Why was it stupid?"

He holds my gaze, and I don't want to break free. As awkward as this should feel, I don't want to move. But I do.

Gently pushing off, I answer, "Because you're right. It's too important to make mistakes. And my pride got the better of me. You do it. I'll . . . I'll go grab coffee or something." I pull strands of my hair out of my mouth.

He stares at me for a moment before nodding. "Good idea." His voice is gruff as he adjusts in his seat.

"Do you, um, want anything?"

"I'm good." His eyes drop to my midsection before he turns away. "You might want to . . . fix your blouse."

I blink down and adjust my shirt—making a mental note to adjust my bra too after I walk out.

Then I think better of it.

What if someone *sees* me adjust my bra outside his office? What will they think?

One thing I've never been is *subtle*. I'm as blunt and awkward as they come.

So when I toss my messenger bag over my head and try to reposition my bra in the same instance, I'm sure I look like a one-woman circus act.

But it gets the job done. Sort of.

When I look over at Wilder, expecting to find an annoyed cowboy, I'm shocked to find his hand lightly covering the smirk on his gorgeous face as he watches me.

"Yeah, well, you try wearing one of these," I mutter on my way out.

The Shack is charming in a way that surprised me the first time Wesley showed me around. It's not all rustic summer camp cafeteria like I'd expected. It's more like a mountain ski lodge.

The kitchen is warm with sheer curtains to allow the sun to soak through and round oak tables that feel more personal and intimate for smaller groups.

The walls are filled with framed memories. I've spotted my brother in several over the last few days. I never truly understood why he loved it here so much until I studied each one. There's life in his eyes. And best of all, he's doing what he loves: cooking, baking, and . . . peopling.

One thing we're both decent at.

It's why I wanted to be a therapist. Still do. But how am I supposed to look at people every day and tell them they're going to be all right, when I don't believe the same for myself?

It's a lie.

Art doesn't lie. It tells a story, lets you use your imagination. But I don't want to make it my life. I want it to be something I do without the pressure of monetizing it. I want to paint when it feels right, not because it's Monday morning and I need to sell seven pieces by the end of the week to make a car payment.

Maybe that's not what being an artist is, but for a while, it might be. And I'm smart enough to know that I need to depend on something else.

Wes is one of the lucky ones. He found it instantly. And he found it here.

My brother storms out of the walk-in fridge with a fresh carton of eggs in one hand and a loaf of bread in the other.

I take another sip of my coffee. "You know I'm on the clock, right? Just toss me another one of those cappuccino muffins and I'll be on my way."

"You're in my kitchen, you eat what I make you." He winks with a smirk, then starts to move around with the kind of ease that comes from years of repetition. It reminds me of all the times he was back home from school, either for the summer or winter break, and showed off all the cool things he'd learned.

"Do you cook for events here too?" I ask, resting my chin on my hand as I watch him whip up some eggs. I've seen the ledgers with parties they book on the ranch. Rodeos, weddings, anniversaries, corporate retreats. I can't imagine he caters them all.

"Our kitchen staff is too small. A few years back we made it a requirement that the hosts choose their own caterer to avoid any complaints or disappointments."

"Smart."

He plates my breakfast. "So, you've been here a whole week. How's it going? Other than the fact that you've been late every day."

I purse my lips. "How do you know?"

Wes leans against the counter with his arms crossed, watching me with an intensity that would make anyone shift in their seat. Or maybe just me, because I'm not sure I've stopped blushing since I left the Saddle Room. "Wild guess."

I glance down at the beverage. "So he hasn't complained?"

Wes hesitates. "No. But I heard some of the guys at breakfast complaining about their paychecks. Take it that's your doing?"

"I just didn't categorize some hours right . . . or the rates."

Wes blows out a heavy breath. "Shit, did he yell at you? Oh no, did you slap him?"

I laugh. "I'm not sure I could reach him if I wanted to. But no, he just said he'd do it himself."

He cocks his head like it's foolish for me to get upset over this. "Cut yourself a break. You'll get the hang of it. I'm not great with numbers either. But I know there's a hell of a lot you *are* good at." He shrugs. "Just have to find how it fits in."

I roll my shoulders back. He's right. "I've got this. If I can survive ranch living, I can handle a grumpy cowboy."

He huffs. “Millie’s old cottage is hardly ranch living. The place looks like Mary Poppins threw up in it.”

I don’t react. I sip my fresh coffee instead. But my brother’s radar is too good.

“Rose?”

“I . . . refused the cottage.”

“What do you mean you refused the cottage?” There’s that tone again.

“Wes, I can’t take Dallas’s dead fiancée’s house. It wouldn’t feel right.”

Another deep exhale. “Where have you been staying?”

“Cabin number four,” I say, like I’m naming some fancy hotel.

Wes laughs. “No, really, where are you staying? You got an Uber taking you back and forth from The Springs Inn?”

“There’s an *inn*? Seriously, when are you going to give me a tour of the town?”

He drops his head in his hands. “Oh my God, you *are* staying in a cabin. Rose. What, are you afraid of a ghost? Millie didn’t die in that house.”

“I know, but it’s weird. It almost feels disrespectful to just use her stuff and sleep on her bed. What if I move things out of place and they get upset?”

Wes smirks.

“What?”

“Does our wild child have a soft side?”

I cock my head. “Only for those who matter to you, big brother.”

Wes shakes his head. “Well, in that case, spare my best friend if he gets a little snippy sometimes.”

"What's his deal, anyway?"

He shrugs. "If you ask me, it's gotten worse since Dallas checked out. Responsibilities doubled. Plus . . ."

"What?"

"Couple of years ago, the tables were reversed." His jaw tightens. "Wilder was . . . leaving. Wanted to give up his share of the ranch, including any rights to buy it back and, well, it caused drama in the Thorne family. Mostly between Wilder, Dallas, and Connor, their father."

"He wanted to leave? Why?"

Wes hesitates, then rolls his eyes. "To follow his heart."

"The man's got a heart?"

"Oh, he did. Her name was Bonnie. Blonde country girl rockstar."

My eyes go wide. "A rockstar?"

"More like a singer. They were together for two years before Bonnie wanted to hit the road. Travel, perform, get discovered or whatnot. He just wanted to make her happy. Anything she wanted." He sighs. "Feud in his family went on, and at the end of the day, he chose her. Not the ranch. Not working alongside Dallas."

"But *you* worked here."

"Yep."

"He was going to just abandon you too?"

That jaw works again. "Yep."

"So what happened? He changed his mind about leaving with her?"

"She changed it for him. Said he's a family man at heart and left."

The love of his life left him? When he was ready to give it all up to be with her? How crushing.

Man, I need to raise my standards. Last year, I dated a guy who made me switch to Hawaiian pizza because he preferred it over pepperoni.

"Who is she? Would I have heard of her?" I'm ready to whip out my phone and google this Bonnie. "Does she have a stage name?"

He almost laughs. "She didn't get very far. Got knocked up by a drummer and lives a few miles outside the ranch."

I set my phone down. "She lives here? With another man?"

Wes nods. "And his baby." He wipes down the countertop. "Dodged a bullet, if you ask me. He deserved better. It all happened too quickly with Bonnie and Tom. Everyone's guess is that they were already sleeping together."

A chill runs through me. "Everyone?"

"Oh yeah, it was the talk of the town."

"How sad. How are things with his family now?"

"That's the thing. They've long forgiven him. It's just not the Thorne way to hold a grudge. Even I felt bad for him. But Wilder's been trying to prove his loyalty ever since."

"Even to you?"

Wes shrugs with a soft chuckle. "I've got nothing here for him to prove his loyalty. But yeah, I guess me too. Said he'd never do anything to compromise our friendship."

My eyes drop to my hands. They tingle with the ghost feeling of his broad chest.

We hear some bustling in the main hall, and Wes straightens. "Anyway, I know you wouldn't know this, but before all that, he used to be a lot more laid-back, fun to be around." He shrugs. "He just took a bad hit."

I humph. "You're right, I wouldn't know."

He clears my plate. "Cabin four, you say? I'd have paid anything to see you survive your first night. But I guess that kind of validates what I told Wilder about you."

"What was that?"

"That you're tougher than you look."

I stare at him. A wave of warmth hitting me. Of all the things I'd expect my brother to say about me—that's never been one of them. "You really think that?"

He perks a brow. "Think you just proved it."

My stomach flutters but I play it down with a coy shrug. "Well, I'd probably surprise you because I think those cabins are kind of cool. In fact, I'm very much enjoying my stay."

He nods like he's waiting for the punchline of a bad joke.

"Now tell me more about this inn," I ask hopefully.

"I knew it. You called his bluff on staying there and now you're puttin' up your white flag."

"Never."

He laughs, and I grin back, missing this between us. He's always so worried about me that being real and unguarded with him hasn't been a choice.

But this . . . it's been nice.

"I should get back to work," I tell him. "See you in a few for lunch?"

"I might skip it. I need to do some damage control with payroll."

And other things . . .

10

Wilder

I'm back at the Saddle Room after doing some rounds at the ranch. The ride did me some good. But a cold shower would be even better.

I settle for a splash of cold water in the washroom and run a hand down my face. Then glare at myself in the cloudy mirror as I grip the sink hard enough to nearly tear it off the wall.

Fuck's sake, this is Wesley's sister.

And I damn near kissed her like the reckless fool I am. A fool I said I'd never be again.

But the urge fell flat when she called herself stupid. Did I make her feel stupid?

Of course I did. Either that or she feels utterly useless since I wouldn't let her fix her mistake.

Damage control.

I need to find a way to make this work with Rose. For Wesley's sake.

Right?

I hear the Saddle Room door swing open, followed by the faint clinking of ice cubes swooshing in a plastic cup. When I turn around, Rose is back. Less flushed and seemingly more . . . perky.

Another reason I hate caffeine.

I hang the towel on the bar and step out of the small room.

I eye the two large cups. "When do you expect to get any work done if you're drinking coffee all day?"

She ignores me and crosses to my desk. "So, I was thinking all this grumpiness could be cured with a little bit of caffeine." She sets the larger one on my desk. "I swear it's the answer to everything."

My reaction is barely an eye roll. It's more of a subtle shift as if to ask if she's done rambling.

When she offers me a wide smile, I take it as a yes and cross to my desk, handing her a note. "Kramer from Red Barn Supplies is expecting your call. Said he'd prefer to talk to the 'lovely lady' regarding next week's deliveries and something about bulk pricing negotiations?" I perk a brow.

She pulls her lips from her straw with a moan. "Oh, I knew he'd come around. I noticed his past two deliveries were late and there was nothing in your contract about credits or guarantees. So I told him we're getting rates from a few competitors who are known for timely deliveries and have been soliciting us for years."

"What competitors?"

She glances up with a shrug. "Oh . . . I googled them on the spot; I think they were . . . Lone Star Supply and . . . Hideaway Springs."

"Hideaway Springs isn't a supplier. That's a town about ten miles north."

She winces. "Well, Kramer didn't seem to notice. Anyway, I told him they promised on-time deliveries and bulk value rates. So he said to give him two days and he'd come back to me with a new proposal and an amended contract that *clearly* covers reliable deliveries."

I cross my arms.

"And I did it all without raising my voice, cowboy," she says softly.

"Fine, looks like you've got a handle on it. When you're done, I left a few things for you on your desk."

She frowns, dropping her gaze to her desk. "Timecards?"

I nod, picking up the iced coffee she brought me. "Said you can fix it, right?"

She frowns. "You pre-signed them."

I blink, hoping it says it all. "That's right. Soon as you're done, just take them over to Ginger, and she'll reissue the checks."

A small smile plays on her lips, but she quickly replaces it with a curt nod. "I'll get them over to her by the end of the day."

I put my hat back on and turn toward the door.

"Wait," she calls.

I turn back slowly, needing to get out of this room.

She holds my gaze for a beat. "I'm sorry about earlier. That was immature. I just really wanted to—"

"No need. I was being a jerk of a boss." I lick my bottom lip irritably. "I apologize."

She smiles. "Sure you don't want to look them over when I'm done?"

And spend more time in close proximity with you?

That wouldn't be wise.

I grip the handle and pull the door open. "I trust you."

The screen door creaks as I push through it to step into the ranch office. Ginger looks up over her red-framed glasses.

"What's doin', boss?"

I still don't like Ginger calling me boss when she practically helped raise me on this ranch. But Dallas and I are done arguing with her. She claims it's easier than our names. "The invoices Rose brought by yesterday have already been paid."

"Terrific. Thanks, Ginger."

She smiles sweetly. "It helps when I get them back quickly instead of having to send you daily reminders to go through 'em."

"Yeah, well, Rose pinned me down Wednesday on your behalf," I tell her.

She nods curtly. "That girl's been doing well here. Real sharp. Organized those files we've been meaning to get done for months."

"She been hangin' out here a lot?"

Ginger shrugs. "Few hours yesterday and for a bit late Wednesday afternoon. Says she's bored. Comes here for somethin' to do."

"Thought I'd given her plenty."

"She's quick."

"You mean she's slick," Brett argues.

Ginger shakes her head. "You hush back there. The girl needed to get around," she barks back.

I scratch the back of my neck, speaking of golf carts. "She complainin' about me yet?"

"Like I'd tell you."

I smirk. "Listen, a few of the guys are going to stop by here with their checks before the end of the day. Going to need them reissued."

She sets her glasses down. "Why?"

"There were some errors."

She winces. "Oh."

"It's no big deal. She'll stop by with the corrected amounts later."

Setting her glasses back over the tip of her nose, she makes a note for herself. I notice it's a long list. Ginger isn't that young anymore. And the additional work will have her leaving here after dark, I'm sure of it.

But the guys need to be paid right today.

"Reminds me," I pull a few bills from my wallet and reach over the desk. "Greatly appreciate it if you get that done tonight."

She perks a brow. "Mighty generous."

I give her a small smile. Dropping a bonus here and there for the extra mile is nothing new to Dallas and me. But we take particular care of Ginger. She was a second mother to us. And we're almost sure she's sticking around past retirement to watch over us. Either that or giving Dad the scoop on the business. I'd like to think it's more sentimental than that.

She stuffs the cash somewhere inside her blouse. "You got yourself a deal, boss."

Before I can utter a thank you, the door swings open behind me. I turn to see a man step inside, his boots scuffing against the wooden floor. He looks to be in his late fifties, maybe early sixties, strong build with a lined face. His hat is worn and his shirt wrinkled, but his posture is steady, confident.

His eyes find mine instantly, sharp but not hostile. "You Dallas?"

I cross my arms. "Wilder, his brother. What can I do for you?"

The man's gaze flicks to Ginger, then back to me. "I'm looking for Dallas."

"I get that. He's unavailable. What can I do for you?" My stomach tightens as I imagine what kind of trouble Dallas got himself into. We don't have many rivals. Callahan Ranch—which just barely crosses the border of Blue River—is the only one. And Dallas and I know that family inside out. He's not one of them.

Maybe this guy owns a bar in town and is here to collect on damage? Damage my brother caused?

"Do you know where I can find him? I was told I could catch him here."

"By who?"

The man shifts at my tone, resting his hand on his belt. He's not threatening in the least. That much, I'm sure. There's a guardedness about him. Like he's been preparing for confrontation. "This is personal business, sir," he states evenly.

I raise an eyebrow, softening, but only a tad. "Well, like I said, he's not here. Maybe I can help? This have anything to do with damage to property? You here to serve him or something?"

The man frowns. "No. Is Dallas a violent man? Should I be worried?" The way he asks isn't sharp or rude, just firm. Still, it hits like a challenge.

"Should I?"

The man stares at me.

"No," I sigh. "He's not a violent man. He's a kind soul who's hurting at the moment, so we're giving him some time. You'll have to excuse me if I'm being protective of my big brother when a stranger stops in demanding to see him."

As if he's been holding it in the entire time, the man releases a steady breath. "I understand. And no, I'm not here for trouble. I'll see myself out."

"Look, mister, we don't get many strangers wandering into our main office asking to see one of the owners. If it's important enough to track him down, maybe you can tell me what's going on."

The man hesitates, his eyes narrowing like he's going to say something. But then he stops, shakes his head again, and backs off. "I'll come back," he says simply, then leaves.

I stare at the door for a long moment, my jaw tight. "You ever seen him before?"

"Nope. But he was cute. Did ya have to kick him out so quickly?"

I shake my head and place my hat back on. "Thanks again, Ginger."

"I'd bet my paycheck he's not done with us yet."

"Yeah," I mutter, my mind already turning over possibilities. None of them are good. "I better go talk to Dallas. See if he has any clue who that might've been."

11

Rose

My muscles ache. The soles of my boots are caked with dirt. My hair is out of control with the humidity. I don't know if it's the week catching up with me or if today just seemed like I'd walked the entire perimeter of the ranch.

Weakly, I push the screen door to the main office. To my relief, Ginger is still here. "Thank goodness I caught you in time. I wanted to bring you these." I hand her the corrected timecards. "Sorry I took a little longer than expected. Things kept cropping up. Phone kept ringing."

"I know all about that, dear. Don't worry, I've been waitin' for ya." She takes them from me and gets started.

"Can I help?"

"Oh Lord, no. This part's easy. You go home now. Get some rest. Although it is a Friday night—I'm sure you young ones have plans."

"Not tonight, unfortunately. I still don't have a car until Wesley figures out a way for me to get around, so I'm stuck here."

She gives me a pointed look. "Well, you've got yourself a brand-new-lookin' cart. Use that."

My eyes widen. "Oh no, Brett said it's not made for roads, potholes and gravel and such."

She pulls down her glasses. "Yeah, well, that didn't keep you from stealing one, did it?"

I press my lips together, wincing playfully. Ginger looks over my shoulder. "Hey, Jake?"

I glance back. Jake is one of the younger ones on staff. Funny and sweet, from our few encounters.

"Hey, Rose." He smiles. "What's up, Ginger?"

"Listen, before you go, boss says the tires on Rose's cart ain't cuttin' it. If she ends up on a dirt road or anywhere rough, they're just gonna tear up. Think you can switch 'em out for somethin' sturdier? Like them all-terrain ones?"

He considers this for a moment, while I bite my lip, then nods. "Yeah, I think I got something." He turns to me. "OK if I drop it off in the morning?"

"Uh, sure," I answer nervously. "It's just outside. I can make it back to the cabins on foot."

He simply dips his hat to me. "I'll go take a look then."

"Ginger," I whisper when he's gone. "I don't want to get in any more trouble."

She gives me a stern look. "Flower, how old are you?"

"Twenty-two."

"And it doesn't bother you that you're being treated like a teenager?"

I sigh. "It did, but then my first night out, I got into trouble with—"

"*Bones* isn't a place for you to be going on your own—they prey on city girls and tourists. But there are other places in town I think you should check out this weekend."

"Like what?"

She shuffles around her desk. "Here are some brochures folks drop off for things to do in Blue River Springs. Take a look. There's a farmers' market, antique shops, a bookstore, museums . . ."

I take the pamphlets from her with some interest but notice she doesn't say much about nightlife. And I'm growing tired of staring at the ceiling all night.

"What about a place *like* Bones? You know, I met the Callahans while I was there."

She shakes her head. "Those two are as much trouble now as they were when they were kids. I babysat for them one night. Frightful children. And I'm not answering your 'place like Bones' question. That's a recipe for disaster, and I'm not getting involved."

I chuckle. "Thanks, Ginger, I'll check these out. Good night."

"Night, dear."

I step out into the warm evening. Exhaustion consumes me when I realize I have to *walk* back. I'll barely have enough energy to walk up the cabin steps, much less the distance from here.

I'm looking forward to the shower in my little cabin. It hasn't been half bad. Wilder thought I wouldn't last a day, but the joke's on him. I've managed four nights just fine.

My cheeks heat at the memory of him catching me this morning. OK, so maybe I fell on top of him, right between his legs—but he still caught me.

I've come in contact with that broad chest a few times now and it still makes my skin sizzle.

What is wrong with me?

I've never been a complete klutz around men. But Wilder brings out the crazy in me. And did I really call myself stupid when he wouldn't let me fix payroll?

That's not like me.

I think it plenty, sure—but I never say it out loud. This attraction has got to stop.

A wind chill runs through my bones, and I fold my arms as I walk, glancing around the familiar road, but not certain where it leads.

"Great," I mutter. Every path seems to split off into more dirt trails winding into the distance. It's dark now and everything just looks the same.

"How hard can this be, really?" The ranch is quieter now, save for the chirping of crickets. Where the hell are those little critters coming from?

I inhale deeply as I keep walking, my feet ready to give out. "Some reset this is turning out to be." Although, despite the blisters, there's something satisfying about the simplicity of it all. No buzzing phones, no broken elevators or crowded subways, just work that feels real. Important. Appreciated.

Inevitably, my thoughts circle back to Wilder and those eyes that seem to see through me, reading me like an open book.

I wonder if he feels what I feel when we touch.

Touch? More like grope him.

Although, if I'm honest, I've yet to feel unwelcome. He might try to act like I'm a nuisance, but I'm not picking up that vibe. The way his mouth twitches into a faint smirk whenever I fumble. The way his whole body stiffens when I press mine against his.

Or maybe it's my body that does that. That goes completely still at the electric circuit shooting through me.

The crunch of hooves on gravel pulls me from my thoughts. I flip around.

At first, I think I'm imagining him since he's on my mind. But I'd know that build anywhere—ran into it enough times.

Wilder rides toward me on a brown horse I've seen him on before, his silhouette outlined against the fading light.

"You lost?"

I hesitate. I'm not a fan of admitting when I don't know what I'm doing.

The sting of embarrassment prickles my skin. "No. Just exploring. It's a Friday night after all, maybe I'm looking for another bonfire or, you know . . . more reasons to aggravate my boss."

He pulls the horse to a stop beside me. "Exploring, huh? Must be why you're about half a mile from your cabin."

"Half a—" I glance around. "How's that?"

He chuckles. "Want a ride back?"

My eyes flick to the horse. I've never been on one before. But I don't want to share that fact just yet. I shrug. "Sure. Why n—"

He swings down like it wasn't really an option for me, holding the reins in one hand as he steps closer. "Come on, then."

He supports me as I hoist myself up. His strong grip rests just above my hip, on the open skin between my waist-tied shirt and jeans.

Jesus, I need to have sex.

That's got to be what this is. It's been too long. I'm drying out over here.

Once I'm settled, I release a breath I'd been holding. I can't tell if it was from climbing a horse for the first time, or Wilder touching me like his hands belong on my skin.

The saddle feels impossibly high, the horse's movements beneath me unsettling. But I'm instantly at ease when Wilder settles behind me.

"Comfortable?" he asks, his tone laced with amusement.

I nod.

He reaches around me to take the reins in both hands, his chest brushing against my back. The heat of him seeps through my shirt and I swallow hard, trying not to melt into him.

Is that even safe to do?

Safe? Maybe you should be asking yourself if it's appropriate.

No. The answer is no. So there will be no leaning or melting of any kind.

"You've never been on a horse before." His breath is on the side of my face. It's warm and masculine.

My cheeks flush hot. I twist my head so he doesn't see me blush—but it backfires.

Because he doesn't move. So when I twist to face away, his lips graze my neck.

I suck in a sharp breath and squeeze my eyes shut. "Oof, I'm sorry." I exhale a laugh, covering my face, because *of course*, I just did that. "I'm an H.R. nightmare, aren't I?"

"A what?"

"Where I'm from, you'd be sending me training videos on sexual harassment and make me sign an acknowledgement of understanding."

His soft chuckle vibrates through me. Then he guides my hands off my face and onto the saddle horn. "Just hold on. The only training I want to give you is how to not fall off a horse," he teases. But with the way his arms are wrapped around me from behind, I am not laughing.

I'm *melting*.

The ride is smooth yet refreshingly . . . gritty. I cling to the saddle horn, my knuckles white as we pick up speed.

"Where's your cart?" he asks.

"Left it with Jake. He said he needed to . . . tune it or something." I don't tell him that Ginger basically ordered the boy to change the tires on that thing so I can ride through town.

Wilder's quiet for a moment, and I wonder if he bought it. Can you even tune a golf cart?

"Thought you called it a day and went home," I say, breaking the silence. And also to find out where he's been the last few hours. If maybe he's keeping his distance because of what happened in the Saddle Room earlier.

"I don't call it a day until everyone else does."

I frown. "How do you manage that?"

"It's my ranch. My staff. Dallas and I tend to do a sweep. I usually check the livestock, storage, closures, all for safety. He'd check on the staff. Make sure no one's over-worked, that the night crew is well rested and prepared."

"Now you do both?"

"Now I do both."

I consider this for a moment. "So this is what, my courtesy ride? Are you on patrol?"

There's a beat before he answers. "No. I came lookin' for you."

My heart skips but quickly fades when I remember how he warned me to try to keep up on my first day.

I hum. "Don't worry, boss. I got it all done."

"Thanks," he mutters. "Sorry I didn't give you a chance to fix things earlier."

Warmth spreads through me at his apology. It almost tells me that he didn't just do it because I was being a brat about it, but that he realized I could.

I shrug. "You did." Then, because I know why he was so adamant about doing it himself, I ask, "I made some people real angry today, didn't I?"

"Nah. These guys aren't like that. It's just that things are a little rocky here these days and I don't want to give them a reason to doubt us. Our integrity."

I frown, wanting to ask him how I can help more, but am thrown off when he pulls up to the beautiful cottage.

He hops off and holds out his hand for me. "What are we doing back here?"

"This is where you're staying," he says, like it's obvious.

"Wilder."

"Cabin four is no longer available," he says tightly. "You're staying *here*."

I suck in a breath and hold it as he lowers me off the horse. I'm on fire until he lets go—almost too quickly—and turns toward the house.

I follow and race to beat him to the door, then twist to face him, blocking his entrance. "I can stay with my brother."

"Rose."

"Wilder, I . . ."

His hands are back on my hips like he can't help himself. Like he's been itching to touch me since he stopped.

This *can't* be all in my head.

"It's OK. I promise you he doesn't mind it. This was Millie's, yes, but for the rest of the summer, it's *yours*."

I bite my lip, looking up at him. "Not the whole summer, just six weeks, right?"

He smirks, pulling his hands off me and sliding them into his pockets. "If you start making it into work on time, I might consider letting you stay the rest of it."

I purse my lips. "You sure you can handle the bruises from my clumsiness?" My eyes drop to his chest.

"You'll have to hit harder if you're tryin' to leave a mark," he rasps out, his breath just above me.

I look up like I might have misheard, but the flirtation in his gaze is unmistakable. "All right," I breathe out. "I'll stay."

"Wise choice. Come on. All your stuff is already inside."

I follow behind, ignoring the daunting name above the mailbox as I walk through the ocean-blue door.

He flicks the light on, and I blink at the brightness as I follow him inside. It's an open floor plan, with a white kitchen and marble countertop, dark hardwood floors with blue and grey oriental rugs.

The décor is right out of a farmhouse magazine. Ivory couch and loveseat, oakwood furniture, plants . . . *everywhere*. It's as beautiful inside as it is on the outside.

"Wilder, this place is so adorable." I step into the kitchen, looking up at the high ceiling. "Is that a skylight? I love those."

He laughs softly as he leans against the counter. "Yeah. We rebuilt it a few years back. There was a small fire in the kitchen. It was no big deal. Millie had a . . . mishap."

"Oh no, was she all right?" It feels awkward to ask that now.

He smiles at the memory. "She was fine. Dallas teased her for weeks, claiming she just wanted a new kitchen." He swipes a finger against the marble. "Didn't stop him from comin' in here every day to build it for her."

I avoid asking questions about Millie, even though I want to know everything. Not just about Millie, but Dallas and Silas too.

About Wilder.

Their parents. I know their dad is still around, but no one talks about their mother.

He clears his throat. "I've got to get going, but there's a fully stocked fridge and cabinets of fresh groceries."

"Really?"

"I raided The Shack earlier. When your brother started asking questions, I told him I was moving you in here tonight."

"What'd he say to that?" I ask as I pop open the fridge.

"He was annoyed. Said he had a bet going with his sous chef on how long you'd make it in a cabin. His money was on you not lasting a week."

I laugh. "Surprised you didn't take that bet."

He doesn't laugh with me. "I wouldn't. I wanted to bring you back here sooner, but knowing how you feel about this being Millie's place, I . . . had to clear some things out first."

"Wilder—"

"It had to get done," he says quickly. "Not like my brother was going to do it." I watch him until he turns to leave. "Anyway, I'll let you get settled."

I follow him out the door. "Wilder," I call until he stops and turns back around. "You're busy enough. You didn't have to come back here and prep this house for me."

He rubs the back of his neck. "Yeah, well, maybe it was for selfish reasons."

"How do you figure that?"

His eyes roam my face. "Maybe now you'll get some sleep and get to work on time." He offers me a small smile. And for once the word "sleep" doesn't sound so evil.

"I sleep plenty," I lie, feeling compelled to prove normalcy.

He scoffs. "No, you don't."

"How can you tell?" I ask, and it's painful because it feels like I'm admitting a flaw.

He looks down at me, his voice equally low as he tucks my hair back, his touch light but deliberate. "How could someone not?"

There's a thick moment between us as I stare back at him. And this time, I know he feels it too.

His arms flex as he pulls back, slipping his fingers back in his pockets, that white shirt looking like it's going to tear off his body as he does it.

"The cottage," I start quietly. "Raiding your staff kitchen just to stock mine. Not firing me for coming in late. And then there's that whole H.R. issue we were talking about." I point a finger at him. "People are going to start claiming favoritism."

He steps closer, a smirk playing on his lips. "Now why would people get the idea that you're my favorite? 'Cause you got boobs?"

"So you've noticed."

He grunts. "Hard not to when you keep pressing them against me."

Heat curls in my stomach. "By *accident*."

He cocks his head. "Yeah."

It totally is. But I'll play his game. Holding his gaze, I risk the question. "Why would I do it on purpose?"

It's a risk not because he's my boss—that's temporary. But because he's Wesley's best friend. And that's forever.

I know enough about bro-code to know the kid sister is almost always off-limits.

I might instigate trouble for myself, but am I willing to risk their friendship?

The immediate answer is no.

Still, eyes locked on his, an imaginary kiss hovering in the space between us, I find myself waiting for Wilder's response. One that just might admit. . . there's something here.

I watch him consider it. See the conflict slowly die out as he lowers his gaze to my lips. Then something hardens in his eyes, and I know. . . he's changed his mind.

"Good night, Rose." He starts down the porch steps.

"Wait," I call and follow him, because there's no way I'm letting that one go.

He doesn't turn back as he reaches his horse. Throwing one arm in the air like he's taking a wild guess, he says, "Maybe a cowboy is on your ride list."

"My what list?"

He doesn't look at me as he adjusts the reins. "Your ride list. It's like a bucket list but no one's dying."

I exhale a laugh. "OK, that's not what I thought you meant."

There's a beat before he adds, "Things you want to try before moving on to the next wild thing Rose chooses."

I drag in a steady breath at the misconception that I'm wild. But I don't contradict him. Because maybe wild is exactly what this wounded wrangler needs.

Maybe we both do.

"A cowboy wasn't on my list." I smirk. "Should it be?"

He turns to me, any playful air between us gone. "Not this cowboy."

I swallow down the disappointment. Not because he's turning me down. But for a moment, I had a glimpse of that playful, laid-back Wilder my brother claimed he once was.

And I liked it. A lot.

"Get some rest, Rose."

I take a step back toward the house, watching him as he climbs his horse. "Sure thing, boss."

11.45 p.m.

Rose: I've got a crush on my boss.

Willow: The cowboy?

Rose: Wesley's friend.

Willow: But he wears a sexy hat and rides a horse? What's the problem?

Rose: He's my brother's best friend. But it doesn't matter. He just shot me down.

Willow: Bummer. Come home.

Rose: I can't. I'm riding this gig out.

Willow: What are you going to do about your crush?

Rose: Ignore it.

Willow: No one does that better than you.

Ouch.

I don't answer her right away. Not because I'm offended. Willow has always been the type to call it how she sees it. But because it's nearly two in the morning in New York. And while I love her always being available for me, she shouldn't have to lose sleep because I do.

I finish setting up my art corner, a perfect space I found by the window in the living room, and try to find some inspiration. I look around the space again.

I was wary coming in here at first. But after making dinner for myself in the clean, fully stocked kitchen, unpacking and taking a hot shower, the place doesn't feel like it belongs to someone's lost love.

It feels like mine. Even for a short while.

I imagine Willow fell asleep since that last text.

I flip through the pamphlets that Ginger gave me, wondering what touristy town things I could do to fill my time this weekend and help me forget I just got shot down.

My eyes widen when I find something happening Saturday night right here in Blue River.

Age group: Twenty to thirty.

Admission: Fifty dollars, drinks included.

Time: Ten to midnight.

End goal: *Forget grumpy cowboy.*

I snap a photo and send it to Willow, figuring she'll get it in the morning.

Rose: What should I wear?

To my surprise, she texts me back.

Willow: Speed-dating???

Rose: Yeah, I was thinking, the white blouse with the royal blue skirt and gold buckle.

Willow: How does this help with getting over your crush? Oh . . . I just got it. 😨 Well, be careful, Rebel. Also, speed-dating sounds fun. Can we do that when you're back home?

Rose: What if we like the same guy?

Willow: I'd be into that . . .

12

Wilder

Not this cowboy.

I'd be lying if I said I'm not usually an ass when a woman's got her eye on me.

Ever since Bonnie, I like to keep things simple. No strings, just a good time. Trust doesn't come easy for me these days.

No one's worth the trouble.

Never mind the fact that I'm not about to one-night-stand my best friend's kid sister, but a girl like Rose—as much fun as we might have—I couldn't give her more.

And I'm one hundred percent sure she wouldn't either.

I don't need another woman changing her mind.

But, man, if it didn't shock the hell out of me to see the hurt in her eyes when I said those three words.

Had she been hoping?

I don't really think her run-ins with me were on purpose. The flush in her cheeks is too real for them to be premeditated.

But fuck if I can't shake the feeling of her in my arms. Her breath on my skin. It's like a flame, a rush of pure fire.

It's bad enough that I've pushed some limits with my self-control lately. But knowing she feels it too—that's a disaster waiting to happen.

On all fronts.

After the evening checks, I take a ride with Tuscan along the river as the sun sets on Saturday. My eyes scan the amber fields for stray cattle or broken lampposts. I'm only half certain I'm paying attention to either. My mind's been on this mystery man that stopped by yesterday.

And what the hell he wants with my brother.

Still can't shake the feeling he'll be back.

Stepping in through the back door, I find Dallas and Dad in the kitchen, the smell of fried onions and ground beef filling the air. Dallas is at the stove, and I can tell from the way Dad's sitting back and watching, he'd come over to drag his grieving son out of bed.

"Dad." I nod curtly and he lifts his chin in response.

"Land looks good tonight," he starts, but he can't end the compliment there. "Check that south gate?"

"I did," I answer flatly, taking my hat off and hanging it on the hook by the door. "Smells good."

Dallas swings his head back. "We'll see if tastes good. Hungry? I'm making meatloaf." He cocks his head back. "Dad's way."

I roll my eyes. "With soy sauce?"

"Didn't hear you boys complainin' when you were eatin' at my house."

I grab a beer from the fridge, peeking over at my brother as he layers on the sauce.

"I invited Wesley, but he's having dinner with Rose over at the cottage," Dallas says, pouring the sauce over the dish and sliding it back in the oven to heat up.

"That's nice. They didn't really get to spend much time together all week."

"Hear you got her staying at the cottage," Dad comments.

Dallas calls over his shoulder. "How's she liking it over there?"

I know better than to tell him she's only been there one night. There's no reason to bring up Millie right now.

"What's not to like?"

Dallas doesn't respond. Instead, he pulls on a batch of scallions and slices. His eyes and breath even, measured, like he's trying to hold it together.

And I suppose now's as good a time as ever to change the subject.

"Someone came by for you yesterday."

"Who?"

"Don't know. He didn't leave a name. Was a little cryptic, honestly. Came by the main office asking for you. Any idea?"

"What'd he look like?" Dad asks.

"About your age. Nothing threatening about him. Was relatively polite."

Dallas shrugs like he's not in the mood. "I don't know. Customer? Competitor?"

"No. This was personal. That much I can tell."

Impatiently, he meets my eyes. "Well then, why the hell should I know more than you?"

"I'm asking if you got into some trouble lately? Maybe something you were too drunk to remember. Bar owner perhaps?"

Not that this guy looked like he owned much of anything. And he certainly didn't come looking like he was trying to even the score.

Plus, I don't see Dallas—even in a drunken state—pouncing on a guy twenty years older than him.

Dallas runs a hand over his face. "If he comes by again, send him over to the house."

"This house?" Dad starts with a firm glare at his oldest son. "Or the one you been buildin' and abandoned?" It's that no-nonsense, weathered tone we all recognize. One that hasn't changed since he started teaching us about responsibility, loyalty, and values.

With a breath, I sit back in my chair.

"Not this again," Dallas grunts and turns to check on the meatloaf.

Dad glances at me, a subtle look that tells me he knows what he's going through. "I walked that line myself, Dal. But after your mom passed, I still had to get up every damn morning—hard as might've been—and do right by everyone countin' on me."

My chest tightens. Dad's not known for his warmth, but he's not wrong. There's a lot riding on Dallas getting back out there. Our staff, the stock, the land—hell, even his old self—all counting on him.

I don't add myself to that category.

Because as much as I need my brother back too, there was a time not long ago when he thought he'd be running this place on his own—while I had my head out in the clouds.

So while I haven't been entirely patient—I've been quiet.

My brother perks a brow. "Look, I don't owe anyone money. I didn't punch some old guy, and I certainly don't go anywhere but Bones to drink. Whoever it is will go away eventually."

"Think the Callahans are involved?"

"Said the guy looked non-threatening?" Dad asks. "Then no."

"Well, I didn't like it." I sit up and turn to Dallas. "I don't like knowing someone is out there looking for you."

"Yeah, why?"

"What if you go missing? How do I know who to kill?"

He smirks. "I can take care of myself."

That used to be true.

He could take care of himself, me *and* Silas back in the day. Our younger brother hardly hung around us. Always preferred the town jocks rather than shooting the shit in the barn. Still, Dallas always knew his whereabouts, who he surrounded himself with and made sure he was alright.

Always the sound one. The one who told me not to trust Bonnie.

The one who was first to forgive me for turning my back on everyone.

"Fine." I set my beer down. "What do you want me to do if he comes back?"

"Tell him to leave. Anyone I need to know, knows how to reach me." He plates our dinner. "You two about done? Cause I'm ready to eat."

Dad and I exchange a worried glance. I nod and push off my chair to help. "Yeah, why not."

Sometime later after Dad leaves, Dallas calls it a night early. Every Saturday night, he and Millie would be out doing something.

Dancing, mingling, riding, anything. Millie hated staying in.

Dallas hated going out. He's a lot like me. I don't people well. I put on a smile for tour groups and the events we hold here at the ranch, but I like a quiet night.

Although tonight . . . a distraction wouldn't hurt. Anything to keep me from taking a short ride to see if the lights are on in the cottage.

They were last night. Pretty late in fact.

It's no wonder the girl's never on time in the morning. Picking up the phone, I text my best friend.

Wilder: Wanna grab a beer?

Wesley: Was just about to text you. Silas is in town with a few of his teammates. Wanna join us?

The fact that I didn't know my little brother is in town and Wes does, gets under my skin. But I don't press on it because I know why Silas didn't tell me he was coming. The last few times he was here, Dallas had been a mess and I was busy prepping for the season.

Silas doesn't think like we do. All he knows is hockey, girls, and staying young and pretty forever. Serious matters like the death of a loved one and running a family business are far from his radar.

Wilder: Sounds fun. You bring your sister with you?

I imagine the question is viable. Warranted even. I'm curious if my new employee is getting her fill of the town.

Wesley: I asked. Said she's tired and going to call it a night early.

Red flags go off in my head.

Wilder: Sounds like something I should do. You boys have fun. Tell Silas I'll call him tomorrow.

Monday night Rose went out after eleven and joined the guys for a bonfire. Tuesday, I found her at Bones about to get in the crossfire of a bar fight.

Then last night, her light was on until after one in the morning.

There's no way Rose is calling it a night at ten o'clock on a Saturday.

But at the same time, I'm relieved she's not going out with Silas's friends.

I let Dallas know I'm stepping out for a bit and don't wait for him to respond.

Hopping on my horse, I casually ride in the direction of the cottage. From this distance, I can see dim lights are on in the living room.

This is ridiculous. What am I doing?

This is borderline stalking.

No. This *is* stalking. I'm basically going to confirm if she's home, when Rose is an adult. She's got every right to leave the premises.

Sure, the idea of her out in the town by herself sends my protective streak out of control, but it's still not my business.

She's my employee and currently not on the clock.

I'm about to turn around when I see a body walking along the path toward the main office.

I ride closer, and he slows down when he spots me. "Hey, boss."

I frown. "Jake?"

He salutes me.

"Everything all right?"

"Sure is. Just did a few checks while I was out. Dropped off Rose's cart a little while ago. She looked very nice."

"Rose's cart?"

"Ginger said you asked me to change up the tires with something more durable. Figure she's going to take it through town."

I growl. "I never said that."

His eyes are wide. "But—"

"It's fine." I hop off the horse. "Will you do me a favor? Take Tuscan back to the stables for me?"

"Sure thing."

Minutes later, I'm in my truck, pulling up to the cottage.

The cart's nowhere in sight. I jog up the steps, banging on the door. No answer. There's no one inside.

Then I remember something Jake mentioned.

She looked very nice.

What's this girl gotten into now?

I try to convince myself that this is Wesley's sister I'm protective over. And that there's no point in ruining his night. I try to convince myself that she now stole parts of my property for her joy ride and I have every right to be the one to go after her myself.

But even I know it's more than that.

Gripping the wheel, I race out the gate of the ranch and onto the streets of my small town.

Deliberately reminding myself it's *small*.

It should be easy to spot a flower-painted golf cart in town, shouldn't it?

A sensible man would call her brother to give him a heads up.

A sensible *sane* man wouldn't be freaking out about what kind of trouble she might get herself into that Dallas and I can't save her from.

A sensible, loyal to his best friend, man *wouldn't* have been relieved knowing she turned down hanging out with a bunch of professional hockey players.

The glow of streetlights casts long shadows on the ground as I make my way through town, my eyes scanning over every corner.

The diner lot, gas station, even the closed shopping strip. All before reaching the street where Bones is.

No Rose-branded golf cart here.

Hell, not even a plain old golf cart to give me false hope.

My frustration is mounting.

She doesn't belong out here—not alone, not at this hour. Rose doesn't know the kind of fast trouble that could show up.

Driving down another block, I finally spot the open, white hooded vehicle. I race toward it, relieved at the unmistakable, caught-red-handed sign.

The Rose.

"Damn stubborn woman," I growl and park my truck at the first empty spot, ready to go door to door.

I look up at the awnings.

This can't be right. The only thing open is an old strip club that shut down ages ago and now only opens for traveling events.

I walk inside like I belong, ignoring the hostess at the front. It's dim, almost too dark, with small round tables and candles filling the room. There must be twenty of them.

The hell is going on here?

Whatever trouble is stirring up here, Rose is sipping on it like it's her favorite drink.

She's sitting at one of the tables, talking to some guy.

She's smiling, her face glowing in the tiny flame.

While mine burns with a new kind of heat, leaving a bitterness in my chest.

"Hi there. Are you signed up for this evening?"

I turn, my eyes dropping to the short woman. She scans me slowly. "Ooh . . . maybe *I* should have too."

"Excuse me? No, I'm not signed up for anything." I turn my focus back to Rose.

"Well, you're in luck; we had a no-show today so we're odd. Go right in."

"Odd? What is this?"

"A place to find your one true love. Or your one true Saturday night, whatever floats your boat." She gives me a push. "Start with table six."

I look up with my jaw tight, watching Rose as another man approaches her table.

Speed-dating?

You have got to be kidding me.

"I'll wait for table nine, thanks," I grit.

Following my gaze, the woman grins. "Nice choice, but that's not how this works. Table six or you can leave."

I grunt and slip her a bill. "Bring me a whiskey when I get to table nine."

13

Rose

I've only gone speed-dating once in New York. Not in hopes of meeting someone special, but for moral support for a college girlfriend of mine. It sounded like fun, and it was. But only when you go with a friend and exchange notes—over lots of drinks.

Willow thinks this is my way of getting the attention I'm not getting from Wilder. But she's wrong.

I do have Wilder's attention. Just not in the way I want.

Tonight is more about having a good time. I don't plan on calling any of them afterwards. Not for a good time and certainly not for forever.

As much fun as it sounded to hang out with Wes and Silas and his teammates tonight, I wanted to be on my own. I really don't want to be talking to a bunch of hockey players—or any guys for that matter—with my brother across the table watching me.

At least that's what I tell myself.

I certainly don't tell myself that I wanted to go out alone tonight—in *hopes* of getting caught.

But I'm on date number twelve and . . . I don't think he's coming.

I've been sitting with Rob or Bob or Andrew for a solid two minutes now. He's been staring at my cleavage since he sat down. Only making eye contact for a few seconds at a time.

I'm not a fan of this one. At least the others made me laugh. Sort of.

Like Todd, the poet, who attempted to come up with a unique poem on the fly that starts with "Roses are red."

Even Gary, who proudly bragged about winning a hot dog eating contest last fall, was funny and sweet. Not in a romantic sense, though.

I fight back a yawn, listening to Bob and mentally counting how many more before I've gone through all sixteen dates.

A towering frame approaches my table. "Clock's up—move along."

My stomach squeezes as I look up. *Wilder*.

Confused, my current date glances between us. "Uh . . . I don't think—"

"I said beat it." Wilder's voice is low but sharp. He doesn't look at me—and something tells me he's *saving* it for when we're alone.

My heart flips with mischievous excitement. Still, I feel some sort of obligation to defend this poor man. I'm about to when I catch date number twelve glance back at an unpaired table six. He smirks as he stands. "Have a nice night, you two."

Wilder's lips are pressed in a thin line as he fills the seat. His jaw is tight. But his eyes, when they finally meet mine, aren't equally angry. They're not tender either, just . . . amused? Challenging?

"Wilder," I say with a steady breath.

"Yes, I'm Wilder, and you are?"

"Surprised."

He leans in and his face is even more gorgeous in the candlelight. "Oh, I was too, but enough about me. How do you plan on getting home tonight?"

I cross my arms. "In my cart."

He shakes his head. "I just had it towed. Stolen property."

"You can't do that. It's mine for the summer. You said so yourself."

"Oh, you'll get it back. When I replace the tires you took without permission."

I glare at him until a waitress sets a drink in front of him. "Thanks, darlin'." He takes a sip and leans back in his chair, watching me. "So, what's a girl like you doin' in a place like this?"

I lean back too, playing his game. And I think I might be better at it. "Lookin' to take the edge off."

He growls to himself, voice strained when he says my name. "Rose."

"What, like I've never done it before?"

His jaw tenses, eyes darkening as he exhales.

The halftime buzzer goes off, signaling we have three minutes left.

"Enough. Now, let's get out of here."

"Why would I do that? You're a terrible date."

"How'd you figure?"

"The second you sat down you accused me of stealing."

"Got a point." He takes another sip of the amber liquid.

"You haven't asked me what my favorite color is."

"Blue," he says in one breath.

"My flaw."

He shrugs. "I don't know . . . trouble sleeping?"

My breath catches in my throat. I didn't think it was noticeable, but then he frowns, sets his drink down, and leans in, his voice low but not judging.

"I'm right, aren't I?"

I swallow. "Sleep is overrated."

"Sorry you feel that way. When that buzzer goes off, we're leaving."

"I'm not going home."

He swirls the remaining liquid in his glass. "Who said anything about going home?"

I look over his shoulder. "I've still got three more dates."

He looks over mine to see what he's got ahead. I watch his face for a reaction, fighting the urge to turn around and see. Are they older? Blonder?

His quick peek doesn't give anything away, but that's not new for him.

I glance at his drink, and he holds it out for me.

I shake my head. "I don't drink."

Wilder cocks his head, narrows his eyes, and watches me for a moment—even after the buzzer goes off.

"To be continued," he says, then inhales the remains of his glass and stands, holding his hand out for me. "Let's go, Blue."

I stare at it for a few short seconds, a smirk playing on my face as I meet his eyes. Because I realize it doesn't matter who's behind me.

Wilder Thorne is leaving with me.

When the hostess tried to stop us from leaving, Wilder looked about as interested in staying as I was.

So he hooked his arm in mine, thanked them for helping him find his soulmate, and we walked out of there laughing.

Well, I was laughing. He seemed annoyed. "You're turnin' me into a liar," he grumbles.

"Oh stop, you enjoyed that," I tease.

He doesn't say another word, but I catch him in another lie as we cross the street. My cart is parked where I left it.

But I don't call attention to it. Just like I don't call attention to the fact that my arm is still tucked under his.

He skims my outfit once more. "Startin' to not believe you had art supplies in two of those suitcases."

I decided against that outfit I told Willow I'd wear. It was too uptown city girl. Instead, I'm wearing a long black skirt with a slit up my thigh and red top. My makeup is minimal, mascara with light shimmery eye-shadow and pink gloss.

"You'd be surprised how many clothes I can fit into one suitcase. Shoes tend to be the problem." I lift my burgundy boots. "And I only brought one pair. Well, and slippers."

He's quiet as we walk along the street, and I wonder what he's thinking. A million things go through my head at the possibilities.

How to fire me without hurting my brother.

How to let me down gently since I'm failing miserably at hiding my attraction.

The best route to Bones, since that's where Wesley and his friends are. There, he'll tell my brother where he found me tonight.

Feeling like a bother to him, I start to slip my arm out of his, but he holds tight, keeping his eyes ahead.

"So, when do you paint?"

The question throws me off, but then I see his thought process. "You think I stay up late painting?"

"When you're not sneaking out, stealing vehicles, caught in a bar fight, or dating random strangers for six minutes at a time, I imagine you might have an actual hobby."

"I used to paint at night. It's how I started actually."

"Now?"

"Now, I . . . paint whenever, I guess."

"So it didn't start as a hobby?"

I get a flashback to a therapy session where I told Dr. Sandra about my art. Which she explained was my outlet. A way to escape stress and overwhelming feelings.

I shake my head. "It was a way for me to focus, help calm me, and keep my head in a better state of mind."

"Wesley says you gave up becoming a doctor for art."

My heart constricts. "Therapists don't heal," I correct.

"Then what do they do?" he challenges, but answering that question will tell him more about me than anyone needs to know.

"Did you know over seventy percent of graduates don't end up in the field they studied?" I deflect.

A smirk touches his lips, his eyes flicking to mine. "I suppose that sounds accurate."

There's a question in his brow, that makes me ask, "And yet . . ."

He lifts a brow with a grin, pleased that I can read him. And it's so sexy, I almost forget what we're talking about. "And yet, something is off with your claim that you're just like that seventy percent of people."

"You think I'm different."

"I *know* you're different."

We turn onto the corner where his truck is parked. There's a bar that looks slightly more upscale than Bones. But not more appealing. A group of women are crowding the front. One smoking a cigarette, the other two laughing. All three are blonde and beautiful.

Wilder pauses, and there's a shift in his vibe I pick up on. It's so abrupt it almost hurts.

"Wilder," I whisper, looking up at him.

He releases a slow breath. "Come on," he mutters low, nudging his head toward his truck, only one storefront away from the girls.

"Bon," one of the girls starts, her tone almost a warning.

Instantly, I know who she is.

Why Wilder stopped and wants to get out of here.

It's her. The woman he was ready to give up everything for.

The woman who betrayed him and gave him up in return.

I pretend I don't see her when we draw close and press myself against Wilder's hard frame, slipping my arm around his back.

Like I'm made to be under the crook of his arm, he tugs me close, with a subtle furrow of his brows.

"Wilder," the blonde I can only imagine to be Bonnie says when we reach them.

Of course her voice is perfect. Angelic with a hint of gruff.

"Hello, Bonnie."

Her eyes are on me, and I give her a small wave and a pretty smile. "Hi there, I'm Rose."

Bonnie perks a brow. "Ya'll look cozy." Her comment isn't directed at me.

"Good to see you."

"Aren't you going to introduce us to your new girl?"

I prepare for Wilder to tell Bonnie and her friends that I'm nothing more than his employee, his best friend's sister.

"She just did that," he says flatly. "This is Rose. And we're on our way home. Excuse us."

The two girls step aside, but Bonnie doesn't move. She scans me just before Wilder takes my hand and walks around her.

When we reach his truck, I plant myself in front of the passenger door. My eyes are on his lips as I tug him close.

"Rose," he warns. "Not doing this. I'm not using you to get to her."

"What if I'm using her to get to you?"

His eyes drop to my lips, but he still hesitates. It's a struggle, like he wants to but is holding back.

Because he doesn't want to use me to make Bonnie jealous? Because of my brother?

Apparently, I'm not above begging.

"Put your morals aside and kiss me, cowboy."

He moves into me like he can't help himself, sets his hands on my hips and growls into my ear. "I said *no*." He pulls me against him and cracks open the passenger door. "Inside."

To our audience, we look playful, like we're drunk on each other and can't wait to make out.

To him, I look like his best friend's kid sister who needs to calm down.

To me, I feel like a fool.

Fifteen minutes later, he parks his truck around the back of the cottage. It almost seems intentional. Like he doesn't want the nearby cabins to see him here this late with me.

"Sorry," he says with a sigh as he helps me out of the passenger seat and shuts the door behind me.

"For what?"

"I said I wasn't taking you home."

I wouldn't have remembered if he hadn't said anything. Because we did walk around for a bit before we ran into his ex.

I shrug with a soft smile. "I guess you owe me."

"I've sent someone for your cart. He'll have it here by morning."

"Let me guess, the tires will be taken off and I'll have to put the old ones back on myself?" I try to make light of his mood because I can tell he's distracted by something.

It's probably her.

He's about to respond but hesitates. And for the first time in a long time, *I'm tired*. This man is exhausting.

"Forget it." I turn, walk up the steps and pull my keys out.

But he's behind me in an instant, flipping me around and pressing me against the door, caging me with his palms. "We need to clear some things up." His hands curl into fists like he's fighting to hold back. "First off, you can keep the tires. On one condition. You only take it outside these gates during the day. You want to go out at night, you call me."

"You adding babysitting to your list now, cowboy?"

"And second, I'm pretty damn sure you wouldn't have wanted an audience for this." His big hands rake into my hair and his lips crash against mine. I suck in a sharp breath, then moan into his mouth, lifting my hands to his face. I kiss him back with equal hunger.

He growls in response and I revel in the sound. The gravelly, masculine, out of control sounds he makes when we're this close.

Lightheaded with heat and lust, I barely feel him unlock the door behind me before it swings open and we move inside.

Wilder breaks the kiss for a moment, shutting the door behind me, but keeping me in his grasp.

The second we're behind the pretty blue door, he hooks his hands under my thighs and lifts me, guiding my legs around him. And *holy crap* what this does to my core.

I whimper into his mouth. I want to cry out his name but fear it will only snap him out of this rage-filled desire.

That's what this is. A release of pent-up frustration that's been driving him mad.

He breaks the kiss with a growl, still holding me with a fist in my hair. "Did you want people watching me devour you like this, Rose? Or did you think it was going to be an innocent little kiss?"

I throw my head back, exposing my neck to him with a plea in my voice. "Wilder."

He nips at my jaw, then yanks me back to face him. "It would do you well to understand what you're asking when you tell a cowboy to put his morals aside."

His eyes drop back to my swollen lips.

"How can I *not* now?" I breathe, lust-eyed and hungry for more.

He growls again, setting me on the kitchen counter and spreading my legs to stand between them. "I'm not crossing this line with you, Rose."

I cradle his strong jaw, stroking it lightly, then lean to kiss along that line I've silently memorized.

His eyes flutter closed. "Fuck, your lips are like a drug." He turns to meet them with his. "The best kind of drug."

He moves me onto the couch, the lights still dim from before I left the house.

Wilder squeezes my thigh, then uses one finger to lift my skirt, dragging it up by the slit.

Anticipation doesn't even begin to describe what I feel in my bones. I want him.

And I'm about to have him.

14

Wilder

There's a hard knock on the door and I jolt back, tearing myself away from the girl I've been struggling *not* to crave for the past week. "Who the hell?"

Rose's eyes are wide and confused, like it's not her door being banged on. "How should I know?"

"Rose, open up."

At the sound of my best friend's voice on the other side, I'm both terrified—and enraged.

Because how dare he waltz onto my property banging on doors of my residents like he owns them?

I'm sitting up on my knees on the sofa, with Rose still under me, her blouse shifted, her skirt—damn her skirt—pulled up high enough for me to see her inner thigh.

I adjust in my jeans, then stand. "He usually come by this late?"

She pushes up off the couch, glancing at the clock over the oven—as if we both don't know it's after one.

"No." Her voice is shaky and now I'm even more outraged. Hell, if I could open this door myself right now—

With that thought, I run a hand through my hair, pacing the small living room. "He can't see me here. Not at this hour."

She looks up at me, almost apologetically—as if she'd done something wrong here. "The bedroom," she whispers. "I'll get rid of him."

I want to bend down to kiss her.

To tell her to get rid of him fast so I can have my hands on her again.

But I hesitate a little too long, and there's another bang. With a single nod, I disappear down the hall, slipping into the bedroom. The lights are off in the hallway, so he shouldn't see me lurking back here.

I hear a sharp intake of breath before the door is pulled open. "Wh—"

Heavy, unrelenting footsteps enter the foyer. "Want to tell me where you were tonight?"

I frown.

Does he know I was with her? Did he see us in town?

"Last I checked, I'm not sixteen and you're not Dad."

She makes a good point, Wes. Back off.

"Cut the shit, Rose. I ran into Jeff at Bones tonight. Said he had to leave to go pick up the golf cart you left outside Starlight. Said it's the second time he's had to do it this week."

Knew I should've gone back for it myself in the morning.

"The hell were you doing at a strip club, Rose?"

I can't help my smile, wondering how she's going to handle this one.

But at the same time, I want to stomp out there and tell him to back off. Because I don't remember her inviting him in.

"It's not a—well, it wasn't tonight. There was this event, and I wanted to go."

This isn't going to end well.

I've been on the other end of this two-way conversation before and it always gets pretty heated.

"What's the event?"

Here we go.

"None of your business," Rose snaps back.

There's silence for a moment and I wonder what's going on.

I hear his footsteps move deeper into the house. Then his voice, as if he's reading from something. My guess is his phone. "Starlight, closed for a private event." There's a pause. "Speed-dating? Really, Rose?"

I hear her laugh, instant relief washing over me. "You should try it sometime, maybe you won't be so cranky if you got laid."

"I'm not cranky. I'm worried about you. And is that what *you* were doing? Trying to get laid?"

I still. Half wondering the answer, the other half wanting to level him.

"Wesley. It's late. I'm tired. Please go."

I hear movement and it sounds like he's landed on the sofa where I was just about to do God-knows-what to his little sister.

He sighs. "Fine, you're right. You're an adult, it's a weekend and you're single. So tell me then, how'd it go?"

"Wesley, enough. Please go."

My heart pounds in my chest because I know if she asks again and he doesn't, then I'm going to have to make my presence known.

"What? I'm curious. Did you meet anyone? Heck, if it worked for you, I might sign up for the next one."

"For God's sake, I wasn't planning on going out with any of them. I just wanted to have fun, explore, get to know people around here."

Another sigh. His voice softening. "Rose, you can't just go out meeting strangers, especially in a strange town."

"Didn't realize I was a prisoner. And if that was your intention here, I'm on the next plane back to New York, Wes."

"I meant I don't want you out *at night* here by yourself."

"Wesley, I don't show up at your door at one in the morning. Please pay me the same respect."

"I'm trying to make sense of what you want so maybe I can help. You wanted to be a doctor, a *therapist*. It's all you ever talked about. Then you pick up a paintbrush—your senior year, no less—and decide to live every day like it's your last? What's going on with you?"

I hang on to every word like it's the key to her puzzle.

But only she holds the missing pieces and something tells me she's not giving them up.

"I asked you to leave." When her voice cracks, I step out into the hallway, about to throw him out—I'm clearly not thinking about the consequences.

But Rose is.

Her gaze meets mine and she shakes her head slightly. There's no fear in her eyes. Just a look that tells me it wouldn't do any good.

I've heard versions of these arguments in the background over the years. I've always been on Wesley's side, commending him for being so responsible and protective of his sister.

But seeing it from the other side now, it feels different. Like he's not taking the time to listen to her. To try to understand.

Wes is still on the couch facing the other way.

In response to her pleading gaze, I tighten my jaw, letting her know I'm not holding off much longer.

Then I retreat, letting her handle her brother her own way.

"How'd you get home?"

No answer.

"Well?"

"I . . . couldn't find my keys. Jeff had a spare, so I called him."

There's silence for a long moment, my stomach twisting at that half-story she told him.

"Fine," he finally says, and I hear movement. "Don't tell me. At least you're back safe. Until the next stupid thing you do."

Heat flares in my chest.

Is that why she called herself stupid the other day? Because of him?

I hear the door opening and there's a pause in movement. Then a deep sigh. "Wilder treatin' you all right?"

"Just fine, thanks." Her response is flat. She's hurt.

"I'm off tomorrow. Maybe I can take you around town?"

"No, thanks. I'm busy making stupid life choices, so I don't see myself making time for my brother anytime soon."

"Rose."

I hear the door close without another word, and I'm torn between following him outside for a heart to heart . . . or just being here for *her*.

I don't get the choice because as I'm stepping out of the dark hallway, Rose slams herself into me, wrapping her arms around my shoulders.

I stroke the back of her head. "Now *that* was definitely on purpose."

She chuckles into my chest.

"You all right?" I rasp against her hair.

I don't bother asking if it's always like this. I know it is. Wesley is exceptionally protective of his sister. One of the qualities I'd always admired about him.

From the living-room window, I watch him drive away, feeling like a traitor. He's always had my back when it comes to family matters. Stood by my side, even when he knew I was wrong.

Is *this* wrong?

Am I risking ten years of friendship for a momentary lapse of self-control?

"The moment's gone, isn't it?" She pulls back slowly, looking up at me. "And after everything you just heard, probably for good."

Hell, how I want to prove her wrong.

"There's nothing wrong with you, Rose." I tuck her hair behind her ear. "He's just not paying attention."

But there *is* something wrong with me risking everything for a night with her.

Because that's all it could ever be.

I drop my hand. "I think we got carried away. No—I got carried away."

When she drops her head, I catch her chin, lifting it. "It's *not* because of those things he said."

She pushes my hand down and steps back a few feet. "Of course it is. And I understand."

My legs carry me toward her and I grip her face this time. Lifting it to mine.

I swear, if I could read those pretty green eyes right now, they're screaming *Get carried away with me again.*

And fuck, I wish I could.

But I know better than to want this. I know better than to let good looks and charm drive me away from everyone I care about.

"If you're going to leave, you should probably do it now."

I nod because she's right. There's no point in dragging this out. I walk out of the house, circle around the back, and hop in my truck.

15

Rose

At around ten the next morning, my doorbell rings, waking me. I pile up my hair in a loose ponytail and step out into the living room with a wide stretch.

Six hours.

The most sleep I've gotten all week. The world needs more Sundays.

If I wasn't so mortified about last night, I'd have texted Wilder to thank him for letting me stay at the cottage.

It's been something of a dream staying here the last few nights. Fully equipped kitchen, my own washer and dryer—it feels like a vacation with a penthouse suite.

I haven't actually been here on a Sunday morning, so I imagine this is a wakeup call of some sorts. I stalk to the door in my pajamas.

My cart is parked outside and I notice something on the seat.

I glance around before striding over and lifting the brown paper bag, immediately smelling what's inside. Coffee and a cappuccino muffin.

There's a note scribbled on the bag.

Love you. Wes.

"An apology would be nice," I grumble.

I bring it inside and close the door, resisting the urge to text him that I'm still not speaking to him.

After breakfast, I flip through the pamphlets that Ginger gave me and circle some ideas for today, since there's no way I'm staying in. I want to see the town, go shopping. Meet people who won't throw me against a wall—even if it is to get me out of the line of fire. Though, Callahan or not, I'm not convinced Dusty is as evil as Wesley and the Thorne brothers paint her.

When I drive my cart outside the gate, it takes me back to Wednesday, when Wilder took me out for breakfast when he thought I was going to pass out from malnutrition.

I'm not angry at him for leaving last night. I'm just mortified. He's got a ranch to run. A family business to keep from crumbling. A brother who's still grieving. And I'm here acting like a girl with a crush.

Stupid.

My first stop is the bookstore. I pick up three books. Two thrillers by authors I recognize, and one romance by an author who is new to me.

At the checkout, I set the romance book aside when I notice it's about a small-town cowboy. Nope, not going there. "Just these two actually."

The checkout girl smirks. "Cowboys not your thing?"

I smile back. "I prefer serial killers. At least you know their next move."

Her eyes widen, but she doesn't say anything.

Thirty minutes later, I'm at the street fair, looking at a pair of beige cowgirl boots that would go with nearly every outfit I brought with me.

My phone pings with a text. I take a quick peek before strongly considering shutting the damn thing off for the day.

My brother.

Wesley: Where are you?

Rose: Just stopped by a warehouse to trade an organ for a pair of boots. Why?

Wesley: Which organ?

I debate on sending back, *My brain, since you don't think I have one.*

Wesley: I'll double whatever they're offering.

I laugh and slide my phone away just as I hear a familiar sweet voice.

"Who's got you laughing?"

I look up, my eyes brightening at the friendly face. "Ginger." I hug her and she pats my back gently. "Took your advice and hitting up everything there is to see in one day."

"That's a mighty long day. Have you eaten?"

"Not yet."

A deep voice comes from behind her. "Well then, you can come have lunch with us."

I look up at the man whose features are strangely familiar. "Hello," I greet him tentatively, my gaze flicking to Ginger.

He extends a hand. "Connor Thorne."

"Thorne? You're Wilder's dad."

He nods, pulling up his belt buckle. "That's one of 'em."

I smile. "I'm Rose."

He nods like he knows everything that goes on at his ranch. "Wesley's sister. You're helping out for the summer. My boy giving you any trouble?"

"I think I'm giving him trouble. He just hasn't fired me yet."

He laughs. "Oh, this should be good. Come to lunch with us, want to hear all about it." The man glances at the item I'm holding in my hands and moves in front of me to pay for the boots.

"Oh, that's not necessary," I try to argue.

"I insist." He thanks the vendor, who bags them up for me and the three of us start walking. "It's been a minute since I bought a pretty lady a pair of cowgirl boots."

I notice that Ginger's arm is tucked under his, and I wonder what the story is there. Are they . . . on a date? Do his sons know? Or maybe it's a secret and these are the few moments they get together.

Suddenly conscious—and slightly uncomfortable—that I might be witness to something no one else knows about, I decline the offer.

"Thank you." I hold up the boots. "These might last me a lot longer on your ranch than the ones I brought."

He nods approvingly. "They were a good choice. Break 'em in right." He winks.

I glance at Ginger. "Well, I appreciate the invite to lunch, but I don't want to intrude. I'm sure you both—"

"You'll come to lunch," he cuts me off with a soft grin and slides his arm beneath mine so he's between Ginger and me. "There's a place just around the corner I think you'll like."

"Cozy and traditional," Ginger adds.

Their warmth spreads through me like a summer breeze, making it hard to argue. And truthfully, I'm not sure I want to.

We stroll into a small restaurant along the street. It's a simple nod of Mr. Thorne's head before we're quickly seated at a table by the window.

It's no wonder. The man exudes power. His presence, his build. But something tells me he's well known. As well as being the original owner of Blue River Ranch, he's also got that confidence about him that tells me he's respected in this town.

"So, there's no Mrs. Thorne?" I ask as we're seated. And immediately feel like I need to justify the question. "Or is she not a fan of cowgirl boots?"

"Oh, she was a fan, all right." He spreads his napkin along his lap. "She's been gone a while now," he says, voice rough. "An accident." And it's all he says. I catch him rub a calloused thumb over the silver band around his finger.

"I'm sorry. What was she like?"

Ginger chimes in energetically. "Oh, she was somethin' fierce. Always smilin', kept fussin' over him and the boys."

Mr. Thorne rubs his chest. "Yeah. I fussed over her fussin'."

I laugh gently. "Sounds like you two were a fun match. Or maybe she just knew how to pull the fun out of you . . ." I narrow my eyes at him. "Even when you were a bit grumpy?"

He scoffs, peering over at me like I'm smarter than I look. "About sums it up."

We order and I try not to ask too many more questions. Instead, I watch the two as I once again try to figure out their relationship. If it's an innocent friendship or . . . courtship.

That's definitely not something I can ask. Maybe I'll wait until Ginger and I are back at work.

"So Rose, how do you like working with Wilder?"

"Oh everyone's been really welcoming," I glance at Ginger in particular. "Truthfully, I don't know a lot about ranching but it's easy to tell you've built quite the legacy."

His brows rise. “What makes you say that?”

I shrug, trying to find the right words for what I feel when I walk the grounds. “There’s a quiet . . . strength to the land. Can tell it’s cared for, appreciated. You poured a lifetime into it, Mr. Thorne, and it shows.”

He watches me for a moment with a subtle nod. “Well, I’m touched and I’m glad you’re feeling welcome. But also wondering if you’re dodging my question on how you like working with my son?”

I smile. “Notice that did ya?”

He grins back. “Just one more of my *quiet strengths*.”

Ginger and I laugh. She nudges me playfully but addresses Connor. “Your boy’s needed a reminder or two on his manners.”

“Which are really unnecessary, Ginger,” I argue with a subtle glare.

He waves me off. “A healthy reminder would do him good.” He points to Ginger. “So if she’s offering, take it. Woman always knew how to set those boys straight better than I did.”

“He’s coming around honestly,” I think of our heated kiss last night at the cottage. The tension and vulnerability I caught when we ran into Bonnie. “Probably just under a lot of stress with the busy season.”

“You’re not wrong there,” Connor offers. “He’s been carrying more than his share lately.” The way he says this almost makes it sound like a lesson or fact of life rather than something that is unfair or unfortunate.

I narrow my eyes, and I’m surprised to hear myself ask, “Why do you sound like you’re OK with this?”

He smirks, then considers his words. "Well, I wouldn't say that exactly. Let's just say it's good to see Wilder holdin' the land together—and damn well. There was a time I wasn't sure he cared enough to."

I absorb this information somewhat in awe. Unsure if I should be offended he'd lost his faith in Wilder—even if it was for a short time. Or if I'm honored he's sharing this with me.

Before I could think of an appropriate response, Ginger nudges Connor with her elbow. "Oh enough of that, tell her some *good* stories about the boys."

He laughs lightly and the two of them shift tunes to a handful of tales about life on the ranch, the boys growing up, and another tidbit or two about Carrie Thorne, his late wife.

But nothing else as to how she died.

"Can I ask about the Callahans?" I finally say after the bill is paid and we're wrapping up lunch. Not that I think her accident and the Callahans are linked, but I can at least rule it out if they aren't. "What's the story there?"

Connor sighs like it's a question he gets often. "It's the river."

"The river?"

"Blue River stretches through both properties, mainly through Blue River Ranch, which got its name because of the generous stretch of it running through our land. While Callahan Ranch has only a short, rocky end of it—barely enough for cattle in dry months."

He holds up a finger as if to make something clear. "Now that's no fault of mine where I built my ranch.

A river always flows where it flows. But over the years, Boon Callahan started accusing me of diverting the water, building dams and whatnot as a way of hurting their ranch and livestock."

Ginger shakes her head, like she remembers the wild accusations. "Their property is bigger. And their business was always better."

"I'd never compete with that," Connor agrees. "But I can't help if the river isn't big enough for it. My ranch is smaller because I took it into consideration from the start." He takes a sip of water. "And I sure as hell wasn't about to sell my land for them to expand."

"He tried to get you to sell?" I ask.

"Came in acting like he was doing me a favor, taking it off my hands. Things spiraled out of control after that. We had spies, break-ins, damaged property, and riled-up livestock. He'd hit every season."

"Is it . . . still going on?" I think about the kind of stress this must put on Wilder, on top of everything else he's dealing with.

Mr. Thorne shakes his head. "Nothing since his kids took over a few years back. Dusty and Ricky. There's been plenty of mishaps on Blue River Ranch since, but nothing ties back to them."

"How do you know? What if they're really good at covering their tracks?" I don't know why I'm so invested. But it just seems strange not to have answers. Like, how did the barn fire start where Millie was killed? What happened to Carrie Thorne?

The man across from me considers this, scratching his well- groomed beard. "Well, take a recently stolen golf cart, or a bush fence left a tangled mess." He pins me with those blue eyes that match his son's. "Callahans could have been Wilder's first guess." He perks a brow at me but it's an amused one with a hint of a smirk. "But was it them, really?"

I roll my lips. "Right."

His chuckle is lighthearted. "Other than . . ." he flicks his wrist in my direction, "recent events, most of the incidents on our ranch have been tied to either recklessness from inexperienced staff or just nature."

It was kind of him to leave me out of the inexperienced staff example. But I don't say as much. "Is there a way to make peace?"

"Would be nice, I suppose. But it's not my decision to make."

"Well, thanks for the background, Mr. Thorne. And for lunch."

"It's Connor, and it was a pleasure. Your brother is like one of my own, so you're part of the family."

My cheeks warm from his tenderness and it's nice to be welcomed—despite myself.

They both walk me to my golf cart parked a few blocks down. Connor has my bags in one hand and Ginger's arm in the other.

I'll have to find out more about these two . . . and a few other things.

12.45 a.m.

Willow: Get anything cute?

I sigh. Bet she set her alarm to check on me at this hour. Stubborn woman. I send her a picture of my boots.

Willow: Oh, cute boots. I'll look good in those when I borrow 'em. You up?

Rose: Nope, sound asleep.

Willow: Hey, I'm allowed stupid questions once in a while.

Rose: Go to sleep, Wil, I'm good.

Willow: Love you.

Rose: Love you more.

I'm painting in the living room. But tonight, I'm not trying to keep my mind from replaying a nightmare from two years ago.

OK, so maybe there's a little bit of that—old habits die hard.

Tonight, my mind's on Wilder.

I've been more than curious about this grumpy cowboy since the day I walked onto his ranch and locked eyes with him.

And now, I've not only kissed him, I let myself get absorbed in the heat of it. In the way his strong arms pulled me close like he had every right to. His lips didn't just claim mine, they gave the promise of claiming all of me.

For those few powerful moments, he was staking his territory, like I already belonged to him.

I've never felt so desired, so incredibly turned on. His touch hit differently. Those calloused fingers against my skin, stroking so tenderly. Nothing like the way his demanding lips possessed me. It was intense and unraveling.

But after my brother left, I knew it was over. I knew Wilder was going to say goodnight. Even if his eyes were saying something else. That he wished we were under different circumstances where I wasn't his best friend's sister.

Because obviously, you don't one-night-stand your best friend's sister.

And that's all I'd be.

Wes said since Bonnie, he's never seen him with the same woman twice.

I'd be no exception.

When the paint strokes start to drift off the canvas, I know it's time for bed.

I move to the door, securing the lock as if it weren't already fastened. Then the windows, reminding myself that this is Blue River Ranch.

Not crime central.

No one's after me here. I'm safe.

That mantra didn't work the first week I was here. It's not going to work my second.

Not even in this pretty house.

I brush my teeth, apply some night cream, and slip into a black cotton nightgown. Willow bought it for me last Christmas. It lands just above the knee and is super soft.

That girl would do just about anything to help me sleep better. She's even invested in some expensive memory foam pillows for me.

I return her text from a few minutes ago checking on me and snap a photo of my bed.

Willow: Wow. And it's not even two yet.

Willow: Sweet dreams.

Rose: Stop waiting for me to go to bed.

Willow: Never.

Shutting off the light, I slip into the comfy bed, taking deep breaths as I close my eyes.

It's not long before I hear the noise.

It's different though. Like footsteps on gravel rather than hardwood.

My eyes fly open.

Crunch. Crunch. Crunch.

Someone's outside.

I jump and quickly slide on my slippers. Racing to the living room, I move to the kitchen and grab a pan off the stove, then turn the light on.

The moment I do, the crunching stops. My heart pounds against my chest. Stupid.

I turn the lights back off and listen. Still no sound. Maybe it's Wesley again.

Maybe it's not.

If there's someone outside this door, I'm going to find out who it is.

Or I'll never sleep again.

This is what you do, Rose. You face your fears. You don't cower. Now open that door and confront.

Swallowing hard and prepared to attack, I unlock the door and leap forward at the hazy, silhouetted body in front of me.

"Whoa, easy, Rose, it's me."

Wilder.

His strong hands grip my wrist to stop me. I'm breathing so hard, I don't say his name out loud. All I hear is the pounding against my chest.

He mutters a curse and shoves us into the house before lifting the pan from my fingers and setting it aside.

"Wha—what are you doing . . . here?" I manage.

Blue eyes rake over me in horror. "You're shaking."

I stare at him like he's the crazy one—not me. "Gee, I wonder why."

Without a word, he lifts me off my feet and carries me to the bedroom, then deposits me onto the bed. He turns the lights on to a dim setting and closes my curtains.

Finally, he turns to me.

"What are you doing here?" I ask again.

He blinks, gathering his thoughts. "I was curious about something."

"You prepping for a fright fest or something?"

"You're up late. It's not an occasional instance. It's every night, isn't it?"

I slide under my covers. The therapist in me would claim I feel seen, but I'm not a therapist tonight. I'm a girl who doesn't know how to answer that question.

"I took a walk over here to check. Saw your light on and waited for a bit. Then when I saw your lights go out, I started to leave. I think that's when . . ."

"I heard you . . ." I finish softly.

"I didn't mean to scare you." He sits on the far end of the bed and I'm oddly relieved he's not leaving. "You know, they have over-the-counter stuff for that."

I nod, adjusting against the headboard. "Comes in gummy form too, I know." I smile weakly, then shake my head.

"How long?"

I suck in a breath. "Since senior year of college."

Understanding crosses his features. He's heard this timeframe before. When I went off the rails, as Wesley calls it.

He stares hard at me, a demanding glare. "What happened?"

I hesitate. But the want . . . no, the need to share this dark part of me with Wilder is too strong to fight.

"You can't tell my brother," I start, my voice small.

"I promise."

I sit up more against the headboard, keeping my eyes on the covers. "In college—early senior year—my roommate and I were attacked in the middle of the night."

He stills, jaw hardening, but he doesn't move, doesn't say anything.

"They broke in. It wasn't even us they were looking for. The girls they were after lived next door. Anyway, one of them stripped my friend of her clothes, laughing the entire time. But the one who came after me, he was . . . aggressive. Or maybe I was. Because I fought him. Hard."

I look up in time to see a hint of pride touching Wilder's eyes. Still, no movement and no words.

"I don't remember how long we fought. I know I gave it all I had until he knocked me against my full-length mirror." I swallow hard. "It crashed into pieces behind me—or beside me, I guess." I lower the blanket to show him the scars from the cuts along my arm.

"Christ, Rose." He moves closer, lifting it to take a closer look.

His touch sends a chill through me and he pulls a throw from the edge of the bed and wraps it around my shoulders. I expect him to step back at this point, but he stays close.

Hot tears flood my eyes and my voice breaks. "I pulled them all out myself. That's how I knew how to take care of Dallas's arm."

His eyes lift to mine, his voice gravelly. "You didn't go to the hospital?"

I shake my head. "The crash was loud enough to wake the entire floor, so they fled. We were both in too much shock to be around people or talk to anyone." Tears stream down my face. "So we never did."

"Rose."

"Stupid, I know."

"I didn't say that."

I look up at him. "Well, then ask me how they broke in."

He watches me wordlessly.

"I didn't lock the door."

I wait for the judgement in his strong features but there's nothing but tenderness. He swipes his thumb against my wet cheek. "Were you hurt anywhere else? Was your roommate . . .?"

"No. The guy managed to strip her but nothing else happened. I think they were there to mess with us—or who they thought we were. And the cuts were the worst of my injuries. The few bruises faded within a week."

He curses under his breath, then stands abruptly, like he's ready for battle. "What did they want from the other girls? Did you ever find out?"

I nod. "They came back two days later. Found the right apartment that time. And they didn't make it out of there in one piece. The cops came and arrested them. The girl they were after was a stripper. Turned down some guy one night and he didn't like it. That's all I know. I didn't ask questions. My roommate and I didn't want any suspicions. If we'd called the police the first time, there wouldn't have been another break-in."

"If you called the police, they might have gotten away and not come back," he points out. After a breath, he asks, "So you never told anyone?"

I shake my head. "Only Willow."

"Was she the other girl?"

"No. I barely knew my roommate at the time. Willow is my best friend. She's been my rock over the last few years. Texts every night to check on me."

"Why didn't you ever say anything? Wesley could have—"

"Blamed me for moving to New York in the first place? Called me stupid for not going to the hospital or locking my door? He wouldn't understand."

Wilder glances at my arm, then looks at me, his voice softer now, calmer. "Have you talked to . . . someone?"

I scoff. "Like a therapist? Yes. For several weeks after. It was worthless. Talking in circles, repeating the worst moment of my life to someone who . . ." I take a breath. "Someone who would never understand." I close my eyes. "It's not like I expected the nightmares and panic attacks to stop overnight. But I got a little tired of hearing 'time will heal' and it wasn't my fault."

He sits back down on the bed. Staying close. "You stopped going."

"I stopped going and I . . . dropped out of NYU. I didn't want to be that person sitting across from someone making it sound like moving on is easy with a few simple steps." I laugh. "After a while, you start feeling pretty dumb. Like, why am I sitting in this room repeating myself and how it felt. Why is she asking the same things different ways? It's like she wanted me to understand something I clearly wasn't."

"Is that what you were taught?"

"Not really. But it's how I felt."

He runs a hand down his face but doesn't stand. Instead, he takes my hand. There's no pity in his features. He actually smiles a little, lightening the mood. "So what do we do, Blue? How do we help you get some sleep?"

"It's better now," I lie. "I have like seven locks in my apartment back home."

"Like seven?"

"Exactly seven, actually. It's overkill, I know. But it was Willow's idea. She thinks the action of locking a door over and over again should reinforce feeling safe. Either that, or assuring I don't get my security deposit back on the apartment." I laugh bitterly.

After a beat, he kisses my forehead then stands, pulling his shirt off. His back is to me as he walks to the armchair, while I try not to drool as I take in every inch of muscle on this man.

"What are you doing?" I ask.

He turns like it's obvious. "There's only one lock on your door here." Gently, he lays the shirt over the backrest and turns to me.

But my eyes are not on his face or his eyes, like they should be.

"Rose," he starts as he moves back toward me. He's about to say something I should probably hear. It may even be a question. But I can't tear my eyes off his broad chest. He's carved perfection. Reaching me, he lifts my chin to meet his warm blues.

"I'm not one to miss the need for a woman's consent when it comes to spending the night." He strokes my cheek. "But I'm not leaving you tonight."

Warmth spreads through me and I feel my shoulders relax. I smile weakly, shifting in my bed.

He straightens, unbuckling his belt, his eyes on me until he slides his jeans off and turns, resting them over his shirt on the chair.

Is this some kind of slow torture? Or a dream . . .?

I wait for him to get under the covers with me, aching to feel his warmth. But he doesn't.

Instead, he tucks me under them securely and settles next to me on top of the covers.

So . . . there's no touching.

I turn to face him. "I'm not afraid to sleep alone, you know."

"Does that mean you want me to leave?"

I shake my head.

"Good. Close your eyes."

When I do, Wilder moves closer. It's quiet for a moment, then a whisper, "Rose?"

"Hmm?"

"Your secret's safe with me." Kissing my temple, he adds, "And so are you."

16

Wilder

Soft, easy breaths ghost across my collarbone. Her weight against my chest, while delicate, grounds me to the bed.

I don't want to get up.

But it's Monday morning. I was due on the field an hour ago. But hell, the ranch could be going up in flames and I'd reason with myself that the guys can handle it.

I slept maybe three hours—good enough for me. But Rose, had to be a solid five—not enough. I watched her for an hour after she fell asleep in my arms.

How did I miss the signs of trauma?

How did Wesley miss them? I try to resettle the anger pulsing through my veins and suck in a slow, calming breath.

The room smells like lavender and something purely . . . Rose. The dim morning light seeps through the thin curtains of her bedroom, turning everything a pale gold.

My jaw clenches as I look down at her, wishing to hell there was something else I could do. I swipe loose strands of hair from across her cheek and forehead.

I watch her as I gently drag my hand down her arm, flicking my gaze to the pink lines there.

She's safe. Curled up against me, her small hand on my ribs like it's her favorite place to touch me, like she belongs there.

Who the hell am I to argue? Because look at her. It's a goddamn miracle how peaceful she looks, knowing the demons that haunt her every night.

Twisting, I drag a hand down my face, careful not to wake her.

I shouldn't want to be her savior. I shouldn't want her, period.

But I do.

Christ, I do. I'm sick to my stomach with the need to keep her just like this. Untouched, unharmed, un . . . assaulted.

She didn't say as much but it's clear she feels ruined by it all.

Maybe I wasn't part of her life then, but it doesn't matter. Someone should have been there for her. Someone should have known what she went through. Anger burns my chest for something neither of us can help.

And like the coward I am, all I can do is lie here and pretend. Pretend that for one night, she's mine to protect.

She groans, fluttering her eyes open. Releasing a breath when she remembers I'm here with her.

"Am I late again, boss?"

I swallow. "Stay in bed." I kiss her temple lightly. "I'll check in on you later." I slide out, feeling enough of the chill for the both of us.

"No. No, I'm going to work."

"Come in later then," I say softly, careful not to treat her like a victim.

"I want to go with you. Remember? Bonus points if I show up before you do?"

I grin down at her but the smile she gives me right back nearly wrecks me. "Fine. Get dressed," I tell her as I zip up my pants.

She slides out of bed in that black nightie she was in last night, and I don't bother turning away this time. I take her all in as she moves to the closet all sleepy and in broad daylight. She pulls on a long-sleeve plaid shirt.

"It's going to be hot today," I remind her, then gesture to her arm. "You don't need to hide that from me."

"It's better to shield from the sun," she tells me without a second thought and slides her arms in.

I imagine it comes naturally to her, making excuses for covering her arms.

I look out her bedroom window and see my men moving about in the distance. I can be careful about slipping out of the house, but us walking onto the field from the same direction as her cottage will raise some brows for sure.

"Is it better if I meet you at the Saddle Room?" she asks, noticing me peeking out the window.

I grind my teeth. It's bad enough she spent the last few years ashamed about her scars and what happened. I'm not letting her feel ashamed now.

I shake my head. "I picked you up this morning. Hauled you out of bed to get to work on time."

She smiles. "Works for me."

She quickly makes a coffee to go and meets me by the front door. Pushing her tumbler into my hand, she slides on what looks like a pair of boots I haven't seen.

"Those new?"

"I got them in town yesterday. Actually, a very kind man by the name of Connor Thorne bought them for me. He was out shopping with Ginger—they ran into me at the street fair."

I rub the back of my neck. "With Ginger, eh?" That one's going to be hard to explain since it's something my brothers and I have been trying to figure out.

She perks her brow at me. "Is that something new?"

"No. They're keeping something from us, that much is clear. I think Dad thinks it's weird since she was a good friend of mom's and works for me and Dallas."

"I think it's sweet that they have each other."

A part of me agrees. But there's another part that wonders if the attraction was there before mom.

I know full well that's a me problem. "Yeah, well, they don't have to be all secretive about it."

Her lips twitch as she looks up at me—eyes dancing with unspoken irony.

With my hand on the door, I roll my eyes with a smirk. "Yeah, well." I scan her—one last look before leaving whatever is happening between us on pause. "You OK?"

She smiles up at me with a reassuring nod. "Thank you, Wilder. For last night. It was good to get that off my chest with someone."

I fight the urge to touch her again. "You call me if you ever need me. If anything scares you at night, you hear anything, just call. I'm not far."

She lowers her chin with a nod and I'm not sure she knows how serious I am. She moves to open the door, but I stop her. "I mean it, Rose."

She sighs. "Can I at least have my coffee first before you start with me, cowboy?"

I press the mug back between her palms. "Fine." I pull the door open, glance around like I'm afraid of my own shadow, and shut it behind us.

Rose is at the Lockup, our storage barn, doing inventory, and I'm thankful for the alone time in my office. Usually, it's the other way around. I'm out on the field while she's here doing what I hired her to do.

Part of me feels guilty for sending her away. The Lockup is not exactly air-conditioned and she's damn insistent on those long sleeves.

It's been two hours since I sent her over and she's been on my mind ninety-eight percent of it.

I want her.

There's no reason in denying it.

Friday night I thought I only wanted her the same way I wanted any woman since Bonnie.

One night. One time.

Zero expectations.

But it's not just her body that's got me out of my mind.

Her laugh. Her curiosity. The light that pours out of her despite the darkness she keeps hiding behind.

Ever since I had a taste of that pretty little mouth, I haven't been the same. Nothing sits right with me anymore.

Like Wesley's relationship with his sister.

There's being protective . . . and then there's calling someone you love stupid when she already feels it.

Hell, I know he doesn't mean it, but it's not a word you throw around lightly.

I growl out loud. Enough of this. I've got work to do.

She's got work to do.

I've got to focus on the ranch—make sure we stay on top of our game with one owner down. And stop thinking with the wrong organ.

A few minutes into my efforts, I fail miserably. Thinking about her meeting Dad.

And he bought her a pair of boots? He doesn't do shit like that.

He despised Bonnie. Said she was a flight risk and had heartbreaker written all over her.

Dad and I had a solid relationship rooted in work, respect, and family values. And I valued his advice more than anything. After everything he'd built, I'd be a fool not to. But I was convinced he was wrong about her—everyone was. When I nearly left, that foundation cracked.

But not deep enough.

Because it didn't take long for us to build most of that back.

Till this day, the man cracks jokes about how I'm "as hardworking and reliable as they come—unless a pretty face shows up."

But I can see what he was thinking when he met Rose. One look at that radiant, easy smile she spreads, that wholesomeness about her, and he was sold.

There's a knock on my door and I all but jump off my seat. Immediately, I think it's Wes here to ask why he—or someone—saw me coming out of his sister's cottage this morning.

"It's open."

Jeff walks in, carrying a bag from the hardware store. "Hey, boss." He empties the contents on my desk. "This was all they got. Want me to put them in?"

I look at the different door locks spread out in front of me. "There are only three."

He looks confused. "Any one of these should do just fine for that door." He points behind him. "Want me to put one in?"

I shake my head. I asked him to get me whatever they had. Not how many per se. "It's not for the Saddle Room. Just leave it here. Thank you."

He watches me for a moment until I look up at him from my desk.

"For Ms. Rose?"

I lean back in my chair, keeping my eyes on one of my more loyal employees.

"I've seen you around her place. Is she feeling threatened by anyone?"

"No." I don't bother asking when or how long he hangs around to notice. He's observant. Always has been. I'm just being paranoid. And protective. "Not exactly. Wouldn't worry about it."

He nods curtly and leaves me with my thoughts.

I tap my pen on the desk. I don't expect to get much done with this bag of locks staring at me. Snatching it off the desk, I march out, hop in my truck, and head to Rose's cottage.

Everything else can wait.

It's nearly six and Rose hasn't come back to the Saddle Room. Against my better judgement, I decide to go check on her at the Lockup. It's next to the stables, so I go on foot, convincing myself I'm heading in that direction anyway to pick up Tuscan for a sweep of the ranch.

Even if I'm an hour early for it.

When I reach the storage, I don't know what I expected after hours of her being here. Maybe she'd still be figuring out what's what and how much of it we need? Maybe even going one step ahead and ordering everything? What I didn't expect is for it to be locked up for the night.

What the hell? Where is she?

I stride to the stables next door, hearing her distinct laughter echoing from inside. I pause when I reach the gate, finding three of my men still milling around after hours.

Rose is propped up on a wooden worktable, laughing. The guys are leaning against stalls, tossing jokes her way like it's some kind of social hour.

Barry and Nelson are shooting the breeze with easy laughter. But Randy—he's standing in the middle, his gaze lingering on Rose in a way I don't like. Not quite with longing or attraction. But more questioning and judgemental.

Heat burns in my veins.

Partly because I never liked the guy.

"Y'all still here?" My voice cuts into the open space, silencing them all—almost exactly the way I intended.

From the corner of my eye, I see the men straighten.

But my eyes are on Rose.

She's hot and sweaty, with strands of hair sticking to her flushed cheeks as she turns to me. She's still catching her breath from laughing, the deep smile lingering. She looks good right there. With those mid-calf boots, her pink cowgirl hat and a plaid shirt—like she damn near belongs on this ranch.

"Hey, boss. Your assistant just finished up inventory over at the Lockup. Asked about your horse, so we brought her over here to meet him," Barry tells me. A little too quick. A little too nervous.

That doesn't add up. She already has.

Rode on him with me too. But I suppose she wouldn't offer up that information.

The air in the room is thick. And I'm going to get to the bottom of it.

I avoid turning my glare over to my newest employee and address the guys. "Day's over. Go on home."

Barry and Nelson spring forward, each tipping their hat over at Rose. "We'll, uh . . . talk later, Ms. Rose."

Talk later? The hell about?

Randy hesitates, watching Rose. "You need a ride back?" he dares to ask.

Before I can process what Randy's intentions are toward Rose—and none of them good—I answer for her. "She's not done. You are."

His gaze flicks to me. Randy isn't a fan of mine. He respects Dallas to hell, but apparently his loyalty doesn't spread to the rest of the Thorne family. Just the man who gave him some sort of superior title.

I'd fire him just for these last sixty seconds if I didn't need him. There's a bit of a stare-off until he winks at Rose. "Yeah, we'll catch up later." He nods to Barry and Nelson like he owns them and the three march out of the stables, boots scuffing deliberately against the dirt.

I curse under my breath and turn to Rose. She wipes her forehead with the back of her hand, lips quirking as she jumps off the table.

"Did you get any work done?" I don't know why I'm being a dick. Rose has yet to slack on the job. It might take her a while to understand what we do here, but she's not one to bullshit around.

But hell . . . she hasn't laughed with me like that.

She blinks, then licks her lips like she was caught doing something wrong. "Not only did I make a list, I ordered everything."

I take the clipboard she hands me and scan it. The order list looks all right, I suppose. But something is still off. She's nervous about something. "From who?"

"Sal's Saddles," she says quickly.

Wait. What? "They weren't on my list of approved vendors." I've heard of them, but Dallas and I never used them. They're too new to be trusted with quality supplies.

I lower the clipboard. "Why?"

She shrugs like they were the obvious choice. "They were cheaper."

"That doesn't mean they're better, Rose. And you can't go using vendors not on the list. We vet them. We check their manufacturers first. If there were any recalls. It's not like buying a pair of shoes."

She doesn't seem the least fazed by my frustration. Tilting her chin, she sets her hands on her hips. "Then maybe you shouldn't have gotten rid of me for the whole day."

"What are you talking about? We had work to do."

"We just did inventory last week. We were fine."

I hold up the clipboard of newly ordered supplies. "Then what was all this?"

She shrugs. "So you'll be a little overstocked. Maybe next time you'll think twice before giving me busy work."

I close the small distance between us but nothing about my advance is inviting. Rose backs up until she hits a stall. The horse rustles behind it.

"Why don't you tell me what you four were talking about before I got here."

Her eyes widen, but she answers quickly. "Rodeos."

My jaw clenches. "What about them?"

"Why don't you hold any here at Blue River Ranch?"

I inhale and decide I'm too tired for this conversation. "Rodeos are a lot to plan. And I've got my hands full this summer. Let's get you home." I turn toward Tuscan's stall.

I half expect her to push me on the subject, but she doesn't.

She's definitely nervous about something. She's avoiding my eyes and there's an unease about her, I feel it down to my bones.

"You comin'?" I ask, leading Tuscan outside.

She watches the horse with new interest and nods.

We ride in silence as the sun sets. She's watching the road. She doesn't lean into me the way she did a few nights ago. In fact, she's stiff as a board.

Hell, why does this feel like our first fight?

Is she being a brat because I gave her busy work today to avoid her? Or is it a decoy from whatever it is she's hiding?

I try not to focus on the distance—since I'm the one who put it between us to begin with.

We're not a couple.

But the hurt in her eyes when she confronted me about getting rid of her today said otherwise.

I haul the horse to a stop in front of her cottage and help her down. "Thanks for your help today, even if you did google a random vendor in Colorado," I mutter.

"It wasn't random," she mutters back.

"No?" I linger in front of her door, not wanting to leave with the tension between us.

"When I called Hideaway Springs Ranch by accident last week thinking they were a supplier, I spoke to a woman named Tessa. She was really cool. Said if I'm looking for someone reliable, I should try Sal's. They're new but they're trying to make a name for themselves. So I knew damn well they weren't on your stupid list." She pouts.

I rub my jaw, covering the humor I find in her attitude. "Levi's ranch, huh?"

She rolls her eyes. "Is that another rival?"

I nearly laugh. "Friend, actually. Competitor, but the owner's kinda hard to hate. Keeps to himself, doesn't start trouble. We trade and help each other out. Good man to have on your side."

"Well then, glad I could help. Good night," she says abruptly and turns to head up the porch steps.

I grab her arm. "You upset with me?"

She barely meets my eyes. "No."

I let go slowly. "Then what's going on?"

Her eyes are on the grass between our feet. "If, um . . . if you had the choice to help someone but you knew they wouldn't like it—would you still do it?"

"What?"

She shakes her head. "Forget it. It's nothing."

I resist the impulse to ask for more. But it doesn't sound like a work-related conversation, and I need to keep things professional.

That word needs to be stitched to my damn shadow since I keep forgetting it.

I clear my throat and glance back at the house. "Listen, I wanted you to feel safe here at night. I've added two porch lights on either side of your door and, uh . . . a few extra locks."

She frowns. "Wha—today?"

I nod. "Sometime after lunch. It's not seven, but it should do the trick. Keep 'em all locked for me, OK?"

Her lips part as she gazes up at me, her eyes glossy with unshed tears. "Thank you."

17

Rose

12.13 a.m.

Rose: I'm feeling conflicted.

Willow: The answer is yes.

Rose: Don't you want to hear the question?

Willow: Fine. shoot.

Rose: There's a rodeo next Friday.

Willow: I stand with my first answer.

Rose: The guys at work . . . they want me to help them sneak Wilder's horse out to compete in a barrel race.

Willow: You lost me. What's a barrel race?

Rose: I'd be helping them steal his horse (granted for a night) to compete in his rival's rodeo.

Willow: Why would you even consider this?

Rose: Randy—he'll be the one riding—says he's sure the horse can win, and it would be huge for our ranch.

Rose: I mean Wilder and Dallas's ranch. They're taking a hit this year and this would help business.

Willow's conflicted too. Or at least confused, because those three dots keep popping up and then disappearing.

Yeah, my thoughts exactly . . .

Willow: And if this Randy guy doesn't win?

Rose: I don't know. Then he doesn't, I guess. Randy said he'll only announce the ranch name if he wins. If not, he'll just bring the horse back and no one has to know, right?

Willow: I don't know, Rose, this seems risky. Just be careful.

Rose: Aren't you the one always telling me to stop looking over my shoulder?

Willow: Not the same thing.

Rose: Right. OK, night babe.

Willow: Rose, I mean it. This doesn't sound like a good idea. Please stay out of it. And maybe even warn him?

Rose: Love you.

Willow: (sigh) Love you.

18

Wilder

For the rest of the week, I've stationed Rose at the main office and asked Ginger to keep her busy. With any luck, some distance will help this boiling pot between us simmer down.

Survey says . . . it's making me want her more.

These feelings, these distractions are all too familiar—but entirely different.

Maybe not entirely. Because everything settling in my chest is that same warm, dangerous feeling I had with Bonnie.

That same natural instinct to be around her, to protect her. To be the hero she never really needed.

Not going down that damn trail again—chasing someone who doesn't see her forever here. Or with me.

Especially not with Wesley's sister.

It's not just my friendship with Wes on the line. I need to focus on the *ranch*.

This crush—or whatever a city girl like Rose would call it—fling, maybe? It's not good for either of us. I don't need to be her distraction and she sure as hell can't be mine.

But I'll be damned if I didn't check on her every night.

With or without her knowing.

I've been driving by the cottage every night since Monday. Once with a text—just like her friend Willow does.

And each night, I stay until her lights are out. Or at least go check on the cattle and redo my evening rounds before circling back toward the cottage.

Which isn't until after two, so yeah, maybe part of my short temper these last few days is from lack of sleep.

But how does a man sleep when the woman he can't get out of his mind . . . is afraid to?

It's now Thursday and she checked in with me a few hours ago in the Saddle Room to sign off on payroll.

She looked good. It's a healthy reminder of why I'm avoiding her.

The other reminder?

I'm on edge this week. The Callahans' rodeo is this weekend and it's the talk of the town, again. We took a hit for a few weeks last year—and the year before that. They keep making it bigger and better each year. As if they have any local competition.

My phone rings with a call from the front office and I answer on the first ring. "What's goin' on?"

"Hey, boss, that nice man is here again, asking to see Dallas," Ginger says.

My gaze flicks to my brother in the kitchen. It's three in the afternoon and he's in pajamas. His hair is a wreck and he hasn't shaved in weeks.

"Give me a second." I lower the phone. "That guy I was telling you about is here again. Told you he'd be back."

Dallas sips his coffee like I just told him one of our hands called out sick. "Fine, let's get this over with. Send him here."

"This is my house, Dallas."

"What do you think we're going to do? Wreck the place with a fist fight? I'll just step outside and see what he wants."

I lift the phone to my ear. "Send him here."

"Both of 'em? Or should I offer to keep the little girl here?"

"He brought his kid with him?"

"Looks a little young to be his. Maybe his granddaughter?"

"Both of 'em," I tell her.

I give Dallas a heads up that this guy isn't looking for a fight if he's brought a kid along—which only confuses him.

I step out as the tourist golf cart approaches the main house.

I nod to Jake that he doesn't have to wait for them. Whatever this is going to be, something tells me it's best kept private for now.

The man I remember from the other day steps out, then reaches for the little girl, lifting her out of the cart and setting her on her feet. She's got dark curly brown hair, pale skin, and heart-shaped sunglasses.

The man looks a little better kept today—at least compared to Dallas.

My brother steps beside me onto the porch, wordlessly. "Hello again," I offer.

The man tips his hat. He's not smiling. Not even scowling. He looks . . . scared.

"Sorry to barge in on you like this again. I'm here to see Dallas."

"How can I help you?" My brother moves down the steps. He hasn't bothered to change or do much of anything since I told him he's got a visitor.

The man surveys him skeptically. "You're Dallas Thorne?"

Well, this isn't going anywhere good.

"Way I see it, you can either believe me or you can leave. No skin off my back if you do," my brother quips.

"Cole. Cole Hartly. That's Ellie."

Dallas glances back at the little girl, who's wandered off to sit on the bench outside my porch.

"What do you need from me?"

The man scans him again. "You don't . . . look so good."

"Well, it's a good thing I didn't ask for your opinion. Any reason you stalkin' me?"

After a beat, Cole shakes his head. "This was a mistake. I'm sorry. Come on, Ellie."

Dallas takes two steps toward the man. "Hey, wait a second. You take one look at me in a state of mourning and decide I'm not worth whatever it is you came here twice to say or do?"

That's what I like about Dallas. He doesn't hold back. Calls people out the way they deserve to be. Some of them at least.

"Three times," Cole corrects.

"Sure sounds important. What, do I owe you money? Wreck your bar during a fight recently?"

Cole chuckles with a headshake, as if to say this just keeps getting better.

"A few years back, you . . ." He glances at the girl. ". . . you were briefly involved with my daughter, Tammy."

I move down the steps, my heart in my throat.

"I'm sorry, I don't remember." Dallas sounds sincere, and I can vouch for his lack of memory. He's not good with faces or people—unless you work for him or are directly related.

Cole removes a picture from his wallet. "Tammy Hartly."

Dallas stares at it, his tone softening. "The singer."

"She was. Died three years ago."

My brother's fingers tremble as he hands the photo back to Cole. "I'm sorry for your loss. She was a great girl. I didn't know her all that well, but she had one hell of a voice."

Cole smiles. "She did. That's her daughter, Ellie."

Dallas's head turns to the girl. Then back slowly. "Why you here?"

Cole's boot drags along the gravel, casually, like he's not about to drop a bomb. "Tammy said she's yours."

Dallas shakes his head. "That's impossible. I don't have—I would have known."

"Don't worry." He sweeps his eyes over him again. "We're not leaving her with you—not yet."

"What's that supposed to mean?"

"My wife, Maya, Ellie's grandmother, is sick. Need to take her to New York for extensive treatment at a good hospital they say they've got there. After that, we're moving down to Florida to stay with her sister until . . . well, it's something I didn't think Ellie should be in the middle of."

My brother's face is a mask as he stares back at Cole. Then a quick glance at Ellie. "You take your daughter's word for it?"

"Dallas," I warn. This is where the disrespect needs to stop.

"It's all right," Cole offers kindly. "I do, Mr. Thorne. Look, I know this can't be easy, finding out you have a six-year-old daughter. And after Tammy, Maya and I never planned on giving her up for anything, but it would be selfish to drag her through all that if she's got . . . someone else who deserves to know her."

Dallas sniffs with a light headshake.

"She goes to Blue River Elementary. She plays soccer."

"Wait, what are you saying?"

Cole hesitates. "Before coming here, we told Ellie she had a father close by. We gave her a choice. And she wanted to meet you."

Dallas glances back at the girl like he's waking up from a dream.

"We'd still be in her life as much as possible, of course, but if this is something you both want . . . she'd live with you."

"You trust me with your granddaughter?"

"Not by a long shot. But you are her father. I've been asking around about you for three years, since Tammy died, and hear nothing but good things." His eyes roam over Dallas once more as if wondering if he's got the right guy.

"Where do you live?" he demands like it's a test.

"East side of town."

"You telling me she's been in Blue River for six years and I didn't know?" Dallas snaps.

Cole scowls. "My wife and I have only known the last three. So you can either ask me to get off your property or you can talk to her while I'm feeling kind."

For a second, I think Dallas is going to tell Cole to take the little girl and get off his property. But instead, he rasps in defeat, "Can I talk to her?"

Cole hesitates.

"I'd just like to sit with her for a minute . . . while you're feeling kind," he grinds.

Cole nods. "Go right ahead."

Dallas starts toward the bench, then turns back. "You say she plays soccer?"

"Only girl on her team. And one of the best."

A ghost of a grin flickers across Dallas's face before he turns and strides toward the bench.

"Was this a bad idea?" Cole asks, and I'm not certain he's asking me or himself. But I answer anyway.

"Bad? No. Brave and . . . selfless, perhaps."

Cole looks at me. "He's in no shape to take care of a child."

No, he's not.

"When you leavin'?"

"Sooner the better." He watches them like he's not sure when that will be.

"If Ellie is his, I'm not sure he'll let you take her with you."

Cole scoffs. "Oh, believe me, I'm counting on him puttin' up a fight."

I nod. "I believe it."

Ellie looks about as interested in talking to Dallas as she is to be dragged out here just to sit on a bench. And Dallas, he's grinning at her, then cocks his head, asking her something. In response she removes her sunglasses.

And damn, if she's not his. Bright blue eyes, high cheekbones, dark hair.

"Ellie, say goodbye now," Cole calls out. "We've got to get going."

Dallas stands and for a second it looks like he's going to reach for her hand. But he shoves them in his pockets instead as they walk back.

"When will we see you again?" There's a shift in my brother's voice. And for the life of me, I can't read it.

"You call me when you're ready. In the meantime, I imagine, you'd want to meet us at the hospital for some tests."

Dallas nods. "If you don't mind."

"Not at all. I'm going to need to make damn sure myself." He tips his hat again.

"Here," I offer, pointing to my truck. "I'll give you a ride back."

When I return, Dallas is back in bed staring at the ceiling. "You've got to be kidding me." It's the wrong thing to say right now. I should ask him how he's feeling about all this. If he wants to talk about it. If he's angry.

"What the fuck's your deal?" he snaps. "Why don't you tell me what's really buggin' you out."

"Running this ranch by myself, for starters."

"Yeah, well, what do you think I was doing years back when you were planning a life on the road with Bonnie? Think that was easy for me? For Dad when he thought I'd be pullin' him out of retirement? Least you got help. Hear Rose is doing just fine."

I glare at him and turn away, storming out of his bedroom.

To my surprise, he follows. "Something I said?"

"Just fuck off and go back to being a lowlife."

"What, is she causing trouble? Flirting with a couple of cowboys?"

My jaw tightens and I glare back at him.

"Heard from Randy you got your feathers ruffled Monday afternoon when you caught them talkin' to her."

"It was six o'clock. They were all hanging around for no reason."

He keeps his gaze on me. "Say a pretty girl is reason enough."

I stalk away from him.

He follows like he's got nothing better to do. "Now is this because you're being protective of your best friend's sister? Or you got your own eye on her?"

I don't lie to my brother. Never have. So I don't answer.

Instead, my eyes flick away, jaw tightening because I can't deny it.

"Oh." Dallas pulls back. "Well then—"

"Look, I'm not the one who's in deep right now." I cut him off because he's clearly deflecting.

He walks past me toward the kitchen. "We don't know she's mine. This could all be—"

"Come on, man. That was your kid."

He rests his palms on the counter. "I can't do this. I can barely take care of myself."

"Well, don't look at me." I stand across from him. "We have to call Dad. This is going to get out soon and I don't want him hearing about it if it ain't from us."

"I can't deal today."

"When *can* you deal? We need to make sure this couple doesn't leave town with *your* kid. Which after one look at you, I wouldn't blame them if they did."

"What if they turned up when Millie was here?"

"Dal, focus on the now."

He shakes his head. "I need a shower. Then maybe I'll go for a ride." He turns back. "The Callahans are throwing their annual rodeo tomorrow."

I nearly scoff like I'm not aware. "They can throw all the rodeos they want. If they got the money and stock to back it up."

He hesitates. "It's gonna be a bit of a hit."

"Nothing we haven't dealt with before. We still got the water, healthier stock. You never worried about it before."

"And I'm not now."

"If you don't think I've got a handle on it, maybe you should come back to work."

He exhales through his nose. "I agree with you and Dad. We don't do rodeos." He shakes his head, glancing out the window at our sprawling fields. "But we gotta do somethin'. Especially these next few weeks."

It's no wonder Silas stays in Denver. Even when hockey season is out.

This place is a shitshow.

Dad comes over and it's hell at my house as he lays into his oldest son. Not for getting a girl pregnant. Not even for the extra seat at the table every other Sunday. But for being so careless to let six years go by without knowing.

I'm surprised the words "town" or "talk" don't slip from his mouth. Then again, since losing mom, his focus has been on family and keeping our bond tight.

When his blame turns on me out of nowhere, I storm out of the house and head straight to Rose's cottage.

If only just to see her light on. Maybe catch her moving inside. It'll be enough for now. Something to keep me steady from the shitshow I just fled.

I hate the distance I forced between us.

Hell, I'm probably the only one suffering from it.

It's stubborn. It's unproductive and . . . I fucking miss her.

Doesn't help that she's been avoiding my eyes when we pass—and I don't blame her for being mad.

The lights are on, but I don't see her movement inside. I imagine her on the floor, painting. Or in the kitchen, cooking. Or hell, maybe wondering when I'm going to text again.

I've been texting nearly every night to check on her.

And I keep doing it until I don't get a response. Or until her lights go out.

I pick up my phone and hesitate. Everything I type feels forced. Placating. Cowardly.

Wilder: Wouldn't believe my night.

Delete.

Wilder: What's it tonight, scenic or a creepy doll?

Delete.

Wilder: Coffee on me tomorrow if you turn your lights out soon.

Delete.

19

Rose

It's Friday night. The night of the heist the guys and I have been planning, and I'm a nervous wreck.

It helps that I've only seen Wilder a total of three times all week.

He's distracted. It can't just be me anymore. Maybe it's Dallas? Maybe the rodeo? I'm anxious to know. I'm anxious to help.

And this whole thing Randy and the others are planning with Tuscan is starting to feel less and less like a good idea.

Oddly enough, the anxiety over it all week helped me fall asleep at a reasonable enough hour. Well, reasonable for me.

The locks on my door have helped too. I do feel safer.

Wes has been coming over for dinner the last few nights and apologized for last weekend. I want to be mad at him for being the reason Wilder's set a wall between us, but truthfully, it doesn't matter anymore. Not now. Not when I can feel the man hurting.

As planned, I leave my lights on in the cottage and sneak out. I don't want to draw attention to myself so I don't take the golf cart. I start on foot, keeping my eyes and ears on alert.

Nelson spots me and waves me down just outside his cabin, and I catch a ride with him in his Jeep.

"That what you're wearin'?"

I'm wearing a long, black, off-shoulder sweater and denim shorts.

"Oh, I'm not going to the rodeo," I say. "I'm just helping with . . ."

"The heist?" Nelson finishes.

I shake my head. "Let's get this over with. Just be careful with him."

"Who you talkin' to? Randy's a helluva rider. He'll win."

"Technically, the horse wins, right? And it'll help get Blue River Ranch more recognition?"

"Absolutely. Come on." He parks in a dark spot on the side of the stables. And I notice the lights are dim around the building. Some even turned off.

"Who shut off the lights?" I say, approaching Randy and Barry, who are already here.

"I did," Randy says.

"That was a bad idea. Someone will notice. Better to keep them the way they always are."

Randy chuckles as he preps Tuscan.

Something tugs in my chest. I start to wonder if he really has Wilder's best interests at heart.

"She might be right," Nelson says. "Should we turn them back on?"

"Well, you can't now. Forget it, how much time do you need to get him ready?" I ask.

Barry and Randy exchange glances and nod in agreement. "Think he's ready."

Nelson glances around the dark open field. "Randy, you sure about this?" he asks.

Randy sighs. "You want to watch Dallas suffer another season because of this? For Blue River to become second rate because of lost business?"

"You know we don't," Barry answers.

Randy turns to me. "You?"

"Of course not."

He scans me. "You comin' tonight? Watch us make a name for this place?"

I swallow, my heart pounding.

Nelson touches my shoulder. "He'd never do it," he says softly, and I know he's referring to Wilder. "But we can do it for him."

"No." I glance back. "I'm not coming. But I can stand guard."

Randy smiles, but there's nothing pleasant about it. "Atta girl."

I run a hand gently down Tuscan's mane. He's Wilder's horse. And Nelson's right. Wilder will never compete. Not at Callahan's anyway. So we will.

I turn on my heel and scurry toward the metal gate. It's dark except for the faint glow of a lantern near the stalls, just enough light for the guys to work without drawing attention. My pulse pounds as I stand by the wide-open gate, arms practically shaking.

With excitement? Anticipation?

Fear?

I listen carefully for any sound beyond the rustle behind me. I wish I could see what they're doing. And why do they need to be so loud?

"Keep it down," I hiss over my shoulder.

"Relax, we'll be in and out," Randy whispers back. A saddle creaks. Hoofbeats shuffle.

My stomach tightens.

I hear another set of boots. Not coming from the stables. But from just around the side.

Dear God let this be someone else Randy enlisted to help tonight.

A tall, shadowed figure steps into the dim light.

My breath catches. Not at the proximity of the massive body in front of me.

But the face glaring back at me. "Wilder," I breathe.

He's ridged, all sharp edges and contained fury.

"What are you doing here so late?" I ask in one breath. The very last I have left.

He lifts a brow, his expression not an ounce softer. That gaze cutting right through me.

It's now that I realize we never decided on a warning word or sound.

Not that I can find the voice to shout back to them now.

Wilder flicks his eyes past me, where the guys are prepping Tuscan. "Move, Rose."

I don't move. I block him using what little I have compared to him.

He huffs before firmly but carefully shoving me aside and striding forward.

I race up in front of him, pressing my palms to his steel body. "Wait."

He ignores me and stares ahead. "What the hell do you think you're doing with my horse?" he seethes at the guys.

They all turn in shock. Then, like I led Wilder here all by myself, they each shoot me a hard glare.

I grip his arms to shift his focus back to me. "Hold on, it's not what it looks like, let me explain—" I don't know why I'm volunteering. Maybe because I feel like a terrible lookout? It was literally my only job.

Or maybe because I need him to know we were doing this for him—not working against him.

A muscle ticks in his jaw, eyes locking with mine. "I'll deal with you in a minute." Then he strides past me to the men. "If you boneheads tell me that you're taking him to the Callahan rodeo, you're all fired."

Randy steps in front of the other two, protectively. "Boss, come on. We were going to represent you. That's why we chose Tuscan. This would be—"

Wilder's nostrils flare. "I catch you sneaking an animal off my ranch and you start with 'Boss, come on'?"

Nelson and Barry glance at each other, then Barry speaks up. "We were trying to help—"

Wilder steps toward Randy—somehow knowing he's the ringleader here. "You were gonna ride him?"

He stares back without a response.

"Course you were. You didn't just take any horse, you took the one that could win. Tell me, you plan on cutting me in on your winnings?"

"Sure did. But the ranch name, that's—"

"That's a load of crock and you know it."

"Boss—" Nelson starts.

"Step away from my horse," he barks. "You all want to go to the rodeo?" Wilder turns his hard glare back on me. "Be my guest. But not with anything that belongs to me."

I keep my eyes locked with his while the men scramble to get the other mares quiet from the commotion. Tuscan stays stationed in the middle, dipping his muzzle into a stack of hay.

I flip back to the sound of crunching gravel as others from nearby cabins appear, alarmed and confused.

Wilder briefly scans over the newcomers but doesn't call the show to an end.

No. His attention shifts back to me, thick with something I can't read.

"You were the lookout?" His voice is low and sharp.

Refusing to shrink under his scowl, I tilt my chin. "I think you're overreacting. We were just trying to help."

"This isn't helping, Rose," he shouts. "This is aiding in a robbery. What if my best horse got hurt tonight? What if he lost? How the fuck would that help anybody?"

I did consider the risks. But I also considered the reward if he won.

It sounds foolish now.

"But I shouldn't be surprised, now, should I?" he continues. "You go out looking for trouble."

My eyes sting, but I fight the urge to let tears loose. Something inside me twists at the heat in his eyes—it's not just anger.

There's something else.

Finally, he lowers his voice. But I prefer yelling over what he says next. "You trying to get my attention, Blue? Well, you've got it." Leaving me with that steely gaze, he turns back to the men.

"Nelson, Barry, you're shoveling stalls tomorrow. Randy, you too. Then on Sunday"—he turns back to me—"I want you to pick up Rose first thing. You can show her how to lift stones from the pastures."

Randy scoffs. "All of them? Sounds good to me." He winks at me.

Jackass.

"Whatever she doesn't finish, you three will," he barks.

"What? Boss, it's supposed to rain tomorrow, the conditions might be—"

"Then I suggest you all dress appropriately. And yes, all of them," he shouts, and it makes me feel sick.

I can't breathe.

Is this . . . punishment?

Is that a thing around here?

My chest is tight with something I can't place. Anger? Betrayal? I have no idea what lifting stones means or how long that might take, but it can't be any worse than the way I feel right now.

My face burns hot and I roll my lips together, barely noticing his eyes drawn to them when I do.

I don't utter another word. I can't. I turn on the toes of my boots and run.

20

Rose

My heart is pounding in my chest. It's so loud, it's all I hear. Even the muffle of voices behind me has faded out.

It's pitch black out now, but I know my way back—I think. It doesn't matter. I'll just keep going until I see something familiar.

Just as I think I'm screwed because I don't in fact know where I am, I see my cottage.

Far left, just past the cabins.

The porch lights that Wilder put in for me are on, thankfully, providing enough glow to guide my way.

I pick up on a slow rhythmic crunch of hooves on dirt behind me. It's not trying to catch up with me as I keep running. It's not threatening.

I don't turn back. I'm sure Wilder sent someone to make sure I got back safely. Like I'm some sort of liability.

Just like he ordered someone to put me to work on Sunday.

But that's just my anger talking. Because I know it's *him*.

"Rose, stop."

My heart twists at the sound of his voice, and I pause for a moment. But I don't turn around. I sprint for my cottage, racing up the steps.

I don't need to be yelled at in private too.

"Rose." It's an exasperated sigh just before I unlock my door, burst through, and shut it behind me.

Killing all the lights, I run to the sofa and throw myself onto a throw pillow like a broken-hearted teenager and silently sob.

I don't do it for long. Because I listen to his horse. The crunch of movement on my front porch.

He's still here.

He doesn't knock. He doesn't call.

He's just here.

Deciding it doesn't matter what he does, I go to the bathroom and wash my face. Then change into an oversized T-shirt.

I reply to a text from Willow and then set my phone aside.

I was positive he'd have left by now, but I still hear Tuscan lingering outside the small house.

My chest squeezes as I decide to get the one-on-one lecture over with.

Marching over, I twist the knob on the four locks and pull the door open.

Wilder is leaning on the door frame, passing out.

"Sorry to wake you," I stammer, partially in defense of what's coming.

He straightens with a groan, instantly towering over me. He blinks a few times, looking into my eyes. "Can I come in?"

"You sure you don't prefer to yell at me where everyone can hear you?"

He doesn't answer. His eyes are glued to my face. He moves toward me, and I stand my ground. "Whether you like it or not, I can actually block you from coming in here."

"You forgot something back at the stables."

I frown.

His chest rises and falls, dragging in a shaky breath as if he'd been running.

"What?"

"To slap me."

I shake my head. "What?"

He steps inside. "You warned me. When people yell, you have a habit of slapping them. I'm not leaving here until you do."

I stare back at him. "I usually get fired after doing that."

He swallows hard, like he's afraid of something. "I was under the impression you were going to leave with or without that."

I narrow my eyes. "And?"

"And I'd let you slap me every day if you stayed."

"Are you drunk?"

"I'm tired, Rose. I'm tired of hiding from this, tired of avoiding you."

I step back, skeptical.

"I'm sorry, baby. I'm sorry I yelled. The audience, the things I said. All of it."

Baby.

He grips my wrists. "Do your worst."

I look at where his hands are. "I can't."

"You can, angel. You've hit me harder without even trying."

Something tells me he's not referring to our run-ins. "Wilder." It's almost a whimper as I start to give in.

He dips to look into my eyes. "I want this, too, Rose. Just not—"

"I know—" I cut him off. "I'm not looking for forever, Wilder. One night. The next day, I'll be on that field picking rocks of some sort—"

And then, as if every ounce of self-control evaporates, his mouth is on mine. Ducking his hands under the hem of my shirt, Wilder grips the back of my thighs and lifts me into his arms.

With my legs securely around him, he twists and presses me against the door, and I'm disappointed he's not carrying me straight to the bedroom.

With barely a free hand, he twists and pulls the latches on all four locks on my door. "Where should we go?" he asks.

"Bedroom." I breathe out what I hope will be the only consent he needs.

"What do you want me to do to you in there, Rose?"

"God, everything. Anything. I want to be yours tonight."

He growls in response and with a few short steps, we're in my bedroom.

He sets me on my feet. "You still mad?"

I shake my head. "No."

"Good."

"Are you?"

"Furious."

I grin. "Good."

He grins back and kisses me hard. I want this passion. This fury and hunger. Every part of him he wants to give. It's wild and addictive, the way I want him.

We're panting as we step apart. He all but rips the shirt off his back and I tug on his belt—half expecting him to stop me so he stays in control.

But he doesn't.

He watches me as I loosen the pants off his waist and shove them down.

He steps out of them then reaches for my hand, kissing it softly before walking me backwards to sit on the bed. "Give me a minute," he says, placing a feathery kiss on my lips. "I'm going to get cleaned up before I touch you."

He waits for my nod, then disappears into the bathroom.

I hear the water run for a few short minutes while my mind races. Will this be a mistake? Will things be awkward after?

No. No mistakes if there are no feelings, right?

For Wilder, at least. For me? I'll be all right. I have to be. Because I want him. I want to give in to . . . whatever this is. To this uncontrollable attraction to a man who makes my skin sizzle when he's near.

And when he's not.

His face is fresh when he returns, hands too. I haven't moved. With our gaze still locked, he strides over to me and lifts me off the bed.

"Baby, you might hear some rustling outside in a little while. It's just Jeff picking up Tuscan for me."

My heart skips because of what that means.

He's staying.

I nod and pull him to me.

He doesn't miss a beat. Cupping my jaw, he kisses me hard, then leaves quick kisses along my jaw and neck.

Before I can tell him to take my shirt off, he drops to his knees and grips my bare thighs, lifting my shirt only slightly for better access to my tingly skin.

Small, barely there moans vibrate from my throat as he kisses and nips the inside of my thigh.

I nearly fall backward with the sensation, but he keeps me firmly in place, slowly kissing his way up my thigh.

"Wilder."

He swears when his face reaches my center and bites gently against my panties.

I cry out.

"Christ, Rose. You're going to end me with your sounds."

I gasp as he nips at me again. "Is—am I too loud?"

He growls and pulls to his feet. "Not loud enough." He lifts the shirt over my head, leaving me in my white panties and bra.

I flush instantly as his gaze travels up my curves. "You're goddamn beautiful, Blue."

I bite my lip. "You going to stare all night or do something about it?"

He chuckles and moves around me to sit on the bed, turning me by my hips. "Always so fresh."

We're almost at eye level with him sitting on my bed and me standing between his legs.

"Rose, I have to ask if this would be . . ."

"Our only time?" *I was expecting as much.*

"Your first time," he corrects.

My lips part. "No, but it's been a while."

He smirks and brushes hair away from my face. "What's a while in your world?"

"Contrary to what you or my brother think, I'm . . . barely an intermediate."

He narrows his eyes, playful with a hint of frustration. "You're going to have to clarify."

"I was . . . intimate . . . with someone. Once. Before . . . it happened. Not since." My sentences are broken and incomplete, but he doesn't question it.

No ounce of judgement. Or pity. Instead, he lifts my hair to kiss my neck. "As for what you thought I was asking . . ." Another kiss to the other side of my neck. "You tell me in the morning if this is our only time."

"In the morning . . ." I mutter lustfully.

"You're not the kind of girl a sane man would walk away from." He strokes my hair gently. "Especially if he has permission to hold her all night."

"Granted."

He grins. "For now, we'll go slow."

I lean into him, kissing his jaw. "Are pep talks your thing, cowboy?"

He groans softly. "Keeping you safe, happy"—he squeezes an ass cheek, increasing my eagerness for him—"and coming for me all night . . . is my thing."

Heat floods my core.

Wrapping me up in his arms, he twists us and lays me flat on the bed, leaning in for a soft kiss before pushing up.

I admire him again from this view. All chiseled, lean, muscular. His body is exquisite. A word I never thought I'd use when it came to describing men.

Especially ones with strength that could overpower me in seconds.

My breath hitches at the invasive thought, and he stops. "Rose? What is it?"

I close my eyes for a moment. Reminding myself to not let my thoughts wander.

I use an elbow to push off the bed. "Can I touch you?"

He smirks. "Anywhere you'd like."

I slide my hands over his hard muscles, arms, chest . . . then his abs. And all the while, he doesn't seem hard. He seems to relax at my touch. Like I'm the relief his hard-working bones need.

He's not a threat in any way.

He's not even guarded right now the way he has been.

He's totally here with me.

By the time I pull my fingers back, he's both amused and aroused, watching me with that quirked lip and . . . lust.

"You trust me?" he asks, as if he knew what this was about for me.

I hook my fingers around his neck and reach up, giving him a kiss for reassurance. "Yes."

He smiles against my lips, while running his fingers along my panties. "Good. Because I'd like to take these off now, beautiful."

I lie back to let him, lifting my hips off the soft sheets.

"Good girl."

My stomach flips at the praise. At the way he watches me as he slides down my soaked panties. He bends my knees and tugs me to the edge of the bed, making me gasp.

I'm a hot ball of nerves when I see him drop to his knees, his face hovering above my center.

He meets my eyes, kissing the inside of my thigh, and I think I hear him shushing me, which only makes me pool hotter between my legs.

"I've wanted to taste you for longer than I'll ever admit, darlin'. But if you don't want me to, say it."

"Wilder," I breathe.

He rises, hovering over my body on the bed, his fingers slicing between my folds. "Yeah, beautiful?"

I writhe under his strokes, panting as I tell him, "Nothing is . . . off-limits. I want . . . you. Longer than . . . I'll ever admit."

He watches me for a moment, and I can only imagine what he's thinking. But whatever it is, it doesn't slow him down. He pushes two fingers inside me, making me lift off the bed for more.

"Wilder," I beg.

"Flower."

I blink. "What?"

"A safe word, in case you find something *is* off-limits. Or too fast. Or too much."

I nod.

"Repeat it."

"Flower," I pant.

"Good." He rubs circles against my clit. "You want my mouth on this pretty pussy?"

"Yes."

"You prepared to beg?"

"No," I stammer.

He grins. "That's all right. You will." With that, he's back on his knees, spreading me open, and there's no more talking.

His hot mouth presses against me, and I'm ruined. His kisses, strokes, and licks drive me wild. He's teasing and taunting instead of driving that tongue into me the way I need.

My back arches, and I cry out, spiraling with pleasure but needing and wanting more.

Catching my clit, he sucks me slow, teasingly, but it's still so good. I can probably last just like this without the need to beg.

He'll have to give in soon, won't he?

I whimper low, fingers digging into the mattress. He picks up speed, finally fucking me with his tongue. "Ohhh," I cry. "Yes, God, yes. Don't stop."

He stops, but doesn't leave me cold. His fingers replace his mouth and I'm ready to sob.

"Give me what I want, Rose." He's relentless.

And I'm shameless.

"*Please*, Wilder. Please don't stop."

He waits as if there's any reason for more. He slides his fingers into me, and I fall backward. "Your mouth, I'm begging for it."

"Good girl." He locks his mouth to me again and it's a whole new ball game.

He's *devouring* me with his expert tongue, chasing my release for me.

I buck my hips and moan in pure anticipation as he builds me up. My thighs tremble as I climb to the edge. I think his name slips from my lips, but all I hear is the long, loud scream as I come hard.

He pushes to his feet, hovering over me with a satisfied grin. The sass in me wants to ask if he's proud of himself for getting his way. But the ordinary girl in me, the one who knows I might never have a man like this again, just relishes what he's given me in return.

And this . . . game he played with me? Making me beg. He's not treating me with kid gloves. Or like I'm anyone's sister.

At this moment, he's my man and I'm his woman.

I grin back, putting my hands on him—because I *can*.

Because he's here with me.

I'm waiting for a comment to ruin it, like *see what happens when you listen*. But there's none of that.

Sincere eyes stare back at me. "You're perfect. Your taste, the way you move." He runs light fingers along my jaw. "The sounds you make for me."

I sit up and reach to frame his face in my hands. "I've got more where those came from, cowboy."

"I'm counting on it."

The straps of my bra have tumbled off my shoulders at this point. He lifts me slightly to unhook and tear it off completely.

He growls at the sight. "Your body is a goddamn dream, you know that, Rose?" He wraps an arm possessively around my back, lowering himself over me on the bed. "I haven't been inside you yet and I already know you're going to be hard to quit."

My lips part at the words and then I cry out when he covers one nipple with his mouth, sucking hard. I welcome the unexpected sensation.

I'd welcome them all.

He mutters for me to get comfortable over the pillows, then stands and sheds his boxers.

His cock, his long, painfully hard cock, the one I felt rub against me more than once tonight, springs out.

This man is jaw-dropping sexy. So incredibly . . . beautifully . . . erotic. I could paint him. I *should* paint him.

He strokes himself with a grin. "Jesus, Rose, if looks can make a man come . . ."

I lift my eyes to his and blush. "Wouldn't want that just yet."

In a flash, he digs a condom out from his jeans, tearing at it like it's a race and slides it on. I bite my lip as he meets me in the middle of the bed.

He settles between my legs and leans down to kiss me. It's a fierce kiss. A kiss that holds a promise of just how wild our night's going to be.

His fingers tease my nipple, making me whimper and arch with need. "Wilder," I pant. "Fuck . . . fuck me."

He lowers his fingers, finding me so very wet. "Slow, Rose," he reminds me.

I'm about to argue, then remember his intimidating size.

He strokes me gently, making me wetter. "I'm going to slide into this pussy nice and slow, baby. You won't be in pain."

I'm so hot with need and desire, I don't care at this point. I want to tell him that he's in dreamland if he thinks he's not going to hurt me.

Gripping his biceps, I pull up to his ear and whisper, "I can take it, Wilder."

"Fuck," he growls then settles between my legs. "Hold on to me."

I keep my hands on him as he sinks into me, nice and slow. I try not to tremble as my pussy pulls him in.

"Breathe."

I exhale, letting him sink further. A low growl escapes him. "That's it, baby." He moves in and out. "I underestimated you, gorgeous."

I look up at him, my hands still on his strong arms. "Faster," I demand. "Harder, Wilder. I'm not above begging for your cock."

His eyes blaze with fire and he rocks his hips, creating a friction I'm newly wild for.

Reaching under, he squeezes my ass as he lifts my hips. The sensation of his fingers digging into my skin makes me clench around him.

"Fuck, yes, baby." He thrusts his hips, but there's palpable hesitation.

"Harder," I plead, giving us both what we want.

Any trace of hesitation is gone as he curses again and slams into me hard and deep, at a flawless rhythmic pace. "So fucking perfect. Taking me so good. Just like I knew you would."

God, these praises. These filthy admirations . . .

I don't want it to end but at the same time we're both chasing our release.

I arch off the bed with a cry as a rush of heat surges through me. A powerful, intense orgasm. "*Wild—*"

He snaps his hips, growling my name once, twice. Then shudders above me, grunting fiercely through his climax. Catching his breath, he stares down at me like he might say something, like he feels something he didn't expect.

Or maybe it's just me.

Deciding against it, he presses soft lips to mine. Then pulls back, looking down at me. "Christ, you're . . ."

I perk a brow, repeating his earlier praise. "Perfect?"

"You're somethin' else, Rose."

Something else. I don't know what that's saying.

But I quickly realize he doesn't know either as he slides out of me. "Be right back." With a quick kiss to my forehead, he disappears to the bathroom.

The water runs for a moment, then shuts off. I try to imagine what's happening in there.

He's staring into the mirror repeatedly, tormenting himself over what he just did with his best friend's sister.

The wild, untamable, out of control, no rhyme or reason, kid sister.

I pull myself to a sitting position, prepared for him to come out here, gather his clothes, and tell me this never happened.

Then I hear the shower starting. And the door opening.

Wilder leans like the Greek god he is against the door frame. "Get that sexy ass in here."

21

Wilder

Rose has been tucked under my arm all night. I wrapped it around her at some point last night when she muttered something about this feeling like her first time.

A selfish thought crossed my mind at that point.

I wish it was.

Then, an even scarier thought. *I should be your only*.

Yeah. That's all it is. Me being selfish. Not possessive. She doesn't belong to me. Not now. Not when I leave here.

And certainly not when *she* leaves here.

It's not fair for me to hope I'd ruined her last night for anyone else.

Because after that first time we came together, I looked into her eyes and thought three words I didn't dare breathe to her.

Made for me.

I'm considerably larger, but she just fits. And not just right here in my arms. The way she moves. The way she turns me on. The way she's had me out of my damn mind for her—it's unnatural.

I kiss her bare shoulder, my cock already hard and it's barely dawn.

But I'm not ready to wake her.

Watching Rose sleep is my new favorite thing. I don't remember ever having a favorite thing.

I knew I wasn't leaving Rose last night. There was nothing sexual about the last time I stayed with her, but it was torture staying away all week.

Especially with visions of someone breaking into her room and attacking her.

She shifts with an adorable groan. Then opens her eyes.

A smile already there. "No."

I frown. "What?"

"You told me to let you know in the morning . . . if that was our only time."

I laugh, kissing the tip of her nose. "You been holding that in since we called it a night?"

"No. Since before we started."

I'm so fucked.

We're naked under the sheets and she has the nerve to twist away from me, her ass brushing my cock in the process.

I growl, gripping her waist. "Fuck, baby, unless you meant right now, you can't move like that."

She peeks over her shoulder, innocently, but I catch the glimmer in her eye. "Did I do something?"

"You asked for it."

She giggles as I turn her onto her stomach. "So?"

"So you're gettin' it."

I reach for my last condom and move over her. I'm relieved she hasn't asked why I had condoms with me. Because I'm not about to tell her I stuffed them in my pocket in a moment of weakness before heading back out last night to play security guard at her cottage.

Which I did for about thirty seconds. It's all it took for me to know she wasn't home. Despite the lights on and her golf cart out front.

I press my lips against her skin before spreading her slightly. She looks over her shoulder, biting her bottom lip with her eyes at my groin. Anticipation all over her beautiful face.

I dip down and nip at her ass cheek while squeezing just under the other one. She fists the sheets and clenches. It's enough to have my cock screaming to be inside her. To slide between where my fingers are heading.

I don't want to rush this. I want to savor her.

I also know that when this is over, I'll need to come clean to my best friend.

But fuck if I give a damn about that right now. Rose is a treasure. Fighting to recover from a horrible night all on her own.

"Wilder," she pleads, rocking against my fingers. "Fuck me."

I rub her slowly. Enjoying the torment more than I should. Tease the fuck out of this clit and have her begging until I thrust deep. I can practically hear the screams of ecstasy, feel her shaking with pleasure, building our friction all the while.

"Open your mouth."

She does without question, and I reach over, setting the condom between her teeth.

She tears at the wrapper without missing a beat.

"That's my girl," I grit out of pure lust for this woman and slide on the condom.

I push inside her, wishing to hell there was nothing between us as I do. She's so wet, I slide to the hilt, making her cry out. "Yes, more."

Fuck, the way she feels, the sounds spilling out of her—it all makes my chest clench tight.

It's a new sensation for me. One I need to force aside, focus on the here and now. I slide in and out of her, my mind racing with every position I want to take her, if I weren't out of condoms.

Rose matches my rhythmic movements so well that I become still and let her take control.

"That's it, baby, keep taking me all the way."

It's almost empowering as she takes the reins, riding me on her hands and knees, taking my cock at her own pace.

"Wilder." Her breath hitches and freezes, clenching around me. I grip her hips, thrusting until she's screaming into the pillow.

It's got me coming undone. I come so hard, my thighs shake. This girl's got me weak in the knees for her pussy.

For her.

I leave a gentle kiss on the small of her back before going to dispose of the condom and washing up.

When I return, Rose's face is still buried.

For a second, I worry that I pushed it with her. But then she peeks over at me with a shyness that melts me. "Jesus, it's broad daylight." She turns over, keeping the sheet above her chest.

I slide back into bed and pull her against me. "And you're goddamn beautiful in it."

Crimson-flushed cheeks press against my chest. "That's nice of you to say."

I lift her chin. "I don't say things I don't mean. You take my breath away in any light."

Her eyes brighten but she plays it off like she doesn't believe me.

"How about some breakfast?"

She scrunches her nose. "How about some coffee?"

I press my forehead to hers. "How about some eggs and bacon with that coffee?"

She grumbles in agreement, and I reward her with a soft kiss, then slide on my boxers.

Stepping into the kitchen, I start the coffee and put the oven on before moving to the living-room window.

It's overcast and rain is expected later this afternoon. I make a mental note of who I've got on weekend rotation today. Not all are experts on wet-weather maintenance.

I'm about to call Jeff—who I trust more than most—and remember the favor I asked last night.

Wilder: At the cottage. Can you pick up Tuscan from here and take him back to the stables?

I owe him an explanation for it at some point. My guess is Jeff's already figured out something's weird about Rose and me.

That's Jeff language for anything that has to do with sex or romance. Like when he noticed Dad coming to the front office a little too often to talk to Ginger or take her to lunch. "Somethin' weird happenin' with those two," he'd say.

Picking up my phone to dial him, I find a message from Dallas.

Dallas: Hey, you all right?

It's barely nine and he's already up? For the last two months it was me asking him if he was all right. I respond with a dodge to his question.

Wilder: You're up early.

Dallas: Jackass. Was going to check things out on the field today. It's getting dark out there. Gonna be a heavy one. Do we have enough hands?

Shit. I'm going to need to be out there. Or at least one of us does.

Dallas: Where are you?

I hear the shower running from the bathroom. I run my hand through my hair. I don't kiss and tell. Ever. But my brother and I have an understanding that when something affects the other—the ranch, or someone we care about—we don't hide shit. We're upfront.

It's why he doesn't lie to me when I ask him where he's been or who his fight was with.

It's how we work. How Dad raised us. And I can trust him.

Wilder: With Rose.

Dallas: Like since this morning?

Wilder: Like since last night.

There's a pause in his response time.

Dallas: Does Wes know?

Wilder: No. Keep an eye on things for me today? Equipment, floods, you know the drill.

Dallas: Yeah, yeah, will do. And thank you.

Wilder: For what?

Dallas: For the biggest smile I've had in months.

Wilder: Well, wipe it off your face.
This is nothing.

Dallas: No. But doesn't mean you're not equally fucked.

Fifteen minutes later, Rose emerges from the bedroom, her dark hair wet and her face glowing with something shiny. She's in that short cotton nightgown I found her in the other night and a grey cotton bathrobe that reaches her knee.

She smells fucking incredible. Like lavender and roses. "I smell bacon."

I push a steaming cup of coffee her way. "Thank you. Why's it so dark in here?"

"It's going to rain and I closed your curtains in case . . . we want the lights on."

She scans the room then turns to me, her eyes brighter than the sun. "Are you staying?"

I finish plating our breakfast and move over to her. "Was thinking about it. You got plans?"

She shakes her head, suppressing a grin.

I lift her off her feet and set her on the counter. "Shame you showered. You're going to get dirty again real soon."

She picks up a strip of bacon and bites into it. "You're teasing me again. I don't believe you're not going out there today."

"Oh, I am. As soon as I feed you, I'm racing back over to my house for more condoms."

Her eyes flash with excitement but she's got nothing but sass this morning as she pokes my chest playfully. "Makin' plans without me, huh?"

I hook my hands behind her knees and slide her against me. She gasps at the contact, that familiar arousal heating her forest-green eyes. "I think I can get you on board with these plans."

She laughs and it's like music. Light, easy, free. A sound that annoyed me when she first got here, and now . . . I think I know why.

I can't *like* the sound of her laugh. Or notice how good it feels to be next to her when she does.

Before anyone gets the wrong idea on what this is—I need to set some things straight.

After we eat, I peek outside and check my messages and the forecast. Still dark but no rain yet.

I'm about to sit her down—wishing I wasn't breaking the mood before noon—when her phone rings.

Rose glances at the screen and looks up at me. "It's Wesley."

I cock my head to the front door. "At least he called first."

She answers on the second ring. "Hey, Wes."

His voice blasts through the speaker and Rose jerks it away from her ear. On instinct, I lift the threat out from her hands and put it on speaker.

Like I'm going to say a damn word.

Rose gives me a pleading look and takes the phone from me but keeps it on speaker.

"I'm sorry," she starts calmly. "I don't understand you when you're loud. Call me back when you calm down."

"Don't hang up. Jesus, you're a real pill. What happened last night?"

Rose looks up at me, wide-eyed. "What did you hear?"

"Don't play dumb, Rose. Randy told me what you were all planning. Stealing stock for the Callahan rodeo? Really? And that you got them all caught."

Her mouth drops, and frankly, I'm fucking offended for her.

She wasn't the reason they were caught. I notice anything and everything unusual on my ranch. And the emergency lights turned off around the stables was a big red flag. That and . . . when I realized Rose wasn't home, I went looking.

I rub my forehead irritably.

"Yeah, well"—she looks up at me, a playful grin on her lips—"maybe I planned on getting caught all along. So technically, I saved Tuscan from being kidnapped."

I cock my head at her with an arched brow, which only amuses her more.

"Good one. Did he yell at you?" Wes asks after a moment.

A relief I wasn't expecting washes over me. He sounds protective. Rose picks up on the tone too and smirks.

"There . . . was yelling, yes."

He sighs, quiet for a moment. "Well, did you slap him?"

She laughs. "No."

"No?"

"He's your friend, Wes, I'm not slapping him. Besides, what kind of precedent would that set if I slapped him in front of all those people?"

I hold back a chuckle.

"Should've slapped him," Wes says, and I have to cover my mouth.

"Want me to come over?"

Her smile disappears and she twists nervously. "No. I'm naked."

I shake my head, pinching the bridge of my nose.

"Jesus, Rose," Wes whines.

"Sorry, it's my way of telling people to keep out when I want to be alone."

"Well, use something else when it's your brother, OK? A simple *I'm busy* would do just fine."

"I'm busy, Wesley."

"Right. What are you painting now? A dead cowboy?"

"Yeah, with the chef's knife next to him as the murder weapon."

He laughs, and shortly after, they end the call.

It's amazing how they work. I've never heard this side to it. Caring, protective, brotherly. As though no matter what kind of trouble she got herself into, he's on her side.

Guilt washes over me. And I know Rose sees it. "We should probably . . . talk," I say gruffly.

She smiles sweetly at me and it's like she's giving me a way out. "I can help with that. Nothing outside these walls. Or this weekend."

Damn, that's more mature than I'd given her credit for.

And yet somehow it slams my chest hard. Because she's right.

"Just one thing outside these walls, Rose." I swallow. "I need to tell Wes. Not today, but eventually. I can't keep something this big from him."

She nods in understanding. "Soon as my plane lands in New York."

Another hard crash against my chest.

"I need to go for a walk." I hadn't meant to say that out loud. But I need to clear my head.

"I'll be here."

"You weren't kidding when you said you had two suitcases of art supplies," I comment, brushing her hair out of her face as she lays on top of me on the couch. The storm was heavy all afternoon but quieted down sometime after supper.

I can say with certainty that Rose did not get the cooking gene that Wesley has. Since we had the time staying in today, she decided to make us homemade pizza. She bought ingredients this week, insisting she was going to make New York style pizza and put this gourmet kitchen to good use.

The cheese was good, sauce was great, but I don't think it was until she was halfway through the second slice that she realized it was cinnamon she had tossed into the mix instead of paprika. And I'm not sure how the crust was burnt on one side and doughy on the other. Still, it was edible.

Hell, I'd eat anything she made with the way she moved around the kitchen. Playful and experimental, the way she bit her lip, like she was creating some sort of masterpiece.

Her cheeks are still in that "just fucked" flush as she glances at the corner where her supplies are laid out over a tarp.

"I imagined I'd be pretty bored here when I'm not working."

"Are you bored?"

She rests her chin on my chest. "Not today."

I kiss her softly, lingering on the sweetness of those lips I thought I'd never taste.

But it's dark out and I'm going to have to leave her soon. I'm on the field tomorrow. Lot to clean up after the mess the weather made today.

"You think you got enough of a workout all day to get some sleep?" It's a cop-out, the way I don't flat-out tell her I can't stay another night.

She hums, stroking the hair on my chest. "I think I got enough of a workout to sleep for three days, cowboy. So technically, you screwed yourself."

I chuckle, wrapping my arms around her.

Fuck, I don't want to leave. But staying wouldn't be right. Staying would imply I'm emotionally available.

Rose—if she even stays in town after the summer—deserves more than some patched-up version of the man I used to be.

The one who will always question where her heart is. If it's with me, some dream she's chasing . . . or another man.

It already feels too much like playing house.

But fuck if it isn't a happy one. Waking up with a beautiful woman, making her breakfast, calling in sick, and going through half a box of condoms.

"I should go."

She sits up, pulling the throw blanket over herself like she heard it coming. The tightness doesn't ease in my chest as I pull on my jeans and watch her.

Rose has got her eyes on an empty canvas resting against the back wall, like she's picturing her next project.

We haven't talked about anything personal the entire time I've been here. And I wonder if human interaction isn't how she expresses herself.

"You gonna paint somethin' tonight?"

"Thinking about it."

"You mind if I stay and watch?"

She lifts her chin to meet my gaze. So much unspoken in those eyes. "I've never done it with anyone watching."

I reach for her hand. "Then let me be your first."

With her one hand in mine, she stands, fisting the blanket in front of her. It's the first time she's shied away from me since last night, and I feel like an ass for nearly walking out on her when things were . . . so damn good.

After Bonnie, I swore to never get so attached to someone that I forget friends and family come first.

The ranch second.

Doesn't leave much interest in a relationship that would just end up in flames.

Rose is a direct contradiction to the friends I put first and the relationships I avoid.

But hell if I give a damn about any of that right now.

She shakes her head. "I don't think so. It takes me a while sometimes. I'm still pretty new. And I don't want to rush it." She smiles playfully. "You need your sleep too."

"I'd like to stay and watch you. Even if it takes all night."

She hesitates, eyes drifting down like she's weighing her options. Finally, biting her bottom lip, she looks up and gives me a small nod. "All right. I just need to get dressed."

Before long, Rose is cross-legged over the tarp with a full set of paints, brushes, charcoal, and paper towels.

I'm sitting on the floor against the wall. I can't see the canvas, but I can see her face, which is all I care to watch at this point.

She's in that oversized T-shirt I found her in last night when I came banging on her door. Her hair is bunched up over her head. Her full lips quirk every time she glances my way. There's warmth and teasing in her eyes, but her focus is undisturbed.

"This why you don't drink? So your strokes stay even?" I ask, breaking my unspoken rule of no personal questions. The less I know, the less protective I become. The easier I can let her go.

So far, like she can't help herself, Rose has been like an open book with me. And I wouldn't trade her trust in me for the world.

But since it might be related to her focus on art, it's not that personal. It's not like I'm here asking if she had a drinking problem. Somehow, I don't think that's it.

She shakes her head. "No."

"Then why?"

"Alcohol tends to knock me out."

I'm about to ask, *Wouldn't that be a good thing?* But then remember why she's anxious to fall asleep.

"You're afraid you won't hear anything if . . ."

She nods, her eyes laser-focused on the tip of her brush.

"Noticed you got a bottle of red on the counter."

She shrugs. "Wes brought it over one night for dinner. He knows I don't drink but he had a glass and left it here. You could have some if you want."

I watch her and barely realize I don't answer.

"I used to *love* wine," she says after a moment. "The red, fruity kind that Wes brought over. Sometimes I think it might be OK. Just a little. But, what's the saying, just because you're paranoid, doesn't mean someone's not trying to get you?"

Something aches in my chest, and I realize it's the unshed tears in her eyes as she keeps them on her creation.

I'm not sure how much time passes. Or how long I've been staring like a man who'd lasso the moon for her, but when she finally finishes, the only thing I want to see is her smile. Proof that she loves it.

"There," she sighs. "I think that's as good as it's going to get." She stands and turns it over to me.

It's my ranch. Or a part of it. One of the barns. It's from a distance so you can see the soft blues of the sky, the trees, the river, and all-around earth tones surrounding it.

"Who's that?" I ask, pointing to a silhouetted figure with Superman muscles and a cowboy hat.

She laughs and dabs on the corner of her eye. "That's you, silly. I can't do people yet, too much detail in that. But I can do silhouette. I met this guy at an art exhibit who told me how much story you can tell with just a silhouette."

"Who is this guy?" I'm on high alert but keep my tone playful.

She glances to the side. "No one important." The response comes too quick and I hate that I question it.

"He an artist too?"

I catch her swallow, keeping her eyes on her work. "I think he was, yes."

I'm rattling her—I can see it. I sure as hell don't mean to but there's something she's not saying.

Stepping closer, I gently lift her chin to look in her eyes. She meets mine, steady, soft, present.

I take a breath before getting in over my head. Pushing her on something I've got no place to. "I think what you did is beautiful."

Her eyes widen. "What is?"

I nod toward the canvas. "This."

She shakes her head. "Oh. Right. I mean, thank you." She bites the corner of her lip. "Honestly didn't think I'd get through it so fast with someone here. You should come over more often." She winces. "Forget I said that."

I smile, reaching for her hand. "Thanks for letting me watch you at work."

"Seemed fair since I like watching you at work."

A quiet ache grips my chest. Because it's *not* fair. Watching me at work is about all I let her know about me. Like it's the only thing that matters. Like nothing else exists or ever did.

I take her hands in mine and kiss them softly. "Have a glass with me."

She starts to shake her head.

"I'll stay tonight. I'll be here so you can knock out soundly, knowing you're safe. Have one with me."

Her eyes brighten with gratitude, but her lips suppress a laugh. "Peer pressure."

I stroke her bottom lip, trying to find the right words. "No pressure. Just want to give you something you want without there being consequences."

She sweeps her gaze over me. "Too late for that." Leaving me with that loaded comment, she walks to the kitchen and reaches for two wine glasses, eyes dancing with delight. "Oh wow, OK. But if I'm doing this, I need to do it right." She holds up a finger. "We should cut some cheese. And chocolate."

I chuckle, meeting her across the island. "And here I thought I'd have to twist your arm."

She pushes the bottle toward me. "You pour, I'll shave."

"I'm sorry—shave?"

"The chocolate. Chocolate shavings, cheese, and wine used to be my favorite thing."

I smile, then feel like kicking myself for even considering leaving her tonight.

22

Rose

I smile as I watch Wilder sleep, still processing that we're lying here together. In a bed that's only temporarily mine.

In a town I'm only staying in for a few more weeks. I swallow hard. *He's going to tell Wesley.*

I tried to play it off that I don't care. That I'm as carefree and wild as everyone thinks I am.

But I'm scared.

I cherish my relationship with my brother. And despite him not trusting my decisions—which is my fault—I can't bear his disappointment.

But Wilder was adamant about telling him. And I'd never let someone bear a secret the way I am.

It's not fair.

It's dawn. The first light in the sky before the sunrise. I can't remember when I've been up this early.

I set my alarm, but it didn't have a chance to go off. I've been up for over an hour.

I knocked out before the movie ended last night. I had two glasses of wine. Wilder had one.

I was hoping to use the extra time we had to get to know him better. Who knows? He might've even opened up about Bonnie and why he hasn't truly moved on.

This cowboy may be single, but it doesn't mean he's available. Wilder is so closed off, a bull couldn't break through his walls.

He's closed off about his family too. He's angry with Dallas but doesn't talk about it. And he's never mentioned a word about his mother.

I only got insight on that from Mr. Thorne.

Something claws at my heart and warning bells go off.

Why should he open up to me? After this short weekend, we're back to being boss and employee.

Well, Boss . . . I'm not going to be late today. I wash up and dress quietly, peeking out the window for Randy. No sign of him yet.

Cripes, it doesn't look good out there.

No worries, a little mud doesn't scare me. Heck, I breathe in worse toxins in some of those old train stations in the city.

The real downer of my day ahead? Which boots to wear. The cute ankle boots I brought from New York?

Or the ones Wilder's dad bought me.

I groan. *I don't suppose barefoot is an option today?*

"You going somewhere?" His voice is rough and sexy.

"Morning. I'm going to work. But you take your time. Need that beauty rest, Superman with a cowboy hat." I wink.

He sits up, confused. "Rose, it's Sunday. Get back in here."

"You forget? Randy's picking me up in a few minutes. He's supposed to supervise me picking rocks from the pastures or something."

He glares at me as if this weren't his idea. "Like hell you are."

"Wilder."

"Rose, the fields are wet and muddy. No goddamn way you're doing any of that now."

I cross my arms. "Are you lifting the punishment from everyone?"

"Fuck no. Rules were broken and you all went against—" His jaw clenches.

I put my hand on my hips and cock my head at him.

He exhales, keeping his anger in check. "But I *will* if that's what it takes."

"You can't do that. It would be out of character for you, and they'll put two and two together."

When the doorbell rings, he hurries out of bed and throws on his jeans.

"That's Randy."

"Rose, you're not going anywhere with him. The guy's an ass, and I don't trust him around you. I don't trust him period."

"You ordered him to have me do this today."

He reaches for his phone. "Well, I'm calling it off."

"Will you stop?"

"Rose, he threw you under the bus when he talked to your brother."

I take a deep breath. He's not letting me out of this because we slept together. I don't want the special treatment.

And . . . I might have a thing for getting him all riled up when it comes to me.

But mostly, I don't want Wilder thinking I can't handle myself out there.

I'm kind of curious if I can.

I reach up and kiss his lips. "Thank you for this weekend. And for looking out for me. But I've got this."

He's about to argue, but I shush him. "Quiet down. He'll hear you."

He growls in frustration and scans me head to toe. I decided on my burgundy boots from home. "You can't go like that. You'll get dirty."

"That was the point, wasn't it?"

He runs his fingers through his hair. "Fuck, I hate this. I'm only punishing myself here."

"I've got to go."

He quits pacing and grips my face. "I'll come check on you in a few hours."

"Please don't," I groan. "I don't imagine it'll be a pretty sight. Just go check on Dallas and do whatever else you boys do after it rains."

He sighs. "Then promise you'll take it easy. Remember, the guys are finishing whatever you don't."

I roll my eyes. "Oh, I remember."

He lets me go, reluctantly, and I have to push him out of sight before I open the door.

Randy's lip curls up. "Ready to get dirty, doll face?"

My eyes widen and I race out, shutting the door before Wilder's temper kicks in. "Don't call me doll face."

"Don't get feisty. Have your coffee this morning?"

Dammit. Knew I forgot something. But there's no way I'm opening that door now. I'm not sure Wilder will let me leave again. "No."

"Me neither. Let's grab some. Hop on." He's got a tractor and I'm relieved to not be taking the cart. I can already see myself getting the wheels stuck in the mud somewhere.

My stomach sinks at leaving Wilder so mad this morning. I have no doubt that this weekend was all we'll have, and I didn't want to end it like that.

We grab a quick bite and a coffee to go from The Shack—which is empty for the most part—then head to work.

"I better be getting paid overtime for this shit," Randy mutters, making me wonder what possessed Wilder to hire him or even keep him around when he's such a jerk.

I ignore him and finish my coffee on the short ride.

"The other guys are clearing the south pasture for you now. It's small—nothing you can't handle. Barry and Nelson will handle the east pasture, that one's pretty wide. We've already moved most of the cattle inside."

"I want the bigger one," I say firmly, suddenly feeling like my early therapy days, when Sandra would "go slow" with me, like I'd break into pieces at any moment.

Or when Wesley insisted I couldn't handle the reality of city living.

I'm not weak.

Just a little flawed.

He glances over at me with a perked brow. "You trying to prove something?"

"Well, you told my brother I'm the reason we got caught, didn't you?" I narrow my eyes at him.

He turns back to the road, leaving my accusation unanswered.

"It's only fair if I take the bigger one." I don't know what I'm doing. Words are just flying out of my mouth. Words I think prove—to no one of importance—that I can handle anything.

"If you say so," he says like he's going to get a kick out of today.

A few minutes later, I follow Randy out of the equipment shed and onto the expanse of the north pasture.

He hands me a silver bucket. "So what am I doing?" I ask.

"Stone pickin'," he says, as if that means anything to me.

I frown at the empty field. *Which ones? How many? I don't see any stones.*

As if reading my mind, Randy nudges the toe of his boot against the dirt, exposing a half-buried rock. "See all these?" He sweeps his arm over the field.

I squint against the sun and see them—rocks of all sizes peppering the dirt like they emerged overnight.

I twist to look back at him. "And we just . . . pick them up?"

He laughs, and I realize I really don't like his laugh. It's creepy and condescending. "That's the gist of it.

Keeps the pasture safe for the cattle, keeps the tractors from bustin' up." He bends, lifts a rock the size of a dollar coin, and tosses it in the bucket. I jerk from the sound. "Think you can handle that?"

I look at my hands.

"Don't worry, princess, I'll get you some gloves."

I sigh, ignoring the comment and crouch down. "I'll pass on those, thanks." I can only imagine how many hands have been in those gloves.

"Don't be a brat. I'll get you the gloves."

I don't wait for him to return from the shed before wrapping my fingers around a rough-edged stone. Damp—but not quite muddy—dirt coats my palms. Lifting it, I toss it in the bucket.

By the tenth rock, my skin is already generously covered and I can see what Wilder meant. It's too wet for this today.

Fantastic.

Randy's sneer comes from behind me. "Ain't so bad, now, is it?"

I brush the dirt from my hands onto my bare knees. "Not yet."

He grins, sweeping his eyes over the enclosed field. "Give it a couple hours." Then he tips his hat. "Back in a little while. Going to check on the other two in their *smaller* pasture."

Three hours in and my back hurts. No, it doesn't hurt, it *burns*. The kind of burn you feel after an extensive workout. An extensive workout in dry heat.

I was thankful for my pink cowboy hat Ginger gave me, keeping my head protected from the sun. That is, until it fell in the dirt an hour ago. And I'm not about to put that thing back over my hair. Not that it would matter since I'm gross everywhere.

Sweat trickles down my spine, making my shirt stick to me like a second skin. The sun beats down ruthlessly on my neck.

I caught myself whimpering like a spoiled city girl a few times and quickly cut that shit out. I'm not cowering out of this.

My fingers are raw and I've filled three buckets' worth so far.

"Not bad," Randy calls, hopping off a horse.

"I thought you were helping," I whine.

He picks up my hat from the ground a few feet away and strolls over, dropping it over my head.

"There. I helped."

"Jerk," I grumble a little too loudly.

On the way back to his horse, he knocks over one of my filled buckets, spilling the rocks back on the ground.

My stomach boils.

"My bad."

I wince. "I don't suppose you want to pick that up?"

"Oh sweetheart, I would but I—"

"You what?" My heart leaps when I see the cowboy pull up on a beautiful horse I haven't seen yet.

Randy turns, hands still on the reins of his horse. "Dallas."

He looks good. He's shaved since I saw him last. Less pale and more . . . alert? Present?

I straighten, rolling my shoulders as if it will help my appearance.

"What's going on here?" Dallas sweeps his gaze over me, and I'm just glad it's not Wilder seeing me like this.

I've been quietly grateful for him leaving me to get this done all morning without "checking on me" like he said he would.

"Oh, well, I was just helping—"

Dallas holds up a sharp hand. "I wasn't asking you." He glances at the knocked-over bucket. "I believe you were just about to pick those up." His voice is steel.

The kind of voice that demands respect.

It's like all the stories I've heard about Dallas being hard-edged and intimidating, suddenly come to life.

His eyes and tone aren't all that softer when he turns back to me, shifting his horse. "Rose?"

I shrug. "I'm stone picking." I'm almost afraid to tell him *why*. I watched this man get into a fist fight for no real reason. If I told him right now that I was involved in attempting to steal a horse—Wilder's horse, no less—he wouldn't hesitate to fire me.

His eyes roam over the empty field. "I can see that. Why?"

"I, um . . ."

Another horse rolls up. One I recognize. Tuscan.

Wilder.

God, he looks so . . . clean. I bet he smells better too.

Wilder doesn't smile when he pulls up next to his brother, holding my gaze like I've done something wrong.

The muscle in his jaw ticks as he glares around the field and back at me.

What, am I not working fast enough for you?

"I . . . assumed you knew," I say to Dallas.

Randy warns me with a vigorous headshake just as Nelson and Barry pull up on a tractor, several stone-filled buckets in the rear cargo.

I take my dirty hat off, setting it over a filled bucket, wincing from the muscle pain when I straighten. "I'll let *Randy* tell you."

The guy glares at me before looking up at his boss in defeat. "Nelson, Barry, and I planned to attend the Callahan Rodeo Friday night. We were going to sneak Tuscan off the ranch to compete. No—to win. In the name of Blue River Ranch."

Dallas releases a deep breath, shaking his head.

"Rose overheard us and . . ."

"I offered to help." I speak up over my pounding heart. I don't know what this is. Heat exhaustion, Wilder's hard glare, or just Randy pissing me off all morning, but I'm about to act out. "In fact, I thought it was a great idea. Even stood guard."

Dallas smirks but keeps his eyes on the men.

"Not very well," Randy mutters.

"Oh right, why don't you tell him the version you told my brother. That *I'm* the reason you were caught."

I catch Wilder rolling his eyes.

Randy shifts. "I exaggerated some parts. Anyway, he should tell his sister to stay out of our business."

This is exactly why I didn't want Wilder letting me off the hook today. I'm not some helpless, ignorant child.

Dallas flicks his gaze between me and Wilder, bored with all the accusations. "I heard enough. What's happening now?"

"Wilder caught us and put the boys and me on stall duty and Rose on stones. Asked me to supervise."

Dallas's eyes drop to the spilled bucket. "I see you're being real helpful."

"Well, I—"

"Grab some gloves and finish the field."

Randy dips to refill the bucket.

"No," I shout.

Wilder snaps his head at me. "Rose. Go get cleaned up. You're done."

"I said no. I'm not finished here. I can do this."

Wilder exhales a frustrated sigh. "Rose, that was—"

"An order?" I demand.

Dallas coughs into his fist. Wilder shoots him a glare.

Dallas rolls his eyes. "She's right. It's not fair. They were all involved. Boys," he calls them over. "Why doesn't everyone just apologize, and you can all call it a day."

I hear them all mutter their apology, admitting it was wrong. While I stand here simmering with rage.

Dallas looks at me. "Rose. We didn't hear you."

"I'm sorry . . . we got caught."

Dallas's brows shoot up and he covers his mouth.

I fold my arms defiantly. "This city girl obviously works best *alone*."

Randy cocks his head. "Excuse me?"

"No pun intended, but who's bright idea was it to shut off the emergency lights?" I put my hand up before anyone can argue. "All I know is I had no problem sneaking out with stolen property my second night here. Couldn't find an exit, so I fucking made one. Meanwhile, three country boys couldn't figure out how to quietly make it to a rodeo with a borrowed horse? Amateurs."

I'm clearly having a tantrum right now. No one gives me enough credit.

Wilder's scowl deepens. "Show's over. I don't care what you all do, just go," he shouts at the men.

Randy and the others don't hesitate to take off.

I stalk over to the buckets, lifting one to carry it back to the shed.

"Drop it," Wilder barks, jumping off his horse. I only grip it tighter.

Dallas jumps off too. "Something you forget to tell me this morning?" he mutters to his brother.

"I've got a handle on it."

The older brother—who looked downright lethal a moment ago—carefully takes the bucket from me, then shuffles my hair. "Nice job, sis."

I frown up at him.

He shrugs. "Wes is family to us, which means you are too. Don't let those guys get to you. And, if it helps, I'll set things straight with your brother."

I hold up my hand. "Don't. I've got a reputation to uphold with my family."

Dallas flicks his gaze between Wilder and me with uncontrolled amusement. "So . . . this all happened Friday night?"

"You got someplace else you could be?" Wilder growls.

He rubs his chin. "I suppose. See you back at the house . . . or not . . . that's cool too." He turns and climbs back over his dark horse, riding off.

Wilder picks up my hat and two of the stone buckets I filled, while I'm trying to figure out why Dallas was being so weird.

My eyes widen when I put it together. "Oh my God, he knows?"

"Grab the other one and follow me to the shed."

I'm frozen in place when he glances back at me. "That's an order."

23

Wilder

I'm not thinking straight. Rose is in pain and hot and I'm having her lift a bucket of rocks.

If I'm not going to hell for fucking my best friend's sister, I'm going to hell for forcing hard labor.

I hold the door open for her, watching her lug the bucket with two delicate hands wrapped around the metal handle.

The moment she's within reach, I take it from her and set it down. She nearly tumbles from exhaustion, and I catch her. Then I shut the door, closing us in the dark shed with nothing but the light seeping through the siding.

I move her to a wall beside the door and cage her in between my arms. Goddamn, she's a sight. Fiery, stubborn green eyes, dirt on her chin, forehead, cheeks.

I want to hold her, bury my nose in her hair and breathe her in. But all I can do is press her against the rough wall—and growl. "You trying to make me mad?" My tone is harder than intended.

"Why would I do that? You're already mad at me." Her voice cracks a little and it nearly breaks me in half.

"What are you talking about?"

"I saw the way you strode up here. I worked really hard today, I'm tired, I hurt everywhere and you're nothing but scowls and orders, and—"

"You knew I didn't want you out here today, and yet I hear you insisted on the bigger field, settled for no help, and let Randy talk to you like you're trash?"

She frowns up at me.

"He's been texting me updates. Said you're a pretty little spitfire who thinks she can handle it all. Now I trust Randy as far as I can throw him, so I rode over here and heard him with you just before Dallas showed up. You know what I didn't hear?"

"What?" she mutters like a teenager with attitude.

"I didn't hear you telling him where he can shove those rocks. I didn't hear you stand up for yourself and tell him he had every part in this."

She rubs the tip of her nose with the back of her hand and sniffs. "I don't need special treatment just because I'm a girl."

"You're not a girl. You're a woman."

You're my woman.

"So act like it," I snap. "Then you pull that shit with the apology? What the hell you tryin' to do to me, Rose?"

"I suppose that pissed you off too?"

I lift her arms over her head, my face hovering over her pretty one. "It fucking turned me on."

"Wilder . . ." she whimpers when I press my hips against her. I'm hard. Painfully hard. The combination of her fierceness, strength, and the sheer memory of her under me turns me into a damn caveman.

"Wilder, I'm dirty. You can't possibly . . ."

"All I wanted to do was throw you over my shoulder, carry you in here, and shut that pretty little mouth up with my cock."

Gasping, she looks down between us. Not that either one of us can see much in here, but I see her, between the thin beams of light cutting into the shed. And she's stunning.

I stroke her jaw, bury my face in her neck, kissing the soft, dusty skin like it's the only thing keeping me alive.

So it's about time I tell her as much.

"I told you, you're gorgeous in any light, didn't I, baby?"

She nods, eyes fluttering shut, head thrown back.

"So hear this—you could be covered in all the dirt, dust, and muck this land's got to offer and I'd still want you more than my next breath."

She's panting hard. But still no words from my angel.

I growl. "I'm sorry. I know you want to get cleaned up. Let me take you home."

She sucks in a breath. "Unbuckle for me."

I stare into her lust-filled eyes. "Rose."

"*Please*," she pleads. "Do it for me. I would, but my hands are—"

I tug on my buckle, loosening it, then pull down the zipper. My cock is straining behind my briefs.

Rose looks at her hands, raw and dusty.

"I'll hold it for you," I rasp out.

She falls to her knees and I slam my hand against the wall to keep from slamming my cock into her mouth as she opens.

I edge in slow to her hot mouth, hissing as I do. Rose moans as she sucks me in, tasting the precum spilling out of me. She drags her tongue up and down my shaft like a popsicle. Then covers me with her mouth, relaxing her throat, taking all of me. And fuck if I'm not impressed and irritated at the same time that she's *so damn good*.

Since she can't do much but grip my thighs to hold still, I buck my hips, slowly fucking her mouth. I rake my fingers into her hair, whispers of praise flooding out of my mouth. My cock vibrates with her moans.

I grip her hair tight. "Rose. Up," I barely grit out, pressing my palm against the wall like it's all I've got holding me up. She doesn't stop, and I come hard. Unexpectedly and uncontrollably hard down her throat. She swallows every drop, licking me clean with a moan. "Fuck, gorgeous."

I lift her off her feet and swipe my thumb under her bottom lip. "Think you can hold on to me real tight for a bit, so I can get you home?"

She nods, lustful eyes fucking me over before I even have a chance to come down.

"Good girl. Come on, baby."

I lather the shampoo into her dark hair again, making sure it's worked through every strand. She's barely moved a muscle in here, and as much as I love touching her, taking care of her in here, I can't wait to get her in bed.

It's only two in the afternoon, but Rose isn't doing anything else today.

When we got back, there was a large paper bag sitting on her porch bench. Food from The Shack.

Dallas must not have been too far from sight, since he texted the minute we got to the cottage that lunch was on him and that he'll see to the ranch the rest of the day.

Rose didn't put up much of a fight when I insisted on feeding her before the shower.

She groans. "Wilder, I'm tired. And I'm clean, really."

"Almost done." I turn her and rinse off the conditioner, watching as the suds trickle down her smooth back and round ass.

I run my hands over it again, fingers slipping between those cheeks and then reaching her slick pussy. She groans in pleasure. "Wilder." It's a tortured breath. "I can't."

"Yes, you can, or you wouldn't be so wet now, would you? One more, baby."

She grins over her shoulder.

"Hands on the tile."

She does as I say and rocks against my touch. I rub circles against her clit, applying pressure.

"Oooh," she breathes, her head falling back.

"That's it."

She rocks faster. "Oh God, Wilder."

"Let me hear you scream."

She opens her mouth, and I cover it with mine, swallowing the moans I've become addicted to.

The *woman* I've become addicted to.

I turn off the water and dry her off, then wrap her in a clean robe. Her lips curve into a grin, satisfied and amused as she watches me.

I thought she was stunning before, but the way she's looking up at me now . . . it's enough to ruin a man.

Rose knocked out in minutes after I settled her in bed.

Closing the drapes, I leave her alone for a while and step out to the living room.

I check my phone for any messages from Dallas.

He's on edge about tomorrow, when we meet Ellie and her grandfather, Cole, at the hospital.

He said he doesn't want anyone with him. But Dad and I are both going. Hell, if anything, it would be good for Mr. Hartly to see that Dallas has help and support. Albeit, there's no female to be a mother figure—unless you count Ginger—but we'll take care of that little girl like our blood runs through her.

And it sure as hell looks like it does.

I had my doubts about how Dallas would take it, but that visit changed my brother. Woke him up.

But what happens if she isn't his?

Will he go back to being no good to anyone? Least of all himself?

Rose's phone rings, and I curse. It's the second time it's rung since she's been asleep. I lift it off the counter to silence it.

Willow.

This is the friend that checks on her daily. I should probably let her know she's all right.

Tired and hurting, thanks to me . . . but all right.

"Rose's phone," I answer.

"Oh, um, hi." The voice sounds feminine but mature. "You're not Wesley."

"This is Wilder, Rose's—boss."

I can hear the smile in her response. "Like cowboy bossman?"

"I suppose."

"Well, howdy. Do you guys say that?"

I laugh. "Rose is asleep."

She gasps. "Are you at her house? Why? Is she all right? Why is she sleeping now?"

Something about her protectiveness warms my heart. "She's good. Just had a long day. I'm making sure she stays asleep for a while."

"Oooh. Well then. Tell her I tried calling her this weekend to see where I should forward her mail, but she didn't return my call, so I mailed it to her brother's apartment."

"Thank you. I'll give her the message."

"Wilder?"

I try not to sigh as I answer. "Yeah?"

"She likes tea, shaved chocolate, tulips, and Tetris."

"Tetris?"

"Sorry, that's not relevant. Thoughtful surprises."

"Um . . . OK."

"Cozy bookstores. Keep her away from thrillers, she reads those so she'll be too afraid to go to sleep."

I add to the mental notes I keep on this girl, but don't say as much.

"The message, just the mail thing, that's it?"

"Do you have a good sense of humor? We need that. I mean *she* . . . she needs that. We're just a team in many things, so I always say 'we.'"

"Thank you, Willow. I'm going to go. It was nice meeting you." *I think*.

"But whatever you do, don't give her a cutesy nickname."

That one makes me pause. After the smudge on her cheek, I've been calling her *Blue*. She seemed to like it.

"Eh . . . that one's more me than her," she adds.

I smile. "Bye, Willow."

There's warmth in her voice and another obvious smile. "Bye . . ."

I shake my head as I hang up and finish scrubbing the dirt off Rose's boots. I twist them in my hands, inspecting every inch. Could use some shine.

I know Millie used to keep leather polish around here. I dig around under the sink and find a small bottle with just enough to get these looking like new.

Few minutes later, I set them down by the door and pull out my phone. I'm about to send a message to Ginger to see if she's been able to find blue cowgirl hats for the shop, when a message pops up.

Dallas: Changed my mind. Come with me tomorrow?

Wilder: Planned on it.

"Look at that. It's not just me you smile at," Rose says, her tiny frame leaning against the hallway wall.

I perk a brow and set my phone down. "How'd you know I'm not looking at you?"

"You got a picture of me on your phone?"

"What's a guy to do when the hottest thing he's ever laid eyes on is on her knees in the dirt because you ordered her to."

"You do not have a picture of me picking rocks out there."

I chuckle. "No. It's Dallas. He's, uh . . ." I look down at my phone. "He doesn't ask for help much, so . . ."

She steps closer, touching my arm. "Does he need more time? I can stay longer if you need me to."

I do a double-take. "You'd do that?"

She shrugs. "It's not like I've got anything else going on."

I push the thought of Rose *staying* out of my mind. "No, it's . . ." I run a hand down my face, no point in keeping it a secret. "Someone showed up at the house the other day. He had a little girl with him. About six. Said she's Dallas's from . . . an old girlfriend."

"Oh my God. That's . . ." She narrows her eyes. "Wait . . . a man, not the mother?"

I give her the short version of the history Cole shared.

"So, where do we go from here?" The way she says "we" tugs at my heart. Like Dallas said, she already feels like part of us.

"I don't know," I rasp. "Right now, we're just trying to find out if she's his. Take it from there. And I just—I know if she is, he won't let her go. Which means I need to count on him getting better. That little girl is too young and innocent to not have it all."

She nods, watching me. "Are you worried she'll be your burden too?"

Damn, she's sharp. "Maybe a little. Can you blame me?"

"I think you don't give him enough credit. This is a human being. And it explains Dallas on the field today. What's making you doubt him?"

That's right. Rose was studying to be a therapist. I pull open the fridge, avoiding her question. "We skipped dessert earlier. Cheesecake?"

She glances at it like I'm giving her a newspaper. "Do you have a preference?"

"What?"

"The little girl. Do you have a preference if it turns out to be his or not?"

"Sounds like a question for my brother, not me."

"It's only natural for you to have a preference. I'm curious."

"Of course you are." I set the plate down and release a breath. "I'd have told you my preference is that she isn't and it's a whole mix-up, but . . ."

"But?"

"But I saw her. And she's got his eyes. And the couple, her grandparents . . . they can't take care of her anymore. It's not like any of us need a kid around right now, but . . . if it turns out she isn't . . . well, something just wouldn't sit right with me for a while."

She watches me for a moment, her face unreadable.

There's no judgement or question. Just understanding.

Rose pulls two forks from the drawer and hands me one. "Cheesecake's my favorite." She dips hers in.

I nudge her with my hip, digging my fork in beside her. "I'll add it to the list."

"List?"

"Willow called. I answered—" I pause when I realize how that might sound. If I ever answered Bonnie's phone, she'd deck me.

Rose rolls her eyes. "Oh Lord, what did she say?"

"She gave me a Rose tutorial."

She breaks into laughter. "I'm sorry. I need to tell her to mind her business. She's protective."

"I like that."

"Between her and my brother, I'm set for life."

I don't know about that.

"She called to let you know she forwarded your mail to Wesley's since she didn't know your address here."

"Oh. Probably just bills my brother will open and check for delinquencies."

I know all about Wes having to take care of his sister because she can't hold down a job. And when she could with something like bartending at night, he'd criticize her judgement.

It sure has got to be frustrating for her.

But hell, if I'm not grateful she ended up here because of it.

"How you feelin'?" I ask, pulling her by the waist.

Her eyes twinkle when she answers, her tone playful. "Like I could go all night."

I bend to kiss the top of her head, trying to match her playful tone but failing. "You got work tomorrow. And I should probably . . ."

She pulls back like she's been burned. "I know. I've taken up so much of your time already."

I see the sun setting and there's one thing I need to set straight with her before the weekend is over. "Come for a walk with me."

Her eyes widen. "Is that OK?"

"Rose, we take walks all the time."

"More like you march ahead of me and boss me around while I try to keep up."

"If I keep my strides even with yours, will you walk with me?"

She nods and there's a hint of apprehension in her eyes, picking up on the shift in mood. This girl is nothing if not perceptive.

Before long, we're walking along the river. The part of my ranch where the water runs slow and smooth. It's a quiet afternoon, ranch humming around us, cottonwood leaning over the fences. I glance down at Rose, liking the way she takes it all in. Her eyes dance from the wildflowers to the daisies that grew thick along the edge this past spring.

She's not in awe of them, her expression is more thoughtful. Like it's more the idea of flowers everywhere she's embracing. "Which one's your favorite?" I ask.

She smirks, glancing up at me. "Which one's yours?"

"Don't have one."

She frowns but it's not playful, there's a subtle sadness that tugs at my chest. "So?" I ask again.

She narrows her eyes as she looks ahead. "Don't have one." Her response is flat and I get the feeling I've offended her.

"Something I said?"

"Of course not. How can it be? You don't say much of anything," she snaps.

I take a deep breath. Feeling like a jackass because she's right. It's not fair. But I can't help that every damn question feels like she's digging into my heart.

It's just a damn flower.

"Sunflower. The wild kind," I tell her.

Her eyes lift as she searches for them.

I point. "They pop up along the west fence line. Tall, strong, resilient."

A small grin plays on her face. "Should've guessed."

Something twists in my gut. Warm and a little painful.

"Lavender," she says, then rolls her eyes with a smirk. "And yes . . . *roses* too."

I bite back a curse. Because she's so damn beautiful. So open and giving, despite how many times I've let her down. And I'm about to again.

She catches me staring, or hell maybe even my jaw working, and clears her throat. "Sorry. I know you didn't bring me out here to talk about flowers."

I soak in what's left of her smile, my gut twisting because I'm about to wash it away. But I can't put this off. Rose broke rules and I've still got a ranch to run.

I glance over at the stables. "Rose, we need to talk about what went down Friday night." I can already hear the warmth draining from my tone.

The brilliant colors disappear from her eyes when she tears them away from the field.

"I got distracted this weekend," I tell her. "We both did. But that doesn't mean I forgot."

"I didn't think you did," she admits.

"It's not just about breaking rules. It's your safety. What if something happened to you over there?"

"It's a rodeo. It's supposed to be fun. And I wasn't going to go, I was just . . . helping."

I stop and turn to face her. "Rose, I can't keep worrying that you're going to run off and do something wild again just to—"

"Just to what?"

I swallow hard and cradle her face so she can't look away. "Just to prove you're brave."

Liquid fills her eyes. "Did Willow tell you that too?" Her voice cracks, and it cuts me in half.

"No," I answer, my voice like gravel.

She looks up at me with something I can't read. Denial? Gratitude? She shakes her head, breaking free of my grasp. "OK, I'm sorry. There, you got your apology."

"I don't want it," I snap. "I told you I *like* that you're not sorry. But I'd also like to know you're safe while you're here."

"You're not my brother. You can't keep me in a bubble." There's a hint of anger and defensiveness in her tone.

"No, but I can ask you to stop tryin' to steal my stuff for an adrenaline rush."

The tension thickens between us but there's still no place else I'd rather be.

When my words sink in, she rolls her eyes and shrugs stubbornly. "I suppose that's fair."

"Thank you," I huff out.

She starts walking. "Still think I should've worked that heist alone."

I walk her back, and we change the subject, flawlessly moving back into a place where we're comfortable just being together.

"So, Wes and Dallas are pretty close too?" she asks.

"His best friend. Now I say this since technically, Dallas doesn't have any other friends."

"Really?"

"His whole circle was Millie's friends. She was a social butterfly." I scoff at a memory. "At her funeral, he joked that at least he didn't have to hang out with her group of friends anymore."

Rose winces but shrugs. "Well, I'm glad you both have Wesley. Even if I don't know what you see in him," she jokes.

It seemed so simple back there by the river. I told her I had a big problem with something and she took the time to listen, understand, bite back a little, which I respect, but we just get each other. And now, we move on, refusing to let a spat ruin our evening like I thought it would.

Like it used to with Bonnie. Or hell, anyone else in my life.

Several instances on our walk back, our hands collide, wanting to grab the other, but we catch ourselves and pull back.

It's the only part of this . . . relationship . . . that feels forced. Keeping my hands off her.

24

Rose

I'm up early on Monday morning. Wilder left after I fell asleep. Just like he told me he would. I'm not upset about it. The last two days have been better than I could have imagined.

Minus the few hours I spent in the heat and dirt picking rocks.

But it was worth it. Not just having the man who put me in that position in agony over it. But the care Wilder gave me when he brought me home.

I know better than to hold on to it. It's understood that this isn't something that can go on for my remaining four weeks here.

Still, the weight of his gaze, the way his deep voice softens for me, the way his rough hands brush along my skin . . . it all lingers on my mind. And it's not going away anytime soon.

I *also* know better than to think none of it meant anything. We shared intimate parts of ourselves. Well, I did anyway. Wilder doesn't talk about himself. And as much as it frustrates me, because I've been nothing but open with him, I know it's better that he doesn't. The less I know about him, the more likely my heart will get the message.

Wilder's not in the Saddle Room when I come in. He must have been earlier, since he left me a note on my desk that he's going to be at the clinic with Dallas this morning, along with a list of things he'd like me to check for him.

Field work?

I run down the list and find some lowly tasks for Randy and Barry to do. They won't be happy.

I text Wilder.

Rose: I can't tell the guys to do these things.

Wilder: Morning. How'd you sleep?

There goes my heart again. He's still tender.

Rose: Morning. Good, you?

Should I have asked? Is it one of those things that your boss just asks but you don't get to ask back?

Wilder: Not as well as the night before.

I want to leap to the ceiling and squeal. But the feeling quickly dies when he follows with another text—shifting to boss mode.

Wilder: I don't expect you to tell them anything. I just need you to make some rounds for me this morning. Report back if the guys are where they should be.

Rose: OK. Will do.

I see the three dots jumping as he works on his response. But they disappear. So I send one of my own.

Rose: How are things over there?

He sees the message but doesn't respond. And there are no little dots jumping around to indicate he's participating in the topic.

As soon as I set my phone down, it rings, Wilder's name on the screen.

"Hi," I answer.

"Hey," he sighs. "We're just waiting now. He's already gone in, but Mr. Hartly and Ellie were late."

"Oh."

"Dallas was a little annoyed until they got here. Then he took one look at her bedhead and sleepy face and all that just melted away."

"Wilder, that's so sweet. Even you have to admit that."

"Yeah, I suppose. He wanted to wait here until she's done. She seemed a little nervous. Soon as they're finished with everything, we'll head back."

"No rush. How long until you know?"

"Couple days."

"Does he know you told me?" I ask.

Another long sigh. "He does."

I bite my bottom lip. "Is he mad at me about the rodeo?"

He chuckles. "Why do you ask?"

"Because since he knows I know, I thought I'd give him some words of encouragement, but if he's mad at me, I'd rather wait."

"Hold on." There's a few seconds before a new voice comes on the line.

"Rose," Dallas says. And I try to recall my earlier psych classes, where I learned to decipher how someone is feeling based on their tone.

"Hey, Dallas. Don't worry, I'm not going to ask how you're doing. I can probably guess. I just wanted to say that no matter what those results say, you've got this. I know you're already going through a hard time and waiting these next few days will feel impossible, but focus on things you can control for now."

If there's one thing I learned from what happened to me, it's that I can't control what happened, but I can control how I move on.

He sighs. "Waiting is gonna be all right, I think. Hardest part for me is trying to not have a preference one way or the other."

I don't ask him what that is.

"It's OK to have one. But whatever the outcome is, try to take the time to think about how you'll handle it. We know you can."

"Do you?"

"The guys on the ranch don't count on you because you're thoughtless and irresponsible. You run a tight ship. You got this."

"Thanks, Rose. Hey, you should come to dinner with the fam next Sunday night. Silas will be in town and Wes usually joins us."

Dinner with the Thorne family? Would Wilder like that?

"Um, I'll let you know. Never know what trouble I'll be up to that night."

He chuckles. "Always time to get into trouble after you eat. Come on by, Dad and Wilder are cooking, and you can listen to your brother play judge."

"Well then, I'll be there."

"Terrific, Wilder will pick you up." Then he hands the phone back to my boss.

"Hey."

"I'm going to get back to work," I say quickly, convincing myself—and maybe him—that I don't need his reaction to the invitation.

"Rose," he starts, a warning in his tone. "Don't engage with the guys. If they're not doing what they're supposed to be, just let me know when I get back, all right?"

"How is that productive, Wilder?"

He sighs. "You know what, forget it, I've got a buddy in town—I'll ask him to do it."

"Wow, that's not insulting at all."

Another sigh. "A drive-by. That's it," he growls.

"Go be with your brother. I'll see you later."

He grumbles when I don't give him my promise.

After we hang up, I work on my usual morning tasks, going through mail, following up with vendors and preparing a blank rotation schedule for next week for Wilder to fill in later.

A drive-by.

How is a drive-by discreet? I'll go on foot.

Leaving my golf cart in front of the Saddle Room, I head to the stables. I'll just go see if Randy and Barry are there and then head back. Just like Wilder asked.

When I reach the building, I move carefully along the side, eyes roaming the edge to where the cowboys are supposed to be mucking out stalls.

I hear a lot of what sounds like shit-talking, but I can't decipher who it's about. Until I do.

"This is some bullshit, I tell you. I've been here sixteen years—back when Connor had rodeos at least once a season."

I frown. "What?" I cover my mouth, then move around toward the front to see if I can hear more. What I'm not hearing is any shoveling.

"Maybe they don't got the money for it now. It ain't cheap," Barry points out.

"But it brings in business. I always liked Dallas, but he's getting weak. They all are. Perhaps it's time to move on."

"His fiancée just died."

"I meant for me."

Barry grumbles in response then pulls himself off the floor where he and Randy have been resting.

Randy doesn't stand; he's picking at his fingernails, and I wonder how much work everyone else does while he just sits around.

With a heavy sigh, I turn to leave before anyone sees me. Then a voice drawls behind me.

"Y'know, if you wanted to watch me sweat, darlin', you could've just pulled up a chair."

Heat floods my cheeks as I spin around.

"Take it the boss sent you to spy?"

I roll my shoulders back. "I'm working. As you should be."

Randy stands and something about his stance is a little threatening. I swallow when he takes slow steps my way. "And what part of your job is this, sweetheart?"

I fight the urge to step back. "That's enough. Why don't you go back to what you were doing. And I'll get back to the office."

"Why don't *you* head on to the kitchen and whip us boys up some lemonade. Then I'll happily let you watch me at work." They both laugh, turning away from me, neither bothering to look remotely busy.

I barely have time for a sharp response before the steady thud of hooves silences their laughter. A deep voice slices through the morning air like a blade. "Something funny, gentlemen?"

Randy scowls as he looks over my shoulder.

I flip around, not recognizing the voice. It's not Wilder or Dallas. And he certainly doesn't work here. I would have remembered seeing *him*.

The man on the chestnut horse has a rugged beard and sharp blue eyes, not as deep as Wilder's though.

His horse shifts beneath him, and he hops off. The cowboys behind me clear their throats. "Just havin' a little fun, sir. Welcome back to Blue River."

"That right? Appreciate the welcome but doesn't look like your jokes are, so might be best if you just get back to work." His scrutinizing gaze sweeps over them before they mumble to themselves and move back to the stalls.

The cowboy's eyes settle on me, and he smiles, reaching a hand. "Levi Reeves."

I accept it with some scrutiny of my own. "Am I supposed to know who you are and why you think I need saving?"

Wilder's soft accusations of my need to prove I'm brave come to mind, but I push them down.

The new cowboy's got a wide grin and a nice set of teeth. "My apologies, protection is an instinct in my family, but you clearly had it under control." He raises his palms in defense.

Is he mocking me?

I'm trying to assess him. He's not threatening in any way. He's quite warm and charming, actually. "I'm Rose. Wilder's assistant for the summer."

He nods. "My wife and I are in town for the night on business. We're staying at one of the guest cabins. He asked me to check in on these two, in particular. Said they've been causing trouble lately."

"So have I. Did he ask you to check on *me*?" I ask defensively.

He grins again with a light chuckle. "You have, huh? Nope, just the guys."

"Oh, you're the friend he told me about earlier. It's not your first visit, I take it?"

"No. We do some business together." He glances around the nearby structures. "Some of these guys here used to work for me at Hideaway Ranch."

"Hideaway Ranch . . . right. I spoke to one of your associates there, Tessa. She helped me out with some vendor recommendations."

He laughs. "That's my wife. She can be very chatty."

"Is she with you? I'd love to meet her."

"Well, hop on."

Five minutes later, we're pulling up to the front of The Shack. It's the guest entrance, not the staff side of the building that I'm used to. A woman with long red curls and a warm smile watches us ride up. Wesley is with her.

When we pull to a stop, she reaches a hand for mine to help me down. "Indie, I leave you alone for ten minutes, and you come riding back with a brunette?" She smiles coyly at me. "You must be Rose." She glances back at my brother. "You two want to join us for lunch?"

"So let me get this straight," Levi starts. "You and those clowns back there tried to sneak Tuscan out to compete at the Callahan rodeo?"

Tessa shakes her head. "Takes guts."

"That's one word," Wes grumbles with a glance my way.

I pick at a piece of cornbread. "Wilder lectured me enough. Can you drop it, now?" I turn to Levi. "We had good intentions, really."

"Not really," Levi comments. "They're a pretty big rival. Believe me, Ricky and his sister would have made sure no rider or horse from Blue River won anything. And if you did, you'd have a bigger problem on your hands."

"Oh, stop being so dramatic, Indie," Tessa snaps.

Levi gives her a sideways glance. "Sounds like somethin' you would do, Whiskey."

"I wouldn't get caught," she mutters.

The pretty redhead and I high-five on instinct, and the guys roll their eyes.

"Whiskey, huh?" I ask. "That your favorite drink or something?"

"Her eyes." The response comes from Levi, and it makes my stomach buzz. The way he sees and adores her.

That small-town love sinks into me, lingering warmly. Like something I suddenly crave.

I exhale softly and perk a brow at Levi. "And . . . Indie?"

"That dark hat and cocky grin," Tessa answers. "Looks like Indiana Jones, doesn't he?"

I don't answer and laugh softly, shifting my gaze before I get any more swoony over these two. "Well, anyway, I still don't understand why Blue River Ranch doesn't host rodeos. So they're a lot of work and money, but wouldn't it be worth it?"

My question earns me a few sideways glances from nearby tables, and one from my brother. "Rose, just drop it, OK?"

Huh. Does he know something?

"You're not the first to ask," Levi offers. "I've only hosted a handful, and the years I don't it's because of the time it takes or staff shortage."

"But they used to," I burst out.

"Really?" Levi asks, interest flickering in his eyes.

"Rose," Wes warns. "I said drop it."

"I heard Randy and Barry talking about it. How Connor used to host regularly. And then Dallas and Wilder took over and it stopped."

Levi cocks his head. "Shame. A ranch like this? Could make a killing. Sponsorships, tourism. A bigger name. Put the ranch on the map in a whole new way."

I don't know what most of that means, but it just sounds like missed opportunities.

"If I can talk him into one, would you be willing to help?" I ask, ignoring my brother as he mutters something about not wasting my time.

Levi points to his beautiful wife. "She can. Tess helped plan one for us last season."

His wife's eyes light up. "I'd love to help you plan one, assuming you've got permission."

"Permission for what?" Wilder's voice comes from behind me, and I look over my shoulder. He's with Dallas, who looks tired, but otherwise his face is void of emotion.

Levi lifts off his seat. "There you two are. How long does it take to run an errand in a small town like this?" The men exchange some greetings, but Tessa doesn't stand. She scooches over to me, practically pressing her lips to my ear. "All right, which one?"

"What?" I tear my eyes off Wilder, who's glaring at me like he's wondering what I'm up to this time.

Tessa pulls back from me, a hint of amusement in her voice. "Never mind, I got it."

The brothers take a seat across from us, and Levi moves to our side of the table next to Tessa. Wes leaves to grab a few rounds, and I take a breath. If I'm going to bring this up, it may as well be now, when I've got a power couple who seem to agree with me and might just back me up.

"I was just saying I overheard Randy and Barry talk about rodeos being hosted on the ranch some time ago. You guys ever think about hosting again?"

Wilder doesn't even look at me. His jaw tightens. "Nope."

I huff. "That's it? Just nope?"

Dallas sighs. "Guys, let's step outside for this."

"There is no *this*," Wilder snaps, then turns back to me, exhaling through his nose, and barely softening his voice. "Rose, I'm not talking about this again with you."

I jerk back at those last two words, blinking away from his hard glare. "I should get back to work."

"I think that's a good idea," Wilder bites out. I catch Tessa's wide eyes at my boss.

Swallowing hard, I slide out of the bench. "It was nice meeting you both." I start for the exit when Wilder pushes to his feet in front of me. "It's not all prize money and good times. Rodeos are a liability."

"I get it," I mutter, trying to move past him.

"Everything's got a risk, but not everyone competing has the sense to take safety measures. Leaving Dallas and me with the biggest risk. And I sure as hell don't want to be held responsible when someone gets tossed by a bull and doesn't get back up."

My heart pounds. Does that *happen*? I'm frowning, but he's not done.

"Broken bones, concussions." He swallows. "Deaths."

"That's enough, Wilder," Wes snaps, his voice harder than I've ever heard it.

I move to my brother's side and whisper softly. "It's fine. I clearly over-stepped. I'm going to go. I'll stop in for dinner later, OK?"

Wes squeezes my arm and nods.

I mutter a quick apology to him and take off toward the cottage. I should have just dropped it.

Something clearly happened to Wilder, or someone he cares about, at one of these events.

This isn't stubbornness—this is personal.

After my shift, Wes takes me to his apartment in town and makes me dinner.

"This place is cool."

"It's small, but I spend all my time at the ranch, so it doesn't matter."

I take a bite of chicken. "Not that this isn't delicious, but why am I here? This about the rodeo?"

"Look, I'm sorry about what happened today. He doesn't usually go off in front of guests like that."

"I'm not packing up just yet, Wes. Don't worry."

He breathes a sigh of relief. "I like having you here. But I should have been more upfront with you. Knowing you'd be curious."

"About what?"

"About what happened to Carrie. Their mom."

My chest is tight with worry. "It have something to do with a rodeo?"

He nods. "She was dared by a Callahan. Not the ones you met. They were too young. Connor Thorne was supposed to compete. But he threw his back out prepping for the event, so she went in his place."

"Was she a cowgirl?"

"One way to put it. She could out-ride and out-rope most men in her day."

A grin tugs at my lips. "Impressive. So what happened?"

He shakes his head. "Missy Callahan, Ricky and Dusty's mother, showed up, brought stock, competed. Missy provoked Carrie. Dared her to compete in her husband's place. Show good faith to her guests."

I cover my mouth, feeling sick to my stomach.

"She got hurt. Rushed to the hospital. Died three days later."

"Oh my God."

"Two years before Dallas took over."

I clutch my heart. "I didn't know." Tears well in my eyes, and I've lost my appetite.

"Look, I'll talk to him," Wes offers.

"And tell him what? Sorry my sister's so unaware?"

"I don't plan on apologizing for anything you said today. You're right. A rodeo, maybe not as big as they used to be, would be huge here. What I meant was he needs to stop acting like people are attacking him for not hosting one."

I shoot him a sour look. "You know I'm no fan of unwarranted apologies either." My shoulders sag in regret. "But this was his *mother*."

He sighs. "And you didn't know."

I glare at him because it doesn't change the fact that I hurt him.

He holds up his hands. "Or . . . you can handle it yourself, like you always do." He watches me. "But you know, Rose, sometimes, it's OK to let people help you, to be there for you."

Stubbornly, I don't say anything.

We finish our dinner with small-talk, and then he drives me home. I'm grateful for the distraction but exhausted. It's been an emotional day. I haven't been able to shake how upset I made Wilder today when I challenged him. And when I found out why, my heart broke for him.

Why does this man carry so much without ever letting anyone in?

The irony of how alike we are doesn't escape me.

I make myself a cup of tea, get in bed, then plug in my phone, finding a text message.

Wilder: Glad you're home safe, I was worried.

My heart tugs and I don't know how to respond. I shouldn't be hurt by the way he lashed out at me today. But I am.

I know I pushed him too far today and as bad as I feel about it, I can't help but also feel resentful for *not knowing* this about his mother. Because he refuses to open up to me.

For Christ's sake, there was an entire production of push and pull just to learn his favorite flower.

I don't want to avoid him. But I'm also not ready to face him.

Rose: I'm sorry I worried you.

Wilder: Can I come by? I need to say a few things.

Rose: I'm tired. Actually, I was hoping it's OK if I work from here tomorrow? I have my laptop.

It's a long moment before he responds.

Wilder: Of course.

Wilder: Your door locks locked?

Rose: All four.

Wilder: Sleep well.

I don't respond and really do try to sleep well. I even consider having a little wine for help. But I'm too tired to get up and eventually fall asleep.

25

Wilder

Rose has been working from the cottage the last two days. And I can't say I blame her.

It's Thursday and she's supposed to bring me payroll to sign off this morning and then get them to Ginger.

I'm at my desk, elbow propped on the wood, running a hand down my face for the tenth time in the last hour. I take another swig of my iced coffee.

I hate it. But the smell and the taste remind me of her. And it helps with keeping me up in the mornings since I haven't been going back to my house to sleep until well after all the lights flicker off in her cottage.

I had to keep myself from knocking on her door several times. Rose clearly asked for space. And I need to give it to her.

Because I'm the asshole who humiliated her when she was just trying to help.

She's so innocent. Sees the best in everything except when it comes to herself.

I swallow back the lump in my throat thinking I made it worse the other day.

The memory is sharp—her face flushing, the way she'd swallowed hard, green eyes blazing with hurt before rushing off. And now, she's avoiding me.

No late morning excuses, no quick-witted comebacks.

Just silence.

The creak of my office door snaps me out of my thoughts, and I sit up straighter as Rose steps inside.

And just like that, she takes my breath away again.

Her hair is tied in a low, loose ponytail, tossed over one shoulder. She's in a denim jumpsuit of sorts that falls just above the knee. A white, long-sleeved fitted shirt underneath.

I resist pushing off my seat and pulling her into my arms when she reaches the other side of my desk.

"Payroll totals are all set. Counted twice," she says, voice even, polite. She barely meets my eyes as she holds them out to me.

"Thank you." I don't grab them from her. I leave her hanging for a bit. I could be a jerk and insist I need her to work with me today. Tell her this isn't a work-from-home job.

But that won't do any good.

I watch her until she looks at me. God, she's stunning. And why the hell do I see guilt in those pretty green eyes? I need a smile.

I glance at the cards. "What's a man got to do for another game of tug-of-war with you over on this side of my desk?" I grin.

She fights one back and sets them down. "Trust me, you don't want me falling all over you."

Oh, I think I do.

But in what sense? Does it matter? Because I'm ready to take what she'll give me.

Self-control fucked, I push off my chair and go to her, lifting her onto my desk and stepping between her legs. The way she opens them for me is doing a number in my pants.

I cup her cheeks, lifting her face to mine. "Baby, I am so sorry. I wanted to come by that night to explain something. Something I want you to know."

She keeps her eyes low, lashes staining with fresh tears. "Wes told me about your mother. I'm the one who should be sorry."

That's it.

That's the guilt I see. Why she stayed away from me.

I should have been the one to tell her. I had an entire weekend to open up to her. But I stayed closed off. Insisting I was there only for her. Not the other way around.

"Why can't you look at me?" The question sounds pitiful from my tongue. Desperate, but I can't find it in me to care. I just want the answer.

She finally replies and it pains me to see how much I've hurt her. "I'm embarrassed for pressuring you to do something that is clearly out of the question."

"What did I tell you about being sorry or feeling ashamed?" I grab hold of her hands and bring her knuckles to my lips.

Her lips curve up, a shred of that familiar light returning to her eyes. I kiss her before she changes her mind and runs off again. I press my impatient, needy lips to hers, and she responds, melting into me.

It's a rough, hungry kiss and I say fuck it. Fuck boundaries, fuck what this means for the rest of the summer, fuck the wheels pulling up to a hard stop in front of the Saddle Room. I'm not taking my hands off this girl.

Rose pulls back with a gasp. "Wilder."

"I don't care," I respond, kissing her soft skin like a starved man. I cup her face again. "I want you, Rose. Not for a night, or the weekend."

Her eyes are wide, flickering with . . . hope, maybe? "Give me the summer."

"Wilder, that could be Wes." There's literal fear in her voice, and I step back just as the door to the Saddle Room flies open.

We both turn, finding Dallas shutting the door behind him. His eyes flick between us, but it's not like he didn't know anything.

Something's off. He looks pale. Even more than he has in the last few weeks. "Dal, you al—"

"Ellie's mine," he states gruffly.

Shock and . . . relief wash over me. And man does it surprise me. I could have sworn I was rooting for a different outcome.

Rose jumps off the desk and rushes to my brother, throwing her arms around his shoulders. "Congratulations," she whispers, a smile in her voice.

I run a hand down my face, still processing as I walk over to them and grip my brother's shoulder. "You're not alone." I said it to him at the hospital and I'll keep saying it. Because no matter what, we stand by each other.

Dallas nods, then looks down at Rose. "You still coming Sunday night? Dinner at Wilder's?"

When she hesitates, I answer for her. "She is."

He releases a breath. "Good. Ellie is coming. I want her to meet everyone, but it's . . . a lot of men."

Rose smiles. "I understand. I'm happy to be there for it."

"Is she . . . with us for good now?" I ask, careful not to ask if he plans on staying at my house with the girl.

"No." He's quick with his answer. "Step by step. I'll be spending a little bit of time with her over the next few weeks until Mr. and Mrs. Hartly leave town for good."

"For good?" I ask.

"They're going to take one or two trips before they move officially at the end of summer. During those trips, they'll leave Ellie with us."

I watch him to see his plan for those . . . sleepovers. Praying he'll take this as a sign that he needs to finish the house he was building for him and Millie.

He turns to Rose and a small part of me hopes he's about to ask for help decorating Ellie's room at the new house.

"I was hoping you could help with that."

Rose's eyes light up. "Of course I'll help. I know exactly what she'll need."

Dallas pinches the bridge of his nose. "The cottage. I'm thinking maybe she can stay with you those nights?"

Rose's smile fades and we exchange a glance. "Oh. I . . . um . . . of course."

"Excuse us, Rose. My brother and I need to take a walk." I grip his collar and shove him out the door.

He doesn't fight me. I don't even know if he's half with it right now. "Hell are you doing, bringing her into this? This is your daughter, Dallas. No doubt the girl's going to feel abandoned by her grandparents not long after losing her mother, now you want to dump her on a stranger?"

"I'm a stranger too," he argues. "At least Rose would be more, I don't know—"

"Not her mother. Not someone she should be getting to know or growing attached to."

"You're fucking one to talk."

"Don't make me hit you right now. I'll do it."

"You're going to stand here and tell me about getting attached to someone? You even tell your best friend you're fucking his sister?"

I shove him hard against his car, growling through my teeth. "I'd hate to give you a black eye this week when you've got dates planned with your little girl. Wouldn't want to send her the wrong message."

He pushes me off. "Maybe that was out of line," he mutters. "But put yourself in my shoes. You think you can become a dad overnight? From a woman you barely remember? What if Ellie asks me if I loved her mother? What if she wants to know how we met or anything about her, what am I supposed to say?"

I blow out a breath. "I don't know. But you need to try, or the first question out of her mouth will be *'Do you even want me here?'*"

I leave him outside and turn back to my office, then I pause, giving him a long side-glance. "Knew she was."

He keeps his eyes on the ground. "So did I."

26

Wilder

The case worker on the custody transition for Ellie suggested Dallas spends some time with Ellie before the official move. So on Sunday morning, he leaves, saying he's taking her to the park and then the street fair.

Which means I've finally got the house to myself.

I should enjoy it, the quiet alone time to breathe, instead of wondering where my grieving brother is.

The hell did I do with myself before he moved in?

Tell you what I didn't do . . . I didn't call over my best friend's sister to spend the day with me.

I pull my door open, and there she is, a smirk playing on her lips. "Hey, cowboy."

"Where you been all weekend, gorgeous?" I growl against her lips, my hand around her throat possessively as I learned she loves.

She moans. "Out on the town, hoping you'd come find me, toss me over your shoulder and haul me back here."

I growl again. And I like that she doesn't ask me where I was last night. Because I don't want to tell her.

Friday and Saturday had been a damn whirlwind for me with disasters left and right on the ranch, two broken-down tractors, a wrecked fence, and the vet canceling when I had two sick calves.

Then Wesley insisted on going out for drinks last night and dodging him again would only raise suspicion that something's off with me.

Sure I could tell him something generic . . .

I want someone. I want her bad.

I've got her. And I'm not ready to quit her.

I'm smart enough to know I need to. To know she's only here for the summer.

But I don't want half-truths with Wesley. And I promised Rose I'd tell him *after* she leaves.

I sweep her hair behind her shoulder. She's in a knee-length dress that hugs her petite body and her arms with those full sleeves.

I run my hands down the fabric. "You and these damn sleeves."

She pulls back self-consciously. "It's going to be a full house tonight."

I sigh, pulling her against me. "But it's just you and me now. And I want to see all of you."

"Aren't you going to show me around?"

I press my lips to hers. "Let's start with the master bedroom." I toss her over my shoulder and carry her up the stairs.

Her shriek is followed by a gentle laugh, but I haven't a funny bone in my body.

My bedroom is considerably larger than the one in her cottage—the bed too. Which is all I'm focused on showing her right now.

"Nice view," she says, staring out my window.

I hum agreeably behind her, untying her dress and pushing it down her arms

Her neck falls to the side. "Do we have time?"

Not enough when it comes to you.

"At least two rounds." I drop to my knees behind her, lifting her feet to remove her dress. She's already topless and these panties are going to go soon too.

She moans. "Finally. Was beginning to think you needed a warm-up."

I like taking my time with Rose, never wanting it to be more than she can handle. But I'm also careful not to treat her like a victim, or with any kind of kid gloves.

"Ah," she squeals when I bite her ass cheek. I pull to my feet, pressing my lips to the side of her face. "Get on the bed before I throw you on it." I slap that same cheek for that comment.

Rose looks good in my bed, her back tucked against my chest. Too good to move, but we're less than an hour away from four other men—and a pint-sized girl—knocking down my door for dinner.

But I've got one thing I need to get off my chest. "Got three weeks here," I start.

"I can count," she says back, barely thrown off by the question.

"Little late to ask, but . . . you got someone back home?"

She takes a moment too long to answer, leaving my heart in my throat. "No, cowboy. I don't."

"Anyone you . . . getting over?"

She doesn't answer that one straight away. Instead, she turns in to me. "Tell me this, if I'm leaving in three weeks—does it matter?"

She's got me there. Not because it doesn't. It sure as hell does. But it's not like I've asked her to stay.

And I want to.

I want to ask her to stay. But for how long? I can't promise her anything.

I put a woman before family and friends once . . . and I'm still proving my loyalty to those I hurt.

After she's gone, I'm telling Wesley about us. Then there's no doubt I'll need to build that friendship and trust back up yet again.

"I suppose not."

She rolls her eyes. "No, Wilder. There's no man I'm trying to get over." Her eyes drop to my chest. "Not yet anyway."

I frown at that confession until I hear a car pull up outside. "Shit. That's Dad."

27

Rose

"You tellin' me they took one look at that girl and still wanted a paternity test?" Wes mutters, leaning beside me at the dinner table.

The long wooden table stretches between the seven of us. Serving dishes are piled with roast beef, green beans, cornbread, and sweet potatoes. Oh, and plain French fries per someone's request—thank goodness for Ellie. I hate sweet potatoes.

Ellie sits across from me, next to Dallas. Wilder at one end of the table and Mr. Thorne on the other. Silas—who I tried not to be all weird around when he introduced himself, because I love hockey—sits on the other side of Wesley. And I've conveniently taken the seat to the right of Wilder.

I nudge my brother for his less than appropriate comment, even though I doubt anyone heard him. But I have to agree. Ellie's features are all Dallas. Dark hair, blue eyes, high cheekbones. She's *beautiful.*

"Can I have jelly on my cornbread?" Her voice, though the smallest at the table, carries the most weight.

"Now there's an idea," Silas calls out. "Wild, you got any here?"

"He does," Dallas answers, then looks at Ellie, his voice soft and a touch playful. "You like grape or strawberry?"

"Strawberry, please."

I watch him disappear into the kitchen. Three days ago, he was coming up with ways to avoid being alone with his daughter. But I'm willing to bet he's got nothing to fear. He's a natural. It could just be his charm—like that first day he met me. But there was an unmistakable twinkle in his eye when he looked down at her to find out which she preferred rather than getting up and just getting whichever they had.

"You've got that look," Wesley mutters.

"Hmm?" I turn to him, but not before noticing he's caught Wilder's attention too, who's to my left.

"That look when you're watching behavioral patterns or whatnot to get insight into their 'mental state.'" He puts air quotes around those last two words because I use them on him often.

"It's called clinical observation." I glance at Wilder and then at Ellie. "And I guess I didn't realize I was."

"And?" Wilder asks.

"My assessment is one day at a time, but I think they'll be all right."

Wesley blows raspberries through his lips. "Three and a half years of tuition and that's all you got?"

I know he's joking, but it still stings because . . . sometimes, I wish I *had* finished. And I really was so close. "You're right. Good thing I quit, huh?"

Shaking his head, he turns to Silas, and they talk about the upcoming hockey season. With my brother's eyes turned away, Wilder reaches for my hand in a comforting way.

And it does comfort me. Instantly. Because I love how in tune he is with me. Even with everyone here.

"I like your name," Ellie says to me, and I smile immediately.

"Thank you. I never liked it. It makes me sound a hundred years old."

She giggles. "I don't think so. Flowers don't live that long."

Dallas chuckles as he hands her the jar of jelly. I frown, wishing he'd thought to spread it for her.

"Well, I like your name. It's kind of a cool-chick name," I tell her.

"What makes it cool?"

I consider it for a moment. "It's strong but soft, short and playful, and . . . it suits you."

She seems pleased with that.

"But it's still not as cool as my best friend Willow's name."

"Willow," Ellie repeats. "I like it."

"It's a pretty name," Dallas agrees. "What's she like?"

"A bit nosy and demanding," Wilder mutters, and I stifle a laugh.

Wes snaps his head over, curiosity in his eyes, and Wilder clears his throat when he realizes his slip-up. "Silas, you staying in town for a while? I can get you in a guest cabin for a few weeks."

Silas shakes his head. "I'm staying with Dad until next week, then I have to head back."

"Uh-oh," Ellie whines, holding her hand up and spreading her fingers.

"Oh no, how did you get jelly all over your wrists?" I ask.

"I almost dropped the cornbread and caught it with my arms."

Dallas smiles down. "I saw that. Nice catch."

Her worried expression softens, and I stand. "Come on, I'll help you wash up."

We hurry to the bathroom and I give her a good scan. "Oh, you've got jelly on your shirt and chin too." I pull up my sleeves to clean up the stickiness she seemed to get everywhere.

"I'm sorry."

"Oh, you don't have to be sorry. Those boys out there are probably making a bigger mess. Can't let them have all the fun."

She giggles, and I take her back out, biting my tongue on the million questions I have for her about how she feels about all this.

Not the place. Not the time. And probably too soon.

We take our seats, and I catch up on the conversation, which seems to have a focus on Silas. Wilder reaches for my hand. "Everything all right?"

I nod, not wanting to say what I'm thinking. Dallas didn't think to help her with the jar. Or take her to the bathroom to clean her up.

They might be all right in the long run, but right now, this man's going to need help.

Maybe I'll get him a book. A few.

"Dallas, how's the house coming along?" Connor asks, his deep voice carrying from the other end of the table.

Dallas's expression shifts to irritation. "Going to spend some time on it this week."

And I don't blame him. Maybe instead of pressuring the man to move out of Wilder's, they can offer help.

Dallas gives some updates on all the things he still needs to do before it's livable.

"What is that?" Wes barks, his eyes sharp on the side of my plate.

I jerk at his tone and then realize he's not looking at my plate. His laser focus is on my arm, resting openly between us.

I pull my arm back.

Wes tugs at it with a good grip, and I stop breathing. "Rose. What are these cuts?"

"Cuts?" Mr. Thorne echoes from the head of the table. "Rose, you didn't hurt yourself on the field, did you?"

"No," I answer quickly. "And can you let go, please?"

"Not until you answer me."

"Wes," Wilder's voice slices like a knife. "Let go."

He releases me and I inhale, glancing at Wilder as if he could help right now.

His expression is the picture of calm. Collected. Like answering Wes's question should be a breeze.

No. No. I'm not ready.

Wilder clears his throat, flashing me a look I'm too clouded to read. "Yeah, Rose. Why don't you tell him?" Wilder suggests all too casually.

I wince and swallow hard. Wilder might be the all-righteous, truth-telling saint, but I'm taking this to my grave.

How do I explain several deep cuts along my arm? Thankfully, they're mostly faded lines now, and Wes never has to know how deep these once were. Wilder will be disappointed, but I have to lie.

"I—"

"Those damn branches didn't just do a number on our golf cart when Rose drove it through the bushes that night. Scraped her arm up pretty good, isn't that right?"

He holds my gaze for a moment, still so cool compared to the turmoil in my stomach right now.

"Holy crap. Did you clean it well?"

Yeah, real well, after I pulled out seventeen shards of glass from my skin.

"Of course I did." My voice is small despite my relief.

Wes shakes his head, and for a moment, I think he's going to say something like *when will you learn?* or *serves you right*, but instead, he runs his fingers gently along the scars. "Keep it out of the sun, OK?"

I nod and lower my sleeves, turning to Wilder with a small, grateful smile.

I can't read his expression. It's stoic but slightly warm with a gratefulness of his own. I can't imagine what for. The only thing that comes to mind is that he's the only other person besides my best friend who knows the truth I don't dare share with anyone else.

28

Rose

We're at Bones again. It's the first time I've been back here since the fight Dallas got into with the Callahan Ranch clan.

It's Saturday night and the bar is full. A comfortable full. Where every seat on the floor-long bar is taken and there's a small crowd along the back wall. Faces seem friendlier somehow tonight. Less intimidating than when I was here alone.

Then again, I didn't have Wilder by my side. And Wesley, Dallas, and even Silas, who was supposed to leave yesterday but stayed the extra night when he found out we were all going out, here too.

I see a few guys from work, including Randy and Barry, on the other side of the bar, sipping their drinks like they're waiting for something.

And then I scan the floor for trouble . . . in other words, Ricky and Dusty. Two out of the several times I've gotten in trouble during my stay, the Callahan duo was somehow involved. Not to blame, no, but involved nonetheless.

"What's the occasion again?" I ask Wilder as he guides me toward the back, where Silas and Wesley are seated at a round high-top table. I've been hearing mixed reasons all day for tonight's outing.

He keeps his hand on my back as we make our way through. "The guys kept it on the low all week, but . . . Randy and Barry are leaving."

"Oh. Did you expect that?"

He shakes his head. "Nope. Barry was supposed to be here for the rest of the summer, at least. But Randy's been here forever. I'm not sad about it. It does put a dent in the schedule though. A big one since he's one of the more experienced."

We reach our table. "You had no notice?"

"None. Both just told Dallas and me two days ago."

"Any idea where they're going?" Wesley asks.

Wilder doesn't answer; his jaw ticks with something I recognize.

"They wouldn't go work for the Callahans, would they?" Silas asks.

Wilder keeps his eyes on the crowd. "Only reason I showed up tonight. To find out."

"So, why you two so late?" Silas asks, changing the subject. There's a smirk on his lips that's a little too suggestive.

He's not wrong though. Wilder and I did get a little delayed tonight. We had dinner together at my place. Then *dessert* . . . and had a little trouble getting dressed after.

"I couldn't figure out what to wear," I say. That, and Wilder kept tossing aside anything I tried to put on.

Wes shakes his head. "I apologize for my sister. I don't know how someone can bring one suitcase of clothes and not figure out what to wear."

Wilder shakes his head, eyes glinting with amusement. "No, no, it's my fault."

I glare up at him.

"I was clearly picking her up too early." He winks.

Silas conceals a chuckle and shakes his head at us. "If you say so." His attention moves behind us. "What are we drinking?" he calls, just as Nelson and Jeff return with a few drinks, Dallas behind them, stuffing his wallet away.

"This a celebration?" I ask.

"It is for me," Wilder mutters. "Good riddance."

"You sure 'bout that?" Silas asks. "Where you going to find two more with their experience in the middle of summer?"

"We'll be fine."

For the second time since we got here, I catch Wesley searching the place again. And I can't tell if he's paranoid . . . or hopeful.

"They're not here," Wilder says, also catching Wes's wandering eyes.

"The Callahans are definitely behind this," Wesley insists. "Something fishy about them just up and leaving. You're not curious where they're going?"

"Not a question I typically ask people who've been a thorn in my side for years," Wilder grumbles. "We'll be all right," he repeats, and I don't believe him. I'm not sure anyone else does either.

Dallas seems to be keeping it together better than Wilder. But there's no mistake—he's pissed about something too. His steely expression doesn't give much away, but I'm picking up an unsettling energy.

"Can I have your attention, please?" A voice cuts through the noise. I remember that voice, and it gives me chills. *Ricky Callahan.*

"Y'all be sure to stop at Callahan's bar Sunday night as we welcome a couple new members to our ranch. Randy Riles and Barry Duke."

I look up at Wilder, who's stiff next to me. "You know about this?" he asks Dallas.

"Had a guess."

"And you didn't think to tell me?"

Dallas sighs. "If I did, you would have blown a fuse, and Ricky and Dusty would'a heard and gotten a kick out of it."

Wilder sucks in a breath as if to say he isn't wrong about that. "Why am I here?"

"To say good riddance." Dallas hands him a beer. "We're better off."

"We needed them," Wilder admits, and it scares me how worried he sounds.

I touch his arm, squeezing his bicep. "We'll be fine," I remind him.

Wilder's eyes soften when he looks down at me. He scans me like he wants to pull me close, but we both know he can't.

"Evening, boys. Nice'a you to come celebrate our new gains," Dusty gloats, cutting through the crowd to our little group.

I take a step away from Wilder. When Tessa was here, she immediately noticed something between him and me. Women tend to be good at that sort of thing. And I wouldn't put it past Dusty to call us out if she did.

Unfortunately, the movement gets her attention. "Oh hey, New York." She glances at Wilder but focuses on me. "See we didn't quite scare you out of town just yet. Love the boots."

Wesley slides out of his chair, moving to my side protectively.

"Take a hike, Dusty. We're only here to wish you luck, 'cause you're going to need it with those two boneheads."

She crosses her arms, acting unimpressed. "Shouldn't you be in the kitchen setting off a smoke alarm or ruining a perfectly nice steak on high heat?"

He narrows his eyes and leans in just enough to match her height. "Don't dish it until you try it."

She rolls her eyes. "Thanks, but I only date cowboys."

"And I prefer real blondes," he says dryly and turns away before she can say another word, and damn, I'm impressed. Also intrigued. There aren't many people who get my brother all fired up like that.

Except me, maybe.

Dusty feigns a yawn. "Well, love to stay and chat but we're celebrating."

"Oh, so are we," I tell her with a wide smile.

"Right," she drawls, then digs in her pocket and hands me a card. "Missed ya at our rodeo couple weeks ago. Call me if you need a ride next time."

I take the card, because even though she's the enemy, there's something sincere about her offer.

Dusty perks a brow at Wilder. "Good luck this season." She starts to make her way past us until she reaches Dallas. He towers over her but doesn't seem affected by her presence. "Oh, and"—she pats his chest—"heard the great news, Daddy. Congrats." She turns back. "Looks like everyone's got their hands full this summer."

29

Wilder

I'm at Rose's cottage again. It's been a shit night. Not just losing two men—I'm not going to lose sleep over that. Ricky might be trying to put us out of business by leaving me to cancel events due to staffing—but it's the least of my worries.

The biggest letdown of the night was not being able to reach out and pull my girl against my chest. Not being able to stand by protectively when someone bumped into her by accident. Or when a few of my men spent a little too much time talking to her.

It might be my imagination, but I swore Wes kept his eye on me all night.

Could just be the guilt. Which is worse since I don't know how to lessen the blow when I tell him about Rose.

I can't tell him it was one time. I can't tell him it was nothing.

And I can't tell him that it won't happen again.

All of that was meant to be the first step in making things right.

But none of it is true.

Metaphorically, it's been a cold evening, not having her by my side for more than a few minutes. But I can't help the feeling of warmth when I shut down for the evening. The locks, the lights, the drapes, and finally, starting the shower for her.

I check the water temp to make sure it's just right, then turn back to her as she undresses.

She looks up at me. It's not playful or seductive, it's just tender. "Are you sure you're all right?"

I like how in tune she is with me. Seems to always be. I like it a whole lot more than I should. Even when I didn't like the idea of her here, I noticed the way she saw me. Knew when I was bothered by something.

I run my thumb gently across her soft cheek. "I am now," I rasp out. "I hate not touching you when he's around."

The thought hits me hard. These *feelings* hit me hard.

It's not just sexual. My hands—and, hell, maybe even another part deep inside me—naturally seek her out, even in public. In stressful situations.

"I know," she sighs. "And I know you don't like lying to people either. Especially your friends and family."

I rub the back of my neck; I have to tell her that Dallas isn't the only one who knows about us. "About that . . . Dad and Silas can pretty much read the room when we're in it together."

She covers her face, but there's a smile behind it. "I can only imagine what they think of me."

"That you're the first girl in years to make me smile."

She searches my eyes. "They didn't say that."

"No," I admit. "The men in my family don't talk like that. But I can read them too."

Her mouth opens, but she doesn't say anything. She doesn't tell me she feels the same. But maybe that's for the best.

I swallow down the disappointment. "Shower. I need to make a call to Dallas about tonight. Then I'll join you."

I stand outside the bedroom door, dialing my older brother. The one who—before he lost himself in grief—was a hardass cowboy willing to kill for this ranch.

I need to see where his head is at about all this. "Hey," he answers on the first ring.

"You home?"

"I'm at my house," he says, like it's obvious.

"Hell you doing over there?"

"Painting."

"It's after midnight," I point out.

"Unless you're offering to help, I'm hanging up."

"A warning would've been nice about the boys," I tell him, even if it isn't the reason for my call.

"I know. But I can't focus on that right now."

"Right." *Ellie.* Which means *I* have to focus on it enough for the both of us. "I'll put an ad out," I tell him. "Get some part-time help. See if Levi can recommend someone he trusts."

"What about the senior group we got staying at the end of the summer?" Dal asks.

"Still on. We'll make it work. Rose and I will rework the schedule."

There's a beat before he comments. "If my calculations are correct, she's leaving next week, isn't she?"

"Two weeks," I correct, listening to the shower running in the other room.

"You planning anything on that front?"

My heart tugs. "Thinkin' of asking her to stay."

"All right. Then what?"

I sigh, running a hand down my face. "I don't know."

"Well, figure it out before you put something like that out there."

I shake my head. Wishing it were that easy.

I've already admitted to myself that I want her, more than physically, more than the summer.

As far as I know, back home, she's got nothing but a friend and a job at a downtown bar to pay the bills.

I can offer her more. But for how long? How long until I start questioning her loyalty to me? I've seen enough to know Rose isn't as wild as Wes drew her out to be.

She's driven but confused. She's talented, but maybe a little stunted.

I trust her.

But I trusted Bonnie too.

Bonnie changed her mind. What if Rose changes her mind?

What if this thing with us is a fleeting adventure for her? Something she does without thinking.

Something she regrets later . . .

I growl low as I pace the living room. The idea of letting Rose go because I'm too scared to trust is both heartbreaking and frustrating.

My eyes drop to the painting of my ranch still drying along the wall. There's another silhouette as well as that superman with a cowboy hat. This time he's got a woman in his arms, lifting her off her feet.

They're in front of a cottage that looks very familiar.

Maybe this is supposed to tell me something. Maybe this is how Rose shows what she wants.

And maybe it's about time I show her how *I* feel.

Tomorrow.

No games. No hesitation.

Tomorrow, I ask the woman I'm wild for . . . to stay.

30

Rose

I've fallen for him.

I know I have. Or I'm sure I have. I don't know how else to explain this gut-wrenching feeling of leaving him in ten days. Or the warmth that spreads through every inch of me when he looks at me, holds me, kisses me.

Everything in my mind tells me this is a fling. A wild summer fling, and I'd be a fool to think it's more.

But my heart is telling me to believe it.

I once heard somewhere that if it's not reciprocated, it's not love. It's lust.

And the possibility of that makes my heart shatter. If I'm as brave as I claim to be, I could ask him how he feels. I could tell him how I feel.

But before I do, I need to know.

Rose: What's love like?

Willow: Uh-oh.

Rose: That bad?

Willow: It's probably just the flu. When you coming home?

Rose: I don't want to.

Willow: Still doesn't mean you're in love.

Rose: I painted us last week.

I attach a picture of my painting and send it to her.

Willow: Cute. Listen, I'm no expert, but I think you need more than great sex and the urge to paint the man.

Rose: He makes me feel like I'm worth something.

Willow: Rose?

Rose: I know . . . I should know what I'm worth with or without him.

Willow: I was going to say . . . let me know when he makes you feel like you're worth *everything*.

I think I know when it happened. That long weekend. No—the night he chose to stay another night. When he watched me paint. When he encouraged me to have a glass of wine so I could feel normal again. Enjoy the things I used to without feeling threatened by it.

I'm not silly enough to think he'd feel the same. He's got a ranch to run. A heart to shield. A friendship to protect.

My heart sinks.

Because Willow has a point.

Wilder makes me feel like I mean something. Not everything.

And everything . . . would be a game-changer.

"I need more time with you." Wilder's husky voice is in my ear. We're still under the covers. Still naked.

I groan, turning in to him, trying not to look too excited about what he might be asking.

"An entire day, naked in bed, more?" I tease.

He shakes his head. "More."

I stroke the hair on his chest.

It's Saturday afternoon. This will be my sixth and last week here. And so far, he hasn't asked me to extend my stay.

Or anything more, for that matter.

I think he attempted to last Sunday when he came over after working on the field all day. He said he had something important to ask. He wasn't expecting to find Dallas here with Ellie watching a Disney movie.

And it's not like we've had much of a chance to talk all week. It's been crazy at the ranch with schedule changes, gossip, and events to try to keep on task.

When he came over last night, he proposed another long weekend. Just him and me . . . uninterrupted. Ellie's with her grandparents, so Dallas is seeing to the ranch.

"A week more?" I don't add that it's when I'd be boarding my return flight.

"Not enough."

I stroke down to that sexy, defined V below his belly. "Through the end of summer?"

"It's a start," he says, eyes closing in on my mouth.

Hope dies a little bit inside me. It's all right though. That flame wasn't all that bright to begin with.

"You think two extra weeks to finish off the summer will be enough, cowboy?"

"No. I said it's a start."

But he's also not asking. Not yet at least.

It's like when Willow's ex said, *I want to spend the rest of my life with you*. But never proposed. Just left her to hope and wait and expect.

Like he was waiting to see if something better comes along.

She finally left him and told me five words that have never resonated so much as they do now. *I want to be enough*.

But is enough *enough*? Is it selfish to want to be someone's everything?

Of course it is. Who am I to demand something like that?

"You have any idea what you do to me?" he continues. His head clearly on something more . . . right now.

"Drive you wild?"

He moves that solid, mountain man of a body over me. "Like you wouldn't believe." Scooping my neck up, he kisses me like a starved man.

He rips the sheet down, exposing us both and twists to sit up against the headboard. "Sit on my lap. With your back to me."

The request throws me off for a second. My lips part, but I don't hesitate for long and shift, settling my knees on either side of his thighs. My back to him.

He strokes my sides gently. "So beautiful." His hand drops between my spread thighs, and I know he finds me soaked. He coats my clit, gliding his thumb in tantalizing circles. His hard cock is in my hands. He reaches over with a condom. "Slide this on me."

He groans from my touch as I roll it down. I'm hot and needy and ready for him. He sucks in a sharp breath like he can't take it anymore and lifts me up, lowering me onto his cock. I guide him in slowly, but with an eagerness I've never possessed.

"Mine. This pussy, this perfect ass . . . is mine, Rose," he growls as he sinks me over his length.

"Yes, yes." My hands press against the mattress in front of me, using it as support as I ride him. The sensation from this erotic position. The declaration of ownership from his dirty mouth . . . it's enough to have me coming apart.

"Wilder," I cry as I ride him.

He threads his fingers into my hair. "Gorgeous. I love the way you move. The way you feel. You were made for me, Blue."

The friction is too much. I'm going to come. "Oh God, Wilder." It's another whimper.

"That's it, baby. Squeeze me just like that. That's my girl. Ride it like it's yours. Because I am. I'm all yours."

I'm trembling, screaming as the build-up becomes impossible to hold back.

"Now come. Come with me." He covers my breasts with his big hands as he thrusts, whispering in my ear, "Stay with me." Then a guttural groan rips from his throat that electrifies me.

My orgasm follows, and I scream, squeezing around him as his pumps become rough and ragged.

We're both breathing hard when he slides out of me and I fall back against his chest.

A moment later, he gives me a sexy, lazy grin as he flips me to face him. "I'm fucking crazy about you, you know that?"

Hours later, we've showered, had lunch and yet somehow neither one of us have real clothes on. I'm still in my little black nightie and cotton bathrobe, and he's in his boxers.

I'm wrapped in his arms, knowing without a doubt in my mind, I've fallen in love with Wilder Thorne.

"You heard what I said earlier?"

I stroke the scruff around his jaw. "That you're crazy about me?"

He lifts my chin. "You own me. Every inch, inside and out."

"Why do you sound sad about it?" I ask, reading too much into the undertone.

"Because it's not easy being owned. Complicates things."

I kiss his jaw. "You're being dramatic."

"Maybe, but I've been burned before, Blue. By someone who I thought lived and breathed the same things I did."

"There's no one else," I assure him.

He brushes his thumb against my bottom lip. "I know. I know it's not the first time I've asked and I'm sorry for that."

I stop him there. "Wilder. Don't be sorry. It's completely justifiable." I touch his cheek. "And I'm not ready to leave you either."

"Then don't. *Stay*, Blue."

"Rose!" A sharp roar cuts through the air, followed by heavy pounding.

What on earth?

Wilder hardens beneath me. His eyes are fiery as he recognizes my brother's voice.

Another bang. "Open this door right now."

"That fucking does it. Stay here," he commands.

"No. No," I plead desperately. "I've got this. Please. It's probably just—oh hell, I don't know what it is this time. Just please wait here and be quiet."

He paces my bedroom. "I don't like it, Rose. He's got no right banging down your door like that."

"Please stay here," I beg quietly.

He glares at me like he's seconds away from losing it.

Then nods.

I race out in my robe and unlock those damn locks, which are beginning to feel ridiculous. I'm fine. I don't need these. Why did I ever think I did?

Except maybe to keep my stupid brother out.

I pull the door open. "Christ, Rose. Hell is with these locks," Wes growls, stalking in like he lives here.

He's carrying a stack of mail—some opened, not surprising. Wesley likes to ensure I'm on top of my bills and pays anything outstanding. Which I'm both grateful and offended for. But I choose my battles.

"It's three in the afternoon. Why aren't you dressed?"

"Because it's Saturday. I'm off. Why are you storming in here? What's going on?"

He crosses my living room, pacing like a lunatic. "I fucking knew it."

My heart starts to thud. Does he know about Wilder?

"I knew I couldn't trust you in the city. You've completely lost your goddamn mind, sis. There's low and then there's this," he shouts, and OK, now I'm a little nervous.

"What are you talking about?"

"Did you need money, is that what it was? Or was this just a regular Monday afternoon for you?"

I watch him, stunned at his behavior. Is he drunk? No. This isn't Wesley drunk. This is Wesley losing his shit the same way he did when I told him I was dropping out of school to paint.

His eyes land on the two plates on the counter behind me. "Someone here?"

"No." I move to block him from going down the hallway.

"Rose," he warns, then grows pale as he stares over my shoulder.

My heart thuds against my chest dreadfully fast as I turn.

Wilder steps out into the living room in nothing but his jeans. And he doesn't look any happier than my brother. "Think it's about time you calmed down, Wes."

"The fuck is this?" It's barely an audible breath.

I swallow hard; my heart is pounding. I turn back to Wesley, and he meets my eyes. "Rose?"

"For fuck's sake, what does it look like, Wes?" I shout.

He glares across the room, disregarding me. "It looks like you're fucking my sister."

Wilder keeps his tone even, taking slow steps. "Can we talk like adults? Calm down for a minute? Then we can explain."

"We? You're a we now? What the fuck? You don't date, Wilder. You fuck around. You—" He pauses, his eyes wide. "Are you using my sister to ease all the stress you're under?"

"No. I'd never do that. Not to you or her."

Wes runs a hand down his face, crossing to the window.

"This is something else." He turns to me. "You're even more out of control than I thought."

"That's enough, Wes. The reality is we don't have to explain anything to you. Rose is an adult. A level-headed, smart, talented, and open-minded human being. Maybe if you took the time to get to know her, she might surprise you."

Wes shakes his head with an unhumorous laugh. "Yeah, real level-headed. A therapist with an eye for art. Or—" He drops a stack of dark eight by ten photos over a manilla envelope onto my counter. "A girl who's lost her identity and does something stupid. And once again, Wilder," he bites, pushing the stack toward him across the counter, "you're too blind to see it."

I catch Wilder swallow hard at my brother's words.

And I don't miss the reference.

How *dare* my brother compare me to Bonnie?

Dropping my eyes to the stack of photos, a chill runs through me. I recognize them instantly. Where I've seen images like it before.

At the gallery.

My stomach sinks as I reach for them. They're *me*. Nude—silhouetted, thank God—images of me, in front of a window, pushing back a curtain, arranging flowers, leaning against a door frame. There must be more than a dozen of them here.

"Get out," I whisper, my eyes fixed on the black and whites.

There's a beat before my brother moves to the door. "Call me when you're ready to talk."

It takes me a moment to recover, but once I do, I race after him onto the porch. He's halfway to his car. "Don't hold your breath," I shout.

Wes turns. "Excuse me?"

"I've had enough of you judging every move I make. You don't know me."

"I don't know you?"

"You've never taken the time to ask what's going on with me. You just assume I'm crazy," I shout, my voice cracking, tears stinging my eyes.

"Fine, let's talk. What was that about?" He motions back into the house, and I'm not sure if he means Wilder or the nude photos.

"You can't just start with that, Wes."

"Seems like as good a place as any to start figuring you out."

"Fine, maybe that was a mistake, but it was mine to make and this was *my* mail."

"Mistakes," he repeats. "It's nothing but mistakes with you." He glances behind me. "And complete disregard for the damage you could be causing."

I swallow, but I'm too hurt and angry to focus on his relationship with Wilder right now. "It's an invasion of privacy, Wes. You crossed a line."

He climbs back up one porch step, head tilted and eyes narrowing. "And you didn't?" he asks, voice low.

When I don't respond, he shoots a final glare into the house and steps down. "Your flight is next Saturday morning. Don't miss it."

My chest tightens at his harsh dismissal, but I can't let it get to me right now.

Stepping back into the house, I shut the door lightly and turn. Wilder isn't looking at me. I don't even think he notices that I'm back inside. His fingers brush the pile of photos on the kitchen counter, spreading them like a deck of cards. His expression blank. Not hard or angry. I wish I could see his eyes.

"That's not what it looks like," I start softly.

He still doesn't look up. "What'd you say these are called? Silhouettes?"

I bite my bottom lip. "You . . . remembered."

"Yeah, I remember." He nods, lifting his eyes to mine. "Who took 'em?"

I look back at him for a beat, my lips barely parting to answer.

"That guy you met at the gallery?" He waits for me to confirm. But not long enough. "The one that got you all rattled up when I asked about him?"

I blink a few times, trying to catch up. "Wilder, slow down."

"Why? Give you time to think of another lie?"

I shake my head, stepping toward him. "I wasn't lying. There was nothing to say."

He perks a brow. "These don't look like nothing, Rose."

"It's just art," I say weakly.

He drops his gaze to them again. "Is the artist usually the subject too?"

"Wilder."

"It's a question, Rose," he snaps.

"No, not usually."

He nods as he pushes them back. Then disappears into the bedroom.

I hurry to the counter and tuck them back into the envelope and into the trash can.

It's too late. I know it is. But still, I want them destroyed.

"Wilder," I try again when he storms out with his shirt on, boots striking hard as he marches to the door. "Wait. Please." I hurry after him.

Without warning, he spins to face me and I nearly crash into him.

He growls to himself and waits, jaw clenched, eyes dark.

It takes me a moment to catch up with my mixed emotions and everything spinning around me. But he's giving me the chance to explain and I'm taking it.

"Patrick—he's a photographer. I met him at a gallery. I looked at his work and didn't see it as . . . provocative. I saw it as expression and beauty, and when he said I'd be perfect, I . . ." I swallow, my voice suddenly getting smaller. "I was captivated by it in the moment."

His eyes soften but it's fleeting.

"I didn't see it as him coming on to me. He's a professional. He barely even looked at me between shots. I was exactly what you said, a *subject*." I'm grasping at anything at this point.

"Forget the damn photos, Rose." He takes a deliberate step toward me. "You got all nervous and lied and I want to know why."

It should be a simple answer and maybe if I had more time, I could dig deep and ask myself why I felt the need to lie about this when I was so open about everything else.

Was I ashamed?

Did I think he wouldn't understand?

I'm so scared that he's giving up on me here, I can't even think straight.

I shrug because I've got nothing else. "I don't know why."

He nods, eyes fixed on the floor. "You know that's exactly what Bonnie said when I asked her the same thing."

My eyes flash wide and I'm left breathless.

Wilder runs a hand down his face. "I'm going to call Ginger. Ask her to make some room for you at the main office this week."

I shake my head. "What? Why?"

"I've got a lot going on, and I need to focus. We'll catch up later this week."

A weight settles in my chest. I'm barely processing as he reaches the door.

How did this happen?

"Wait." My tone is pleading, and he turns. "I know you're upset right now. But can we please talk tomorrow?"

He looks out the window, to where my brother just left. "How long before you wake up and realize this was a mistake too?" He gestures between us. "Just a misstep. Something that seemed like a good idea at the time . . ."

"Wilder—" I move toward him. "Stop."

I freeze in my tracks, eyes burning.

He rubs his chin roughly like he's fighting to say what's on his mind. "Fuck." Then, like he can't help himself, he reaches for me, pulling me the rest of the way until I'm flat against his chest. "I'm sorry. I never want to hurt you, I just . . . need a day."

I nod and push against his chest, giving him the space he's asking for. I can do this. A day is nothing. A day is easy. "Yeah, OK. We'll talk when you're ready."

I know he's trying, but there's no warmth when he says goodbye and walks out of the cottage.

I have a nauseating feeling that I'm never going to see him again.

At least not in the same way.

It's midnight when I get the text I've been expecting. Waiting for.

Willow: Evenin' lady. Got company or want some?

I swipe at my puffy eyes, ready to cry again.

Rose: I did something stupid.

Willow: You fell in love, I know, I heard.

Rose: Would that be stupid?

Willow: The stupidest. Take it from me.

Rose: Then it's the second stupidest thing I've done.

Willow: What was the first?

I snap a photo and wince as I send it. Then toss the photos back in the trash where they belong.

There's no text back. And I hold my breath.

My phone rings and I swipe to answer right away.

"Holy shit, is that you?" Willow shrieks.

"It's me," I grumble.

"Hot stuff." She really means it too, and somehow—even though it goes against everything I tried to convince Wilder of—it makes me feel better.

"It's not hot, it's art."

She chuckles. "If you say so, missy."

"I do say so."

"Oh yeah?" she challenges. "Then why am I only hearing about it now?"

"Wise ass," I mutter. Then I give her a quick rundown of my afternoon.

"How did Wes even—oh no. Is this what I mailed him?"

I hadn't even considered that. "Yeah, but—"

"Shit, this is all my fault. I say you call the feds on the guy. He opened your mail."

"It's not your fault, and I'm not calling the feds. He's my brother. I can hear his argument now: *She didn't call anyone when I was paying her bills, did she, Your Honor?*"

She grumbles. "Want to chat for a while?"

"No. I'm pretty tired."

I don't need to tell her I've been crying for the better part of the day since my brother and Wilder walked out.

"Well, I'll be up for a little while if you need to chat. Also, does this mean you're coming home early? I've been looking at apartments for us."

"You don't want me as a roommate. I'm unpredictable and impulsive."

"No. You're my best friend and I love you. You don't need to be tamed. You just need to find what makes you happy."

"Thanks, Wil. Talk tomorrow?"
"Night."

Willow: And Rose?

Rose: Yeah?

Willow: You look hot in those silhouettes. Keep 'em.

Not if my life depended on it.

31

Wilder

“Looks good, Larry,” I comment, giving the fence a good nudge. We had to move the cattle to the smaller pasture for a few days till the fence was repaired.

He tips his hat.

“Listen, I know you’re off this weekend, but we’re a little short-staffed. You mind doing a shift?”

“Happy to. Just let me know where you need me, Wilder.”

I thank him and I separately want to thank Rose too. She spent all of last week manipulating the schedule, overtime, and budget so that we’re covered through the summer.

She emailed me the final schedule yesterday and sent someone to the Saddle Room with a hard copy.

It’s organized, color coded, and gives me some kind of reassurance that we can pull this off until the season is over.

Assuming no one else leaves.

It's early Tuesday morning. Two whole days have passed and I'm not any more ready to talk to Rose than I was when I walked out.

I took Tuscan out for a ride these last two nights, running by the cottage. OK, maybe not running by. More like waiting. Waiting with my heart in my throat until the lights went out.

And even then, it was tough to leave.

After an easy ride along the river, checking the fields, I find myself steering Tuscan back in her direction. The ache in my chest has nothing to do with the land. Or the work, for that matter.

It's the woman the stubborn part of me is slowly letting go.

How could she be so reckless? How could I be so reckless?

I fell hard for a woman who, in every reality—was never mine to keep.

This is who Rose is. She pushes boundaries, rides the edges like she's got nothing to lose. Strips naked for strangers like it's part of her road to self-discovery.

The anger is still fresh.

Her wildness had a spark that lit me up. I thought her unpredictability would bother me, but I lived for it.

I *lived* to keep her safe through it instead of controlling it.

Seeing those photos, as innocent as her gullible little heart thought they were, made me see that she's not thinking straight.

She's on some road that I can't follow. A road I might not have a place for down the line.

And that's the part that scares me.

My phone dings with a message, and I hope it's one from Wes. I've been trying him all day, yesterday and Sunday.

I swipe the screen.

Rose: Can we please talk tonight?

Rose: I know I didn't say much the other day. It just all happened so quickly.

Rose: I know I can fix this.

That last one makes my heart ache for her. I'm going to have to talk to her eventually. But I just need one more day.

One day to make sense of my doubts. It's been hard.

Because every time I try to explain it to myself, I hear her in my mind. Telling me how ridiculous I am for not seeing she's crazy about me too.

It's mid-afternoon when I get another one from her.

Rose: Can I leave early today?

I type out a response that basically says to ask Ginger, since I've left her in charge of Rose. But it's a dick response. One she doesn't deserve.

Wilder: Yes.

I'm tempted to follow it with a question asking why, but I think better of it.

I spend the rest of the afternoon making a few calls and feel somewhat productive.

The door to the Saddle Room swings open without a knock. Dallas stalks over to me, hands shuffling through some cards. "Pink, purple, or rose?"

I blink. "What?"

"I mean the color."

I shake my head. "This for Ellie's room?"

"Well, it's not for mine."

I sigh. "Why don't you ask Ellie?"

"And look like I'm clueless?"

I glare at him, hoping it answers his rhetorical question.

Then I sigh. "Pink."

He nods then tosses the swatches to the side. "Figured I'd find you in here, sulking."

"What do you mean?" I haven't told him about Rose.

"Got a pretty angry call from Wes the other day, asking me if I knew what was going on with you and his sister."

"Sorry," I grumble. Probably should have warned him.

Dallas leans back in his chair. "I've never been more afraid of another man in my life."

I chuckle. "Wish I could've seen it." I reach for a stack of old invoices that don't need my attention. "Not sulking. I'm working."

"You're hiding. And seein' as how Ginger is giving Rose busy work in the front office, I take it you ended it."

I shake my head, avoiding eye contact.

"Can I ask why her brother finding out about you two made you walk out on her?"

"It's none of your business."

He stands. "Well, I know better than to try to get anything out of you when you're like this."

"Where you going?"

"Pick up Rose. Got to put good talent to useful work."

"Leave her alone. She's leaving early today," I snap.

He grins. "I know." He tips his head. "Said she's got ideas for Ellie's room. We're going to go to the hardware store, then back to the new house. Figured you wouldn't mind."

I shrug as my teeth clench and my heart sinks. "She's as much your employee as she is mine. But if she falls off any ladders, I'll personally break every bone in your body."

He stands, lifting his black hat off the table. "Ladders. Good one. Better than that B.S. story about Rose's arm you told her brother."

My eyes snap to his. "What do you know about that?"

"I know you were lying. Those scars weren't fresh. Noticed them that night she took care of mine."

I lower my gaze. "I'll see you tomorrow."

At the end of the day Wednesday, I stop at The Shack to talk to Wes.

I haven't been able to get over the things those two said to each other outside. How he'd never taken the time to listen to her.

How much she needs him to.

We're not quite closed yet, but it's the end of the day and he's usually the last one here, taking inventory and working on the menu.

As expected, I find him behind the bar, closing out the register. He eyes me as I lock the door and flip the sign on the door to Closed.

"Can we talk?"

He glances at the sign. "Doesn't look like I've got much of a choice, boss."

"I'm not here as your boss. I never am. Just want to make sure we're not interrupted."

He scoffs. "Explains all the locks on Rose's door."

"No, it doesn't," I snap.

He jerks at my tone. And I'm not sorry for it because he doesn't know why I put them there.

And he needs to.

"Look, I know you're not ready to talk to me or even see me. And I know from experience, you don't forgive easily."

Wesley's jaw locks, muscles flexing as he remains behind the bar.

"But I need you to talk to Rose."

I miss saying her name. Miss calling her *Blue*. The nickname reminds me of the time she tried to get a reaction out of me for vandalizing my cart. And all I saw was that bright blue smudge on her right cheek.

He turns his chin to the side at the mention of her name. And I'm damn sure it's the memory of her calling him out—and then shutting him out.

Something hard hits my chest but I push it aside to focus on what matters here. And that's my best friend's relationship with his sister. "You said her flight is Saturday and not to miss it."

"Yeah, so?"

"You really want to find out what happens after she gets on that plane? Are you that unafraid that you're willing to let her go back without talking to her?"

My gut twists at my own words.

He slams the register. "This town not big enough for you or something? Not enough women throwing themselves at you?"

I don't know what Wesley sees, but women don't throw themselves at me. "Think you're confusing me with Silas."

He rolls his eyes and maybe I'll give him that. I haven't had a problem getting a date for a night here and there since Bonnie.

But that's all they've been. Sometime in the last three years I stopped seeing the women I'm with as who they are. I only see Bonnie.

No. I only see what Bonnie *did*.

And no one was worth trying something more with. Until Rose.

"This ain't about me or our friendship." He scoffs. "It never was."

"Make her talk, Wes," I shout impatiently. "And take the time to listen. You might lose her if you don't."

He frowns, narrowing his eyes at me. "Do you know something I don't?"

I don't deny it. "I've known you for over ten years. Trust me when I say this is the best advice you'll ever get from me. Don't fuck it up."

32

Rose

It's been five days since he left my cottage with a promise to talk soon.

But he can't avoid me today. It's Thursday and he needs to sign off on payroll.

He wouldn't avoid me—not when I'm supposed to leave in two days.

I came in early today to total up the cards a few times before going to see him. I've been too anxious and can't have it show in my work.

Ginger swings back in her chair. "You going to run those over soon? I can get started on them early today. It's a little slow."

"Yep, just finishing up," I tell her.

"Great, and then . . ." She looks around. "Well, maybe you can rearrange some of the display shelves over by the gift shop?"

I swallow. "Ginger, you don't really have anything for me to do, do you?"

"Not really, you've been pretty efficient."

I smile at her. "Well, I'll go get these signed off for you and then maybe take a long lunch."

"There you go." She swivels back to her desk.

My heart sinks to my stomach. Will he want to see me? Will he finally talk to me?

I've been looking forward to seeing him all morning, and now, I don't know if I can stomach it.

I hop in my golf cart and ride over. It's a nice breezy day today, a bit gloomy, but we're not supposed to be getting any rain.

Maybe it's just me?

I'm holding my breath as I walk up to the door of the Saddle Room. Pushing it open, I freeze at the threshold.

"Oh hey, Rose," Dallas greets me from Wilder's chair.

I step in tentatively, closing the door behind me. "Where's Wilder?"

"We were just in here going through the budget, then he said he had to run out for a bit."

Run out.

He knew I was coming.

And he left.

My chest is tight with something even I can't figure out. I'm not disappointed.

I don't even think I'm hurt.

This is more of a hollow ache. Like something that was never mine to lose.

"Rose?"

I blink up as Dallas pushes off the chair like I'm about to faint.

"Are you all right? You look pale."

"I'm cold," I whisper honestly. Because I do feel cold. And empty.

He left, knowing I was coming.

My hands shake as I cross the room to the desk and place the cards down.

"Oh, here." Dallas pulls his black hoodie off and hands it to me. "Take this."

"Thank you." I accept it because I can't do anything else. A reality that I've been avoiding hits me like a ton of bricks.

No one is waiting for me.

I'm the one who's waiting.

And what I'm waiting for, I won't find in this room.

In my haze, I see his eyes drop to the stack. "I'll have Wilder take a look at these."

I stare at them as my mind searches for the next right thing.

"You sure you're all right?"

"I just remembered"—I snap my head up—"I have something I need to do tomorrow," I mutter. "Would you do me a favor?"

"Anything."

I shuffle for my timecard. I cross off the hours I prepopulated for Friday. "Will you sign off on this for me?"

He studies it, then looks at me. "But, uh . . . I might need you tomorrow. You did an amazing job in Ellie's room. The detail on those flowers along the back wa—"

I drop the card and flip around. "Forget I asked." I head to the door.

"Rose, wait."

I pause midway and turn.

"Tell me what happened. Maybe I can help." He shoves his hands in his pockets. "Millie and I didn't fight much, but when we did, I usually knew how to fix it."

I shake my head. "Something bad happened—not with Wilder—with me, a few years ago. Life's been . . . different since." Tears build up in my eyes. "Like a long pause filled with mistakes and wasted energy." I take a breath. "But with him, I found something steady, something safe and fun, and warm. He doesn't share much, but he listens, he's patient. . ." I swallow. *And up until a few days ago, he didn't judge.*

Dallas tilts his head to the side. "Then what on earth's the problem?"

"Something I did caught up with me and it tested his patience. I've been . . . waiting for him to get past it."

"You just need to give him t—"

"No, I think . . ." I blink with a low headshake. "I think I've been waiting for the wrong person to get past it."

He watches me for a moment. His features are naturally hard, but he's warm and understanding.

Without a word, he walks back to the desk and lifts my timecard, signing it. "I'll bring these back to Ginger myself."

I release a breath. "Thanks."

"You got my number. Call if you need anything. I mean it."

"I know. Thank you."

I take the rest of the afternoon to make calls. I know which ones I've needed to make for a while and now . . . I'm ready.

Wilder and Wesley giving up on me shouldn't have been my push, my wake-up call. But the silence they left behind didn't settle—it itched like a question I couldn't shake.

What am I doing?

I've been holding on to Wesley finally understanding. To Wilder choosing me over everything that holds him back. I'd forgotten that I came here for a reset.

A chance to recharge, reorganize my thoughts, my objectives, and most of all, my sanity.

I've been blaming myself when the answer all along was to *move on*. Not change who I am or question my ability to help others.

I may have lost two years, but I can catch up quickly.

I've always wanted to be a therapist. I let the idea that I couldn't help someone when I could barely help myself derail me, confuse me, and take control.

Sandra, the therapist I ghosted several months ago, was my first call. I made an appointment at her office next week, but she wanted to take some time to catch up first. So I filled her in and she talked me through a few crucial next steps.

I felt unshackled. Like I'd been carrying something heavy for too long.

Through a new perspective, I was in complete awe listening to her. The care, attention, and knowledge she provided. The checklist she insisted I make. And the constant reassurance that I'm not alone.

I called my dad next, and he agreed to pay for the remaining credits I need to graduate. Then I scheduled a call for Monday with an advisor at NYU.

Finally, after dinner, I pack.

I've got an early morning, so at nine o'clock, I start to shut down. I send a quick text to Willow letting her know I'm good for tonight and to stop setting her alarm in the middle of the night just to check on me. After tomorrow, the two-hour time difference will never be an issue for us again.

I linger by the front door for a moment, turning the latch on one lock.

Good enough. It's good enough.

I lock one more, shut off the light, and go to bed.

Friday morning, I step back into the house just after eight. I wash the white paint off my hands and change out of my stained clothes.

Painting the cart back to white was painful, but no one around here needs a reminder of the wild Rose and "the bullet the bossman dodged."

OK, so maybe no one would say that last part, but the more I convince myself I'm not wanted here . . . the easier it will be to leave.

Fortunately, I was able to find a cheap last-minute flight to New York. Unfortunately, I can only afford to check one bag. So whatever is left of my supplies has to stay.

There's a knock on my door as I spot-check the rooms. "Almost ready," I call out, then grab my suitcase and open the door.

I frown. "Wesley."

His eyes drop to my bag. "Where are you going? Your flight is tomorrow."

I start to close the door on him.

"Wait." He pushes against it and I don't fight him. "Can we talk?"

I step back and start moving about the floor, looking for any contents I may have left behind.

He watches me for a moment. "Rose, slow down. Can we sit or something?"

"I don't have time to sit or talk. But you're free to."

He rubs his forehead. "I guess it's over with you and Wilder?"

"Yes. Is that all?" I peel my eyes off the trashcan near the kitchen, that manilla folder still peeking out.

Definitely not taking *those*.

"No. That's not all. Wilder says there's something you need to tell me?"

I release a breath then shake my head.

"Come on, Rose. You can tell me anything." He steps closer but a little awkwardly. There's tenderness in his voice but I'm too hurt and angry to accept it.

I pause and lock eyes with him, "No. I really can't."

He blinks but doesn't back down. After a beat, he chances another step closer. "I promise you, you can." He stuffs his hands in his pockets. "You know everything Wilder said about you is true. You're smart, talented, maybe a little too open-minded sometimes, but that's better than not at all, I suppose."

I glare at him impatiently.

His shoulders sag. "I'm sorry," he rasps. "I messed up and I know it. I thought I was protecting you but all I did was hurt you. And I know I violated your privacy and I'm so sorry for that. It's just that, Rose . . . I *know* half-truths when I hear them. And that's all you ever give me. *Something's* been going on with you and I hate not knowing what it is." His eyes glisten as he glances at my packed bag. "Rose, please don't go yet. I was blindsided and angry, I shouldn't have blown up at you like that. And I certainly shouldn't have shown those photos to him. It was private, it was yours, and I was out of line."

I stand still, my heart heavy because this changes nothing. This is guilt. A last-minute apology so I don't hate him when I leave.

And this isn't the therapist in me. This is the scorned sister in me.

"What do you need to tell me?" he asks softly.

"Need is a strong word. Maybe you should be asking what you deserve to know."

He drops his head with a nod. "I take it that isn't much?"

My shoulders slump with a breath. "I fell in love with your best friend."

He lifts his brows. "In love?"

"This is the part where you tell me I don't know what that is."

He runs his hand along his face like this is something he wasn't expecting. "Have you told him how you feel?"

There's a honk outside my cottage. I swallow. "That's my ride."

He stiffens. "Wait. That wasn't what you need to tell me. There's something else, I know there is. What have I been missing, Rose? Please just tell me so I can help you."

"I don't need your help," I shout. "I needed you to listen. How can I tell you what's going on with me when you'd just—"

"I'd what?"

"You'd just blame me," I choke out, tears threatening.

He reaches for me, but I step back, taking off my sweater and holding out my arm to show him the scars again. "This didn't happen here. They happened two years ago when someone came into my dorm room and attacked me and my roommate."

He pales. "What?"

"I was able to fight him off but just barely. The only reason he stopped is because he threw me against a mirror and it shattered over me. He and his friend ran."

"Rose—"

"My door wasn't locked, Wes." I shrug. "I didn't lock it like you always told me to. I didn't call the police, I didn't even go to the hospital."

"Ro." He releases a breath. "Why didn't you call me? I would have been there."

"You warned me about staying safe out there. And I didn't even lock the door."

He pulls me into his arms, and I let him hold me for a long moment, my arms at my sides. "I'm so sorry," he whispers.

There's a hard knock on my door. "I've got to go."

"Don't go," he pleads softly, holding me tight.

"I'll miss my flight."

He pulls back, looking at me, his eyes red. "Don't go at all," he begs. "I know I've been hard on you, but I want to make things right."

I nod, grabbing my suitcase. "Great. You know where to find me."

"Ro, I don't want to lose you. I love you. We need each other." The desperation in his voice makes me turn.

I watch him, my expression hard, and it's not fair. It's not the way to fix this. I release my suitcase and take a breath. "I love you too. But I can't stay. I've got a plan now, I'm taking care of it." I glance out the window. "I don't know if New York is for me, but I'm going to get my school records and maybe . . . move back home for a bit. Willow will kill me since we planned on moving in together, but I can't go to school *and* pay rent."

He starts to argue, but I stop him. "And you won't either."

He smirks. "We could get our own place together here, you know? Denver's got some great schools. Less than an hour commute."

I give him a small smile. "Thanks, but I don't think living with my brother in his prime is the best idea."

I roll my suitcase around him and open the door.

"Christ, you New Yorkers," Dusty mutters. She points a finger at me. "Consider this the last favor I do you."

"Dusty Callahan?" Wesley barks behind me. "You called *her*?"

"Wes, I've been up for hours. I've got a long flight, please don't start with me."

"Want me to deck him?" Dusty offers.

"No. Then I'd have to tell our parents I let a girl hit him."

"Your brother. Explains a lot."

Wes reaches for my suitcase, ignoring the blonde. "Rose, I'll take you to the airport."

"The lady said no," Dusty growls.

"Like you've got any manners," he bites back.

I put a hand on his shoulder. "I'll call you from the airport."

"If you get there," he mutters, still glaring at Dusty.

She rolls her eyes. "I'll be in the car."

10:30 a.m.

Rose: Heading to airport.

Willow: Really?

Rose: Why wouldn't I be?

Willow: Just thought there'd be some last-minute proclamation of love or something.

I laugh, and Dusty glances over at me from behind the wheel.

Rose: No. I'm coming home.

Willow: Airport. There's going to be an airport chase. Someone's going to get arrested.

Rose: Wanna get dinner later?

Willow: Check your voicemail before you board. You don't want that Ross and Rachel thing where she almost doesn't get off the plane.

I roll my eyes.

Rose: I'm with Dusty. I've got to go.

Willow: Who's Dusty? Is he cute?

"Thanks for coming," I say to the not-so-intimidating blonde.

She keeps her eyes on the road. "Only gave you my number to piss off the boys. Didn't think you'd actually use it."

I grin. "Yet here you are."

She cocks her head. "Here I am."

I do get to the airport on time and in one piece, so there's something to be said for trusting my instincts.

Can't say the same for my heart.

Because like a fool, I wait for him at the airport and even look back before I board.

33

Wilder

Gut-wrenchingly hollow. With a heavy weight of regret stuck in my chest. If I'm honest, it's been there all week, but it's especially strong this morning.

I can still see her. That look in her eyes begging me to understand the innocence in what she did.

Fuck, I still don't. I never will.

But that little misstep is not what made me walk out. It just opened my eyes. Because all I saw was myself being that mistake for her down the line.

I watched the light in her eyes flicker out. Watching her swallow hard, give me a small nod like she understood when I asked her to give me time. No, a day. I asked for a day.

And I've been a coward all week. Albeit busy with damage control at the ranch, but nonetheless, a coward.

She was right in that text she sent me. It all happened so fast.

One minute I'm asking her to stay with me. We'd work the rest out. Her brother, her dreams, we'd figure it all out. I'd make it number one on all my lists until we do.

Next, I tell her I need time and leave her in tears.

All because of that part in me that never wants to feel not enough, a second thought . . . like someone you can walk away from.

I growl, pinching the bridge of my nose hard as I realize the irony of my actions.

Shit.

Why does it feel too damn quiet here? And empty.

What day is it? Rose is supposed to come here with the timecards for payroll. I check the time. Almost eleven. She always has them ready for me before noon on Thursdays.

I stand and pace, my heart racing as I think of what I'm going to say to her. If I'm even ready to say it.

An hour later, I nearly leap out of my seat at the sound of an engine humming outside the Saddle Room, even if it is too loud to be some decked-out golf cart.

Sure enough, Dallas bursts through the door like he owns half the place.

"Hey," I grumble.

Unlike me, he's a heavy coffee drinker. And right about now I'll take any scent that reminds me of her.

I check the time again.

Where is she? It's almost noon.

Rose's lights were out already by the time I rode by last night so I'm assuming she didn't have a late start today.

I pull up the schedule again for a distraction, even though I've already memorized it and know we're in good shape for the weekend. Rose made sure of it.

The only real problems I've got now are two sick animals and a head chef not talking to me.

"Look, man, I know things are a little hectic right now, but you need to slow down," Dallas says, taking a seat at Rose's desk. "You've been running around all week like a chicken without a head."

"Just need to make sure we've got it all covered." I sigh. "You seen Rose today? Need to see what we owe for last week's payroll."

"Nine thousand, five hundred and two."

I look up at him. "How could you possibly know that?"

He gives me a smug grin. "Signed off on it yesterday. Lost my favorite hoodie in the process, but I'll manage."

I shake my head. "I don't understand. Today's Thursday—"

He sits up, intrigued. "Today's Friday. Rose came by *yesterday*."

I push off my chair. "She was here? And you didn't say anything?"

"You left. Figured you didn't want to see her."

"I left because Landry called and said the vet was here and I met him over by the barn." I realize I'm shouting.

Because it's fucking Friday.

I told her I needed one day. And I took a fucking week.

I pace the floor. No doubt she thought I left to avoid her and left Dallas to sign off instead.

"I need to go find her."

"Wilder." His deep voice stops me in my tracks. "I don't think you're going to find her."

"Like hell I won't."

I always find her.

"What difference would it make?" he shouts as I pull the door open. "Every girl you lay eyes on you compare to Bonnie."

I don't move.

"You screwed something up with Wesley's sister and this poor girl is here blaming herself."

I turn to face him. "What do you mean? What did she say?"

"Nothing I'm sure you don't already know deep inside. You want to run yourself out of a future with someone special? You go right ahead. But not Rose. She's too young to deal with your insecure shit."

I glare at him and the man doesn't even blink. "I'll find her," I repeat.

And chant it all the way to her cottage.

My stomach drops like a stone when I reach it minutes later and find a freshly painted golf cart parked out front.

No. No, no.

I push her unlocked door open and fly in. Wesley is in the corner of the living room, cleaning up her art supplies.

She's not here. It feels too empty.

"Don't worry," he says, groaning as he pushes to his feet. "I'll have this all cleaned up and tossed soon."

"Where is she?" I pant.

He's not surprised by my question. He checks his watch. "Probably over Indiana right about now."

Any breath I have left is knocked out of me. "She left?"

Wes nods. "Three hours ago."

"You let her go?" I shout.

He dusts his hands with an exasperated sigh. "No. *You* let her go."

I run a hand down my damp face, glancing down the hall as if she'd magically appear. "I mixed up my days. I missed her."

"Yeah, I don't know what that means, but I'll come back and clean up here later. I need to get back to work."

"Don't touch any of it," I growl, my heart pounding like I've just lost everything.

Relief rolls through me when I find the familiar yellow envelope still tucked inside the tin trashcan. Bending, I lift it up and shake off the excess trash.

From the corner of my eye, I see Wes lingering by the door. "You put these in?"

I turn to him in a daze. "What?"

"The locks. You do this?"

I swallow, having no clue if Rose told him yet—like I hoped she would. "Yeah."

Another nod. "Thank you."

I slide the envelope safely into a drawer and cross to the living room. "You don't think she's nuts for needing them?" I ask.

And it's almost accusatory and defensive.

"I think she's my sister and I love her. And because I am the way I am, she didn't tell me about the one thing in her life that scared her half to death." He looks at me. "But she told you."

I wait for the blow. The claims of betrayal. "Why are you here?" he asks.

I swipe at my brow. "I asked her for a day. I took six."

He frowns like this means nothing to him. "Why are you here?"

I look around the small house. It's not Millie's anymore. It's hers. And hell, some nights, it felt like ours. The bed, the showers, the cooking, the painting, the chocolate shavings.

My eyes fall to the canvas resting up against the back wall. With the cowboy lifting up the city girl into his arms like I'm her damn hero.

I swallow hard. "I'm here because I fell in love with your sister."

He stares at me for a long moment, then breaks with a scoff. "Unbelievable."

"Wes. You know I'd never do anything to hurt our friendship again otherwise."

"I feel a *but* coming on . . ."

"But I need to go find her."

His eyes drop for a moment, like he's remembering something. Maybe something she told him? He lifts his gaze to mine. "You don't get another chance here, Wild. You screw this up . . . you hurt her . . . we're through too."

I swallow at the thought, even if I know I'd never let it happen. I manage an easy grin. "This a 'three-strikes and you're out' kind of thing?"

He deadpans me. "This is a 'hurt her again and you're dead to me' thing."

34

Rose

"That was amazing," I tell Willow when she finishes her set on Saturday night at the Lock Bar. It's not a fancy place to work, but then again, neither was stone-picking in the mud. So, technically, this is a dream job.

"Thank you." My redheaded friend does a little bow for me and takes an empty seat at my bar. "I'll take that margarita now."

"You gonna tip me?" I tease.

She slaps a pack of cigarettes on the bar. "Some joker put that in my jar. You believe that?"

"The nerve," I agree. Then shrug and swipe it from the counter.

"Hey," she shrieks.

"What? I'm entitled to breaks."

"You don't smoke."

I pop the lid, inspecting it. "Look at that, it's a fresh pack, too."

"Throw it out this instant."

"All right, all right." I toss it behind the counter and start mixing her drink. "You know you don't have to wait for me. My shift isn't over for another two hours."

"I know. But I've missed you. And what am I going to do at home? Pack more boxes so I can move into our new place *alone*?"

I wince. "I'm sorry. But hey, you're not married to the city either. Come to South Carolina with me. You'd love Charleston." I set the watermelon margarita in front of her.

She takes a sip. "So, did you keep the photos? You only showed me the one. I want to see all of them."

I swat my rag at her with a coy smile. "No, pervert."

She takes a few more sips, watching me. Her expression saddens. "You OK?"

I spread my arms wide like it's obvious how well I am doing. "Hey, Billy kept his word and put me back on the closing shift so there's that. My school records are in the mail, and based on what I looked up at the school in Charleston, I can start my Masters by next spring and begin supervised practice hours within a year."

She holds up her glass. "You lost me at school records."

I laugh, then scan her outfit. Willow's got a typical city-girl style about her, but with comfort. So, jeans—not the skinny kind—an off-shoulder lightweight sweater, and low heels.

But when she's playing, she dresses the part. Today, it's a low-cut sleeveless top that hugs her body, and a pair of embroidered leggings. I can tell she's uncomfortable. "Put something on before I turn into your jealous ex-boyfriend and throw my jacket over you."

"Actually, I wouldn't mind it. Someone knocked into me when I got here and spilled beer over my sweater."

"Jerks. Here." I pull out the hoodie Dallas gave me the other day and hand it to her across the bar.

"Someone leave this behind?"

"No. It belongs to a friend."

She buries her nose in it. "Mmm . . . smells nice. Woodsy." She smiles as she slides the oversized black hoodie over her head. "Thanks."

"Keep it. It looks good on you." And it's better that she does. Even though Dallas isn't the one I'm hurting over, I don't need any reminders of Blue River.

She passes her empty glass to me. "Take an Uber tonight, OK?"

"Will do," I lie. "Love you."

I wave goodbye and get back to the few customers I've got at the bar. It's slow tonight—or became slow after Willow finished her set.

"Refill?" I ask the two guys at the far end finishing their beer. I hope they say yes. I don't like this place when it's too quiet. Too empty. Especially when I'm closing.

"Yes, ma'am. This round's on me," one of them says, handing me his card.

I smile. "Be right with you." I fill up their drafts to the brim and place the glasses carefully in front of them. "The next one's on me, boys."

They lift their glasses with a grateful nod, and there's a sudden shift in the air. A pull in my chest. It's raw and sends a toe-curling chill through me.

I turn to look at the door, but there's no one there. It's like I'm seeing things—or feeling things that aren't real.

Like I did for a brief moment back at the airport because of Willow's dumb cliché movie reference.

I shake it off and move to another customer with a glass half full, leaning on my elbows. "Too strong for ya?"

"You tryin' to get me drunk?"

I smile. "Is it working?"

The old man with kind eyes laughs with a blush. "I'll let ya know." He takes another sip, returning to his newspaper.

I wave to the high-top waiter closing with me, letting him know I'm stepping outside for a minute. Then I swipe up the carton of cigarettes and a lighter from behind the bar and step out.

It takes a few tries, but I finally light the damn thing. Placing it between my lips, I inhale slowly.

And there's that ghost of a feeling again that someone's watching me.

My skin tingles as I turn and lock eyes with him.

Stepping toward me in dark jeans, a white shirt, and silver buckle. The man who asked for a day and left me waiting.

Wilder.

He lifts the cigarette from between my fingers and brings it to his mouth. After one drag, he flicks it aside.

Playfully, I take out another one. A challenge in my eyes. "What are you doing here?"

He doesn't let me light it before pulling it from my lips. "What does it look like?" he asks, holding up the unlit cigarette with a perked brow. "Sensed trouble and came running."

My heart flips, but I force it steady. He's come for me before. And he's left before, too.

I smirk with a nod. "Well then"—I press the pack against his warm chest—"crisis averted. You can go home."

I release, and he catches the pack just as I turn and walk back into the bar.

Wilder follows, taking an empty seat at the end, his eyes on me like I'm the only one in the room as I check on my few customers.

I fill a glass of ice water and set it in front of him. "You're on the wrong side of the country, cowboy."

"I'm exactly where I want to be. Thanks for the water." I meet his eyes again for a moment. That deep blue steady, like he was memorizing me. Like I might disappear if he blinks.

"Why are you here?" I ask, my voice soft despite wanting to stay strong.

"Because I haven't been able to breathe all week," he says roughly.

My pulse flutters, but I frown because maybe he doesn't realize that I haven't either. "That sounds terrible."

A muscle ticks in his jaw. "I know. It's not fair. But if you give me a chance to explain—"

"Hey, sweetheart, next one's on you, right?" It's the two guys from the opposite side of the bar.

I wink back at them. Then turn back to Wilder. "I'm working."

He relaxes in his chair with his ice water as if to show he's not going anywhere.

Two hours later, I'm locking up for the night. It took me longer than usual after closing since my hands were shaky and my mind in shambles.

Wilder is outside, leaning against a meter, watching the busy downtown street. I turn and start down the sidewalk for my long walk home.

Here, I walk like I belong, matching the city's pace. Not like six weeks ago, when I was struggling to keep up with Wilder's long strides as he showed me around town.

He catches up with me, now sprinting like *I'm* too quick. "We headin' home?"

"*I'm* heading home."

He doesn't say anything but follows behind me, pulling me to a stop when I reach a cross street. A taxi zooms past two feet in front of me. "Rose."

"What, I saw him coming."

"Christ," he mutters, but releases me.

Wordlessly, he follows me for another two blocks until my patience starts to boil.

I spin around abruptly—nearly colliding with him. But we don't.

His sure and steady arms come around me, catching me. "Saw that coming a mile away," he says with that knowing grin.

It still takes my breath away. Still makes my heart race. I swallow hard and pull away. "Why don't you just say what you came here to say," I whisper, my voice giving away that I'm ready to break.

He moves me out of the way of a couple walking along the sidewalk, then hails a cab like an expert.

The ride back to my apartment is quick, and he hasn't said a word in response to my asking why he's here.

"Can I come in?" he asks when we reach my door.

I pull my keys out and look up at him. He looks so sincere. And tired. "It's late, Wilder."

He looks over my shoulder. "I know. I didn't exactly think this through when I booked the first flight out today." He brushes my hair back. "I just knew I had to get here."

I look back at my door but don't make a move to go inside.

"Can we please talk soon then? I can wait," he asks gruffly, like he hears the irony and knows my response.

I should say it. *I need a day.*

The scorned girl in me wants to. But the sharp, level-headed woman in me who just wants to move on doesn't.

I shake my head. "I don't think so," I say softly. "You have a ranch to run. A friendship to protect. And a heart to shield." I repeat the reasons I used to convince myself *it wasn't me* for the past week.

I touch his cheek. "I never want to hurt you. So please don't wait," I tell him in all sincerity. Then I unlock my door and step inside, shutting it softly.

My eyes burn as I close them, listening for his departing footsteps.

They don't come.

And I don't wait for him to leave before turning in for the night.

35

Rose

"In the middle of a set?" I ask Willow when she sits down during a quick break and asks for a margarita.

"If I'm going to smell like alcohol, I might as well be drinking it."

The door swings open, and I don't have to look up to know it's him. There's a weight to his presence, a shift in the air, like my body knows he's near before my mind can catch up.

But I don't pause in shaking up the mixer before pouring my friend's favorite drink into a salt-rimmed glass.

Willow must sense my tension because her head turns toward Wilder as he strides in.

He leans against the bar next to her. "Drinks any good here?"

He's so effortlessly . . . rugged. He's wearing a dark green fitted shirt, his scruff from yesterday now neatly trimmed. He looks well rested, which is refreshing.

But it's also confusing to me how he can be so relaxed. I'd have sworn by now he'd be impatient to get back to the ranch.

I smooth my hands over the towel at my hip.

Willow frowns, about to turn and tell this guy where to shove it until her big brown eyes take him in. She gasps, flipping back to me. "It's him, isn't it?"

I cock my head at my not-so-subtle friend.

He chuckles and holds out his hand. "Wilder Thorne."

She takes it. "Willow."

He nods. "I figured. OK if I sit?"

"OK with me." She looks over my shoulder where my boss is probably lingering. "Besides, I've got to go finish my set before Billy fires me." She points to her piano and scurries off.

"An unlikely event," Billy calls after her. Wilder takes her seat, his eyes on me.

"Where you staying?" I ask casually, like I would any tourist hanging around my bar.

The soft, melodic notes of Willow's piano drift from the other side of the bar, drawing heads toward the sound. Except Wilder's. "Courtyard Inn across the street from you."

"When's your return flight?"

"Bought a one-way ticket."

"Wilder," I release a breath.

"Rose," he breathes back, and damn it, I hate the way my name sounds in his voice. Like it belongs there.

"You should go home. Dallas needs you. Your staff. The ranch. You couldn't step away all week and now—" My voice breaks, and I shake my head.

He leans in. "Please give me a chance to explain."

I grab a glass and toss it into the ice to give me something to do, then fill it with whiskey and set it in front of him.

He narrows his eyes. "How you know what I drink?"

"You had a whiskey on the rocks during our speed-date."

He laughs, and it makes me smile as he lifts his glass. "You keeping notes on me, Blue?"

My smile fades because it makes me think of my cart. "They're not all gems, cowboy."

He exhales sharply, like I knocked the wind out of him. He glances at my boss, who no doubt is only focused on Willow. "When can we talk?"

And for this one instance, I'm weak again. My eyes sting with hurt. "I don't know. Sunday through Thursday of last week, maybe?" I shrug with a hard swallow.

Pain flickers in his eyes. "Rose, I'm sorry. You have to know I didn't leave that day because of you or because of those photos."

My eyes well and I have to look away. "Of course it was," I whisper, but I'm not sure he heard me.

He leans in, voice dropping to something just between us. "No, it wasn't." His throat bobs, like he's swallowing down words he's not sure he can say. "It's just . . . when I saw them, I immediately thought of the guy you *told* me was no one."

I snap my head back to him, just barely controlling my outrage. "It was irrelevant. But it was still a hell of a lot more than you ever shared with me."

His jaw hardens. "I know. It wasn't fair to you. It just . . . triggered something for me." He twists the glass in his hands. "I want to tell you what happened with Bonnie."

I shake my head. "You don't have to. Wesley did. I know what she did and I get you're protecting yourself."

He meets my eyes. "I hurt a lot of people choosing her, trusting her. Never realizing her head and heart were somewhere else. A road I had no place for." His eyes linger on me like it's the only thing he's allowed now. "I was afraid down the line . . . I'd lose you the same way."

My whole body screams to reach for him. To say his name and convince him that he'd have all of me if he'd given me a chance.

Someone hails for a refill, and I slide another drink down the bar and turn back.

"I didn't understand," I tell him honestly. "But I do now."

"You do?"

I nod. "And I don't blame you. Giving your heart to someone just because they're here now doesn't mean you'll have them forever."

With that, I turn and avoid him for the rest of the night.

36

Wilder

Three days later

Wilder: How are things?

Dallas: Hilarious.

Wilder: What?

Dallas: Dad's helping out and he's commissioned Silas for the next two weeks.

Sounds about right. Silas's attempts on the ranch are downright comical. He moves like a fish out of water.

The way he tries to saddle a horse, you'd think he was defusing a bomb instead of tightening a cinch.

Wilder: When's he due back on the ice?

Dallas: Mid-September. How are things over there?

Wilder: Remember that time Silas tried to herd cattle?

Dallas: Ha. Yeah.

Wilder: He had a smoother handle on it than I do right now.

Dallas: I'll see you Friday?

Wilder: See you Friday.

37

Rose

Wilder's been here every night since last Saturday, closing the place down with me. Then taking me home in a city cab. He walks me up to my door, says good night, and I can almost count on seeing him the next day. Same place. Same time.

It's almost like . . . having a boyfriend.

He hasn't been pushy. But he's been talking. And I've been listening.

This week, Silas started working at the ranch with Connor and Dallas. Which, based on the stories Wilder told me about Silas's ranch skills, I'm devastated I didn't get to witness in person.

Then he told me more about his relationship with his younger brother. They're not close. Would kill for each other, but don't talk as much as they probably should—Wilder's words.

And I make a mental note of it.

Because as much as I'm fighting it, I want to be part of his life.

I haven't asked about their mother, Carrie, but she's slowly been coming up more in conversation. Nothing about her accident. Just how things were when she was around. There was less . . . tension, which I think is the word Wilder was thinking of. He grumbled something about there not being "so much barbed wire" between them back then.

He's been asking about my progress with registration for the fall semester. I don't offer much. Since technically . . . I don't *know* much.

It turns out the new school back home in South Carolina wants me to retake certain courses to match their curriculum after the transfer. So I've been holding off on committing.

And . . . maybe there are other reasons I've held off.

The other day, I looked into the school Wesley was telling me about in Denver. Just browsing the site and taking note of their application deadline. No calls made yet.

No submissions. Just . . . an open mind.

I clap with the crowd as Willow finishes her first set of the night on Friday evening. She takes a small bow and moves to sit at my bar.

"Boy, you're just giving up, aren't you?" I laugh, taking in her look. Not that she doesn't look gorgeous, she's just dressed down tonight.

Her auburn hair hangs in loose waves around her shoulders, framing a face with minimal makeup. She's in jeans and that oversized black hoodie I gave her last week.

She shrugs coyly. "Choosing comfort over big tips today."

I grin. "Big what?"

"Tips, tips," she calls out.

I laugh, wiping down a bottle before setting it behind the bar.

Willow settles in her chair and looks around, confused. "Is he here yet? I haven't seen him."

I don't follow her gaze. I know he's not here. It's an hour past his usual arrival time and I'm trying hard not to care—not to notice, not to let my heart sink.

I talked to Sandra about him briefly the other day during our first session. She, of course, didn't say much since he's not the focus of my healing. But apparently, he's a big part of my road to self-worth and trusting again.

Still trying to figure out what the difference is.

She also reminded me not to wait too long to let him in or I might lose him.

I swallow, because maybe she was right.

He gave it a week . . . and left. I'd be a hypocrite to be hurt by it since it's exactly what I did.

"Margarita?" I ask cheerfully.

"Rose?" She narrows her eyes.

"Babe, you've only got ten more minutes. You want it or not?"

She looks to the door and purses her lips, her expression matching my inner disappointment. "Just water tonight, thanks."

I dig a glass into the ice.

"Make that two." That familiar deep voice sends a shiver down my spine.

I lift my gaze. Wilder flashes me a crooked smile, with a quick glance at my friend. "Evening, ladies."

Willow pulls up her hood, her eyes flashing with delight as she covers her chuckle.

I'm glad she finds my turmoil of emotions funny.

I set her glass down and swallow as Wilder takes an empty seat two down from her. "Lime?" I ask him, my voice stuck in my throat.

It's a stupid question. Wilder doesn't want lime, but I had to say something or he'd see right through my composure.

He keeps his gaze on me, that ghost of a grin still there. "No, thanks."

I brush my wet hands down my apron just as another voice comes from behind him.

"Hope you got something stronger than that for me."

I look up at the dark and handsome cowboy. "Dallas," I breathe with a smile.

He steps between Wilder and Willow and reaches over to give me a hug. He looks good. A little tired, but good.

"What are you doing here?"

He jerks his head like he's offended. "Hopefully, not drinking water. You come all this way for this?" he asks me.

"Not quite."

"I'm here for the weekend with Ellie. Her grandmother is having a procedure at a hospital up here and they wanted to take Ellie around town, show her the sights."

"How nice of you to bring her. What can I get you?"

"Whiskey, ne—" His eyes land on my friend, who's had her head covered in that hood, swirling the small straw in her ice water. "Nice hoodie."

Willow snaps her head up, meeting his eyes. A thick moment stretches, and it's like the rest of the room doesn't exist.

Willow lowers her hood and blinks. "Yeah, uh, it's . . . my boyfriend's. I wear his clothes all the time." She shrugs, and I want to roll my eyes.

I get that my friend has sworn off men, but these white lies to repel the opposite sex are getting a little ridiculous.

Last week she told a guy she's in a committed relationship with her cat.

Which would have been fine . . . if she had a cat.

"Is that right?" Dallas mutters.

I clear my throat. Grabbing Willow's attention, I shake my head subtly and point to Dallas.

She rolls her lips and assesses him. "This is yours, isn't it?"

He nods.

Then she leans her nose into him, ghosting it over his torso, then draws back. "Checks out."

Dallas's brows shoot up. "I'm glad. Can I have it back?"

"No." She hops off her chair. "Time for round two."

Willow sets her drink over a coaster on her piano and settles into her chair.

Wilder pulls his gaze back toward me. "Sorry I'm late. We had to drop off Ellie first, then grab a late dinner."

"I wasn't waiting," I lie. "I was relieved, actually; they need you back home on that ranch."

"Sorry to disappoint."

I set Dallas's whiskey at the bar—not that he's focused on a drink anymore. Or anything other than the soft music from the corner of the bar.

"You heading back with your brother?"

Wilder takes a breath and considers it. "No."

"What are you waiting for?"

He keeps his eyes on me, making my stomach flip.

"Wilder."

"Can we talk tonight?"

I give him a small smile. "I'm actually leaving early tonight."

He checks his watch. "It's eleven. What's your idea of early?"

"Midnight. There's a tattoo parlor open late in the Village and I want to go see if they can do something for me." I pull a piece of paper from my back pocket where I mocked up a concept I've been working on and show it to him.

I watch his expression as he studies it, shifting his gaze briefly from my arm to the artwork. "Is this a river?"

I nod, admiring the sketch again. It's an outline of a narrow river which would flow from my upper arm to just above my wrist. Blue roses and petals float along the surface like an endless, gentle journey.

He smiles. "I can already see it. And I love it."

I lean in, challenging him, keeping my tone playful but also being serious. "You don't think it's impulsive or wild or . . . something I'll regret later?"

He doesn't blink as he holds my eyes. "I think you know exactly what you want. It's what I love about you . . ." He leans back with a smile like he's totally here for it. "Ride hard, think light."

That smile is contagious, and I take a moment to settle my heart from what he's just said before I lean in with another question.

"What if I . . . change my mind?"

His eyes are full of gravity. "What if you don't? What if it turns out to be the best thing you ever did? Think that's a risk worth taking."

I nibble on the corner of my lower lip.

Wilder glances back at his brother, checking if he's still distracted with the entertainment. "You regret having those pictures taken of you?"

I've been thinking about those a lot these last few days and the truth is, no. I'm not saying it was a good idea, but it also doesn't fall under the category of "greatest mistake." It was exhilarating at the time. I felt flawless, beautiful, not scarred. I didn't feel compelled to shrink into myself, which I sometimes do while fully dressed.

I shrug coyly. "Only after you saw them."

His eyes soften and he tilts his head to the side with a smirk. "Well then, you won't mind that I kept them for you."

My heart swells because of how much he's saying between the lines with that look, that comment. The fact that he kept them.

A thick moment passes before someone snaps for a refill behind me. Dallas turns on instinct, like a wolf, ready to protect his own.

I break from Wilder's gaze and get back to work.

"Thank you for coming with me," I tell Wilder as he follows me into my apartment.

Dallas also tagged along to the tattoo parlor, before we parted ways and he went back to Wilder's hotel room.

He frowns, and I can tell he's nervous about it. Probably more than I am. "Guy seemed to know what he was talking about. Four hours, huh? That's a long time to sit there while someone pokes you with needles."

I laugh. "I'll be all right."

He reaches for me. "I'll make sure of it, holding your other hand."

My shoulders sink because now, the guilt of him staying is weighing on me. "Wilder. The appointment is next week. You can't—"

"I'm not leaving, Rose," he says quietly. He sets my things on the kitchen counter then takes my hands in his again. "I will if that's what you want, but I'm not giving up until you're back where we both know you belong."

Warmth blooms in my stomach. I poke him playfully. "Before Wes came that day . . . you asked me to stay."

"Yes."

"I was going to say yes."

He swallows because we both know what happened after. "I know."

"How do I know you won't change *your* mind?"

He pushes back my hair, not the least bit surprised by my question. "You know what I felt when Bonnie left me? *Before* I knew there was someone else?"

I watch him without answering.

"Angry. Confused. Played." He grips my hands tighter. "But when *you* left, I felt it in my bones before anyone said a word. I was hollow. A shell. You took a part of me with you. A part of me that belonged to you since our first date."

A flutter jumps in my chest. Then I frown. "First date?"

"You don't remember? It was six whole minutes."

I laugh as he tugs me playfully.

"The difference is, Rose, Bonnie walked away with my pride. But you have my heart."

My eyes well with tears.

"So tell me, what on earth do I have to go back to if you're not there?"

"*Everything*," I breathe like he's crazy.

He watches me. "Something," he agrees. "Not everything."

I melt as he pulls me against him. "Now quit it with your what-ifs." He rests his forehead on mine. "I love you, Rose."

I suck in a breath, my hands coming up to hold his face. "I love you."

He presses his lips to my forehead, breathing me in. "Come back with me. Come home."

I give a small nod and that's all it takes. He comes alive, crashing his lips against mine in one powerful, all-consuming kiss. Heat flares between us as our tongues collide relentlessly. I moan into his mouth, overcome with emotion and desire.

He pulls back almost abruptly and walks to my door. He turns the locks—all of them.

"Oh, you don't need to do all those—"

"I know. I'm making sure your brother doesn't interrupt us."

Epilogue

Rose

Three weeks later

Wesley gently twists my right arm, sweeping his eyes over the ink that covers those faint scars I've been hiding for too long.

"I love that you designed it," he says softly. "It's beautiful, Ro."

I smile back at him, pulling my sleeve down since the skin is still a little raw. "Thank you."

He leans back on the couch, his eyes dancing with that familiar mischief. "You know what else you do beautifully?"

I cross my arms in front of my chest. "What's that?"

"Telling your big brother he was right when he brought you down here."

I nod thoughtfully. "Mmhmm. Tell me, do you consider validation to be something you need from everyone close to you? Or only from family members?"

Wes tosses his head back with a groan. "Not this again. Glad you're back on track—but you're not licensed yet, so cut that shit out."

I laugh and sit back, taking a sip of my wine. We're at my cottage for a little welcome home party Wesley put together for me.

Ginger is here, and so are Connor, Dallas, and Ellie. Jack from the kitchen stopped by too, and I'm told others will be dropping by for my official welcome to Blue River.

Initially, the plan was for the guys to help me unpack the boxes I had shipped here last week. But then there was food, and hugs, and alcohol, and no boxes were being unpacked.

After my tattoo appointment, I convinced Wilder to go home while I stayed back to tie up loose ends in the city.

Once he returned, he took my brother out for a few beers. Wesley claims he was kidnapped, but in any case, they talked.

Neither one will tell me what was said, but supposedly, they're OK now. And I hope that's true. Because it would break my heart to weaken their bond.

Wilder reaches for my hand and lifts me off the couch. "Leave him alone, Blue. Should know by now, he can dish it but can't take it." He grins at his friend.

My brother's eyes shift between us like we're going to take some getting used to, and he pushes off the couch. "Better go refill the . . . cheese platter or something."

I watch as he heads to the kitchen wordlessly. Then with a frown, I step into Wilder's arms.

“He’ll be fine,” he assures me.

“Maybe we can find him a nice girl to distract him for a while.”

Wilder scoffs. “Good idea. Then I can come banging on *his* door when *they’re* trying to be alone.”

Peeling my eyes off my brother, I watch Ginger and Connor with Ellie. They’re playing a “guess which hand” game with her while she’s propped up on the kitchen counter near the bowl of Skittles.

Dallas is watching them from the window in the dining room. His face is neutral. Then his eyes roam over the place, and I’m sure he’s remembering a different time in this cozy cottage.

Wilder turns my chin to him. “Everyone’s fine. How are you? You tired? Want me to kick everyone out?”

I press against his chest like he’s crazy. “No way. I never get parties. We’re going all night.”

“I kind of had other plans to last all night,” he grumbles.

I hum low, wanting that too. But I’ll settle for a kiss. I lift on my toes, then pause, still feeling awkward with my brother watching. “Come outside with me.”

He follows my lead as I step out to the porch and shut the door behind us.

Without missing a beat, he presses me against the siding, snakes his hands into my hair, and kisses me. It’s a soft, long kiss. But he pauses briefly. “I thought we weren’t hiding anymore,” he says.

“We’re not. I just didn’t want an audience.” I smile against his lips.

He growls low. “Wise ass.”

I giggle, pulling him close. We're interrupted by the sound of tires crunching on gravel, followed by a double honk.

An ice-blue SUV slows in front of the cottage. Silas hops out of the driver's seat, and he's brought a friend. I narrow my eyes as a familiar face steps out of the passenger side. I gasp. "Is that—"

"Chase," Wilder sighs, then, taking me with him, jogs down the steps to greet his brother. I try not to gawk at the man they call King of the Ice, but it's hard when he comes around, holding out his hand.

"You must be Rose. Chase Reeves."

I know who you are, I'm about to say. Then pause mid-handshake. "Wait, Reeves?"

"Levi's brother," Wilder says dryly.

"And captain of the Denver Kings," I point out.

"Finally, someone who doesn't acknowledge me as someone's kid brother." He squeezes my shoulders like he likes me already. "Welcome. Hope you love it. Silas and I had to wrangle a set of season tickets to get this color."

I frown in question, but he's already heading to the house. "Silas, one beer, then I've gotta get back to the wife."

I turn back to the guys. "What does—"

I don't have a chance to ask before Silas wraps me in a hug. "Welcome back. And look, I don't run pick-up favors for nothing. You're going to be in Denver a lot, I'm going to expect rides into town." He winks, then drops the keys into Wilder's hand. "See you inside."

I turn my gaze back to the car, pulling my bottom lip between my teeth. Wilder watches as I run my finger along the shiny blue exterior.

"It's yours," he confirms.

My lips part with no words as I look up at him.

"You're going to need it to get to and from school three days a week."

"Wilder, it's beautiful. But this is too much."

He shrugs. "Figured I'd better get you something before *my* truck suddenly goes missing one night."

"You've already given me a place to live and I'm not even working here anymore."

He wraps his arms around my waist. "About that. Wesley and I had an idea last week. In New York, you told me that art was your therapy, how you relieved stressful emotions and that maybe one day . . . you want to teach it."

"I do." I frown as he twists me to face the cottage, keeping his strong arms around me.

"What if there was a place you could do that now?"

"Art therapy? Here?"

"Wes and I were talking. We could turn it into a studio for you. Hold classes all year round. On your terms, your schedule. If you want."

I lean back against him as I picture it all. "That would be amazing, Wilder."

"Only problem is . . ." He lowers his lips to the side of my face. "You'd have to move in with me."

I grin, twisting to face him. "Have to, huh?"

"Best view in town. Deluxe coffee machine I'm making Dallas leave behind. And me . . . every morning. And every night."

"Wine and chocolate shavings?"

"The works," he promises.

"Locks?"

"Just the one. It's all you need."

I press my lips together, my eyes stinging as I nod. "It's all I want."

His eyes gleam and now—I really wish the house was empty.

Wilder looks over my shoulder at the crunch of another set of tires pulling up to the cottage. "I forgot one more thing." He steps back. "Something I'm going to need you to do first thing tomorrow," he says sternly.

My smile dims as I turn. Jeff pulls up in my cart. My very white and boring old cart.

"Evenin', Rose. Good to have ya back." He unloads a bucket, two paint cans and a set of brushes from the cart.

"Did I miss a spot?" I grumble.

He laughs and tips his hat, then heads inside. I cock my head at Wilder.

He shrugs. "In case you need a vehicle that fits through the bushes."

I laugh and we walk over to it. I notice something on the seat and gasp. "Is that . . ."

"Ginger finally found 'em. Blue cowgirl hats. Shop's filled with them now."

I jump inside and pop it on my head. He follows and sits beside me. "It's perfect," I tell him, part giddy and part heartbroken.

Because something feels off. It's definitely my cart, but doesn't feel . . . *mine* anymore.

My shoulders sink as I stare at the front hood, remembering how hard it was to paint it all back to white.

"Paint it back for me, Blue?" Wilder whispers beside me.

I sniffle and lean into him. "Now is that you asking nicely or specifying a color?"

"I want it exactly the same." He holds up a finger. "With one minor change."

My brows shoot up. "Oh?"

"I'm not sure *The Rose* is quite right."

"Then what do I call it?"

"*Wild Rose*."

If you loved *Wild Rose*, don't miss the next instalment in the Blue River Springs series. Saddle up for Dallas and Willow's irresistible love story in *Fallen Willow*!

Available to Order!

Acknowledgements

Wild Rose surprised me in the best ways and has been such a joy to write. The idea of Rose's character grabbed my heart from the very first thought, and unlike many of my heroines—she came to me fully formed. As if waiting for me to tell her story.

I wasn't completely sold on him for her until Wilder and Rose finally shared a page.

The banter, the run-ins, the quiet electricity between the two—they just worked. And had me buzzing to write their happily ever after.

But their story might never have found your hearts if it weren't for the people I want to take the time to thank and acknowledge.

First and always a huge thank you to my family. To my husband for believing in me and cheering me on every single day. And for silently refilling my tea and M&M's when I'm glued to my keyboard. To my son, who is still always so proud and amazed when mommy's first proof copy comes in the mail.

Thank you to my fantastic team of bloggers, bookstagrammers and everyone in my Reader Group (*Roxanne's Rocks*). You guys are all truly amazing and make all of this worthwhile.

My assistant, Zsuzsanna at Midnight Readers PR, for everything you do everyday to keep what *I* do organized and stress-free. I'll always be grateful for the day we met.

To Betty, for your remarkable designs and graphics. To Emma (*Booktastic Blonde*) for your support, inspiration, and services.

My beta readers; Kerri, Liz and Steph for all your helpful feedback and for loving this story even when it was a mess.

My agent, Sarah Hornsley. Thank you for taking a chance on my stories so that more people can. Sincere and lasting gratitude for your guidance and our partnership.

And finally, my editor, Bea Grabowska and the entire team at Embla Books. I'm forever grateful that *Wild Rose* has captured your hearts the way I've meant it to. Thank you for believing in this series—and in me. A special thanks to your hard (and quick) work on this release to get it in top shape for the world.

About the Author

Roxanne grew up in New York City, where she studied theater and screen writing. Her passion for storytelling started very young—even if it never made it on paper.

She now writes contemporary small-town romance with strong realistic heroines, steam, banter, and a healthy dose of angst.

A mom of two, when she's not writing, Roxanne enjoys baking, jogging with her golden-doodle, and practicing flirty banter with her real-life male hero.

Website: https://www.roxannetully.com
Newsletter: https://geni.us/rtnewsletter
Instagram: https://www.instagram.com/roxtully.author/
TikTok: https://www.tiktok.com/@roxtully

About Embla Books

Embla Books is a digital-first publisher of standout commercial adult fiction. Passionate about storytelling, the team at Embla believe our lives are built on stories – and publish books that will make you 'laugh, love, look over your shoulder and lose sleep'. Launched by Bonnier Books UK in 2021, the imprint is named after the first woman from the creation myth in Norse mythology. Embla was carved by the gods from a tree trunk found on the seashore; an image of the kind of creative work and crafting that writers do, and a symbol of how stories shape our lives.

Find out about some of our other books and stay in touch:

X, Facebook, Instagram: @emblabooks
Newsletter: https://bit.ly/emblanewsletter